FERNANDO VALLEJO

La Virgen de los Sicarios

punto de lectura

Título: La Virgen de los Sicarios
© 1994, Fernando Vallejo
© de la edición de Aguilar, Altea, Taurus, Alfaguara, S.A. de C.V.
© De esta edición: enero 2001, Suma de Letras, S.L.
Juan Bravo, 38. 28006 Madrid (España) www.puntodelectura.com

ISBN: 84-663-0164-X
Depósito legal: B-35.204-2004
Impreso en España – Printed in Spain

Diseño de cubierta: Sdl
Fotografía de portada: © Foto promocional del filme
  La Vierge des Tueurs de Barbet Schroeder
Diseño de colección: Suma de Letras

Impreso por Litografía Rosés, S.A.

Quinta edición: septiembre 2002
Sexta edición: noviembre 2003
Séptima edición: mayo 2004
Octava edición: julio 2004

117 / 01

FERNANDO VALLEJO

La Virgen de los Sicarios

las comunas -
~~39-41~~ 39 - 41
57-61
86-88

It's like the readers are tourists &
Fernando's the guide
- fascination w/ violence, drugs etc.

the only past is his childhood
- not nostalgic for the collective past

ia vida ni la muerte son únicas
   los muertos pueden volver

el es invisible al fin
   - todo el mundo está muerto

pregnant women killed - they're producing more ppl
   for him to hate, contaminating
   - mentions a crazy man who injects pregnant
     women w/ poison

Había en las afueras de Medellín un pueblo silencioso y apacible que se llamaba Sabaneta. Bien que lo conocí porque allí cerca, a un lado de la carretera que venía de Envigado, otro pueblo, a mitad de camino entre los dos pueblos, en la finca Santa Anita de mis abuelos, a mano izquierda viniendo, transcurrió mi infancia. Claro que lo conocí. Estaba al final de esa carretera, en el fin del mundo. Más allá no había nada, ahí el mundo empezaba a bajar, a redondearse, a dar la vuelta. Y eso lo consté la tarde que elevamos el globo más grande que hubieran visto los cielos de Antioquia, un rombo de ciento veinte pliegos inmenso, rojo, rojo, rojo para que resaltara sobre el cielo azul. El tamaño no me lo van a creer, ¡pero qué saben ustedes de globos! ¿Saben qué son? Son rombos o cruces o esferas hechos de papel de

7

china deleznable, y por dentro llevan una candileja encendida que los llena de humo para
que suban. El humo es como quien dice su
alma, y la candileja el corazón. Cuando se lle-
nan de humo y empiezan a jalar, los que los están elevando sueltan, soltamos, y el globo se
va yendo, yendo al cielo con el corazón encendido, palpitando, como el Corazón de Jesús.
¿Saben quién es? Nosotros teníamos uno en la
sala; en la sala de la casa de la calle del Perú de
la ciudad de Medellín, capital de Antioquia;
en la casa en donde yo nací, en la sala entronizado o sea (porque sé que no van a saber) bende-
cido un día por el cura. A él está consagrada
Colombia, mi patria. Él es Jesús y se está seña-
lando el pecho con el dedo, y en el pecho
abierto el corazón sangrando: goticas de sangre rojo vivo, encendido, como la candileja del
globo: es la sangre que derramará Colombia,
ahora y siempre por los siglos de los siglos
amén.

    ¿Pero qué les estaba diciendo del globo, de
Sabaneta? Ah sí, que el globo subió y subió y
empujado por el viento, dejando atrás y abajo
los gallinazos se fue yendo hacia Sabaneta. Y
nosotros que corremos al carro y ¡ran! que
arrancamos, y nos vamos siguiéndolo por la

8

carretera en el Hudson de mi abuelito. Ah no, no fue en el Hudson de mi abuelito, fue en la carcacha de mi papá. Ah sí, sí fue en el Hudson. Ya ni sé, hace tanto, ya no recuerdo… Recuerdo que íbamos de bache en bache ¡pum! ¡pum! ¡pum! por esa carreterita destartalada y el carro a toda desbarajustándose, como se nos desbarajustó después Colombia, o mejor dicho, como se "les" desbarajustó a ellos porque a mí no, yo aquí no estaba, yo volví después, años y años, décadas, vuelto un viejo, a morir. Cuando el globo llegó a Sabaneta dio la vuelta a la tierra, por el otro lado, y desapareció. Quién sabe adónde habrá ido, a China o a Marte, y si se quemó: su papel sutil, deleznable se encendía fácil, con una chispa de la candileja bastaba, como bastó una chispa para que se nos incendiara después Colombia, se "les" incendiara, una chispa que ya nadie sabe de dónde saltó. ¿Pero por qué me preocupa a mí Colombia si ya no es mía, es ajena?

A mi regreso a Colombia volví a Sabaneta con Alexis, acompañándolo, en peregrinación. Alexis, ajá, así se llama. El nombre es bonito pero no se lo puse yo, se lo puso su mamá. Con eso de que les dio a los pobres por ponerles a los hijos nombres de ricos, extravagantes, extranjeros: Tayson Alexander, por ejemplo, o Fáber o Eder o Wílfer o Rommel o Yeison o qué sé yo. No sé de dónde los sacan o cómo los inventan. Es lo único que les pueden dar para arrancar en esta mísera vida a sus niños, un vano, necio nombre extranjero o inventado, ridículo, de relumbrón. Bueno, ridículos pensaba yo cuando los oí en un comienzo, ya no lo pienso así. Son los nombres de los sicarios manchados de sangre. Más rotundos que un tiro con su carga de odio.

Ustedes no necesitan, por supuesto, que les explique qué es un sicario. Mi abuelo sí, necesitaría, pero mi abuelo murió hace años y años. Se murió mi pobre abuelo sin conocer el tren elevado ni los sicarios, fumando cigarrillos Victoria que usted, apuesto, no ha oído siquiera mencionar. Los Victoria eran el basuco de los viejos, y el basuco es cocaína impura fumada, que hoy fuman los jóvenes para ver más torcida la torcida realidad, ¿o no? Corríjame si yerro. Abuelo, por si acaso me puedes oír del otro lado de la eternidad, te voy a decir qué es un sicario: un muchachito, a veces un niño, que mata por encargo. ¿Y los hombres? Los hombres por lo general no, aquí los sicarios son niños o muchachitos, de doce, quince, diecisiete años, como Alexis, mi amor: tenía los ojos verdes, hondos, puros, de un verde que valía por todos los de la sabana. Pero si Alexis tenía la pureza en los ojos tenía dañado el corazón. Y un día, cuando más lo quería, cuando menos lo esperaba, lo mataron, como a todos nos van a matar. Vamos para el mismo hueco de cenizas, en los mismos Campos de Paz.

La Virgen de Sabaneta hoy es María Auxiliadora, pero no lo era en mi niñez: era la Virgen del Carmen, y la parroquia la de Santa Ana. Hasta donde entiendo yo de estas cosas (que no es mucho), María Auxiliadora es propiedad de los salesianos, y la parroquia de Sabaneta es de curas laicos. ¿Cómo fue a dar María Auxiliadora allí? No sé. Cuando regresé a Colombia allí la encontré entronizada, presidiendo la iglesia desde el altar de la izquierda, haciendo milagros. Un tumulto llegaba los martes a Sabaneta de todos los barrios y rumbos de Medellín adonde la Virgen a rogar, a pedir, a pedir, a pedir que es lo que mejor saben hacer los pobres amén de parir hijos. Y entre esa romería tumultuosa los muchachos de la barriada, los sicarios. Ya para entonces Sabaneta había dejado de ser un pueblo y se había convertido en un barrio más de Medellín, la ciudad la había alcanzado, se la había tragado; y Colombia, entre tanto, se nos había ido de las manos. Éramos, y de lejos, el país más criminal de la tierra, y Medellín la capital del odio. Pero estas cosas no se dicen, se saben. Con perdón.

Por Alexis volví pues a Sabaneta, acompañándolo, la mañana que siguió a la noche en que nos conocimos. Puesto que las peregrinaciones son los martes, nos tuvimos que conocer un lunes: en el apartamento de mi lejano amigo José Antonio Vásquez, sobreviviente de ese Medellín antediluviano que se llevó el ensanche, y cuyo nombre debería omitir aquí pero no lo omito por la elemental razón de que no se pueden contar historias sin nombres. ¿Y sin apellido? Sin apellido no te vayan a confundir con otro y por otras cuentas después te maten. "Aquí te regalo esta belleza —me dijo José Antonio cuando me presentó a Alexis—, que ya lleva como diez muertos". Alexis se rió y yo también y por supuesto no le creí, o mejor dicho sí. Después le dijo al muchacho: "Vaya lleve a éste a conocer el cuarto de las mariposas". "Éste" era yo, y "el cuarto de las mariposas" un cuartico al fondo del apartamento que si me permiten se lo describo de paso, de prisa, camino al cuarto, sin recargamientos balzacianos: recargado como Balzac nunca soñó, de muebles y relojes viejos; relojes, relojes y relojes viejos y requeteviejos, de muro, de mesa, por decenas, por gruesas, detenidos todos a distintas horas burlándose de la eternidad, negando el tiempo. Estaban en más desarmonía esos relojes que los habitantes de Medellín. ¿Por qué esa obsesión de mi amigo por los relojes? Vaya Dios a saber. La que sí le habían curado los años era la de los muchachos: pasaban por su apartamento y por su vida sin tocarlos. Perfección a la que aún no he llegado yo pero de la que ya estoy cerca: lo cerca que estoy de la muerte y sus gusanos. En fin, por ese apartamento de José Antonio, por entre sus relojes detenidos como fechas en las lápidas de los cementerios, pasaban infinidad de muchachos vivos. O sea, quiero decir, vivos hoy y mañana muertos que es la ley del mundo, pero asesinados: jóvenes asesinos asesinados, exentos de las ignominias de la vejez por escandaloso puñal o compasiva bala. ¿Qué iban a hacer allí? Por lo general nada: venían de aburrirse afuera a aburrirse adentro. En ese apartamento nunca se tomaba ni se fumaba: ni marihuana ni basuco ni nada de nada. Era un templo. Y ni eso, vaya: vaya a la Catedral o Basílica Metropolitana para que vea rufianes fumando marihuana en las bancas de atrás. Distinga bien el olor del humo, que no se le confunda con el incienso. Pero bueno, entre tanto reloj callado tronaba un televisor furibundo transmitiendo telenovelas, y entre telenovela y telenovela las alharacosas noticias: que hoy mataron a fulanito de tal y anoche a tantos y a tantos. Que a fulanito lo mataron dos sicarios. Y los sicarios del apartamento muy serios. ¡Vaya noticia! ¡Cómo andan de desactualizados los noticieros! Y es que una ley del mundo seguirá siendo: la muerte viaja siempre más rápido que la información.

¿Y qué se ganaba José Antonio con ese entrar y salir de muchachos, de criminales, por su casa? ¿Que le robaran? ¿Que lo mataran? ¿O es que acaso era su apartamento un burdel? Dios libre y guarde. José Antonio es el personaje más generoso que he conocido. Y digo personaje y no persona o ser humano porque eso es lo que es, un personaje, como sacado de una novela y no encontrado en la realidad, pues en efecto, ¿a quién sino a él le da por regalar muchachos que es lo más valioso?

"Los muchachos no son de nadie —dice él—, son de quien los necesita". Eso, enunciado así, es comunismo; pero como él lo ponía en práctica era obra de misericordia, la decimoquinta que le faltó al catecismo, la más grande, la más noble, más que darle de beber al sediento o ayudarle a bien morir al moribundo.

"Vaya lleve a éste a conocer el cuarto de las mariposas", le dijo a Alexis, y Alexis me llevó riéndose. El cuarto es un cuartico minúsculo con baño y una cama entre cuatro paredes que han visto quietas lo que no he visto yo andando por todo el mundo. Lo que sí no han visto esas cuatro paredes son las mariposas porque en el cuarto así llamado no las hay. Alexis empezó a desvestirme y yo a él; él con una espontaneidad candorosa, como si me conociera desde siempre, como si fuera mi ángel de la guarda. Les evito toda descripción pornográfica y sigamos. Sigamos hacia Sabaneta en el taxi en que íbamos, por la misma carreterita destartalada de hace cien años, de bache en bache: es que Colombia cambia pero sigue igual, son nuevas caras de un viejo desastre. ¿Es que estos cerdos del gobierno no son capaces de asfaltar una carretera tan esencial, que corta por en medio mi vida? ¡Gonorreas!

(Gonorrea es el insulto máximo en las barriadas de las comunas, y comunas después explico qué son.)

Algo insólito noté en la carretera: que entre los nuevos barrios de casas uniformes seguían en pie, idénticas, algunas de las viejas casitas campesinas de mi infancia, y el sitio más mágico del Universo, la cantina Bombay, que tenía a un lado una bomba de gasolina o sea una gasolinera. La bomba ya no estaba, pero la cantina sí, con los mismos techos de vigas y las mismas paredes de tapias encaladas. Los muebles eran de ahora pero qué importa, su alma seguía encerrada allí y la comparé con mi recuerdo y era la misma, Bombay era la misma como yo siempre he sido yo: niño, joven, hombre, viejo, el mismo rencor cansado que olvida todos los agravios: por pereza de recordar.

No sé si entre aquellas casitas campesinas que quedaban estaba la del pesebre, o sea, quiero decir, la del pesebre más hermoso que hayan hecho los hombres desde que se estableció la costumbre de armar en diciembre nacimientos o belenes para conmemorar la llegada a esta mísera tierra a un establo, a una pesebrera, del Niño Dios. Todas las casitas

es una representación de su vida

campesinas de la carretera, desde que salíamos caminando de Santa Anita hacia Sabaneta tenían pesebre, y abrían las ventanas de los cuarticos que daban al corredor delantero para que lo viéramos. Pero ningún pesebre más hermoso que el de la casita que digo yo: ocupaba dos cuartos, el primero y el del fondo, llenos de maravillas: lagos con patos, rebaños, pastores, vaquitas, casitas, carreteritas, un tigre, y arriba de la montaña, en lo más alto, la pesebrera en la que el veinticuatro de diciembre iba a nacer el Niño Dios. Pero estábamos apenas a dieciséis, en que empezaba la novena y en que hacíamos los pesebres, y faltaban exactamente ocho días para el día, la noche, más feliz. Ocho días de una dicha interminable en espera. Mira Alexis, tú tienes una ventaja sobre mí y es que eres joven y yo ya me voy a morir, pero desgraciadamente para ti nunca vivirás la felicidad que yo he vivido. La felicidad no puede existir en este mundo tuyo de televisores y casetes y punkeros y rockeros y partidos de fútbol. Cuando la humanidad se sienta en sus culos ante un televisor a ver veintidós adultos infantiles dándole patadas a un balón no hay esperanzas. Dan grima, dan lástima, dan ganas de darle a la humanidad una patada en el culo

17

y despeñarla por el rodadero de la eternidad, y que desocupen la tierra y no vuelvan más.

Pero no me hagas caso que te estoy hablando de cosas bellas, de diciembre, de Santa Anita, de los pesebres, de Sabaneta. El pesebre de la casita que te digo era inmenso, la vista de uno se perdía entre sus mil detalles sin saber por dónde empezar, por dónde seguir, por dónde acabar. Las casitas a la orilla de la carretera en el pesebre eran como las casitas a la orilla de la carretera de Sabaneta, casitas campesinas con techitos de teja y corredor. O sea, era como si la realidad de adentro contuviera la realidad de afuera y no viceversa, que en la carretera a Sabaneta había una casita con un pesebre que tenía otra carretera a Sabaneta. Ir de una realidad a la otra era infinitamente más alucinante que cualquier sueño de basuco. El basuco entorpece el alma, no la abre a nada. El basuco empendeja.

Mira Alexis: Yo tenía entonces ocho años y parado en el corredor de esa casita, ante la ventana de barrotes, viendo el pesebre, me vi de viejo y vi entera mi vida. Y fue tanto mi terror que sacudí la cabeza y me alejé. No pude soportar de golpe, de una, la caída en el abismo. Pero dejemos esto, sigamos por esa noche de caminata hacia Sabaneta. Íbamos todos, mis padres, mis tíos, mis primos, mis hermanos y la noche era tibia, y en la tibieza de la noche parpadeaban las estrellas incrédulas: no podían creer lo que veían, que aquí abajo, por una simple carretera, pudiera haber tanta felicidad.

El taxi pasó frente a Bombay, esquivó un bache, otro, otro, y llegó a Sabaneta. Un tropel entre un carrerío llenaba el pueblo. Era la peregrinación de los martes, devota, insulsa, mentirosa. Venían a pedir favores. ¿Por qué esta manía de pedir y pedir? Yo no soy de aquí. Me avergüenzo de esta raza limosnera. En el oleaje de la multitud, entre un chisporroteo de veladoras y rezos en susurros entramos al templo. El murmullo de las oraciones subía al cielo como un zumbar de colmena. La luz de afuera se filtraba por los vitrales para ofrecernos, en imágenes multicolores, el espectáculo perverso de la pasión: Cristo azotado, Cristo caído, Cristo crucificado. Entre la multitud anodina de viejos y viejas busqué a los muchachos, los sicarios, y en efecto, pululaban. Esta devoción repentina de la juventud me causaba asombro. Y yo pensando que la Iglesia andaba en más bancarrota que el comunismo... Qué va, está viva, respira. La humanidad necesita para vivir mitos y mentiras. Si uno ve la verdad escueta se pega un tiro. Por eso, Alexis, no te recojo el revólver que se te ha caído mientras te desvestías, al quitarte los pantalones. Si lo recojo me lo llevo al corazón y disparo. Y no voy a apagar la chispa de esperanza que me has encendido tú. Prendámosle esta veladora a la Virgen y oremos, roguemos que es a lo que vinimos: "Virgencita niña, María Auxiliadora que te conozco desde mi infancia, desde el colegio de los salesianos donde estudié; que eres más mía que de esta multitud novelera, hazme un favor: Que este niño que ves rezándote, ante ti, a mi lado, que sea mi último y definitivo amor; que no lo traicione, que no me traicione, amén". ¿Qué le pediría Alexis a la Virgen? Dicen los sociólogos que los sicarios le piden a María Auxiliadora que no les vaya a fallar, que les afine la puntería cuando disparen y que les salga bien el negocio. ¿Y cómo lo supieron? ¿Acaso son Dostoievsky o Dios padre para meterse en la mente de otros? ¡No sabe uno lo que uno está pensando va a saber lo que piensan los demás! En la iglesita de Sabaneta hay a la entrada un Señor Caído; en el altar del centro está Santa Ana con San Joaquín y la

Virgen de niña; y en el de la derecha Nuestra Señora del Carmen, la antigua reina de la parroquia. Pero todas las flores, todos los rezos, todas las veladoras, todas las súplicas, todas las miradas, todos los corazones están puestos en el altar de la izquierda, el de María Auxiliadora, que la remplazó. Por obra y gracia suya esta iglesita de Sabaneta antaño apagada hoy está alegre y florecida de flores y milagros. María Auxiliadora, la virgen mía, de mi niñez, la que más quiero los está haciendo. "Virgencita niña que me conoces desde hace tanto: Que mi vida acabe como empezó, con la felicidad que no lo sabe". Entre el susurro de las voces dispares mi alma se fue yendo hacia lo alto como un globo encendido, sin amarras, subiendo, subiendo hacia el infinito de Dios, lejos de esta mísera tierra.

Le quité la camisa, se quitó los zapatos, le quité los pantalones, se quitó las medias y la trusa y quedó desnudo con tres escapularios, que son los que llevan los sicarios: uno en el cuello, otro en el antebrazo, otro en el tobillo y son: para que les den el negocio, para que no les falle la puntería y para que les paguen. Eso según los sociólogos, que andan averiguando. Yo no pregunto. Sé lo que veo y olvido. Lo que sí no puedo olvidar son los ojos, el verde de sus ojos tras el cual trataba de adivinarle el alma.

"Toma", le dije cuando terminamos y le di un billete. Lo recibió, se lo guardó y siguió vistiéndose. Salí del cuarto y lo dejé vistiéndose, y dejé también de paso mi billetera en mi saco y el saco en la cama para que se llevara lo que quisiera: "Todo lo mío es tuyo, corazón —pensé—. Hasta mis papeles de identidad". Después, más tarde, conté los billetes y estaban los que había dejado. Entonces entendí que Alexis no respondía a las leyes de este mundo; y yo que desde hacía tiempos no creía en Dios dejé de creer en la ley de la gravedad. Al día siguiente nos fuimos a Sabaneta y en adelante siguió conmigo hasta el final. Y al final dejó el horror de esta vida para entrar en el horror de la muerte. "A la final", como dicen en las comunas.

Hombre, fíjese usted, que me viniera a dar el destino acabando lo que me negó en la juventud, ¿no era un disparate? Alexis debió llegarme cuando yo tenía veinte años, no ahora: en mi ayer remoto. Pero estaba programado que nos encontráramos ahí, en ese apartamento, entre relojes quietos, esa noche, tantísimos

Fernando Vallejo
autor vs. narrador/personaje

años después. Después de lo debido, quiero ¡este
decir. La trama de mi vida es la de un libro ab- / libro!
surdo en el que lo que debería ir primero va
luego. Es que este libro mío yo no lo escribí, didn't
ya estaba escrito: simplemente lo he ido cum- have a
pliendo página por página sin decidir. Sueños say in
con escribir la última por lo menos, de un tiro, his own
por mano propia, pero los sueños sueños son y life
a lo mejor ni eso.

Este apartamento mío está rodeado de terrazas y balcones. Terrazas y balcones por los
cuatro costados pero adentro nada, salvo una
cama, unas sillas y la mesa desde la que les escribo. "¡Cómo! —dijo Alexis cuando lo vio—.
¿Aquí no hay música?" Le compré una casetera y él se compró unos casetes. Una hora de
estrépito aguanté. "¿Y tú llamas a esta mierda
música?" Desconecté la casetera, la tomé, fui a
un balcón y la tiré por el balcón: al pavimento
fue a dar cinco pisos abajo a estrellarse, a ca-
llarse. A Alexis le pareció tan inmenso el crimen que se rió y dijo que yo estaba loco. Que
no se podía vivir sin música, y yo que sí, y que
además eso no era música. Para él era música
"romántica", y yo pensé: a este paso, si eso es
romántico, nos va a resultar romántico Schön-
berg. "No es música ni es nada, niño. Aprende

a ver la pared en blanco y a oír el silencio".
Pero él no podía vivir sin ruido, "música", ni
yo sin él. Así que al día siguiente le compré
otra casetera y aguanté otra hora el estrépito
antes de explotar y de ir a desconectarle el
monstruo para tirarlo por el balcón. "¡No!"
gritaba Alexis abriendo los brazos en cruz
como Cristo tratando de detenerme. "Niño,
así no podemos vivir, yo no soporto esto. Prefiero incluso que fumes basuco, pero en silencio, callado". Y él que no, que nunca había fu-
mado basuco. Y yo: "Yo prejuicios no tengo.
Lo que pasa es que tengo los oídos rotos".

Entonces, extrañado por ese comporta-
miento irracional mío me preguntó si me gustaban las mujeres. Le contesté que sí y que no,
que dependía. "¿De qué?" "De sus hermanos".
Se rió y me pidió que hablara en serio. Le expliqué, en serio, que por cuanto a la fisiología se
refería, las únicas dos con que me había acostado sí, sí me habían gustado, pero que ahí acababa la cosa pues más allá no había nada porque
para mí las mujeres era como si no tuvieran
alma. Un coco vacío. Y que por eso con ellas
era imposible el amor. "Es que yo estudié con
los curitas salesianos del colegio de Sufragio.
Con ellos aprendí que la relación carnal con las

mujeres es el pecado de la bestialidad, que es cuando se cruza un miembro de una especie con otro de otra, como por ejemplo un burro con una vaca. ¿Ves?" Después, sabiendo que me iba a contestar que sí, por no dejar, le devolví la pregunta y le pregunté si a él le gustaban las mujeres. "No", contestó, con un "no" tan rotundo, tan inesperado que me dejó perplejo. Y era un "no" para siempre: para el presente, para el pasado, para el futuro y para toda la eternidad de Dios: ni se había acostado con ninguna ni se pensaba acostar. Alexis era imprevisible y me estaba resultando más extremoso que yo. Conque eso era pues lo que había detrás de esos ojos verdes, una pureza incontaminada de mujeres. Y la verdad más absoluta, sin atenuantes ni importarle un carajo lo que piense usted que es lo que sostengo yo. De eso era de lo que me había enamorado. De su verdad.

Tengo muy presentes los sucesos de mis primeros días con Alexis. La mañana, por ejemplo, en que salí dejándolo en el apartamento en su estrépito, a comprar en la farmacia de abajo unos tapones para los oídos. Cruzando la Avenida San Juan, de regreso, presencié un atraco: veo que en la fila de carros detenidos por el semáforo un hombre grasoso, un cerdo, está atracando con un revólver un jeep que maneja un muchacho: uno de esos muchachitos linditos, riquitos, hijos de papá que me fascinan (también). El muchacho sacó las llaves, saltó del jeep, echó a correr y de lejos le gritó al hombre: "¡Te quedé conociendo, hijueputa!" El hombre, enfurecido, sin poderse llevar el jeep porque no tenía las llaves, con el atraco frustrado, burlado, hijueputiado, se dio a perseguir al muchacho disparándole. Uno de los tiros lo alcanzó. Cuando cayó el muchacho el hombre se le fue encima y lo remató a balazos. Por entre el carrerío detenido y el caos de bocinas y de gritos que siguió se perdió el asesino. El "presunto" asesino, como diría la prensa hablada y escrita, muy respetuosa ella de los derechos humanos. Con eso de que aquí, en este país de leyes y constituciones, democrático, no es culpable nadie hasta que no lo condenen, y no lo condenan si no lo juzgan, y no lo juzgan si no lo agarran, y si lo agarran lo sueltan… La ley de Colombia es la impunidad y nuestro primer delincuente impune es el presidente, que a estas horas debe de andar parrandiándose el país y el puesto. ¿En dónde? En Japón, en México… En México haciendo un cursillo.

26

Del presunto asesino no quedó sino el "presunto" flotando sutilmente en el aire de la Avenida San Juan, hasta que en el smog de los carros la presuntez se esfumó. O la presunción, si prefieren y les da por la corrección del idioma en este que fuera país de gramáticos, siglos ha. De los ladrones, amigo, es el reino de este mundo y más allá no hay otro. Siguen polvo y gusanos. Así que a robar, y mejor en el gobierno que es más seguro y el cielo es para los pendejos. Y mire, oiga, si lo está jodiendo mucho un vecino, sicarios aquí es lo que sobra. Y desempleo. Y acuérdese de que todo pasa, prescribe. Somos efímeros. Usted y yo, mi mamá, la suya. Todos prescribimos.

"El pelao debió de entregarle las llaves a la pinta esa", comentó Alexis, mi niño, cuando le conté el suceso. O mejor dicho no comentó: diagnosticó, como un conocedor, al que hay que creerle. Y yo me quedé enredado en su frase soñando, divagando, pensando en don Rufino José Cuervo y lo mucho de agua que desde entonces había arrastrado el río. Con "el pelao" mi niño significaba el muchacho; con "la pinta esa" el atracador; y con "debió de" significaba "debió" a secas: tenía que entregarle las llaves. Más de cien años hace que mi viejo amigo don Rufino José Cuervo, el gramático, a quien frecuenté en mi juventud, hizo ver que una cosa es "debe" solo y otra "debe de". Lo uno es obligación, lo otro duda. Aquí les van un par de ejemplos: "Puesto que sus hermanos se enriquecen con contratos públicos y él lo permite, también el presidente debe de ser un ladrón". O sea, no afirmo que lo sea, aunque parece que lo creo. Y por parecer creer no hay difamación, ¿o sí, doctor? ¿Por tan poca cosa se puede uno ir a la cárcel cuando nos están matando a todos vivos? Y "debe" a secas significa que se tiene que, como cuando digo: "La ley debe castigar el delito". ¡Pero cuál ley, cuál delito! Delito el mío por haber nacido y no andar instalado en el gobierno robando en vez de hablando. El que no está en el gobierno no existe y el que no existe no habla. ¡A callar!

Los tapones de algodón no sirven definitivamente para los oídos. Dejan pasar la música disco o "heavy metal". O no es que la dejen pasar, es que vibra el hueso, el temporal, y la vibración taladra el cerebro. Así que el problema de la casetera de Alexis y mi amor por él no tiene solución. Sin solución me voy solo a la calle. Solo como nací, a jugarme la vida y a visitar iglesias.

Señor Procurador: Yo soy la memoria de Colombia y su conciencia y después de mí no sigue nada. Cuando me muera aquí sí que va a ser el acabóse, el descontrol. Señor Fiscal General o Procurador o como se llame, mire que ando en riesgo de muerte por la calle: con las atribuciones que le dio la nueva Constitución protéjame.

¡Qué iglesia iba a haber abierta ni qué demonios! Las mantienen cerradas para que no las atraquen. Ya no nos queda en Medellín ni un solo oasis de paz. Dicen que atracan los bautizos, las bodas, los velorios, los entierros. Que matan en plena misa o llegando al cementerio a los que van vivos acompañando al muerto. Que si se cae un avión saquean los cadáveres. Que si te atropella un carro, manos caritativas te sacan la billetera mientras te hacen el favor de subirte a un taxi que te lleve al hospital. Que hay treinta y cinco mil taxis en Medellín desocupados atracando. Uno por cada carro particular. Que lo mejor es viajar en bus, aunque también tampoco: tampoco conviene, también los atracan. Que en el hospital a uno que tirotearon no sé dónde lo remataron. Que lo único seguro aquí es la muerte.

Los treinta y cinco mil taxis señalados (comprados con dólares del narcotráfico porque de dónde va a sacar dólares Colombia si nada exporta porque nada produce como no sea asesinos que nadie compra) llevan indefectiblemente los radios prendidos transmitiendo: partidos de fútbol, vallenatos, o noticias optimistas sobre los treinta y cinco que mataron ayer, quince por debajo del récord, aunque un soldado al que le pasó por el cuello un tiro libre (o sea que salió) me asegura que día hubo en Medellín en que mataron ciento setenta y tantos, y trescientos ese fin de semana. Sabrá Dios, que es el que ve desde arriba. Nosotros aquí abajo lo único que hacemos es recoger cadáveres. Si uno le dice al taxista: "Por favor, señor, bájele un poco a ese radio que está muy fuerte", el hideputa (como dice Cervantes) lo que hace es que le sube. Y si uno abre la boca para protestar, ¡adiós problemas de esta vida! Mañana te estarán comiendo esa lengua suelta los gusanos. Bueno, objetará usted, si los taxistas andan desocupados, ¿por qué tratan tan mal a los clientes? Por eso, porque les da uno trabajo, y "El trabajo degrada al hombre" dijo un sabio. ¿Y en los buses? ¿Se puede viajar en bus sin música? Tanto como se puede respirar sin oxígeno.

El vacío de la vida de Alexis, más incolmable que el mío, no lo llena un recolector de basura. Por no dejar y hacer algo, tras la casetera le compré un televisor con antena parabólica que agarra todas las estaciones de esta tierra y las galaxias. Se pasa ahora el día entero mi muchachito ante el televisor cambiando de canal cada minuto. Y girando, girando la antena parabólica al són de su capricho y de la rosa de los vientos a ver qué agarra para dejarlo ir. Sólo se detiene en los dibujos animados ¡Plas! Caía un gato malo sobre el otro y lo aplastaba: lo dejaba como una hojita finita de papel que entra suave por el rodillo de esta máquina. Sin saber ni inglés ni francés ni japonés ni nada sólo comprende el lenguaje universal del golpe. Eso hace parte de su pureza intocada. Lo demás es palabrería hueca zumbando en la cabeza. No habla español, habla en argot o jerga. En la jerga de las comunas o argot comunero que está formado en esencia de un viejo fondo de idioma local de Antioquia, que fue el que hablé yo cuando vivo (Cristo el arameo), más una que otra supervivencia del malevo antiguo del barrio de Guayaquil, ya demolido, que hablaron sus cuchilleros, ya muertos; y en fin, de una serie de vocablos y giros nuevos, feos, para designar ciertos conceptos viejos: matar, morir, el muerto, el revólver, la policía… Un ejemplo:

"¿Entonces qué, parce, vientos o maletas?" ¿Qué dijo? Dijo: "Hola hijo de puta". Es un saludo de rufianes.

El televisor de Alexis me acabó de echar a la calle. Alexis, por lo visto, no requería de mi presencia. Yo sí de la de él, en ausencia de Dios. Vagando por Medellín, por sus calles, en el limbo de mi vacío por este infierno, buscando entre almas en pena iglesias abiertas, me metí en un tiroteo. Iba por la estrecha calle de Junín rumbo a la catedral, llegando al parque, viendo, sin querer, entre la multitud ofuscada una señora de culo plano que iba adelante, cuando ¡pum!, que se enciende la balacera: dos bandas se agarraron a bala. Balas iban y venían, parabrisas explotaban y caían transeúntes como bolos en la barahúnda endemoniada. "¡Al suelo! ¡Al suelo!" gritaban. ¿Al suelo quién? ¿Yo? ¡Jamás! Mi dignidad me lo impide. Y seguí por entre las balas que me zumbaban en los oídos como cuchillas de afeitar. Y yo pensando en el viejo verso ¿de quién? "Oh muerte ven callada en la saeta". Pasé ileso, sano y salvo, y seguí sin mirar atrás porque la curiosidad es vicio de granujas.

"Hoy en el centro —le conté a Alexis luego hablando en jerga con mi manía políglota—

dos bandas se estaban dando chumbimba. De lo que te perdiste por andar viendo televisión". Se mostró interesado, y le conté hasta lo que no vi, con mil detalles. Le desplegué por todo Junín un tendal de muertos. Me sentía como Don Juan presumiéndole a Don Luis de las mujeres que se había echado. Luego procedí a contarle mi retirada, cómo pasé incólume por entre el plomero, sin agacharme, sin inmutarme, sin ni siquiera apurar. "¿Tú qué habrías hecho?" le pregunté. "Tocaba abrirse", contestó. ¿Huir yo? ¿Abrirme? Jamás de los jamases. Jamás. A mí la muerte me hace los mandados, niño.

¿Tenía una compensación ese tormento a que me sometía Alexis, mi éxodo diurno por las calles huyendo del ruido y metido en él? Sí, nuestro amor nocturno. Nuestras noches encendidas de pasión, yo abrazado a mi ángel de la guarda y él a mí con el amor que me tuvo, porque debo consignar aquí, sin jactancias ni presunción, lo mucho que me quería. Es de poca caridad, ya sé, exhibir la dicha propia ante la desgracia ajena, contarle historias de amor libre a quien vive prisionero, encerrado, casado, con mujer gorda y propia y cinco hijos comiendo, jodiendo y viendo televisión. Mas dejemos el aparato y sigamos, exhibiendo plata ante el mendigo. ¡Y qué! ¡Los pobres pobres son y por la verdad murió Cristo! Hénos pues en la cálida noche silenciosa, ardiendo la chimenea de nuestro amor en el calor del verano. "Abre las ventanas niño —le pedía— para que entre la brisa". Y mi niño se levantaba desnudo como un espejismo de las Mil y Una Noches y su imaginación desaforada, con sus tres escapularios, y abría el balcón. Brisa no entraba porque brisa no había, pero sí la música, el estrépito, del hippie de al lado y sus compinches, los mamarrachos. "Ese metalero condenado ya nos dañó la noche", me quejaba. "No es metalero —me explicó Alexis cuando se lo señalé en la calle al otro día—. Es un punkero". "Lo que sea. Yo a este mamarracho lo quisiera matar". "Yo te lo mato —me dijo Alexis con esa complacencia suya atenta siempre a mis más mínimos caprichos—. Dejáme que la próxima vez saco el fierro". El fierro es el revólver. Yo al principio creía que era un cuchillo pero no, es un revólver. Ah, y transcribí mal las amadas palabras de mi niño. No dijo "Yo te lo mato", dijo "Yo te lo quiebro". Ellos no conjugan el verbo matar: practican sus sinónimos. La infinidad de sinónimos que tienen para decirlo: más que los árabes para el camello. Pero antes de seguir con lo anunciado y de que mi niño saque el fierro, oigan lo que él me contó y que les quiero contar: que le habían dado un día "una mano de changón" en su barrio. Qué es un changón preguntarán los que no saben como pregunté yo que no sabía. Era una escopeta a la que le recortaban el tubo, me explicó mi niño. "¿Y para qué se lo cortan?" Que para que la lluvia de balines saliera más abierta y le diera al que estuviera cerca. ¿Y los balines qué? ¿Eran como municiones? Sí, sí eran. Pues tres de esos balines le metieron en el cuerpo a mi niño y ahí quedaron, sin salir: uno en el cuello, otro en el antebrazo y otro en el pie. "¿Justo donde llevas los escapularios?" "Ajá". "¿Y cuando te dispararon ya los llevabas?" "Ajá". "Si ya los llevabas entonces los escapularios no sirven". Que sí, que sí servían. Si no los hubiera llevado le habrían dado un plomazo en el corazón o en el cerebro. "Ah…" Contra esa lógica divina ya sí no se podía razonar. Lo que fuera. Ver a mi niño desnudo con sus tres escapularios me ponía en delirium tremens. Ese angelito tenía la propiedad de desencadenarme todos mis demonios interiores, que son como mis personalidades: más de mil.

Bajé en el acto la escalera, salí a la calle, compré una pesa o balanza, y volví a subir y lo pesé desnudo para descontarle, digamos, unos doscientos gramos de los balines. "Yo no sé si vas a crecer más o no niño, pero así como estás eres la maravilla. Mayor perfección ni soñarla". La pelusita del cuerpo a la luz del sol daba visos dorados. ¡Cómo no le tomé una foto! Si una imagen vale más que mil palabras, ¡qué no valdría mi niño vivo! "Vístete mi amor no te vayas a resfriar y vámonos a la Avenida Jardín a comernos una pizza". Fuimos y volvimos vivos, sin novedad. La ciudad se estaba como desinflando, perdiendo empuje. ¡Qué va! Amaneció a la entrada del edificio un mendigo acuchillado: les están sacando los ojos para una universidad…

Fue la tarde de un martes (pues en la mañana habíamos vuelto en peregrinación a Sabaneta) cuando el punkero "marcó cruces". "¡Ahí va! ¡Ahí va!" exclamó Alexis cuando lo vio en la calle. Ni tiempo tuve de detenerlo. Corrió hacia el hippie, se le adelantó, dio media vuelta, sacó el revólver y a pocos palmos le chantó un tiro en la frente, en el puro centro, donde el miércoles de ceniza te ponen la santa cruz. ¡Tas! Un solo tiro, seco, ineluctable, rotundo, que mandó a la gonorrea esa con su ruido a la profundidad de los infiernos. ¡Cuántas veces no he pasado la escena por mi cabeza en ralenti! Veo sus ojos verdes viéndolo. Verdes turbios. Embriagados en lo irrepetible del instante. ¡Tas! Un solo tiro, sin comentarios. Alexis guardó el revólver, dio media vuelta y siguió caminando como si nada. ¿Por qué no le disparó por detrás? ¿Por no matar a traición? No hombre, por matar viendo los ojos.

Cuando el hippie se desplomó pasaba en ese instante una moto. "¡Ahí van!" le señalé a una señora, el único transeúnte que pudo haber sido testigo del suceso. "¡Lo mataron!" exclamó la vieja. "Ajá", contesté: era una constatación evidente. Torpezas tales sólo se oyen en el cine mexicano, que suele poner en boca de los personajes obviedades, simplezas. Era evidente que estaba muerto: muerto está el que no resuella. ¿Pero quién lo mató? "¡Cómo que quién, señora! ¡Pues los de la moto! ¿No los vio?" Claro que los había visto, y que siguieron hacia la plaza de la América. Unos niños entre tanto se apuraban unos a otros: "¡Corran! ¡Corran! ¡Vengan a ver el muñeco!" El "muñeco" por si usted no lo sabe, por si no los conoce, es el muerto. El vivo de hace un instante pero que ya no. Todo lo alcanzó a ver la señora, y así se lo contaba al corrillo que se formó en torno al muerto y su protagonismo callado, una empalizada humana de curiosidad gozosa. Alcanzó a ver incluso ella que uno de los de la moto llevaba una camiseta estampada con calaveras y cruces. Fíjense nomás...

Antes de alejarme le eché una fugaz mirada al corrillo. Desde el fondo de sus almas viles se les rebosaba el íntimo gozo. Estaban ellos incluso más contentos que yo, ellos a quienes no les iba nada en el muerto. Aunque no tuvieran qué comer hoy sí tenían qué contar. Hoy por lo menos tenían la vida llena.

Mis conciudadanos padecen de una vileza congénita, crónica. Ésta es una raza ventajosa, envidiosa, rencorosa, embustera, traicionera, ladrona: la peste humana en su más extrema ruindad. ¿La solución para acabar con la juventud delincuente? Exterminen la niñez.

Y que no me vengan los alcahuetas que nunca faltan con que mataron al inocente por poner música fuerte. Aquí nadie es inocente, cerdos. Lo matamos por chichipato, por bazofia, por basura, por existir. Porque contaminaba el aire y el agua del río. Ah, "chichipato" quiere decir en las comunas delincuente de poca monta, raticas, eso.

Volví al apartamento y al rato llegó Alexis, con un garrafón de aguardiente: dos botellas y media pues. "Hubieras comprado también una copitas —le hice ver—. Ya ves que aquí no hay ni en qué tomar". "De la botella". Abrió la botella, se tomó un trago y me lo dio en la boca. Así, tomando yo en su boca, él en la mía, en el delirio de una vida idiota, de un amor imposible, de un odio ajeno nos empacamos el garrafón. Amanecimos en un charco de vómito: eran los demonios de Medellín, la ciudad maldita, que habíamos agarrado al andar por sus calles y se nos habían adentrado por los ojos, por los oídos, por la nariz, por la boca.

Las comunas cuando yo nací ni existían. Ni siquiera en mi juventud, cuando me fui. Las encontré a mi regreso en plena matazón, florecidas, pesando sobre la ciudad como su desgracia. Barrios y barrios de casuchas amontonadas unas sobre otras en las laderas de las montañas, atronándose con su música, envenenándose de amor al prójimo, compitiendo las ansias de matar con la furia reproductora. Ganas con ganas a ver cuál puede más. En el momento en que escribo el conflicto aún no se resuelve: siguen matando y naciendo. A los doce años un niño de las comunas es como

comunas

quien dice un viejo: le queda tan poquito de vida… Ya habrá matado a alguno y lo van a matar. Dentro de un tiempito, al paso a que van las cosas, el niño de doce que digo reemplácenlo por uno de diez. Ésa es la gran esperanza de Colombia. Como no sé qué sabe usted al respecto, mis disculpas por lo sabido y repetido y sigamos subiendo: mientras más arriba en la montaña mejor, más miseria. Uno en las comunas sube hacia el cielo pero bajando hacia los infiernos. ¿Por qué llamaron al conjunto de los barrios de una montaña comunas? Tal vez porque alguna calle o alcantarilla hicieron los fundadores por acción comunal. Sacando fuerzas de pereza.

Los fundadores, ya se sabe, eran campesinos: gentecita humilde que traía del campo sus costumbres, como rezar el rosario, beber aguardiente, robarle al vecino y matarse por chichiguas con el prójimo en peleas a machete. ¿Qué podía nacer de semejante esplendor humano? Más. Y más y más y más. Y matándose por chichiguas siguieron: después del machete a cuchillo y después del cuchillo a bala, y en bala están hoy cuando escribo. Las armas de fuego han proliferado y yo digo que eso es progreso, porque es mejor morir de un tiro en el corazón que de un machetazo en la cabeza. ¿Tiene este problemita solución? Mi respuesta es un sí rotundo como una bala: el paredón. Otra cosa sería buscarle la cuadratura al círculo. Una venganza trae otra y una muerte otra muerte, y tras la muerte vienen los inspectores de policía oficiando el levantamiento de los cadáveres. Pero digo mal, los inspectores no: la nueva Constitución dispone que lo realicen en adelante los agentes de la Fiscalía. Y éstos, sin la experiencia secular de aquéllos, copados por la avalancha de cadáveres, sin darse abasto, han eliminado el expedienteo y la ceremonia misma y se la han dejado a los gallinazos. ¿Cómo llenar, en efecto, veinte pliegos de papel sellado consignando la forma en que cayó el muñeco, si nadie vio aunque todos vieran? Para eso se necesita imaginación y los funcionarios de hoy en día no la tienen, como no sea para robar y depositar en Suiza. Acto jurídico trascendental, oficio de difuntos, ceremonia de tinieblas, el levantamiento del cadáver, ay, no se realizará más. Una institución tan entrañable, tan colombiana, tan nuestra… Nunca más. El tiempo barre con todo y las costumbres. Así, de cambio en cambio, paso a paso, van perdiendo las sociedades la cohesión, la identidad, y quedan hechas unas colchas deshilachadas de retazos.

Yo hablo de las comunas con la propiedad del que las conoce, pero no, sólo las he visto de lejos, palpitando sus lucecitas en la montaña y en la trémula noche. Las he visto, soñado, meditado desde las terrazas de mi apartamento, dejando que su alma asesina y lujuriosa se apodere de mí. Millares de foquitos encendidos, que son casas, que son almas, y yo el eco, el eco entre las sombras. Las comunas a distancia me encienden el corazón como a una choza la chispa de un rayo. Sólo una vez subí, y bajé, y nada vi porque me lo impidió tremendo aguacero. Uno de esos aguaceros de Antioquia en que el cielo cargado de rabia se desfonda.

Pero estoy anticipando, rompiendo el orden cronológico e introduciendo el desorden. ¡Cuánta agua de alcantarilla no arrastró el río antes de mi subida a las comunas! En tanto, por lo pronto, suelo divisarlas desde mis terrazas con Alexis a mi lado. Mi corazón a mi lado. Esas de allá, niño, rumbo al mar, hacia el norte, son la nororiental y la noroccidental, las más violentas, las más famosas: enfrentadas en opuestas montañas viéndose, calculándose, rebotándose sus odios. Corrígeme si me equivoco. Pero si Alexis no conoce el mar para qué lo menciono. No conoce ni siquiera el Cauca que está aquí abajo, el río de mi niñez que tiene una "u" en medio. Ese río es como yo: siempre el mismo en su permanencia yéndose. Alexis sólo conoce arroyos turbios, desaguaderos. "Señálame, niño, tu barrio, ¿cuál es?" ¿Es acaso Santo Domingo Savio? ¿O El Popular, o La Salle, o Villa del Socorro, o La Francia? Cualquiera, inalcanzable, entre esas luces allá a lo lejos... Ha de saber usted y si no lo sabe vaya tomando nota, que cristiano común y corriente como usted o yo no puede subir a esos barrios sin la escolta de un batallón: lo "bajan". ¿Y si lleva un arma? Se la "bajan". Y bajado el fierro le bajan los pantalones, el reloj, los tenis, la billetera y los calzoncillos si tiene o trusa. Y si opone resistencia porque éste es un país libre y democrático y aquí lo primero es el respeto a los derechos humanos, con su mismo fierro lo mandan a la otra ribera: a cruzar en pelota la laguna en la barca de Caronte. Usted verá si sube.

En lo alto de mi edificio, en las noches, mi apartamento es una isla oscura en un mar de luces. Lucecitas por doquiera en torno, en las montañas, palpitando en la nitidez del cielo porque aquí no hay smog: lo tumba la lluvia. Al atardecer nuestras montañas son tan nítidas, tan resaltadas, que haga de cuenta usted que las recortó un niño con tijeras de una foto del Colombiano. (El Colombiano es el periódico de Medellín, el que da los muertos: tantos hoy, ¿mañana cuántos?) Sí señor, Medellín en la noche es bello. ¿O bella? Ya ni sé, nunca he sabido si es hombre o mujer. Lo que sea. Como esas lucecitas ya dije que eran almas, viene a tener más almas que yo: tres millones y medio. Y yo una sola pero en pedazos. "Virgencita niña de Sabaneta, que vuelva a ser el que fui de niño, uno solo. Ayúdame a juntar las tablas del naufragio". Las veladoras de María Auxiliadora palpitaban al unísono como las lucecitas de Medellín en la unánime noche, rogándole al cielo que nos hiciera el milagro de volver a ser. A ser los que fuimos. "Yo ya no soy yo, Virgencita niña, tengo el alma partida".

¿Cuántos muertos lleva este niño mío, mi portentosa máquina de matar? Uno hasta donde sé y ahora. De los de más atrás no respondo. Yo no suelo preguntar como los curas que quieren saberlo todo para ellos solos, sin compartir, en secreto tumbal de confesión. Que cómo, que cuándo, que con quién, que por dónde. ¡Por donde sea! ¡Absuelvan en bloque carajo y desensotanen esa curiosidad rabiosa! Un padrecito

44

ingenuo de la Facultad de Teología de cierta católica universidad me contó una confesión diciendo el milagro pero callando el santo. O sea, revelando el secreto pero sin violarlo. Héla aquí: Que un muchacho sin rostro se fue a confesar con él y le dijo: "Acúsome padrecito de que me acosté con la novia". Y preguntando, preguntando que es como se llega a Roma que es adonde ellos quieren ir, el padre vino a saber que el muchacho era de profesión sicario y que había matado a trece, pero que de ésos no se venía a confesar porque ¿por qué? Que se confesara de ellos el que los mandó matar. De ése era el pecado, no de él que simplemente estaba haciendo un trabajo, un "camello". Ni siquiera les vio los ojos… "¿Y qué hizo usted padre con el presunto sicario, lo absolvió?" Sí, el presunto padre lo absolvió. De penitencia le puso trece misas, una por cada muerto, y por eso andan tan llenas de muchachos las iglesias.

Y aprovechando a este padrecito que están tan escasos desde que volvieron Centro Comercial al seminario yo le pregunto una cosa: ¿De quién es el pecado de la muerte del hippie? ¿De Alexis? ¿Mío? De Alexis no porque no lo odiaba así le hubiera visto los ojos. ¿Mío entonces? Tampoco. Que no lo quería, confieso.

45

¿Pero que lo mandé matar? ¡Nunca! Jamás de los jamases. Jamás le dije a Alexis: "Quebráme a éste". Lo que yo dije y ustedes son testigos fue: "Lo quisiera matar" y se lo dije al viento; mi pecado, si alguno, se quedó en el que quisiera. Y por un quisiera, en esta matazón, ¿se va a ir uno a los infiernos? Si sí yo me arrepiento y no vuelvo a querer más.

He ido a esa católica universidad huyendo de la música de Alexis. No se extrañe pues usted de encontrarme en los sitios más impensados. Aquí y allá y en el más allá. Huyendo de ese ruido infernal me estoy volviendo más ubicuo que Dios en su reino. Y así voy por estas calles de Medellín alias Medallo viendo y oyendo cosas. Desquitándole a la muerte, cruzando rápido antes de que me atropelle un presunto carro. Con eso de que les dio por tirarle el carro a uno tratando presuntamente de agarrarlo como si fuera uno cualquier presunto conejo siendo uno y ellos todos presuntos cristianos...

Impulsado por su vacío esencial Alexis agarra en el televisor cualquier cosa: telenovelas, partidos de fútbol, conjuntos de rock, una puta declarando, el presidente. El otro día se estaba rasgando este maldito las vestiduras porque dizque unos sicarios habían matado a un senador de la República. ¡Ay, de la República! Como si aquí hubiera senadores de los departamentos, tonta. Esto no es los Estados Unidos. Además los senadores en Colombia tampoco son unas peritas en dulce. Que les va a cargar a los que lo mataron "todo el peso de la ley", dice la original. Como si supiera quién. ¿Y hoy qué? Hoy dando parte a la nación porque veinticinco mil soldados habían dado de baja al presunto capo-jefe del narcotráfico, contratador de sicarios. Que no prevalecería el delito, como si el delito con sus hermanos contratos no le pisara la cola. Y que vamos en la dirección correcta: "in the right direction", como oyó decir en inglés. Y yo sólo pregunto una cosa: ¿la ley en Colombia matando presuntos? Ah, y que les va a dar el parte de la victoria a los gringos en su lengua, porque también él es políglota. Y lo creo muy capaz: les lee el discurso que le escribieron en inglés con esa vocecita chillona, montañera, maricona, suya, y con el candor y acento de un niño de escuela que está aprendiendo: "This is my nose. That is your pipi". "¡Apaga a ese bobo marica —le dije a Alexis—, que pa maricas los de aquí adentro!" Se rió de verme tan desquicia-do, tan enojado, y oh milagro, lo apagó. Y aña-dió: "Si querés te quiebro a esa gonorrea", con esos calificativos suyos que adoro. "¿Y cuándo vas a quebrar la casetera?" pregunté. "Ya". Y la tomó, corrió al balcón y la tiró por el balcón. Le hice ver lo irresponsable de esos arrebatos incontrolados suyos que podían matar, con un poquito de suerte, a algún presunto transeúnte que pasara.

Con la muerte del presunto narcotraficante que dijo arriba nuestro primer mandatario, aquí prácticamente la profesión de sicario se acabó. Muerto el santo se acabó el milagro. Sin trabajo fijo, se dispersaron por la ciudad y se pusieron a secuestrar, a atracar, a robar. Y sicario que trabaja solo por su cuenta y riesgo ya no es sicario: es libre empresa, la iniciativa privada. Otra institución pues nuestra que se nos va. En el naufragio de Colombia, en esta pérdida de nuestra identidad ya no nos va quedando nada.

Pero concentrémonos en Alexis que es la razón de esta historia. ¿Cuándo pensaba quebrar el televisor? Mi mente acariciaba la idea como a un gatico de raso. ¿Qué lo va a inducir? ¿Lo puedo inducir yo con mi mente poderosa? Mucho lo dudo porque yo me he concentrado días y días en que se muera Castro y sigue ahí, entronizado. (Castro es Fidel y Fidel es Cuba y Cuba el universo mundo y su revolución socialista.)

De los muertos de Alexis, cinco fueron gratis, por culebras propias; y cinco pagados, por culebras ajenas. ¿Qué son "culebras"? Son cuentas pendientes. Como usted comprenderá, en ausencia de la ley que se pasa todo el tiempo renovándose, Colombia es un serpentario. Aquí se arrastran venganzas casadas desde generaciones: pasan de padres a hijos, de hijos a nietos: van cayendo los hermanos. Bueno, ¿que cómo supe lo de Alexis si yo no pregunto? Sin preguntar, me lo contó La Plaga. Él es un niño divino, maldadoso, malo, que se quedó también sin trabajo. Tiene quince añitos con pelusita que te desarman el corazón. Creo que se llama Heider Antonio, un nombre bello. Y cuando no está matando está jugando billar: en el Salón de Billares X… (No digo el nombre porque de pronto le da al dueño por iniciarme una "acción de tutela" como marca la nueva Constitución, y después me cargan todo el peso de la ley.)

A La Plaga lo conocí también en el cuarto de las mariposas, pero nuestro amor no prosperó: me dijo que tenía novia y que la pensaba preñar pa tener un hijo que lo vengara. "¿Y de qué, Plaguita?" No, de nada, de lo que fuera. De lo que no alcanzara él. Este sentido previsor de nuestra juventud me renueva las esperanzas. Mientras haya futuro por delante fluye muy bien el presente. En cuanto al pasado... Pasado es el que yo tengo y el que me mantiene así.

A todo se le llega en este mundo su día: pasa el alcalde, pasa el ministro, pasa el presidente y el Cauca sigue fluyendo, fluyendo, fluyendo hacia el ancho mar que es el gran vertedero de desagües. ¿Que por qué lo digo? Hombre, mire, vea, fíjese, porque se le llegó también su día al televisor. La muerte de este maldito es digna de un poema. Lo estoy pensando en versos de arte mayor, en alejandrinos de catorce sílabas que me salen tan bien. Yo soy de respiración pausada y de tiro largo.

Los hechos ocurrieron así: llegué una tarde cansado, derrumbado, derrotado, sin un carajo de ganas de vivir. Yo no resisto una ciudad con treinta y cinco mil taxis con el radio prendido. Aunque vaya a pie y no los tome, sé que ahí van con su carraca, pasando noticias de muertos que no son míos, de partidos de fútbol en los que nada me va, y declaraciones de funcionarios mamones de la teta pública que están saqueándome a mí, Colombia, el país eterno. "Yo te los quiebro —me repite Alexis—, decíme cuál". Nunca digo. ¡Para qué! Eso es tirarle a langostas con escopeta. "Niño —le dije a Alexis—, préstame tu revólver que ya no aguanto. Me voy a matar". Alexis sabe que no bromeo, su perspicacia lo siente. Corrió al revólver y para que no me quedara una sola bala se las vació al televisor, lo único que encontró: estaba hablando el presidente, para variar. Que no sé qué, que el peso de la ley. Fue lo último que dijo esta cotorra mojada, y nunca más volvió a abrir su puerco pico en mi casa. Después silencio, silencio en mis noches calladas que están cantando las cigarras, arrullándome el oído con su eterna canción, que oyó Homero.

Mayor error no pude cometer con la quiebra de ese televisor. Sin televisor Alexis se quedó más vacío que balón de fútbol sin patas que le den, lleno de aire. Y se dedicó a lo que le dictaba su instinto: a ver los últimos ojos, la última mirada del que ya nunca más.

Las balas para recargar el revólver se las compró este su servidor, que por él vive. Fui directamente a la policía y les dije: "Véndanmelas a mí, que soy decente. Aparte de unos cuantos libros que he escrito no tengo prontuario". "¿Libros de qué?" "De gramática, mi cabo". ¡Era un sargento! Este desconocimiento mío de las charreteras era vívida prueba de mi verdad, de mi inocencia, y me las vendió: un paquetote pesado.

"¡Uy, vos sí sos un verraco! —me dijo Alexis—. Consigámonos una subametralladora". "Niño, 'consigámonos' somos muchos. A mí no me incluyas". ¡Pero cómo no incluir en el amor!

Los próximos muertos de Alexis fueron tres soldados. Íbamos por el parque de Bolívar, el principal, cuando los vimos de lejos en una requisa. Si Alexis traía el fierro, lo mejor era desviarnos. "¿Y por qué?" "Hombre, niño, porque nos van a requisar y te lo van a quitar. ¿No ves que somos sospechosos?" Me incluí en el "somos" por delicadeza; aquí nadie sospecha de los viejos, que ya están probados: atracadores viejos no los hay, unos con otros hace mucho que se mataron, pues si bien es cierto que perro no come perro, atracador sí atraca a atracador. "Desviémonos". Que no, y seguimos. Y claro, nos detuvieron. Más les valía no haber nacido. ¡Tas! ¡Tas! ¡Tas! Tres tiros en las puras frentes y tres soldados caídos, tiesos. ¿Cuándo sacó Alexis el revólver? Ni alcancé a ver. Los soldados me iban a requisar a mí ya que me metí en el charco a alborotar los tiburones, para seguir con mi niño. Ya no siguieron. Aunque en su ultimísimo instante en vida querían, ya no pudieron. Los muertos no requisan. De un tiro en la frente a cualquiera le borran la computadora.

A mató 3 soldados

Era tan asombroso el suceso, tan imprevisto el suceso que no sabía qué hacer. Alexis tampoco. Se quedó viendo los cadáveres como hipnotizado, mirándoles los ojos. "Se me hace que lo mejor es que nos vamos yendo, niño, a almorzar". Aquí el almuerzo era a las doce, pero con este cambio de las costumbres se ha ido pasando para la una y media. Alexis se guardó el revólver y seguimos caminando como si nada. Es lo mejor en estos casos: como si nada. Correr es malo. El que corre pierde la dignidad y se cae y lo agarran. Además, aquí desde hace mucho, pero mucho es mucho, ya nadie persigue ladrones. En mi niñez, recuerdo, los transeúntes viles, amparados por la dizque ley, solían correr tras el ladrón. Hoy nadie. El que lo alcance se muere, y el alma colectiva, gregaria, ruin, la jauría cobarde y maricona ya lo sabe. ¿Muchas ganas de perseguir? Se queda quietecito y nada vio, si quiere seguir viendo. Policías en torno no había y mejor para ellos: tres tiros le quedaban a mi niño en el fierro para ponerles a otros tantos en la frente su cruz de ceniza. Para morir nacimos.

Almorzamos sancocho, que es lo que se come aquí. Y para abrir más el apetito, cada quien una Pilsen, y no es propaganda porque son muy malas, es la pura verdad. Una cerveza Pilsen nos tomamos y yo pedí para el sancocho un limón. A todo le pongo. "Y nos trae, señorita, unas servilletas, caramba, ¿o con qué cree que nos vamos a limpiar?" Esta raza es tan mezquina, tan mala, que aquí las servilletas de papel las cortan en ocho para economizar: ponen a los empleados cuando no hay clientes a cortarlas: pa que trabajen, los hijueputas. Así es aquí.

Me limpié con el papelito la boca y se me embarraron los dedos... ¿Y en los sanitarios? En los sanitarios (le voy a explicar a usted porque es turista extranjero) no pueden poner papel higiénico porque se roban el rollo: cuando inauguraron el aeropuerto nuevo de Medellín, que costó una millonada, un solo día lo pusieron y nunca más. Fue la multitud novelera con sus niños a conocerlo y se robaron hasta los sanitarios. Ah, y los maleteros, o sea los que cargan las maletas, son los que inician los robos. Que ese "man" que va allá trae un fajo de billetes y dos maletadas de contrabando: en cualquiera de las tres bajadas del aeropuerto a Medellín lo bajan. La otra vez, cuando volvía de Suiza, vi a un cristiano bajando a pie por una de esas carreteras como si anduviera en Grecia en una playa nudista, o sea como Dios lo echó al mundo a funcionar. Mi taxista no lo quiso

54

recoger no fuera a ser un gancho para robarle el taxi. ¡Y yo convencido de que los taxistas eran los atracadores! No señor, o sí señor, aquí la vida humana no vale nada.

¿Y por qué habría de valer? Si somos cinco mil millones, camino de seis… Imprímalos en billetes a ver qué quedan valiendo. Cuando hay un cinco —digamos seis— con nueve ceros a la derecha, uno es un cero a la izquierda. Vale más un mono tití, de los que quedan pocos y son muy bravos. Nada somos, parcerito, nada semos, curémonos de este "afán protagónico" y recordemos que aquí nada hay más efímero que el muerto de ayer. ¿Quién sabe de los tres solداditos del parque que dizque nos iban a requisar? No salieron ni en El Colombiano, y el que no sale en El Colombiano es porque sigue vivo o está muerto. ¿Y "parcerito" qué es? Es aquel a quien uno quiere aunque uno no se lo diga aunque él bien que lo sabe. Sutilezas de las comunas, pues.

La fugacidad de la vida humana a mí no me inquieta; me inquieta la fugacidad de la muerte: esta prisa que tienen aquí para olvidar. El muerto más importante lo borra el siguiente partido de fútbol. Así, de partido en partido se está liquidando la memoria de cierto candidato a la presidencia, liberal, muy importante, que hubo aquí y que tumbaron a bala de una tarima unos sicarios, al anochecer, bajo unas luces dramáticas y ante veinte mil copartidarios suyos en manifestación con banderas rojas. Ese día puso el país el grito en el cielo y se rasgaba las vestiduras. Y al día siguiente ¡goool! Los goles atruenan el cielo de Medellín y después tiran petardos o "papeletas" y "voladores", y uno no sabe si es de gusto o si son las mismas balas de anoche. Se oyen tiros en la oscuridad, por aquí, por allá, y uno antes de volverse a dormir se pregunta: "¿A quién habrán sacado ya de la fiesta?" Después usted vuelve a las ondas alfa, beta, gamma del sueño, arrullado por los tiros. Dormirse con tiroteo es mejor que con aguacero. Se siente uno tan protegido en su cama… Y yo con Alexis, mi amor… Alexis duerme abrazado a mí con su trusa y nada, pero nada, nada le perturba el sueño. Desconoce la preocupación metafísica.

Mire parcero: no somos nada. Somos una pesadilla de Dios, que es loco. Cuando mataron al candidato que dije yo estaba en Suiza, en un hotel con lago y televisor. "Kolumbien" dijeron en el televisor y el corazón me dio un vuelco: estaban pasando la manifestación de los veinte mil en el pueblito de la sabana y el tiroteo. Cayó el muñeco con su afán protagónico. Muerto logró lo que quiso en vida. La tumbada de la tarima le dio la vuelta al mundo e hizo resonar el nombre de la patria. Me sentí tan, pero tan orgulloso de Colombia… "Ustedes —les dije a los suizos— prácticamente están muertos. Reparen en esas imágenes que ven: eso es vida, pura vida".

El próximo muertico de Alexis resultó siendo un transeúnte grosero: un muchachote fornido, soberbio, malo que es lo que es esta raza altanera. Por Junín, sin querer, nos tropezamos con él. "Aprendan a caminar, maricas —nos dijo—. ¿O es que no ven?" Yo, la verdad, veo poco, pero Alexis mucho, ¿o si no cómo esa puntería? Pero esta vez, para variar, bordando sobre el mismo tema su consabida sonata no le chantó el pepazo en la frente, no: en la boca, en la sucia boca por donde maldijo. Y así, quién lo iba a creer, la última palabra que dijo el vivo fue "ven", como pueden ver volviendo a ver su frase. Nunca más vio. A estos muertos se les quedan los ojos abiertos sin ver. Y ojos que no ven, aunque uno los vea, no son ojos, como atinadamente observó el poeta Machado, el profundo.

Cuando el incidente íbamos para la Candelaria y para la Candelaria seguimos, sin más preámbulos, en el tropel. Esta iglesia es la más hermosa de Medellín, que tiene ciento cincuenta y que las conozco yo: cien con Alexis, esperando a veces horas enteras a que las abran. Pero la Candelaria nunca la cierran. Tiene a la entrada en la nave izquierda un Señor Caído de un dramatismo hermoso, doloroso, alumbrado siempre por veladoras: veinte, treinta, cuarenta llamitas rojas, efímeras, palpitando, temblando, titilando rumbo a la eternidad de Dios. Dios aquí sí se siente y el alma de Medellín que mientras yo viva no muere, que va fluyendo por esta frase mía con los ciento y tantos gobernadores que tuvo Antioquia, a tropezones, como don Pedro Justo Berrío, quien sigue afuera, en su parque, en su estatua, bombardeado por las traviesas e irreverentes palomas que lo abanican y demás. O como don Recaredo de Villa a quien, apuesto, usted no ha oído ni mencionar. Yo sí, lo conozco. Yo sé más de Medellín que Balzac de París, y no lo invento: me estoy muriendo con él.

¿Estuvo bien este último "cascado" de Alexis, el transeúnte boquisucio? ¡Claro que sí, yo lo apruebo! Hay que enseñarle a esta gentuza alzada la tolerancia, hay que erradicar el odio. ¿Cómo es eso de que porque uno se tropieza con otro en una calle atestada le van soltando semejantes vulgaridades? No es la palabra en sí (porque los maricas son buenos en esta explosión demográfica): es su carga de odio. Cuestión pues de semántica, como diría nuestro presidente Barco, el inteligente, que nos gobernó cuatro años con el mal de Alzheimer y le declaró la guerra al narcotráfico y en plena guerra se le olvidó. "¿Contra quién es que estamos peliando?" preguntó y se acomodó la caja de dientes (o sea la dentadura postiza). "Contra los narcos, presidente", le contestó el doctor Montoya, su secretario y memoria. "Ah…" fue todo lo que contestó, con esa sabiduría suya. El que no sea capaz de convivir que se vaya: a Venezuela, a ultratumba, a Marte, adonde sea. Sí niño, esta vez sí me parece bien lo que hiciste, aunque de malgenio en malgenio, de grosero en grosero vamos acabando con Medellín. Hay que desocupar a Antioquia de antioqueños malos y repoblarla de antioqueños buenos, así sea éste un contrasentido ontológico.

Pero retomando el hilo perdido del discurso, el hilo de Machado y sus meditaciones trascendentales sobre el ojo, volvamos a los del muerto para preguntarnos: ¿por qué será que no los cierran? Abiertos, brillantes todavía de rabia mala, siguen reflejando sin parpadear al corrillo alegre, a la chusma vil que se arremolina en torno. Una vez, a uno, por caridad, se los quise cerrar para que no viera tanto alborozo, pero se le volvían a abrir como los de esos viejos muñecos de hace años que decían: "Mamá".

¿Difuntos? ¡Difuntos los que aquí hacemos! En el barrio de Aranjuez, la cuna de los Priscos que fueron la primera banda de sicarios, los que iniciaron la profesión, los pioneros, y que como tales ya están todos cascados, muertos, en el parque de ese barrio digo, estaba yo con Alexis (o si prefieren él conmigo) esperando a que abrieran la iglesita de San Nicolás de Tolentino para conocerla, cuando me volví a encontrar con El Difunto. Meses hacía que no lo veía, y lo noté muy recuperado, muy "repuesto". "Ábranse —nos dijo—, que los van a cascar". "Carambas, si alguna sospecha tengo yo a estas alturas del partido, parcero, es que soy más incascable que vos —le contesté—. Pero gracias por la advertencia". ¡El Difunto! Así llamado porque en un salón de billares lo encendieron a plomo y le empacaron cuatro tiros y murió pero no: cuando estaban en el velorio borrachos los parceros, abrazados al ataúd y cantándole "Tumba humilde" con un trío, tumbaron el ataúd, que al caer se abrió, y al abrirse salió el muerto: fue saliendo

El Difunto pálido, pálido, dicen, y que con una erección descomunal. Esto, en términos psicoanalíticos, yo lo llamaría el triunfo de Eros sobre Thánatos. ¡Pero qué carajos, si el psicoanálisis está más en bancarrota que Marx! Al Difunto también me lo regalaron, recién salido del ataúd, y no eran sino los restos de lo que fue, del joven fornido y sano. Y ahora exangüe, anémico, fantasmal… ¡Pero qué, quién se resiste a acostarse con el ahijado de la Muerte! Siempre es bueno tener abogados que intercedan por uno ante tan caprichosa señora. ¿Pero a santo de qué estoy hablando de éste? Ah, porque dizque nos iban a matar en Aranjuez, un barrio alto pero muy bajo: alto en la montaña y bajo en mi consideración social. Ahí, cuando yo nací, terminaba esta ciudad delirante. Ahora ahí empiezan las comunas, que son la paz.

Nos levantamos de la banca del parque y dimos una somera vuelta por detrás de la iglesia tras despedirnos, por supuesto, del Difunto. Al regresar ahí estaban: bajándose de una moto, en el atrio, pensando que estábamos adentro pero no, estábamos afuera, y detrás de ellos. Sin muchas averiguaciones, ipso facto, en plena calle, Alexis les hizo lo mismito que otros le habían hecho al Difunto en el salón de billares: los

61

encendió a bala. Estos difuntos, sin embargo, hasta donde yo sé, no regresaron nunca de su oscuro reino. Ahí están todavía esperándome, a mí con mis dudosos lectores.

¿Qué cómo llegué a saber, a confirmar? Hombre, de lo más simple, de lo más sencillo, de lo más fácil: lo dijo el taxi. Llevaba el radio prendido cacariando, el asqueroso, cuando tras la noticia de otra matazón dieron la de ésta: que dos víctimas más, inocentes, de esta guerra sin fin no declarada, habían caído acribillados en el atrio de la iglesia de Aranjuez cuando se dirigían a misa, por dos presuntos sicarios al servicio del narcotráfico. ¿Yo un presunto "sicario"? ¡Desgraciados! ¡Yo soy un presunto gramático! No lo podía creer. Qué calumnia, qué desinformación. A ver, ¿quién me pagó? ¿Qué narcotraficante conozco yo como no sea nuestro embajador en Bulgaria porque salió en el periódico? ¿Sicario el que se defiende? ¿Qué policía había que nos defendiera a nosotros cuando nos iban a matar? De haber habido, nos habrían detenido para extorsionarnos. Pero no, andaban extorsionando en el centro. En la agonía de esta sociedad los periodistas son los heraldos del enterrador. Ellos y las funerarias son los únicos que se lucran. Y los médicos. Ése es su modus vivendi, vivir de la muerte ajena. En Italia a los periodistas los llaman "i paparazzi", o sea los papagayos; estos de aquí son buitres.

¡Y vuelta a ese apartamento vacío con una cama! La cama para el amor sólo sirve los primeros días; después el amor debe nutrirse de otras fuentes. ¿Cómo por ejemplo cuáles? Como por ejemplo digamos, montar una empresita juntos. Lo de la empresita lo pensé y lo deseché: ¡qué empresa va a prosperar aquí con tanta prestación, jubilación, inseguridad, impuestos, leyes! Impuestos y más impuestos pa que a la final nu haiga ni con qué tapar un hueco. El primer atracador de Colombia es el Estado. ¿Y una industrica? La industria aquí está definitivamente quebrada: para todo el próximo milenio. ¿Y el comercio? Los asaltan. ¿Y servicios? ¡Qué servicios! ¿Poner una casa de muchachos? No los pagan. El campo también es otro desastre. Como está tan ocupado en la procreación, el campesino no trabaja. ¿Y de qué viven? Viven del racimo de plátanos que le roban al vecino, hasta que el vecino no vuelve a sembrar. No, el amor aquí no tiene alicientes. Es una chimenea sin leños que se mantiene como por milagro, ardiendo apagada.

Si por los menos Alexis leyera… Pero esta criatura en eso era tan drástico como el gran presidente Reagan, que en su larga vida un solo libro no leyó. Esta pureza incontaminada de letra impresa, además, era de lo que más me gustaba de mi niño. ¡Para libros los que yo he leído! y mírenmé, véanmé. ¿Pero sabía acaso firmar el niño? Claro que sí sabía. Tenía la letra más excitante y arrevesada que he conocido: alucinante que es como en última instancia escriben los ángeles que son demonios. Aquí guardo una foto suya dedicada a mí por el reverso. Me dice simplemente así: "Tuyo, para toda la vida", y basta. ¿Para qué quería más? Mi vida entera se agota en eso.

Saliendo de conocer la iglesia de Robledo (un galponcito desangelado en donde a duras penas se para mi Dios), decidimos seguir pendiente arriba en busca de un mirador en la montaña para divisar a Medellín, para apreciarlo en su conjunto con la objetividad que da la distancia, sin predisposiciones ni amores. A mano izquierda subiendo, en una finquita vieja, un rodadero con un platanar seco, abandonado, leíase el siguiente anuncio en mayúsculas torcidas y desflecadas, como para cartel de Drácula: SE PROHÍBE ARROJAR CADÁVERES. ¿Se prohíbe? ¿Y

64

esos gallinazos qué? ¿Qué era entonces ese ir y venir de aves negras, brincando, aleteando, picoteando, patrasiándose para sacarle mejor las tripas al muerto? Como un niño travieso, haga de cuenta usted, jalándole la cuerda a un payasito de cuerda que ya no hará más payasadas en esta vida. ¿El cadáver de quién? ¡Y yo qué sé! Nosotros no lo matamos. De un hijo de su mamá. Cuando pasábamos ya estaba ahí, y en plena fiesta los gallinazos e invitando más. Lo tostaron y ahí lo tiraron violando el anuncio, de donde se deduce que: mientras más se prohíbe menos se cumple. ¿Sería en vida una bellecita? ¿O un "man" malevo? "Man" aquí significa como en inglés, hombre. Nuestros manes, pues, no son los espíritus protectores. Por el contrario, son humanos e hideputas, como dijo Don Quijote.

Dije arriba que no sabía quién mató al vivo pero sí sé: un asesino omnipresente de psiquis tenebrosa y de incontables cabezas: Medellín, también conocido por los alias de Medallo y de Metrallo lo mató.

¿Que si tiene el país cosas buenas? Pero claro, lo bueno es que aquí nadie se muere de aburrición. Va uno de bache en bache desquitándole al atracador y al gobierno. Compañero, amigo y paisano: no hay ave más hermosa que el gallinazo, ni de más tradición: es el buitre del español milenario, el "vultur" latino. Tienen estas avecitas la propiedad de transmutar la carroña humana en el espíritu del vuelo. Mejores pilotos nadie, ni los del narcotráfico. ¡Mírenlos sobre el cielo de Medellín planeando! Columpiándose en el aire, desflecando nubes, abanicando el infinito azul con su aleteo negro. Ese negro que es el luto de los entierros… Y aterrizan como los pilotos de don Pablo: en un campito insignificante, minúsculo, cual la punta de este dedo. "Me gustaría terminar así —le dije a Alexis—, comido por esas aves para después salir volando". A mí que no me metan en camisa de ataúd por la fuerza: que me tiren a uno de esos botaderos de cadáveres con platanar y prohibición expresa, escrita, para violarla, que es como he vivido y como lo dispongo aquí. Desde el morro del Pan de Azúcar hasta el Picacho vuelan los gallinazos con sus plumas negras, con sus almas limpias sobre el valle, y son, como van las cosas, la mejor prueba que tengo de la existencia de Dios.

En tanto, mientras llamamos a Éste a pedirle cuentas, sigamos ajustándoselas a nuestros paisanos de aquí abajo. Después de los dos sicarios de Aranjuez con moto ¿quién siguió? ¿Siguió la empleada grosera, o el taxista altanero? Aquí si ya no sé, con esta memoria cansada se me empiezan a embrollar los muertos. ¡Para Funés el memorioso nuestro ex presidente Barco! Como el orden de los factores no altera el producto, que pase primero el taxista altanero. Sucedieron así las cosas: frente a la antigua estación del Ferrocarril de Antioquia (ya desmantelado porque se robaron los rieles), tomamos un taxi entre buses atestados. Pues, para variar, llevaba el taxista el radio prendido tocando vallenatos, que son una carraca con raspa y que no soporta mi delicado oído. "Bájele al radio, señor, por favor", le pidió este su servidor con la suavidad que lo caracteriza. ¿Qué hizo el ofendido? Le subió el volumen a lo que daba, "a todo taco". "Entonces pare, que nos vamos a bajar", le dije. Paró en seco, con un frenazo de padre y señor mío que nos mandó hacia adelante, y para rematar mientras nos bajábamos nos remachó la madre: "Se bajan, hijueputas", y arrancó: arrancó casi sin que tocáramos el piso, haciendo rechinar las llantas. De los mencionados hijueputas, yo me bajé humildemente por la derecha, y Alexis por la izquierda: por la izquierda, por su occipital o huesito posterior, trasero, le entró el certero tiro al ofuscado, al cerebro, y le apagó la ofuscación. Ya no tuvo que ver más con pasajeros impertinentes el taxista, se licenció de trabajar, lo licenció la Muerte: la Muerte, la justiciera, la mejor patrona, lo jubiló. Con el impulso que llevaba el taxi por la rabia, más el que le añadió el tiro, se siguió hasta ir a dar contra un poste a explotar, mas no sin antes llevarse en su carrera loca hacia el otro toldo a una señora embarazada y con dos niñitos, la cual ya no tuvo más, truncándose así la que prometía ser una larga carrera de maternidad.

¡Qué esplendida explosión! Las llamas abrasaron al vehículo malhechor pero Alexis y yo tuvimos tiempo de acercarnos a ver cómo ardía el muñeco. De lo más de bien, como dicen aquí con este idioma tan expresivo. "¡Que una soda para apagarlo!" pedía a gritos un transeúnte imbécil. "Y de dónde vamos a sacar una soda, hombre. ¿Acaso somos James Bond que lleva todo lo que se necesita encima? Déjelo que se acabe de quemar para que ya no sufra". Treinta y cinco mil taxis había en Medellín; quedaban treinta y cuatro mil novecientos noventa y nueve.

Y llegado aquí sí me quito el sombrero ante el ex presidente Barco. Tenía razón, todo el

problema de Colombia es una cuestión de semántica. Vamos a ver: "hijueputa" aquí significa mucho o no significa nada. "¡Qué frío tan hijueputa!", por ejemplo, quiere decir: ¡qué frío
tan intenso! "Es un tipo de una inteligencia la
hijueputa" quiere decir: muy inteligente. Pero
"hijueputas" a secas como nos dijo ese desgraciado, ah, eso ya sí es otra cosa. Es el veneno
que te escupe la serpiente. Y a las serpientes ve-
nenosas hay que quebrarles la cabeza: o ellas o
uno, así lo dispuso mi Dios. Muerta la serpiente seguimos con Eva, la empleada de la cafetería: murió de un tiro en la boca. Cuando nos tiró el café la delicada, porque le pedimos una
servilleta entera y no esos triangulitos de papel
minúsculos con los que no se limpia ni la trom-
pa una hormiga, a Alexis lo primero que se le
ocurrió fue la boca, y por la boca se despachó a
la maldita. Guardó su juguete y salimos de la
cafetería como si tales, limpiándonos satisfe-
chos con un palillo los dientes. "Aquí se come
muy bien, hay que volver". Como usted comprenderá nunca volvimos. Eso de que se vuelve
al sitio son pendejadas de Dostoievsky. Volvería
él cuando mató a la vieja, yo no. ¿Para qué?
¿Habiendo tanta cafetería en Medellín y tan
atentas?

Por esos días de tanto refuego se empeñó Alexis en que le comprara una mini-Uzi. "Por ningún motivo, ni lo sueñes, una mini-Uzi jamás. Eso es muy visible, nos pone muy banderas". Para mí era casi como una erección en el bus. ¿Se imaginan ustedes a uno andando con una subametralladora acomodada entre los pantalones? ¿Que cómo son? Ah, yo no sé, nunca se la compré. Según él, que la policía me la vendía, que yo era muy verraco pa convencer. "Seré yo muy verraco, ¿pero qué les voy a alegar a ésos?" ¿Que la necesito para defenderme del televisor y sus continuos atentados al idioma? No, aunque mi más profundo deseo fuera complacerlo, definitivamente no. Ahora, pasado el tiempo, me río de esos adverbios en "mente", tan largos pero tan desinflados. Son meras apariencias. Si hubiera insistido un poquito, yo me conozco, hubiera ido adonde el mismísimo general comandante en jefe a comprarle su mini-Uzi. El último gramático de Colombia, que tuvo tantos y tan famosos, no puede andar con menos que con una mini-Uzi para su protección personal, ¿o no, mi general? Otra cosa es que tenga uno tiempo para sacarla. En este oeste…

Tampoco le compré la moto. ¿Me pueden ver a mí, con esta dignidad, con estos años, abrazado a él de "parrillero" en una moto enve- nenada, todos ventiados? No, que ni lo soñara. "Así que me va apagando ese radio, señor taxis- ta, que hoy no ando pa discusiones". Y santo re- medio, lo apagaban. Algo oían en mi tono de perentorio, la voz de Thánatos, que les quitaba toda gana de disentir: o lo apagaban o lo apaga- ban. ¡Qué delicia viajar entre el rüido en el si- lencio! El süave rüido de afuera entraba por una ventanilla del taxi y salía por la otra purificado de agresiones personales, como filtrado por el silencio de adentro.

Y ahora qué, sin mini-Uzi, sin moto, ¿qué nos ponemos a hacer? "Pónte a leer Dos Años de Vacaciones, niño". ¡Qué iba a leer! No tenía la paciencia. Todo lo quería ya, como un tiro por entre un tubo. Por lo menos era martes, día de peregrinación a Sabaneta: cuando llegamos en plena plaza se estaban encendiendo a bala dos bandas que no se podían ver, pero que ni en pin- tura. Se estaban dando plomo a lo loco estos dos combos "por cuestiones territoriales", como de- cían antes los biólogos y como dicen ahora los sociólogos. ¿Territoriales? ¿Dos bandas de la comuna nororiental, que como su nombre lo indica está en el Norte, agarradas de la greña en Sabaneta, que está en el Sur, en el otro extremo?

Sabaneta goza de extraterritorialidad, amigos, y aquí no me vengan a dirimir sus querellas de barrio: esto es mar abierto para todos los tiburones. ¡O qué! ¿Creen que María Auxiliadora es propiedad privada? María Auxiliadora es de todos y el parque de nadie: que ninguno sueñe con que es propio porque orinó primero, porque en este parque nadie orina.

Eso que dije yo es lo que debió decir la autoridad, pero como aquí no hay autoridad sino para robar, para saquear a la res pública... Y así me encuentro a Sabaneta, el pueblo sagrado de mi niñez, en el bochinche y la guachafita, en el más descarado desorden que me están introduciendo estos cabrones. Mi indignación no podía más, me estaba dando un ataque de ira santa. "¡Uuuuuu! ¡Uuuuuu!" aullaba una ambulancia con su letrero de ambulancia escrito al revés para que uno tenga que leerlo patas arriba dando la vuelta; paraba en seco y se bajaban dos camilleros a recoger a los muertos. Dos, tres, cuatro... ¿Esto es la guerra de Bosnia-Herzegovina o qué, una masacre? Y hé aquí otro ejemplo de lo hiperbólico que se nos ha vuelto el idioma en manos de los "comunicadores sociales". ¿Una masacre de cuatro? Eso es puro desinflamiento semántico. ¡Masacres las de ahora tiempos!

Cuando los conservadores decapitaban de una a cien liberales y viceversa. Cien cadáveres sin cabeza y descalzos porque el campesino de entonces no usaba zapatos. ¡Ésas sí son masacres! Ustedes muchachitos de hoy en día no han visto nada, les está tocando muy bueno. ¡Masacres!

Treinta y tres millones de colómbianos no caben en toda la vastedad de los infiernos. Hay que dejar un espacio prudente entre dos de ellos para que no se maten, digamos una cuadra, de suerte que si no se pueden ver por lo menos se divisen. ¡Pero miren qué hacinamientos! Millón y medio en las comunas de Medellín, encaramados en las laderas de las montañas como las cabras, reproduciéndose como las ratas. Después se vuelcan sobre el centro de la ciudad y Sabaneta y lo que queda de mi niñez, y por donde pasan arrasan. "Acaban hasta con el nido de la perra" como decía mi abuela, pero no de ellos: de sus treinta nietos. Mi abuela no conoció las comunas, se murió sin. En santa paz.

Entramos en la iglesia, pasamos ante el Señor Caído, y seguimos hasta el altar del fondo en la nave izquierda, el de María Auxiliadora, la virgencita alegre con el Niño, flotando sobre un mar de ofrendas de flores y constelada de estrellas. Adultos y viejos llenaban la iglesia y, cosa

sicanos in confesional

notable, muchachos con el corte de pelo de los punkeros, rezando, confesándose: los sicarios. ¿Qué pedirán? ¿De qué se confesarán? ¡Cuánto daría por saberlo y sus exactas palabras! Saliendo como una luz turbia de la oscuridad de unos socavones, esas palabras me revelarían su más profunda verdad, su más oculta intimidad. "Yo debo de ser muy malo, padre, porque he matado a quince". ¿Eso, por ejemplo? La presencia de tantos jóvenes en la iglesita de Sabaneta me causaba asombro. Pero ¿asombro por qué? También yo estaba allí y veníamos a buscar lo mismo: paz, silencio en la penumbra. Tenemos los ojos cansados de tanto ver, y los oídos de tanto oír, y el corazón de tanto odiar. "Madre Santísima, María Auxiliadora, señora de bondad y de misericordia, posternado a vuestros pies y avergonzado de mis culpas, lleno de confianza en vos os suplico atendáis este ruego: que cuando llegue mi última hora, por fin, acudáis en mi socorro para que tenga la muerte del justo. Ahuyentad al espíritu maligno y su silbo traicionero, y libradme de la condenación eterna, que la pesadilla del infierno ya la he vivido en esta vida y con creces: con mi prójimo. Amén".

A ver, ustedes que dizque son tan buenos católicos ¿me sabrán decir en qué iglesia de

Medellín está San Pedro Claver? En la de la Sagrada Familia no. En la del Carmelo no. En la del Rosario no. En la del Calvario tampoco. ¿Dónde pues? En la iglesia de San Ignacio, en la nave derecha. ¿Y en dónde está el beato de la Colombière? ¿En la de la Asunción? ¿En la de la Visitación? ¿En la de Cristo Rey? ¿En la de Jesús Obrero? No, no, no y tampoco. En ninguna de ésas está: está también en la de San Ignacio, en el altar mayor, al lado de éste. ¿Y saben, por lo menos, en cuál está San Cayetano? Pues sepan por si no lo saben que en la de San Cayetano, como San Blas en la de San Blas, y San Bernardo en la de San Bernardo. Ciento cincuenta iglesias tiene Medellín, mal contadas, casi como cantinas, una exageración, y descontando las de las comunas a las que sólo sube mi Dios con escolta, las conozco todas. Todas, todas, todas. A todas he ido a buscarlo. Por lo general están cerradas y tienen los relojes parados a las horas más dispares, como los del apartamento de mi amigo José Antonio donde conocí a Alexis. Relojes que son corazones muertos, sin su tic-tac.

Ha de saber Dios que todo lo ve, lo oye y lo entiende, que en su Basílica Mayor, nuestra Catedral Metropolitana, en las bancas de atrás se venden los muchachos y los travestis, se comercia en armas y en drogas y se fuma marihuana. Por eso, cuando está abierta, suele haber un policía vigilando. Pregúntenle a ver si invento. ¿Y Cristo dónde está? ¿El puritano rabioso que sacó a fuete a los mercaderes del templo? ¿Es que la cruz lo curó de rabietas, y ya no ve ni oye ni huele? Al olor sacrosanto del incienso se mezcla el de la marihuana, la que sopla desde afuera, desde el atrio, o la que se fuma adentro. La mezcla te produce cierta religiosa alucinación y ves o no ves a Dios, dependiendo de quien seas. Años hace que no venía a esta catedral al Oficio de Difuntos, a rezar por Medellín y su muerte, pero ahora Alexis, mi niño, me acompaña. He dejado de ser uno y somos dos: uno solo inseparable en dos personas distintas. Es mi nueva teología de la Dualidad, opuesta a la de la Trinidad: dos personas que son las que se necesitan para el amor; tres ya empieza a ser orgía. *companing relationship to relig ion.*

Viniendo de la catedral, en el parque de Bolívar donde Junín desemboca a éste, en ese Centro Comercial de ladrillo que construyeron sobre el sitio mismo en que se levantaban, siglos ha, arqueológicamente, las dos cantinas de mi juventud, el Metropol y el Miami, ahí presenciamos la escena: un gamincito sucio y grosero insultaba llorando a un policía: "¡Gonorrea! —le decía—. ¡Por qué me pegaste, gonorrea!" Y tres de los espectadores del corrillo defendiéndolo. Son esos defensores de los "derechos humanos", o sea los de los delincuentes, que aquí surgen por todas partes espontáneamente para sumársele al "defensor del pueblo" que instituyó la nueva Constitución que convocó el bobo marica. Yo no sé por qué le pegaría el policía y si le pegó, pero la palabra en boca de ese niño era la más cargada de rencor y de odio que he oído en mi vida. ¡Y miren que he vivido! "¡Gonorrea!" El infierno entero concentrado en un taco de dinamita. "Si este hijueputica —pensé yo— se comporta así de alzado con la autoridad a los siete años, ¿qué va a ser cuando crezca? Éste es el que me va a matar". Pero no, mi señora Muerte tenía dispuesto para esta criaturita otra cosa esa tarde. El policía, uno de esos jovencitos bachilleres que están reclutando ahora para lanzarlos, sin armas y atados de manos por las alcahueterías de la ley, al foso de los leones, no sabía qué hacer, qué decir. Y los tres defensores enfurecidos, abogando por el minúsculo delincuente y cacariando, amparados desde la valentía cobarde de la turbamulta, que dizque estaban dispuestos que dizque a hacerse matar, que dizque si fuera necesario, del que no tenía armas. Pues se hicieron pero del que sí: sacó el Ángel Exterminador su espada de fuego, su "tote", su "fierro", su juguete, y de un relámpago para cada uno en la frente los fulminó. ¿A los tres? No bobito, a los cuatro. Al gamincito también, claro que sí, por supuesto, no faltaba más hombre. A esta gonorreíta tierna también le puso en el susodicho sitio su cruz de ceniza y lo curó, para siempre, del mal de la existencia que aquí a tantos aqueja. Sin alias, sin apellido, con su solo nombre, Alexis era el Ángel Exterminador que había descendido sobre Medellín a acabar con su raza perversa. "Vaya a buscar a su superior —le aconsejé al pobre policía jovencito cuando lo vi tan perplejo— y le cuenta lo que pasó, y que después decidan ellos, con cabeza fría, cómo ocurrieron las cosas". Y seguí mi camino tras Alexis, y sin más tomamos el primer taxi que pasó. "¿Qué pasó?" preguntó el desgraciado taxista viendo el tropel que se armaba afuera, y subiéndole instintivamente al radio a ver si daban la noticia. "Nada —contesté—. Cuatro muertos. Y apague el loro que venimos supremamente ofuscados". Se lo dije en uno de esos tonos que he cogido que no admiten réplica, y dócil, sumiso, vil, lo apagó.

78

De las comunas de Medellín la nororiental es la más excitante. No sé por qué, pero se me metió en la cabeza. Tal vez porque de allí, creo yo, son los sicarios más bellos. Mas no pienso subir a constatarlo. Si la Muerte me quiere, si está enamorada de mí, que baje aquí. "Enamorada" dije y efectivamente, en el sentido de las comunas. Como cuando un muchacho de allí dice: "Ese tombo está enamorado de mí". Un "tombo" es un policía, ¿pero "enamorado"? ¿Es que es marica? No, es que lo quiere matar. En eso consiste su enamoramiento: en lo contrario. Cualquier sociólogo chambón de esos que andan por ahí analizando en las "consejerías para la paz", concluiría de esto que al desquiciamiento de una sociedad se sigue el del idioma. ¡Qué va! Es que el idioma es así, de por sí ya es loco. Y la Muerte una obsesiva laboradora. No descansa. Ni lunes ni martes ni miércoles ni jueves ni viernes ni sábados y domingos, fiestas civiles y de guardar, puentes y superpuentes, días del padre, de la madre, de la amistad, del trabajo… ¡Del trabajo, carajo, ni ése descansa! Pero trabajando así, con tanto tesón, sin crear nuevas fuentes de empleo disminuye el desempleo que aquí, según dicen los tanatólogos, es el que trae más violencia. O sea que mientras más muertos menos muertos. Mi señora Muerte pues, misiá, mi doña, la paradójica, es la que aquí se necesita. Por eso anda toda ventiada por Medellín día y noche en su afán haciendo lo que puede, compitiendo con semejante paridera, la más atroz. Este continuo nacer de niños y el suero oral le están sacando canas.

Las comunas son, como he dicho, tremendas. Pero no me crean mucho que sólo las conozco por referencias, por las malas lenguas: casas y casas y casas, feas, feas, feas, encaramadas obscenamente las unas sobre las otras, ensordeciéndose con sus radios, día y noche, noche y día a ver cuál puede más, tronando en cada casa, en cada cuarto, desgañitándose en vallenatos y partidos de fútbol, música salsa y rock, sin parar la carraca. ¿Cómo le hacía la humanidad para respirar antes de inventar el radio? Yo no sé, pero el maldito loro convirtió el paraíso terrenal en un infierno: el infierno. No la plancha ardiente, no el caldero hirviendo: el tormento del infierno es el ruido. El ruido es la quemazón de las almas.

Cada columna está dividida en varios barrios, y cada barrio repartido en varias bandas: cinco, diez, quince muchachos que forman una jauría que por donde orina nadie pasa. Es la tan mentada "territorialidad" de las pandillas que se estaba decidiendo la otra tarde en Sabaneta. Por razones "territoriales", un muchacho de un barrio no puede transitar por las calles de otro. Eso sería un insulto insufrible a la propiedad, que aquí es sagrada. Tanto pero tanto tanto que en este país del Corazón de Jesús por unos tenis uno mata o se hace matar. Por unos tenis apestosos estamos dispuestos a irnos a averiguar a qué huele la eternidad. Yo digo que a perfume neutro. Pero no nos desviemos de las comunas de aquí abajo y sigamos subiendo, viendo: ojos secretos nos espían por las rendijas: ¿Quiénes seremos? ¿Qué querremos? ¿A qué vendremos? ¿Seremos sicarios contratados, o vendremos a contratar sicarios? Asolados por las bandas, se ven aquí y allá negocitos entre rejas: una venta, por ejemplo, de aguardiente, o un "granero" con su extenso surtido de cuatro plátanos, cuatro yucas y unos limones podridos. Los limones de Colombia son una vergüenza, no se dan; el musgo de la humedad los asfixia. Aquí nunca tendremos limones buenos. Ni cine: al que le da por filmar le roban las cámaras. Si no, ¡qué película no te harías para Colombia y la eternidad que nos diera la palma de oro del Festival de Cannes! Por estas callejuelas empinadas, por estas escalinatas de cemento que van subiendo lentamente, cansadamente, dolorosamente rumbo al cielo, que no es nuestro, ascendiendo de escalón en escalón y los escalones tallados en las laderas de la montaña, en su tierra amarilla y yerma, en el mismo barro de que hizo Dios al hombre, su juguete, perdiéndonos en el laberinto de los callejones y de los odios, tratando de desentrañar lo inextricable, la trama enmarañada de los rencores y los ajustes de cuentas que se heredan de padres a hijos y se pasan de hermanos a hermanos como el sarampión, ¿qué decía? Que qué película tan hermosa, tan dolorosa no haríamos. Pero no, ésos son sueños y los sueños sueños son. Y a Medellín, además, el cine y la novela le quedan muy chiquitos. Algún día, cuando menos lo pensemos, queriendo o no queriendo, iremos a dar a la morgue a ver si sí o si no, a contar cadáveres, a sumárselos a las cifras desorbitadas de la Muerte, mi señora, la única que aquí reina. Sí señor. La lucha implacable es a muerte, esta guerra no deja heridos porque después se nos vuelven culebras sueltas. No señor.

Antaño, en época de lluvias bajaban por los barriales resbalando, patinando; eran montañas sin calles, tierreros, pero por donde se podía transitar libremente. Estos barrios cuando los fundaron eran, como se dice, "barrios de puertas abiertas". Ya nunca más. Las guerras de las bandas están casadas: de barrio con barrio, de cuadra con cuadra. Una muerte trae otra muerte y el odio más odio. Esto es así, la ley del gato que gira y gira queriendo agarrarse la cola. Y las rachas de violencia que no apagan los entierros… Por el contrario, las encienden. Se diría que en las comunas los destinos de los vivos están en manos de los muertos. El odio es como la pobreza: son arenas movedizas de las que no sale nadie: mientras más chapalea uno más se hunde.

¿Cómo puede matar uno o hacerse matar por unos tenis? preguntará usted que es extranjero. Mon cher ami, no es por los tenis: es por un principio de Justicia en el que todos creemos. Aquel a quien se los van a robar cree que es injusto que se los quiten puesto que él los pagó; y aquel que se los va a robar cree que es más injusto no tenerlos. Y van los ladridos de los perros de terraza en terraza gritándonos a voz en cuello que son mejores que nosotros. Desde esas planchas o terrazas de las comunas se divisa a Medellín. Y de veras que es hermoso. Desde arriba o desde abajo, desde un lado o desde el otro, como mi niño Alexis. Por donde lo mire usted.

83

Rodaderos, basureros, barrancas, cañadas, quebradas, eso son las comunas. Y el laberinto de calles ciegas de construcciones caóticas, vívida prueba de cómo nacieron: como barrios "de invasión" o "piratas", sin planificación urbana, levantadas las casas de prisa sobre terrenos robados, y defendidas con sangre por los que se los robaron no se las fueran a robar. ¿Un ladrón robado? Dios libre y guarde de semejante aberración, primero la muerte. Aquí el ladrón no se deja, mata por no dejarse o se hace matar. Y es que en Colombia la posesión de lo robado y la prescripción del delito hacen la ley. Es cuestión de aguantar. Después, poco a poco, de ladrillito en ladrillito, va construyendo uno la segunda planta de la casa sobre la primera, como el odio de hoy se construye sobre el odio de ayer. Parados en una esquina de las comunas, los sobrevivientes de las bandas esperan a ver quién viene a contratarlos o a ver qué pasa. Ni nadie viene ni nada pasa: eso era antes, en los buenos tiempos, cuando el narcotráfico les encendía las ilusiones. No sueñen más, muchachos, que esos tiempos, como todo, ya pasaron. ¡O qué! ¿También se creyeron ustedes eternos porque se estaban muriendo rápido? Parchados en una esquina de las comunas, viendo correr las horas desde una encrucijada del tiempo, los muchachos de las antiguas bandas hoy son fantasmas de lo que fueron. Sin pasado, sin presente, sin futuro, la realidad no es la realidad en las barriadas de las montañas que circundan a Medellín: es un sueño de basuco. En tanto, la Muerte sigue subiendo, bajando, incansable, por esas calles empinadas. Sólo nuestra fe católica más nuestra vocación reproductora la pueden contrarrestar un poco.

Si de las comunas la que más me gusta es la nororiental, de los presidentes de Colombia el que prefiero es Barco. Por sobre el terror unánime, cuando plumas y lenguas callaban y culos temblaban le declaró la guerra al narcotráfico (él la declaró aunque la perdimos nosotros, pero bueno). Por su lucidez, por su memoria, por su inteligencia y valor, vaya aquí este recuerdo. Pensando que todavía era ministro del presidente Valencia, que gobernó veintitantos años atrás, le expresaba lo siguiente al doctor Montoya, su secretario, el suyo: "Voy a aconsejarle al presidente, en el próximo Consejo de Ministros, que le declare la guerra al narcotráfico". Y el doctor Montoya, su memoria y conciencia, le corregía: "El presidente es usted, doctor Barco, no hay otro". "Ah… —decía él pensativo—.

85

Entonces vamos a declarársela". "Ya se la declaramos, presidente". "Ah… Entonces vamos a ganarla". "Ya la perdimos, presidente —le explicaba el otro—. Este país se jodió, se nos fue de las manos". "Ah…" Y eso era todo lo que decía. Después tornaba a su obnubilación, a las brumas de su desmemoria. Tumbado de la tarima el candidato ambicioso, montándose sobre su cadáver subió, después de Barco, la criaturita que hoy tenemos, el lorito gárrulo. Y las encuestas lo favorecen, todos decimos que sí, que sí, que sí. Que lo está haciendo "de lo más de bien", como dicen.

Al Sumo Pontífice o capo de los capos o gran capo, para protegerlo de sus enemigos, los otros capos, esta ocurrencia que tenemos de presidente le construyó una fortaleza con almenas llamada La Catedral, y pagó para que lo cuidaran, con dinero público (o sea tuyo y mío, que lo sudamos), un batallón de guardias del pueblo de Envigado que el gran capo escogió: "Quiero a éste, a aquél, a aquel otro. A ese de más allá no lo quiero porque no le tengo confianza". Así fue escogiendo a sus guardianes o guardaespaldas. Un día, harto de la catedral y de jugar fútbol con tres compinches en el patio, con sus propias paticas el gran capo fue saliendo, dejando a su batallón comiendo pollo. Y se les perdió año y medio durante el cual el lorito gárrulo ofreció para el que lo encontrara, por televisión, una recompensa en dólares, en billete verde de los que aquí fabricamos o lavamos, grandísima, como de la revista Forbes, y puso veinticinco mil soldados a buscarlo por cuanto hueco había, menos en los del Palacio de Nariño donde él vive. Yo decía que estaba allí, encaletado, en cualquier resquicio del presupuesto. Pero no: estaba a la vuelta de mi casa. Desde las terrazas de mi apartamento oí los tiros: ta-ta-ta-ta-tá. Dos minutos de ráfagas de metralleta y ya, listo, don Pablo se desplomó con su mito. Lo tumbaron en un tejado huyendo, como a un gato en desgracia. Dos tiros tan sólo le pegaron, por el su lado izquierdo: uno por el su cuello, otro por la su oreja. Se despanzurró como el susodicho gato sobre el "entejado", su tejado caliente, quebrando, entre él y sus veinticinco mil perseguidores, más de un millón de tejas en la persecución. La recompensa no me la gané yo, pero estuve a tres cuadras.

Muerto el gran contratador de sicarios, mi pobre Alexis se quedó sin trabajo. Fue entonces cuando lo conocí. Por eso los acontecimientos nacionales están ligados a los personales, y las

87

Alexis' whole band was killed but him his band was really famous, it was a big deal

pobres, ramplonas vidas de los humildes tramadas con las de los grandes. La tarde en que La Plaga me habló de Alexis en el salón de billares me contó del exterminio de su banda: diecisiete o no sé cuántos, que fueron cayendo uno por uno, religiosamente como se va rezando el rosario, y de los que no quedó sino mi niño. Ese "combo" fue una de las tantas bandas que contrató el narcotráfico para poner bombas y ajustarles las cuentas a sus más allegados colaboradores y gratuitos detractores. A periodistas, por ejemplo, de la prensa hablada y escrita con ánimos de "figuración" así fuera en cadáver; o a los ex socios del gobierno: congresistas, candidatos, ministros, gobernadores, jueces, alcaldes, procuradores, y cientos de policías que ni menciono porque son pecata minuta. Todos se fueron yendo, como avemarías del rosario. ¿Pero algún inocente habría, preguntará usted que es sano, entre los del gobierno? Sí, como en Sodoma y Gomorra. Haciéndose los de la boca chiquita los muy bocones y todos bien untados. Todo político o burócrata (que son lo mismo, puesteros) es por naturaleza malvado, y haga lo que haga, diga lo que diga no tiene justificación. Jamás presumas de éstos su inocencia. Eso es candor.

Y sigamos con los muertos, que es a lo que vinimos. Pues que vamos por Junín abajo mi niño y yo, y que de entre la chusma va saliendo El Difunto a manifestarnos que: Uno, que anoche uno de sus compinches, de sus "parceros", un guardaespaldas de un capo, se había matado jugando a la ruleta rusa. Que sacó cuatro balas del tambor del revólver, se lo llevó a la sien y que jaló el gatillo: la primera de las dos balas que dejó, sin darle chance a la segunda, le despeputó los sesos. Y dos, que nos "pisáramos" que nos venían a matar y que con balas rezadas y que esta vez era en serio. "Vamos por partes", le contesté. Uno: "¿Era el guardaespaldas suicidado una bellecita?" Que él no sabía, que él no se fijaba en esas cosas. "Pues te tienes que fijar, Difunto, ¿o para qué te dio Dios esos ojos si no es para ver y el corazón para latir al sentir la belleza? Que la pinta no era gran cosa. "Entonces no se perdió gran cosa". En cuanto a lo segundo, que no se preocupara, que las balas rezadas no bien tocaban mi sagrada túnica, mi ropa santa se desintegraban. Entonces surgieron los de la moto de entre una nube de polvo y la multitud disparando. ¿Saben a quién le dieron, adónde desvió sus balas mi señora Muerte? A otra señora, embarazada. Le entamboraron de plomo la barriga y allí mismo, en pleno Junín, falleció con su feto. ¿Y los de la moto, se fueron? ¡Ja! Se fueron con el impulso de la muerte rumbo al derrumbadero de la eternidad: por sus respectivos occipitales, cuando huían, Alexis les voló la cabeza. Y otra vez a irnos yendo entre el tropel, entre el escándalo, en esta ciudad tan alharacosa y caliente. Y ese olor espantoso de fritangas con aceite rancio…

Las balas rezadas se preparan así: Pónganse seis balas en una cacerola previamente calentada hasta el rojo vivo en parrilla eléctrica. Espolvoréense luego en agua bendita obtenida de la pila de una iglesia, o suministrada, garantizada, por la parroquia de San Judas Tadeo, barrio de Castilla, comuna noroccidental. El agua, bendita o no, se vaporiza por el calor violento, y mientras tanto va rezando el que las reza con la fe del carbonero: "Por la gracia de San Judas Tadeo (o el Señor Caído de Girardota o el padre Arcila o el santo de tu devoción) que estas balas de esta suerte consagradas den en el blanco sin fallar, y que no sufra el difunto. Amén". ¿Que por qué digo que con la fe del carbonero? Ah yo no sé, de estas cosas no entiendo, nunca he rezado una bala. Ni nadie, nadie, nadie me ha visto hasta ahora disparar.

¿Qué es lo que está diciendo este vallenato que oigo por todas partes desde que vine, al desayuno, al almuerzo, a la cena, en el taxi, en mi casa, en tu casa, en el bus, en el televisor? Dice que "Me lleva a mí o me lo llevo yo pa que se acabe la vaina". Lo cual, traducido al cristiano, quiere decir que me mata o lo mato porque los dos, con tanto odio, no cabemos sobre este estrecho planeta. ¡Ajá, conque eso era! Por eso andaba Colombia tan entusiasmada cantándolo, porque le llegaba al alma. No había reparado en la letra, yo sólo oía la carraca. Por este restico de año, por lo que falta, hasta año nuevo, Colombia seguirá cantando alegre, con amor de fiesta, su canción de odio. Ya después se le olvidará, como se le olvida todo.

Cuando a una sociedad la empiezan a analizar los sociólogos, ay mi Dios, se jodió, como el que cae en manos del psiquiatra. Por eso no analicemos y sigamos: "Con el radio apagado, señor taxista, que ya tengo muy oído ese vallenato, y no-lo-re-sis-to". Nos bajamos en el parque de Bolívar, en el corazón del matadero, y seguimos hacia la Avenida La Playa por entre la chusma y los puestos callejeros caminando, para calibrar el desastre.

¿Las aceras? Invadidas de puestos de baratijas que impedían transitar. ¿Los teléfonos públicos? Destrozados. ¿El centro? Devastado. ¿La universidad? Arrasada. ¿Sus paredes? Profanadas con consignas de odio "reivindicando" los derechos del "pueblo". El vandalismo por donde quiera y la horda humana: gente y más gente y más gente y como si fuéramos pocos, de tanto en tanto una vieja preñada, una de estas putas perras paridoras que pululan por todas partes con sus impúdicas barrigas en la impunidad más monstruosa. Era la turbamulta invadiéndolo todo, destruyéndolo todo, empuercándolo todo con su miseria crapulosa. "¡A un lado, chusma puerca!" Íbamos mi niño y yo abriéndonos paso a empellones por entre esa gentuza agresiva, fea, abyecta, esa raza depravada y subhumana, la monstruoteca. Esto que véis aquí marcianos es el presente de Colombia y lo que les espera a todos si no paran la avalancha. Jirones de frases hablando de robos, de atracos, de muertos, de asaltos (aquí a todo el mundo lo han atracado o matado una vez por lo menos) me llegaban a los oídos pautadas por las infaltables delicadezas de "malparido" e "hijueputa" sin las cuales esta raza fina y sutil no puede abrir la boca. Y ese olor a manteca rancia y a fritangas y a gases de cloaca… ¡Qué es! ¡Qué es! ¡Qué es! Se ve. Se siente. El pueblo está presente.

Pero volvámonos un momento atrás que se me olvidaron al bajar del taxi dos muertos: un mimo y un defensor de los pobres. Abajito del atrio, en las afueras de la catedral, estaba el mimo arremedando, imitando en la forma de caminar a cuanto transeúnte desprevenido pasara, pero siempre y cuando fuera alguien indefenso y decente, jamás a un malhechor de la canalla por miedo a una puñalada. Y la gentuza del corrillo riéndose, a las carcajadas, celebrándole la burla. ¡Qué gracia la que les hacía este émulo de Marcel Marceau, este prodigio! Si usted camina, él camina. Si usted se para, él se para. Si usted se suena, él se suena. Si usted mira, él mira. La genialidad, pues. Cuando nos bajamos del taxi estaba remedando a un pobre señor honorable, uno de esos seres antediluvianos, desamparados, que aún quedan en Medellín para recordarnos lo que fuimos y lo que ya no somos más y la magnitud del desastre. Al darse cuenta de lo que pasaba y que era el hazmerreír del corrillo, el señor se detuvo avergonzado sin saber qué hacer. Y el mimo detenido sin saber qué hacer. Entonces el ángel disparó. El mimo se tambaleó un instante antes de caer, de desplomarse

93

con su máscara inexpresiva pintarrajeada de blanco: chorreando desde su puta frente la bala le tiñó de rojo el blanco de su puta cara. Cuando cayó el muñeco, uno de los del corrillo en voz baja, que creyó anónima, comentó: "Eh, qué desgracia, aquí ya no dejan ni trabajar a los pobres". Fue lo último que comentó porque lo oyó el ángel, y de un tiro en la boca lo calló. Per aeternitatis aeternitatem. El terror se apoderó de todos. Cobarde, reverente, el corrillo bajó los ojos para no ver al Ángel Exterminador porque bien sentían y entendían que verlo era condena de muerte porque lo quedaban conociendo. Alexis y yo seguimos por entre la calle estática.

Ay qué memoria la mía, me quedó faltando un cascado más, al final del parque. Acabando nosotros de cruzarlo, cuando todavía no se sabía en este extremo lo que pasó en el otro, estaba un grupo de Hare Crishnas danzando al son de sus panderetas, trayéndonos su mensaje de paz y amor del Oriente (de ese amor que jamás sintió Cristo el tremebundo), y de respeto a todo lo vivo, empezando por los animales y acabando por el prójimo. Pues que se había metido a bailar con ellos, con un desprecio irrespetuoso, inmenso, una de estas roñas zafias que abundan en

94

Medellín y que creen que la única verdad es la suya, la católica cerrazón del puñal y del basuco. Fue este granuja burlón el cascado del final del parque. Y ya sí seguimos sin mayor tropiezo, a tropezones por entre la turbamulta.

Quinientos años me he tardado en entender a Lutero, y que no hay roña más grande sobre esta tierra que la religión católica. Los curitas salesianos me enseñaron que Lutero era el Diablo. ¡Esbirros de Juan Bosco, calumniadores! El Diablo es el gran zángano de Roma y ustedes, lambeculos, sus secuaces, su incensario. Por eso he vuelto a esta iglesia del Sufragio donde sin mi permiso me bautizaron, a renegar. De suerte que aunque siga siendo yo yo ya no tenga nombre. Nada, nada, nada. El bautisterio ya no estaba, con un muro de cemento lo habían tapado. Era que todo lo mío, hasta eso, se acabó. Un poco más, un poco más y viviría para ver exterminada de esta tierra la plaga de esta roña.

Desde las terrazas de mi apartamento, con el cielo arriba y Medellín en torno, empezamos a contar (a descontar) las estrellas. "Si es verdad que cada hombre tiene una estrella —le decía a Alexis—, ¿cuántas has apagado? Al paso a que vas vas a callar el firmamento". Para hacer un cascado se necesita una simple bala más un revólver, y mucha, mucha, mucha voluntad.

Hay un sitio en las inmediaciones de la Avenida San Juan que se llama "Mierda Caliente": un atracadero, un matadero. Con ésos siguió el ángel. Yo le decía que no, que mejor burócratas de la Alpujarra o monseñor obispo, el cardenal López T. antes de que se nos escapara a Roma impune con las joyas que se robó, pero estando como estábamos en nuestro apartamento, ese sitio nos quedaba más a la mano. En la noche borracha de chicharras bajó el Ángel Exterminador, y a seis que bebían en una cantinucha que se prolongaba con sus mesas sobre la acera, de un tiro para cada uno en la frente les apagó la borrachera, la "rasca". ¿Y esta vez por qué? ¿Por qué razón? Por la simplísima razón de andar existiendo. ¿Les parece poquito? No, si esta vida no es cualquier canto de pajaritos, yo siempre he dicho y aquí repito, y que el crimen no es apagarla, es encenderla: hacer que resulte, donde no lo había, el dolor. Cuando volvíamos de hacer nuestra cotidiana obra de caridad bajaba por San Juan un borrachito prendido gritando: "¡Vivan las putas! ¡Vivan los marihuaneros! ¡Vivan los maricas! ¡Abajo la religión católica!" Le dimos mi niño y yo un billetico para que pudiera seguir tomando.

Hubo aquí un padrecito loco, desquiciado, al que le dio dizque por hacerles casita a los pobres con el dinero de los ricos. Con su programa de televisión "El Minuto de Dios", que pasaba noche a noche a las siete, se convirtió en el mendigo número uno de Colombia. Su cuento era que "los ricos son los administradores de los bienes de Dios". ¿Habráse visto mayor disparate? Dios no existe y el que no existe no tiene bienes. Además el que ayuda a la pobreza la perpetúa. Porque ¿cuál es la ley de este mundo sino que de una pareja de pobres nazcan cinco o diez? La pobreza se autogenera multiplicada por dichas cifras y después, cuando agarra fuerza, se propaga como un incendio en progresión geométrica. Mi fórmula para acabar con ella no es hacerles casa a los que la padecen y se empeñan en no ser ricos: es cianurarles de una vez por todas el agua y listo; sufren un ratico pero dejan de sufrir años. Lo demás es alcahuetería de la paridera. El pobre es el culo de nunca parar y la vagina insaciable. El mal que le hizo ese padrecito a Colombia no tiene nombre. Visto el éxito del programa, montó un banquete anual, el "del millón", a millón la entrada y de cena caldo

Maggi. Hasta que logró, claro, lo que las sectas protestantes gringas llaman "la fatiga de los donantes". No le volvimos a dar. Entonces se acordó de los nuevos ricos de Colombia, los narcotraficantes explotadores de bombas, y se les puso a su servicio para ayudarles a tramar sus tretas. Para él no había dinero malo o bueno, sucio o lavado. Todo le servía para sus pobres y que pudieran seguir en la paridera. Él fue el que arregló la entrada del gran capo a la catedral. Poco después murió y le hicieron tamaño entierro. Fue el éxito de este curita pedigüeño haberse dejado llevar por su instinto, su espíritu limosnero, con el cual coincidía con lo más natural y consubstancial de este país damnificado y mendicante, su vocación de pedir, que viene de lejos: cuando yo nací ya Colombia había perdido la vergüenza.

Pero dejemos que este curita descanse en paz y pasemos a palabras mayores, al cardenal López T., el que se quería despachar Alexis. Muy delicadito él, de modales finos y adamados, perfumados, se empeñó en hacer negocios con el narcotráfico, el único que tenía aquí dinero contante y sonante. Cartas quedan de este cardenal al gran capo ofreciéndole en venta terrenos de la Curia. ¿Y no le importaban al cardenal —preguntará usted— los incontables muertos de las bombas, de las muchas que mandó estallar el gran capo, todos ellos gentecitas humildes y buenas, del "pueblo"? Sí, tanto como a mí. Un muerto pobre es un pobre muerto, y cien son cien. No lo critico por eso. Lo que no le perdono, lo que me está quitando el sueño y más que el café, es que se haya ido a Roma con las joyas que se robó y su afeminamiento. Un cardenal afeminado no es un príncipe de la Iglesia, es un travesti, y su sotana una bata: así la siente. Bueno, lo último que quería hacer aquí esta eminencia nuestra pontificable antes de que se tuviera que escapar a Roma, era venderle al narcotráfico los predios de la Universidad Pontificia Bolivariana, que no era suya pero que valen una millonada, para comprárselos en joyas. Más joyas para él. Yo me lo imaginaba poniéndoselas ante un espejo de cristal de roca renacentista para irse luego a divisar, todo enjoyado, a la ciudad santa desde Villa Borghese. A ver volar palomas sobre las cúpulas, y entre esas palomas el Espíritu Santo. ¡Él allá disfrutando de semejante espectáculo, y yo aquí viendo volar gallinazos sobre los botaderos de cadáveres! No podía dormir de la indignación, no podía conciliar el sueño, no podía pegar un ojo. Desde un punto de vista estrictamente religioso, para acabar con este espinoso tema, yo prefiero a un cardenal cínico perfumado un cardenal humilde maloliente, que huela a rayos, que huela a diablos.

No sé por qué pero López, con perdón de ustedes si así se llaman, me suena a ratero cínico. Es que aquí hay tantos… López M., López C., López T. Etcétera, etcétera, etcétera. A veces los unos son los hijos de los otros pero no siempre porque también en ocasiones, por guardar el celibato, hay López que se van a Roma a casarse con el primer guardia suizo que encuentran. López me sugiere un zorro o una comadreja que se escapa por entre los matorrales con su presa, la gallina que se robó. No es culpa mía, es cuestión de semántica. Qué culpa tengo yo si los apellidos me sugieren cosas… ¡Zorros voraces! Después, impunes, todos despatarrados, se van los López a banquetiarse la gallina y a rascarse las pelotas. Ya ni se ríen: todo tesoro público que les entra a sus bolsillos sin fondo se les hace cosa natural.

El próximo muerto de Alexis fue un vivo en el cementerio. En el Cementerio de San Pedro donde yacen descansando todas las notabilidades de Antioquia menos yo. El vivo muerto era

100

el joven guardián de una tumba, y la tumba un mausoleo-discoteca con casetera sonando a todas horas para entretener en su vacío eterno, esencial, a una temible familia de sicarios allí enterrada, cuyos miembros fueron cayendo, uno por uno, uno tras otro "sacrificados", según rezaban sus lápidas pero sin decir por qué causa, por la blanca causa de la coca. Encerrada entre rejas para que no se la robaran en un descuido de su guardián (por ejemplo cuando iba al baño), la casetera tocaba día y noche sin parar vallenatos, la música predilecta de los difuntos cuando pasaron por aquí abajo todos ventiados. Al pasar frente a esa tumba mi niño y yo meditando (meditando sobre los sinsabores de esta vida terrena y las incertidumbres humanas comparadas con lo seguro de la eternidad), el guardián de la tumba, un muchacho, una belleza, se disgustó porque sin querer miramos. "¡Qué! —dijo todo malgeniado—. ¿Se les perdió algo?" Y luego, en voz baja, como rumiando, con uno de esos odios suavecitos que me producen por lo intensos una especie de excitación sexual nerviosa que me recorre el espinazo musitó: "Malparidos…" ¡Qué hermosa voz! Creen los tanatólogos que ellos son los dueños y señores de la muerte porque tienen empleo con el gobierno en sus "consejerías para la paz", mientras que este su servidor no tiene "destino". ¡Jua! La muerte es mía, pendejos, es mi amor que me acompaña a todas partes. El ángel levantó el revólver a la altura de la frente del otro y disparó. El trueno del disparo se fue culebriando por entre esos recovecos y socavones llenos de tumbas llenas de eternidad y de gusanos, y se quedó resonando por un rato con una voracidad de infinito. El eco del eco del eco... Muchísimo antes de que el eco se extinguiera el guardián de la tumba se desplomó. Luego el eco murió en sus armónicos. El Ángel Exterminador se había convertido en el Ángel del Silencio. Cuando nos alejábamos, la casetera se encendió sola y rompió a tocar importuna un vallenato, "La gota fría", que es el que les canté arriba.

Pero aquí la vida crapulosa está derrotando a la muerte y surgen niños de todas partes, de cualquier hueco o vagina como las ratas de las alcantarillas cuando están muy atestadas y ya no caben. En las afueras del cementerio, cuando salíamos y Alexis recargaba su juguete, dos de esos inocentes recién paridos, como de ocho o diez años, se estaban dando trompadas de lo lindo azuzados por un corrillo de adultos y otros niños, bajo el calor embrutecido del sol del trópico. Dale que dale, con sus caritas encendidas por la rabia, sudorosas, sudando ese odio que aquí se estila y que no tiene sobre la vasta tierra parangón. Como la única forma de acabar con un incendio es apagándolo, de seis tiros el ángel lo apagó. Seis cayeron, uno por cada tiro; seis que eran los que tenía el tambor del tote: cuatro de los espectadores y mánagers, y los dos promisorios púgiles. Cada quien con su marquita en la frente escurriendo unos chorritos rojos como de anilina, unos hilitos de lo más pictóricos. Mi señora Muerte con su sangre fría les había bajado el calor y ganado, por lo menos, este round. Y vamos para el siguiente a ver qué pasa. Suena la campana.

Pasando de prisa El Difunto nos advirtió que venían los de la moto. Y venían, en efecto, y en contra vía los muy cabrones, violando las más elementales y sagradas leyes de Colombia, las del tránsito, que te impiden ir contra la corriente y te mandan seguir la flecha, la del chocolate Luker que las patrocina, en cada esquina, para eso están. ¿Es que no la vieron, desgraciados? Sí la vieron pero no las balas con que mi niño Alexis los recibió, éstas sí en la dirección correcta, "in the right direction" como dijo arriba en inglés nuestro primer mandatario el políglota, tan atinadamente, y como marcaba la flecha de ese chocolate infalible que se tomaba de a pastillita por taza pero que ay, ay, ay, ya no se toma más. Perdimos la costumbre del chocolate y la de las musas y la de la misa, y nos quedamos más vacíos que el tambor de hojalata que el enano sidoso no volverá a tocar. Todo lo tumbaron, todos se murieron, de lo que fue mío ya nada queda. Les evitaría el final de los de la moto por evidente, pero no, que sufran: se chocaron contra un carro que venía a toda "in the right direction", y acabaron en el techo del susodicho. De ahí, del techo, de la capota, los tuvo que bajar el agente de la fiscalía que vino a realizar el levantamiento de los cadáveres. ¿Se imaginan un "levantamiento" bajando? Así andamos de mal.

Nada funciona aquí. Ni la ley del talión ni la ley de Cristo. La primera, porque el Estado no la aplica ni la deja aplicar: ni raja ni presta el hacha como mi difunta mamá. La segunda, porque es intrínsecamente perversa. Cristo es el gran introductor de la impunidad y el desorden de este mundo. Cuando tú vuelves en Colombia la otra mejilla, de un segundo trancazo te acaban de desprender la retina. Y una vez que no ves, te cascan de una puñalada en el corazón. En nuestro Hospital San Vicente de Paúl, en la sala de urgencias que llaman "la policlínica", siempre atestada, un pabellón de guerra en nuestra paz, son expertos en coser corazones: con cualquier hilo corriente de atar tamales los cosen y tan bien que vuelven a latir y a suspirar y a sentir el odio. Como aquí el que vive se venga, los que te cascaron se meten al hospital y te rematan saliendo de la operación exitosa: de cuatro o cinco o veinte tiros en el coconut a ver si los médicos antioqueños son tan buenos neurocirujanos como cardiólogos. Después van saliendo muy tranquilos, muy campantes, guardando el tote, a fumarse un "varillo" o a meter basuco. Un "varillo" es un simple cigarrillo de marihuana, y el basuco ya lo expliqué.

Curitas salesianos apologéticos, eminentísimos, profundísimos señores: ¿Que mis críticas son superficiales, triviales? Pues para mí, mula que pisa firme y no da traspié porque calcula paso por paso antes de ir a meter la pata, toda religión es insensata. Si uno las considera así, desde el punto de vista del sentido común, de la sensatez, se hace evidente la maldad, o en su defecto la inconsubstancialidad, de Dios, para decirlo con una palabreja escurridiza como un conejo que me saco de la manga de mi toga de prestidigitador escolástico para designar su no existencia.

¡Claro que no existe! Pongo mis cinco sentidos alerta más la antena del televisor a ver si lo capto, pero no, nada, todo borroso. Lo único que existe es lo que veo: un conejo. Y el conejo se va... En cuanto a Cristo, ¡cómo se va a realizar Dios, que es necesario, por los caminos contingentes, concretos, de un hombre! Y rabioso. Me gustaría ver a ése funcionando en Medellín, tratando de sacar a fuete a los mercaderes del centro; no alcanza a llegar vivo a la cruz: se lo despachan antes de una puñalada con todo y fuete. ¿Rabieticas aquí?

Hace dos mil años que pasó por esta tierra el Anticristo y era él mismo: Dios es el Diablo. Los dos son uno, la propuesta y su antítesis. Claro que Dios existe, por todas partes encuentro signos de su maldad. Afuera del Salón Versalles, que es una cafetería, estaba la otra tarde un niño oliendo sacol, que es una pega de zapateros que alucina. Y que de alucinación en alucinación acaba por empegotarte los pulmones hasta que descansas del ajetreo de esta vida y sus sinsabores y no vuelves a respirar más smog. Por eso el sacol es bueno. Cuando vi al niño oliendo el frasquito lo saludé con una sonrisa. Sus ojos, terribles, se fijaron en mis ojos, y vi que me estaba viendo el alma. Claro que Dios existe.

Entre las infamias que comete Dios por mano del hombre quiero citar aquí la de los caballos de Medellín, cargados de materiales de construcción, vendados, arrastrando sus pobres vidas sin ver y las pesadas carretas, bajo el rabioso sol de su rabioso cielo. "Carretilleros" llaman aquí a los que explotan esos caballos, de los que habiendo tanto carro quedan cientos. Íbamos en un taxi mi niño y yo cuando rebasamos a uno que iba al trote, bajo una lluvia de latigazos: frente a los edificios mismos de la Alpujarra, nuestro centro administrativo, el de los burócratas que no sienten porque no ven porque tienen el corazón ciego pero la boca llena mamando del presupuesto. "¡Los caballos no tienen por qué trabajar, el trabajo lo hizo Dios para el hombre, hijueputa!" le grité al carretillero sacando la cabeza por la ventanilla del taxi. Al oírse llamar como dije el carretillero miró, y así, al volver la cabeza, le quedó en posición perfecta para Alexis, quien con un tiro en la frente me le remarcó lo dicho y como quien dice le tomó la foto. El carretillero cayó al pavimento y al soltar las riendas el caballo paró. Un carro que venía a toda verraca, ventiado, se detuvo en seco contra el carretillero estripándolo pero no lo mató: no lo mató porque ya estaba muerto. Y perdón por la palabrita que grité arriba pero es castiza: son los mismos "hideputas" que dijo Don Quijote aunque elevados a la enésima potencia. De todos modos, con perdón. Es que los animales son el amor de mi vida, son mi prójimo, no tengo otro, y su sufrimiento es mi sufrimiento y no lo puedo resistir.

Por cuanto a nuestro taxista se refiere, siguió el mismo camino del conductor de carretas, en caída libre rumbo a la eternidad como quien baja sin frenos por la pendiente de Robledo. Le aplicamos su marquita frontal visto que nos quedó conociendo. Son los riesgos de su oficio, y de oír cuando no hay que oír y de ver cuando no hay que ver en una ciudad tan violenta. Taxistas inocentes, por lo demás, no los conozco.

Alexis y yo diferíamos en que yo tenía pasado y él no; coincidíamos en nuestro mísero presente sin futuro: en ese sucederse de las horas y los días vacíos de intención, llenos de muertos. Cuando Alexis llegó a los cien definitivamente perdí la cuenta. Ya una vez me había pasado, en mi remota juventud, cuando por el cincuenta y tantos de mis amores los números se me enredaron y no volví a contar. Mas para darles una somera idea de sus hazañas digamos que se despachó a muchos menos que el bandolero liberal

Jacinto Cruz Usma "Sangrenegra", que mató a quinientos, pero a bastantes más que el bandolero conservador Efraín González, que mató a cien. Para hablar en cifras redondas, pongámoslo en doscientos cincuenta, que es un punto intermedio. En cuanto al gran capo que tanto ruido hizo y tanto dio de que hablar, ése más de mil, pero por interpósita persona, por manos de sicarios, que no cuentan. ¿O es que usted cuenta como amores los que tan sólo ve, por ejemplo a través de un hueco? Ése es el pecado lamentable del voyerismo.

Hombre vea, yo le digo, vivir en Medellín es ir uno rebotando por esta vida muerto. Yo no inventé esta realidad, es ella la que me está inventando a mí. Y así vamos por sus calles los muertos vivos hablando de robos, de atracos, de otros muertos, fantasmas a la deriva arrastrando nuestras precarias existencias, nuestras inútiles vidas, sumidos en el desastre. Puedo establecer, con precisión, en qué momento me convertí en un muerto vivo. Fue un anochecer, bajo las lluvias de noviembre, yendo con Alexis a lo largo de una avenida del barrio Belén por cuyo centro corría una quebrada descubierta, uno de esos arroyos de Medellín otrora cristalinos y hoy convertidos en alcantarillas que es en lo que acaban todos, arrastrando en sus pobres aguas la porquería de la porquería humana. De súbito presencié la escena: un perro moribundo había ido a caer al arroyo. Hubiera querido seguir y no ver, no saber, pero el perro con una llamada muda, angustiada, ineludible me llamaba arrastrándome hacia su muerte. Resbalando, bajo el aguacero, bajé con Alexis al caño: era uno de esos perros criollos callejeros, corrientes, que en Bogotá llaman "gozques" y en Medellín no sé cómo, o sí, perros "chandosos". Cuando traté con Alexis de levantarlo para sacarlo del agua descubrí que el perro tenía las caderas quebradas, de suerte que aunque lo sacáramos no había esperanzas de salvarlo. Un carro lo había atropellado y el animal, arrastrándose, había logrado llegar a la quebrada pero se había quedado atrapado en sus aguas al intentar cruzarla. ¿Cómo iba a poder salir de allí herido, destrozado, si se nos dificultaba a nosotros sanos? Los bordes de cemento que encauzaban el arroyo le impedían salir. ¿Cuánto llevaba allí? Días tal vez, con sus noches, bajo las lluvias, a juzgar por su deterioro extremo. ¿Habría tratado de volver acaso, herido, a su casa? ¿Pero es que tendría casa? Sólo Dios sabrá, él que es culpable de estas infamias: Él, con mayúscula, con la mayúscula que se suele usar para

110

el Ser más monstruoso y cobarde, que mata y
atropella por mano ajena, por la mano del hombre, su juguete, su sicario. "No va a poder volver
a caminar —le dije a Alexis—. Si lo sacamos es
para que sufra más. Hay que matarlo". "¿Cómo?" "Disparándole". El perro me miraba. La
mirada implorante de esos ojos dulces, inocentes, me acompañará mientras viva, hasta el su-
premo instante en que la Muerte, compasiva,
decida borrármela. "Yo no soy capaz de matarlo", me dijo Alexis. "Tienes que ser", le dije.
"No soy", repitió. Entonces le saqué el revólver
del cinto, puse el cañón contra el pecho del perro y jalé el gatillo. La detonación sonó sorda,
amortiguada por el cuerpo del animal, cuya al-
mita limpia y pura se fue elevando, elevando
rumbo al cielo de los perros que es al que no en-
traré yo porque soy parte de la porquería humana. Dios no existe y si existe es la gran gonorrea.
Y mientras el aguacero arreciaba enfurecido y se
iba cerrando la noche entendí que la felicidad
para mí sería en adelante un imposible, si es que
acaso alguna vez antaño, en mi ayer remoto, fue
una realidad, escurridiza, fugitiva. "Sigue tú
matando solo —le dije a Alexis—, que yo ya no
quiero vivir". Y me llevé el revólver al corazón.
Entonces, otra vez, como meses atrás en mi

apartamento, Alexis desvió el tiro, que fue a salpicar el agua. En el forcejeo acabamos de caer al caño hundiéndonos por completo en la mierda, de mierda como ya estábamos hasta el alma. Creo recordar que Alexis también lloraba, conmigo, sobre el cuerpo del animalito. Al día siguiente, en la tarde, en la Avenida La Playa, lo mataron.

Íbamos por la Avenida La Playa entre el gentío —por la calle lateral izquierda para mayor precisión, e izquierda mirando hacia el Pan de Azúcar— cuando de frente, zumbando, atronadora, se vino sobre nosotros la moto: pasó rozándonos. "¡Cuidado! ¡Fernando!" alcanzó a gritarme Alexis en el momento en que los de la moto disparaban. Fue lo último que dijo, mi nombre, que nunca antes había pronunciado. Después se desbarrancó por el derrumbadero eterno, sin fondo. Jirones de frases y colores siguieron, rasgados, barridos en el instante fugitivo. Alcancé a ver al muchacho de atrás de la moto, el "parrillero", cuando disparó: le vi los ojos fulgurantes, y colgando sobre el pecho, por la camisa entreabierta, el escapulario carmelita. Y nada más. La moto, culebriando, se perdió entre el gentío y mi niño se desplomó: dejó el horror de la vida para entrar en el horror de la

112

muerte. Fue un solo tiro certero, en el corazón. Creemos que existimos pero no, somos un espejismo de la nada, un sueño de basuco.

Cuando mi niño cayó en la acera me seguía mirando desde su abismo insondable con los ojos abiertos. Traté de cerrárselos pero los párpados se le volvían a abrir, como los de ese muñeco lejano que otro día, en otro sitio, en virtud de otro muerto también recordé. Ojos verdes, incomparables los de mi niño, de un verde milagroso que no igualarán jamás ni siquiera las más puras esmeraldas de Colombia, esas que se llaman "gota de aceite". Pero los muertos muertos somos y en esencia todos iguales, de ojos negros, cafés o azules, y el corrillo empezaba a cercarnos: con sus rumores, sus murmullos, su tumulto, con su infamia. Entonces entendí lo que tenía que hacer: llevármelo, substraerlo de la curiosidad infame pretendiendo que estaba herido antes de que nadie dijera que estaba muerto. Para privarlos del espectáculo del levantamiento del cadáver que es el que nos toca dar a los que morimos en la vía pública, y que tan íntimo gozo les produce a los que creen que siguen vivos porque están de pie arremolinados, con su vileza en torno. Al primero que vi, un basuquero de esos que se han apoderado de la

avenida y que duermen en sus bancas, le pedí el
favor: que me detuviera un taxi y me ayudara a
subir a mi niño. Él fue el que me lo detuvo, él
fue el que me lo ayudó a subir. Le di unas mone-
das y el taxi arrancó.

Hay al otro lado de la avenida, por la calle lateral de enfrente, una clínica privada de rateros,
lo cual es un pleonasmo que me sabrán discul-
par los señores académicos que me leen habida
cuenta de mi desesperación y de la prisa. Es la
Clínica Soma, la primera en su género que hubo en Medellín y que fundaron tiempos ha, en
mi matusalénica niñez, un grupo de médicos es-
pecialistas, de delincuentes, que se juntaron para explotar más a conciencia la candidez y desesperación del prójimo y verles más a fondo, hasta
el fondo, como Dios manda, con rayos X, los
bolsillos de sus clientes, perdón, pacientes. "A
estos hijos de puta les voy a dejar el cadáver", se
me ocurrió con esa lucidez de relámpago que
infaltablemente me ilumina en los momentos
culminantes de mis desastres, y le indiqué al taxista que dando un rodeo, el que fuera, y cobrando lo que quisiera, me llevara allí, a la acera
opuesta. "Aquí les traigo a este muchacho que
acaban de herir en la calle", les dije en la recepción. Al darse cuenta de la real situación, que

ellos no eran funeraria para poderle sacar partido a un cadáver, fue tal la desesperación que les acometió que la mía se hizo chiquita, y en medio del alboroto me mandaron adonde el director, a que muy humanamente me aconsejara el caritativo señor que me llevara a mi niño a la policlínica, la del gobierno, donde me lo podían atender gratis porque allí sí tenían los recursos para un caso tan grave y urgente. "Pues si eso es lo que se necesita y procede, apreciadísimo señor doctor —le contesté—, yo no lo llevo: lo lleva usted". Y me di media vuelta y fui saliendo tirándole en las narices la puerta. En sus sucias narices por las que el asqueroso se suena.

Y qué más da que nos muramos de viejos en la cama o antes de los veinte años acuchillados o tiroteados en la calle. ¿No es igual? ¿No sigue al último instante de la vida el mismo derrumbadero de la muerte? Me lo iba diciendo para tratar de no pensar, pensando por entre el gentío que tenía que encontrar una iglesia. Las de San Ignacio y San José, las más cercanas, por las leyes de Murphy iban a estar cerradas. Quedaba la Candelaria, que siempre estaba abierta, y hacia la Candelaria me dirigí, a pedirle a Dios que se acordara de mí y me mandara la muerte. Mientras le rogaba al Señor

Caído entre el chisporroteo de sus veladoras, me acordé de que le había dejado a Alexis el revólver en la cintura. No se lo había sacado. Era mi horrorizada aversión a las armas de fuego, que me impide pensar que existen. ¡Claro, se lo había dejado y ahora les quedaba a los delincuentes de la clínica! Que les aprovechara, que con ese mismo los mataran... Dejé la iglesia y salí a la calle y todo seguía igual, el mismo sol, el mismo ruido, la misma gente, sin que pesaran sobre nadie en concreto los negros nubarrones del porvenir. Y cuando pasé por el parque alzaron, como siempre, su precavido vuelo las palomas.

Alejándome segundo a segundo del instante atroz de la muerte de Alexis y paso a paso por el centro, volví a dar a esa avenida funesta del barrio Belén con su quebrada, en los confines del día. Más empantanado mi destino que un sumario, huyendo del dolor volvía a él. De súbito, sin anunciarse cómo había llegado esa tarde la Muerte, cayó la noche. Desemboqué en un cruce de avenidas. Hileras de luces de carros avanzaban con lentitud por las vías atestadas, como gusanos luminosos, luciérnagas terrestres que se arrastraran resignadamente por los atascaderos de esta vida. Eran los infinitos carros

comprados con dineros del narcotráfico que en
los últimos años embotellaban la ciudad. Dejé el
lento río de las luces y me adentré en la oscuridad. Oí unos tiros. La noche de alma negra, delincuente, tomaba posesión de Medellín, mi
Medellín, capital del odio, corazón de los vastos
reinos de Satanás. Algún carro desperdigado me
alumbraba por un instante la calle, iluminando
con sus faros hasta cuatro palmos el porvenir.

En los días que siguieron mi nombre dicho
por Alexis en su último instante me empezó a
pesar como una lápida. ¿Por qué si durante los
siete meses que anduvimos juntos pudo evitarlo
tenía que pronunciarlo entonces? ¿Era la reve-
lación inesperada de su amor cuando ya no tenía
objeto? Si así fuera, con ese nombre que apenas
si reconozco yo que no me atrevo a mirarme en
el espejo, Alexis me estaba jalando a su abismo.
Mi nombre en boca suya en el instante irreme-
diable me seguía repercutiendo en el alma. No
se me borraba, como dicen que no se les pueden
borrar a los sicarios los ojos de sus víctimas. ¿Y
cómo lo supieron? Nadie sabe lo de nadie.

Podríamos decir, para simplificar las cosas,
que bajo un solo nombre Medellín son dos ciu-
dades: la de abajo, intemporal, en el valle; y la de
arriba en las montañas, rodeándola. Es el abrazo

de Judas. Esas barriadas circundantes levantadas sobre las laderas de las montañas son las comunas, la chispa y leña que mantienen encendido el fogón del matadero. La ciudad de abajo nunca sube a la ciudad de arriba pero lo contrario sí: los de arriba bajan, a vagar, a robar, a atracar, a matar. Quiero decir, bajan los que quedan vivos, porque a la mayoría allá arriba, allá mismo, tan cerquita de las nubes y del cielo, antes de que alcancen a bajar en su propio matadero los matan. Tales muertos aunque pobres, por supuesto, para el cielo no se irán así les quede más a la mano: se irán barranca abajo en caída libre para el infierno, para el otro, el que sigue al de esta vida. Ni en Sodoma ni en Gomorra ni en Medellín ni en Colombia hay inocentes; aquí todo el que existe es culpable, y si se reproduce más. Los pobres producen más pobres y la miseria más miseria, y mientras más miseria más asesinos, y mientras más asesinos más muertos. Ésta es la ley de Medellín, que regirá en adelante para el planeta tierra. Tomen nota.

Existe en las comunas una guerra casada desde hace años, de barrio con barrio, de cuadra con cuadra, de banda con banda. Es la guerra total, la de todos contra todos con que soñó Adamov, el dramaturgo, mi amigo, que ya murió y pobre y viejo, pero en París. Todos en las comunas están sentenciados a muerte. ¿Que quién los sentenció, la ley? Pregunta tonta: en Colombia hay leyes pero no hay ley. Se sentenciaron unos a otros, solitos, y a sus parientes y amigos y a cuantos se les arrimen. El que se arrime a un sentenciado es hombre muerto, cae con él. Demográficamente hablando, así nos vamos controlando aquí. En mi Colombia querida la muerte se nos volvió una enfermedad contagiosa. Y tanto, que en las comunas sólo quedan niños, huérfanos. Incluyendo a sus papás, todos los jóvenes ya se mataron. ¿Y los viejos? Viejos los cerros y Dios. Cuánto hace que se murieron los viejos, que se mataron de jóvenes, unos con otros a machete, sin alcanzarle a ver tampoco la cara cuartiada a la vejez. A machete, con los que trajeron del campo cuando llegaron huyendo dizque de "la violencia" y fundaron estas comunas sobre terrenos ajenos, robándoselos, como barrios piratas o de invasión. De "la violencia"… ¡Mentira! La violencia eran ellos. Ellos la trajeron, con los machetes. De lo que venían huyendo era de sí mismos. Porque a ver, dígame usted que es sabio, ¿para qué quiere uno un machete en la ciudad si no es para cortar cabezas? No hay plaga mayor sobre el planeta que el campesino colombiano, no hay alimaña más dañina, más mala. Parir y pedir, matar y morir, tal su miserable sino.

Los hijos de estos hijos de mala madre cambiaron los machetes por trabucos y changones, armas de fuego hechizas, caseras, que los nietos a su vez, modernizándose, cambiaron por revólveres que el Ejército y la Policía les venden para que con el aguardiente que fabrican las Rentas Departamentales se emborrachen y se les salgan todos los demonios y con esos mismos revólveres se maten. Con el dinero que le producen las dichas rentas, el aguardiente, el Estado paga los maestros para que les enseñen a los niños que no hay que tomar ni matar. Y no me pregunten por qué este contrasentido. Yo no sé, yo no hice este mundo, cuando aterricé ya estaba hecho. Es que la vida es así, cosa grave, parcero. Por eso vuelvo y repito: no hay que andar imponiéndola. Que el que nazca nazca solo, por su propia cuenta y riesgo y generación espontánea. Apuntalado en una precaria legitimidad electorera, presidido por un bobo marica, fabricador de armas y destilador de aguardiente, forjador de constituciones impunes, lavador de dólares, aprovechador de la coca, atracador de impuestos,

el Estado en Colombia es el primer delincuente. Y no hay forma de acabarlo. Es un cáncer
que nos va royendo, matando de a poquito.

Sí señor, Medellín son dos en uno: desde
arriba nos ven y desde abajo los vemos, sobre todo en las noches claras cuando brillan más las
luces y nos convertimos en focos. Yo propongo
que se siga llamando Medellín a la ciudad de
abajo, y que se deje su alias para la de arriba:
Medallo. Dos nombres puesto que somos dos, o
uno pero con el alma partida. ¿Y qué hace Medellín por Medallo? Nada, canchas de fútbol en
terraplenes elevados, excavados en la montaña,
con muy bonita vista (nosotros), panorámica,
para que jueguen fútbol todo el día y se acuesten
cansados y ya no piensen en matar ni en la cópula. A ver si zumba así un poquito menos sobre el
valle del avispero.

A fuerza de tan feas las comunas son hasta
hermosas. Casas y casas y casas de dos pisos a
medio terminar, con el segundo piso siempre en
veremos, amontonadas, apeñuzcadas, de las que
salen niños y niños como brota el agua de la roca por la varita de Moisés. De súbito, sobre las
risas infantiles cantan las ráfagas de una metralleta. Ta-ta-ta-ta-tá… Son las prima donnas, las
mini-Uzi con que soñaba Alexis cosiendo el aire

121

con sus balas, cantando el aria de la locura. Se guindaron a candela los de arriba con los de abajo, los del lado con los de al lado, los unos con los otros. ¡Qué mano de changonazos, Dios mío, qué lluvia de balines como rociada de agua bendita! Y van cayendo los muñecos mientras sopla sobre Santo Domingo Savio y la mañana caliente su ráfaga fría y refrescante la Muerte. Santo Domingo Savio es un barrio que de santo no tiene más que el nombre: es un verdadero asesino. Después vienen los inspectores a recoger los cadáveres y luego nada, como si nada, a seguir los vivos viviendo hasta la próxima balacera que nos sacuda el aburrimiento.

Además de los enemigos que les dejaron sus difuntos padres, hermanos y amigos, cada quien en las comunas se consigue por su propia cuenta los propios para heredárselos a su vez, todos sumados, a sus hijos, hermanos y amigos cuando lo maten. Es la herencia de la sangre, el río desbordado. Las comunas sólo se pueden entender desenredando la trama enmarañada de estos odios. Cosa imposible e inútil. Yo no le veo a este asunto más solución ni remedio que cortar como hizo Alejandro, de un tajo, el nudo gordiano, e instaurar el fusiladero: una tapia larga, larga, encalada de

122

blanco, que anuncie en letras grandes y negras la Urosalina, ese remedio milagroso de mi niñez que se deletreaba así, en el radio, a toda carrera: U-ere-o-ese-a-ele-i-ene-a. ¡Urosalina! Y que vayan cayendo los fumigados, y aterrizando sobre ellos los gallinazos.

¿Qué cómo sé tanto de las comunas sin haber subido? Hombre, muy fácil, como saben los teólogos de Dios sin haberlo visto. Y los pescadores del mar por las marejadas que les manda, enfurecido, hasta la playa. Además sí subí, una tarde, en un taxi, que me cobró una fortuna porque dizque vida no hay sino una y que él tenía cinco hijos. Arriba me dejó, en Santo Domingo Savio o Villa del Socorro o El Popular o El Granizal o La Esperanza, en uno de esos mataderos, solo con mi suerte. Hasta allá subí a buscar a la mamá de Alexis y de paso a su asesino. Vi al subir los "graneros", esas tienduchas donde venden yucas y plátanos, enrejados ¿para que no les fueran a robar la miseria? Vi las canchas de fútbol voladas sobre los rodaderos. Vi el laberinto de las calles y las empinadas escaleras. Y abajo la otra ciudad, en el valle, rumorosa… En una callejuela de muy arriba en la montaña encontré la casa. Llamé. Me abrió ella, con un niño en los brazos. Y me hizo pasar. Otros dos niños de pocos años se arrastraban, semidesnudos, por esta vida y el piso de tierra. Pensé en una humilde mujer de mi niñez, una sirvienta de mi casa, que me la recordaba. Evidentemente aquella lejana mujer, que por la edad podía haber sido mi madre, no era la que tenía enfrente, que podía ser mi hija. Además, ¡cuánto no haría que esa sirvienta de mi casa se murió! ¿Sería que por sobre el abismo del tiempo se repetían las personas, los destinos? Lo que fuera. Ni en esta pobre mujer ni en ninguno de sus niños reconocí un solo rasgo de Alexis, nada pero nada nada de su esplendor. Los milagros son así, burleteros. Hablamos muy poco. Me contó que su actual esposo, el padre de estos niños, la había abandonado; y que al otro, el padre de Alexis, también lo habían matado. En cuanto al muchacho que mató a Alexis, era de los lados de Santa Cruz y La Francia y le decían La Laguna Azul. No se asombren de que ella que no lo vio supiera más que yo del asesino, yo que lo vi disparando. En las comunas todo se sabe. Tenga por seguro que si a usted lo matan en el parque de Bolívar (y no lo quiera mi Dios), no bien esté acabando de caer allá kilómetros abajo, aquí kilómetros arriba ya lo están celebrando. O llorando. Sentí una inmensa compasión por ella, por sus niños, por los perros abandonados, por mí, por cuantos seguimos capotiando los atropellos de esta vida. Le di algo de dinero, me despedí y salí. Cuando emprendía la bajada, sin decir agua va ni mediar provocación ninguna (¿porque quién alborota esta furia?) se soltó el aguacero.

Quiero explicarle por si no lo sabe, por si no es de aquí, que cuando a Medellín le da por llover es como cuando le da por matar: sin términos medios, con todas las de la ley y a conciencia. Es que aquí no se puede dejar vivo al muerto porque entonces a uno lo quedan conociendo y después el muerto es uno, cosa grave para uno en particular pero alivio para los demás en general. Por eso los que caen a la "policlínica", el pabellón de urgencias del Hospital San Vicente de Paúl, nuestro hospital de guerra, es a que les cosan el corazón. El cielo que nos mira desde arriba vive tan enojado como los cristianos de abajo, y cuando se suelta este loco a llover es a llover, con una demencia desbordada. Arroyos torrentosos empezaron a saltar por las escaleras de cemento como cabras locas desbalagadas y a confluir en ríos por las desbarrancadas calles. Me hice a un lado para que el río-tromba que bajaba atronando, atrabancado, atropellando, pasara y no me llevara. Íbamos para el mismo lado, para abajo, pero yo sin tanta prisa. Y mientras el loco frenético de arriba se despanzurraba de la ira, nadie en las desiertas calles de las comunas. Ni un alma, ni un asesino. Y ni un alero tampoco para guarecerme en tantas casas miserables, mezquinas, construidas con el egoísmo del sálvese quien pueda. Añoré mi viejo barrio de Boston donde nací, de nobles casas con alero para que cuando lloviera nos escampáramos los parroquianos que íbamos a misa.

¿Se les hace impropio un viejo matando a un muchacho? Claro que sí, por supuesto. Todo en la vejez es impropio: matar, reírse, el sexo, y sobre todo seguir viviendo. Salvo morirse, todo en la vejez es impropio. La vejez es indigna, indecente, repulsiva, infame, asquerosa, y los viejos no tienen más derecho que el de la muerte. En la laguna azul sombría me estaba hundiendo. Era azul de nombre pero de aguas verdes, traicioneras. Su alma pantanosa enredada en mohos y en algas pegajosas me jalaba hacia el fondo. Las algas soltaban un veneno verde que era el que le daba su color falaz a la laguna azul. ¿Y quién dijo que yo lo iba a matar? Para eso están aquí los sicarios, para que sirvan, como las putas, y los contraten los que les puedan pagar. Ellos son los cobradores de las deudas incobrables, de sangre o no. Y valen menos que un plomero. Es la última ventaja que nos queda en este cuadro de desastres. Mientras en las comunas seguía lloviendo y sus calles, ríos de sangre, seguían bajando con sus aguas de diluvio a teñir de rojo el resumidero de todos nuestros males, la laguna azul, en mi desierto apartamento sin muebles y sin alma, solo, me estaba muriendo, rogándoles a los de la policlínica que le cosieran, como pudieran, aunque fuera con hilo corriente, a mi pobre Colombia el corazón. Luego entraba adonde el director a pedirle que mandara cerrar las puertas del hospital porque por todas partes venían a rematarla asesinos contratados, sicarios. Después me iba con Alexis rumbo al centro. A lo lejos, sobre el mar de bruma alucinada que cubría el centro, flotaba la alta cúpula de la iglesia de San Antonio. Hacia allá nos dirigíamos pero rasgando para poder seguir, para poder pasar, las densas capas de bruma. Entrábamos a la iglesia y resulta que era un cementerio. Tumbas y tumbas y tumbas mohosas. Y yo solo, muriéndome, sin un alma buena que me trajera un café ni un novelista de tercera persona que atestiguara, que anotara, con papel y pluma de tinta indeleble para la posteridad delirante lo que dije o no dije. Una mañana me despertó el sol, que entraba por las terrazas y los balcones a raudales, llamándome. Y una vez más, obediente, obsecuente, le hice caso a su llamado y me dejé engañar. Me levanté, me bañé, me afeité y salí a la calle. Camino al parque del barrio de La América por la Avenida San Juan, en una cafetería que tenía el radio prendido me tomé un café. ¿Cuántos meses habrían pasado, cuántos años? Semanas si acaso porque seguía el mismo presidente, la misma lora gárrula leyendo con su vocecita inarmónica los mismos discursos zalameros, embusteros, que le hicieron. Repitiéndose, como si se hubiera detenido el tiempo. Cuando paró de retransmitirse el pajarraco deslenguado, el radio, reconfortante como un café caliente, oficioso y mañanero, pasó a darnos las noticias de la noche que acababa y las cifras de los muertos. Que anoche no habían sido sino tantos… La vida seguía pues.

"Tened fe y veréis qué cosa son los milagros", dijo San Juan Bosco y en efecto, la iglesia de La América estaba abierta. Entré, y en el primer altar, el del Señor Caído, arrodillándome, le pedí al Todopoderoso que puesto que no me mandaba la muerte me devolviera a Alexis. A Él, que todo lo sabe, lo ve, lo puede. Desde el altar mayor presidiendo la iglesia, de negro, aureolada por los destellos de su pequeño resplandor dorado, la Virgen Dolorosa me miraba. La iglesia estaba desierta. Más vacía que la vida de un sicario que quema los billetes que le sobran en el fogón.

De mala sangre, de mala raza, de mala índole, de mala ley, no hay mezcla más mala que la del español con el indio y el negro: producen saltapatrases o sea changos, simios, monos, micos con cola para que con ella se vuelvan a subir al árbol. Pero no, aquí siguen caminando en sus dos patas por las calles, atestando el centro. Españoles cerriles, indios ladinos, negros agoreros: júntelos en el crisol de la cópula a ver qué explosión no le producen con todo y la bendición del papa. Sale una gentuza tramposa, ventajosa, perezosa, envidiosa, mentirosa, asquerosa, traicionera y ladrona, asesina y pirómana. Ésa es la obra de España la promiscua, eso lo que nos dejó cuando se largó con el oro. Y un alma clerical y tinterilla, oficinesca, fanática del incienso y el papel sellado. Alzados, independizados, traidores al rey, después a todos estos malnacidos les dio por querer ser presidente. Les arde el culo por sentarse en el solio de Bolívar a mandar, a robar. Por eso cuando tumban los sicarios a uno de esos candidatos al susodicho de un avión o una tarima, a mí me tintinea de dicha el corazón.

Yendo por la carrera Palacé entre los saltapatrases, los simios bípedos, pensando en Alexis, llorando por él, me tropecé con un muchacho. Nos saludamos creyendo que nos conocíamos. ¿Pero de dónde? ¿Del apartamento de los relojes? No. ¿De la televisión? Tampoco. Ni él ni yo habíamos salido nunca en la televisión, o sea que prácticamente ni existíamos. Le pregunté que para dónde iba y me contestó que para ninguna parte. Como yo tampoco, bien podíamos seguir juntos sin interferirnos. Tomando hacia ninguna parte por la calle Maracaibo desembocamos en Junín. Al pasar por el Salón Versalles recordé que llevaba días sin comer y le pregunté al muchacho si había almorzado. Me contestó que sí, que antier. Entonces invité a almorzar al faquir. Mientras almorzábamos los dos faquires le pregunté su nombre: ¿Se llamaba Tayson Alexander acaso, para variar? Que no. ¿Y Yeison? Tampoco. ¿Y Wílfer? Tampoco. ¿Y Wílmar? Se rió. ¿Que cómo lo había adivinado? Pero no lo había adivinado, simplemente eran los nombres en voga de los que tenían su edad y aún seguían vivos. Le pedí que anotara, en una servilleta de papel, lo que esperaba de esta vida. Con su letra arrevesada y mi bolígrafo escribió: Que quería unos tenis marca Reebock y unos jeans Paco Ravanne. Camisas Ocean Pacific y ropa interior Kelvin Klein. Una moto Honda, un jeep Mazda, un equipo de sonido láser y una nevera para la mamá: uno de esos refrigeradores enormes marca Whirpool que soltaban chorros de cubitos de hielo abriéndoles simplemente una llave… Caritativamente le expliqué que la ropa más le quitaba que le ponía a su belleza. Que la moto le daba status de sicario y el jeep de narcotraficante o mafioso, gentuza inmunda. Y el equipo de sonido ¿para qué? ¡Para qué más ruido afuera con el que llevábamos adentro! ¿Y para qué una nevera si no iban a tener qué meter en ella? ¿Aire? ¿Un cadáver? Que se tomara su sopita y se olvidara de ilusos sueños… Se rió y me dijo que anotara a mi vez, por el reverso de la servilleta, lo que yo esperaba de esta vida. Iba a escribir "nada" pero se me fue escribiendo su nombre. Cuando lo leyó se rió y alzó los hombros, gesto que prometía todo y nada. Le pregunté si se le ponía tilde a "Wílmar" y me contestó que daba igual, que como yo quisiera. "Entonces digamos que sí".

131

Dejando el Salón Versalles que de Versalles no tiene un aplique, un carajo, tomando por Junín abajo rumbo a ninguna parte se soltó a llover. Estábamos frente a la iglesia de San Antonio, que no conocía. ¿O sí? ¿No la había visto pues en sueños con Alexis vuelta un cementerio en brumas? Le dije a Alexis, perdón, a Wílmar que entráramos. La iglesia tiene dos entradas: una por la fachada de la cúpula, otra por la de las torres. Por la de la cúpula entramos. Subiendo por la escalinata del pórtico, bajo unas bóvedas góticas, antes de entrar uno a la iglesia ve a la derecha una inmensa cripta de osarios. Susurros de almas en pena rasgaban las brumas del tiempo eterno. ¡Claro, ése era el cementerio de mi delirio! Pasamos a la iglesia y miré hacia arriba, y por primera vez vi desde adentro la alta cúpula que había visto desde afuera mi vida entera dominando el centro de Medellín. A todo se le llegaba pues su día, su muerte. Los engranajes del destino girando inexorables me habían traído, con el engaño de la lluvia, a la iglesia de San Antonio de Padua, la de los locos. Y no lo digo por mí que sé dónde estoy parado, lo digo por ellos, sus dueños, los mendigos locos que duermen afuera bajo ese puente cercano que es un cruce de vías elevadas y que vienen al amanecer, cuando arrecia el frío, a la primera misa y a pedirle a Dios, por el amor que le tenga a San Antonio, un poquito de calor, de compasión, de basuco. Adentro un Cristo pendía de la alta cúpula, suspendido en el aire sobre las miserias humanas y los avatares del tiempo. Como escapados de una pintura medieval, unos frailes franciscanos cruzaron furtivamente por la iglesia y la realidad delirante. Cuando Wílmar y yo salimos, por el pórtico de las torres, pensé que íbamos a hundirnos en un mar de bruma pero no, el día estaba claro, recién bañado por la lluvia. "Domus Dei Porta Coeli" leí bajo el reloj detenido, en la fachada de las torres. Bajé los ojos y vi la casa cural, contigua a la iglesia: una vieja casona del Medellín de antes, de dos plantas, con alero. Con un alero caritativo para las lluvias de ayer, de hoy y siempre.

De muchacho mi superstición me decía que el día que entrara a la iglesia de San Antonio ése iba a ser el último mío. ¡Qué va! Aquí sigo vivo. De haberme muerto además mi superstición no habría podido reprocharme: "Te lo advertí, te lo dije". Los muertos no ven ni oyen ni entienden, y les importa un carajo lo que les advirtieron o no.

"¡Cómo! —exclamó Wílmar al conocer mi apartamento—. ¡Aquí no hay televisión ni un

equipo de sonido!" ¿Cómo podía vivir yo sin
música? Le expliqué que me estaba entrenando
para el silencio de la tumba. "¿Y el teléfono?
¿Desconectado?" "Ajá, y el agua y la luz también, tampoco por lo general funcionan. Cuando más las necesito se van". Eran las leyes de
Murphy, niño, las más seguras, que estipulaban
que: Que lo único seguro de esta vida son cada
mes sin faltar las cuentas de la luz, el agua y el teléfono. Entonces, arrodillado en el piso, con un
cuchillo de la cocina a falta de destornillador,
Wílmar lo reconectó. No bien lo reconectó y
sonó el maldito. Me precipité sobre el aparato
monstruoso, alarmado de que alguien me pudiera llamar. ¿Quién? Nadie, un idiota equivo-
cado preguntando si aquí compraban higuerillo. Le contesté que sí. Y él: ¿Que a cómo lo
estaba pagando? Y yo: ¿Que a cómo lo estaba
vendiendo? Que a tanto el bulto. Le ofrecí la
mitad. Y yo subiendo de a poquito y él de a poquito bajando nos encontramos en el camino y
le compré veinte bultos. ¿Que adónde me los
mandaba? Pues a mi depósito, adonde me estaba hablando, en la Central de Abastos; que pre-
guntara por fulanito de tal. Y le di el nombre del
ministro de Hacienda. Me prometió que a primera hora, sin faltar, me llevaba los veinte

bultos en un camión contratado. Colgó y colgué. Wílmar, que no entendía, me preguntó que para qué era el higuerillo. Le contesté que para hacer aceite. Se quedó convencido de que yo tenía una fábrica de aceite de higuerillo.

Vuelvo y repito: no hay que contar plata delante del pobre. Por eso no les pienso contar lo que esa noche antes de dormirnos pasó. Básteles saber dos cosas: Que su desnuda belleza se realzaba por el escapulario de la Virgen que le colgaba del pecho. Y que al desvertirse se le cayó un revólver. "¿Y ese revólver para qué?" le pregunté yo de ingenuo. Que para lo que se ofreciera. Pues sí, pregunta tonta la mía, un revólver es para lo que se pueda ofrecer. Y abrazado a mi ángel de la guarda me dormí, no sin que antes de que me desconectara el sueño me entrara el futurismo, el fatalismo y me diera por pensar en los titulares amarillistas del día de mañana: "Gramático Ilustre Asesinado por su Ángel de la Guarda", en letras rojas enormes, que se salían de la primera plana. Luego, recapacitando, me dije que los dos periódicos de Medellín eran serios, no como los pasquines sensacionalistas de Bogotá. La página roja, incluso, la habían reducido en los últimos tiempos a una columnita. ¿Sería que hablar en Medellín de asesinados era como decir en época de lluvias "¡Aguaceros Torrenciales!" o en verano "Nos estamos asando del calor"? ¿Dar como noticia lo obvio? No, era que todavía nos quedaba un poquito de dignidad, de decencia. Y tuve fe en el futuro, en el ajeno, porque el mío, como bien lo sabía desde muchacho, se acababa ahí, el día que conocí la iglesia de San Antonio. Y con esta nota de desolado optimismo me dormí.

Amaneció martes y yo vivo y él abrazado a mí y radiante la mañana. "¿Qué día es?" me preguntó abriendo los ojos el ángel. "Martes", le contesté. De él fue entonces la idea de que fuéramos a Sabaneta adonde María Auxiliadora. "¿A qué vas? —le pregunté—. ¿A dar gracias, o a pedir?" Que a ambas cosas. Los pobres son así: agradecen para poder seguir pidiendo.

Encontré a Sabaneta más bien fría de fieles, desangelada. La plaza desahogada, sin congestionamientos de buses ni atropellamientos de peregrinos. Y los puestos de estampitas y reliquias de María Auxiliadora sin un cliente. ¿Qué pasó? ¿Sería que esta raza novelera desertó también de la Virgen? ¿Por el fútbol? ¿Y que ya no creía más que en los milagros de sus propias patas? Entramos a la iglesia: semidesierta, con unos cuantos viejos y viejas de poca monta y ni

136

un sicario. ¡Carajo, también esto se acabó, como todo! Y me arrodillé ante la Virgen y le dije: "Virgencita mía, María Auxiliadora que te he querido desde mi infancia: cuando estos hijos de puta te abandonen y te den la espalda y no vuelvan más, cuenta conmigo, aquí me tienes. Mientras viva volveré". ¿De qué le estaría dando gracias Alexis, perdón, Wílmar a la Virgen? ¿Qué le estaría pidiendo? ¿Ropas, bienes, antojos, mini-Uzis? Decidí hacerlo feliz ese día y darle en nombre de ella lo que quisiera.

Salimos de Sabaneta por la vieja carretera de mi infancia caminando, y caminando, caminando, conversando como en mis felices tiempos, Wílmar me preguntó que por qué si tenía una fábrica tenía que andar a pie como pobre, sin carro. Le expliqué que para mí el mayor insulto era que me robaran, y que por eso no tenía carro: que prefería mil veces seguir andando a vivir cuidándolo. En cuanto a la fábrica, ¿de dónde sacó tan peregrina idea? ¿Darles yo trabajo a los pobres? ¡Jamás! Que se lo diera la madre que los parió. El obrero es un explotador de sus patrones, un abusivo, la clase ociosa, haragana. Que uno haga la fuerza es lo que quieren, que importe máquinas, que pague impuestos, que apague incendios mientras ellos, los explotados, se rascan las pelotas o se declaren en huelga en tanto salen a vacaciones. Jamás he visto a uno de esos zánganos trabajar; se la pasan el día entero jugando fútbol u oyendo fútbol por el radio, o leyendo en las mañanas las noticias de lo mismo en El Colombiano. Ah, y armándome sindicatos. Y cuando llegan a sus casas los malnacidos rendidos, fundidos, extenuados "del trabajo", pues a la cópula: a empanzurrar a sus mujeres de hijos y a sus hijos de lombrices y aire. ¿Yo explotar a los pobres? ¡Con dinamita! Mi fórmula para acabar con la lucha de clases es fumigar esta roña. ¡Obreritos a mí! Pero cuando la cara se me encendía de la ira pasamos por Bombay, la "bomba de gasolina" de mi infancia, que era a la vez cantina, y los recuerdos empezaron a ventiarme suavecito, como una brisa con rocío, refrescante, bienhechora, y me apagaron el incendio de la indignación. ¡La bomba de Bombay, qué maravilla! Era un simple surtidor de gasolina afuera y adentro una cantina, ¡pero qué cantina! Allí en las noches alborotadas de cocuyos y chapolas, a la luz de una Cóleman, encendidos por el aguardiente y la pasión política se mataban los conservadores con los liberales a machete por las ideas. Cuáles ideas nunca supe, ¡pero qué maravilla! Y la nostalgia de lo pasado, de lo vivido, de lo soñado me iba suavizando el ceño. Y por sobre las ruinas del Bombay presente, el casco de lo que fue, en una nube desflecada, rompiendo un cielo brumoso, me iba retrocediendo a mi infancia hasta que volvía a ser niño y a salir el sol, y me veía abajo por esa carretera una tarde, corriendo con mis hermanos. Y felices, inconscientes, despilfarrando el chorro de nuestras vidas pasábamos frente a Bombay persiguiendo un globo. Con su aguja gruesa una vitrola en la cantina tocaba un disco rayado: "Un amor que se me fue, otro amor que me olvidó, por el mundo yo voy penando. Amorcito quién te arrullará, pobrecito que perdió su nido, sin hallar abrigo muy solito va. Caminar y caminar, ya comienza a oscurecer y la tarde se va ocultando…" Y los ojos se me encharcaban de lágrimas mientras dejando atrás a Bombay, para siempre, volvía a sonar a tumbos, en mi corazón rayado, ese "Senderito de Amor" que oí de niño en esa cantina por primera vez esa tarde. Y qué hace sin embargo que volvía con Alexis por esta misma carretera, agotándose instante por instante en la desesperanza nuestro imposible amor… Wílmar no lo podía entender, no lo podía creer. Que alguien llorara porque el tiempo pasa… "¡Al diablo con la bomba de Bombay y los recuerdos! —me dije secándome las lágrimas—. ¡Nada de nostalgias! Que venga lo que venga, lo que sea, aunque sea el matadero del presente. ¡Todo menos volver atrás!" Unas cuadras después pasamos frente a Santa Anita, la finca de mi infancia, de mis abuelos, de la que no quedaba nada. Nada pero nada nada: ni la casa ni la barranca donde se alzaba. Habían cortado a pico la barranca y construido en el hueco una dizque urbanización milagro: casitas y casitas y casitas para los hijueputas pobres, para que parieran más.

De regreso a Medellín le compré a Wílmar los famosos tenis y la dotación completa de símbolos sexuales: jeans, camisas, camisetas, cachuchas, calcetines, trusas y hasta suéteres y chaquetas para los fríos glaciales del trópico. De pantalón en pantalón, de camisa en camisa, de tienda en tienda recorriéndonos todos los centros comerciales con resignación y constancia (resignación mía y constancia suya) fuimos encontrando poco a poco, exactísimamente, lo que él quería. Los muchachos son tan vanidosos como las mujeres y más insaciables de ropa. Y de un tiempo a esta parte les ha dado por ponerse en el lóbulo de una oreja (pero no sé si en el de la derecha o en el de la izquierda) un arete.

Que por qué no me compraba yo algo. Le dije que por cuestión de principios no despilfarraba plata en ropa para mí, que yo ya no tenía remedio. Que con el traje negro que mantenía en un closet planchado me bastaba para los entierros. Ni me oyó. Iba y venía por los pasillos como enajenado buscando trapos entre trapos. Haga de cuenta usted un gato revolviendo en un cofre mágico y sacando de entre sus sorpresas la felicidad. Mensaje al presidente y al gobierno: El Estado debe concientizarse más y comprarles ropa a los muchachos con el fin de que ya no piensen tanto en procrear ni en matar. Las canchas de fútbol no-bas-tan.

Con la ropa nueva de Wílmar mis tres míseros closets vacíos quedaron atestados, atiborrados, y mi pobre traje negro relegado, arrinconado, apabullado por tanto color vistoso. De inmediato Wílmar quiso salir al centro a estrenar. Más me valiera no haber salido, no haber nacido porque volvimos a lo de Alexis. Iba un hombre por Junín detrás de mí silbando. Detesto pero detesto que la gente silbe. No lo tolero. Lo considero una afrenta personal, un insulto mayor incluso que un radio prendido en un taxi. ¿Que el hombre inmundo silbe usurpando el sagrado lenguaje de los pájaros? ¡Jamás! Yo soy un protector de los derechos de los animales. Y así se lo comenté a Wílmar, disminuyendo el paso para que el hombre nos pasara y se fuera. ¡Quién me mandó abrir la boca! Adelantándosele a su vez al asqueroso, Wílmar sacó el revólver y le propinó un frutazo en el corazón. El hombre-cerdo con vocación de pájaro se desplomó dando su último silbo, desinflándose, en tanto Wílmar se perdía por entre el gentío. Como al difuntico al caer se le abrió la camisa, se le despanzurró la barriga; y así pude ver que llevaba bajo el cinturón un revólver. ¡Jua! Le iba a servir en la otra vida para matar cuanto sus puercos pies para caminar. Los muertos no matan ni caminan: caen en caída libre rumbo a los infiernos como una piedra roma. Con la conciencia tranquila del que va a misa seguí mi camino, pero empecé a sospechar que lo conocía. ¿De dónde? ¿Quién podía ser? Y que se me enciende el foco. ¡Era el que había visto atracando en San Juan meses antes, el que mató al muchacho por robarle el carro! Bendito seas Satanás que a falta de Dios, que no se ocupa, viniste a enderezar los entuertos de este mundo. Me devolví a constatar la identidad del caído, pero me fue imposible llegar: el cerco de curiosos, festivo, jubiloso, se había acabado de cerrar, y no había arrimadero ni para un inspector de policía que viniera a levantar un cadáver. Cuadras adelante me encontré con Wílmar y estaba radiante, jubiloso, riéndose de felicidad, de dicha. Con una dicha que le chispeaba en sus ojos verdes. Mi niño era el enviado de Satanás que había venido a poner orden en este mundo con el que Dios no puede. A Dios, como al doctor Frankenstein su monstruo, el hombre se le fue de las manos.

Aquí no hay inocentes, todos son culpables. Que la ignorancia, que la miseria, que hay que tratar de entender… Nada hay que entender. Si todo tiene explicación, todo tiene justificación y así acabamos alcahuetiando el delito. ¿Y los derechos humanos? ¡Qué "derechos humanos" ni qué carajos! Ésas son alcahueterías, libertinaje, celestinaje. A ver, razonemos: si aquí abajo no hay culpables, ¿entonces qué, los delitos se cometieron solos? Como los delitos no se cometen solos y aquí abajo no hay culpables, entonces el culpable será el de Allá Arriba, el Irresponsable que les dio el libre albedrío a estos criminales. ¿Pero a Ése quién me lo castiga? ¿Me lo castiga usted? Mire parcero, a mí no me vengan con cuentos que yo ya no quiero entender. Con todo lo que he vivido, visto, "a la final" como bien dice usted, se me ha acabado dañando el corazón. ¡Derechitos humanos a mí! Juicio sumario y al fusiladero y del fusiladero al pudridero. El Estado está para reprimir y dar bala. Lo demás son demagogias, democracias. No más libertad de hablar, de pensar, de obrar, de ir de un lado a otro atestando buses, ¡carajo!

Íbamos en uno de esos buses atestados en el calor infernal del medio día y oyendo vallenatos a todo taco. Y como si fueran poco el calor y el radio, una señora con dos niños en pleno libertinaje: uno, de teta, en su más enfurecido berrinche, cagado sensu stricto de la ira. Y el hermanito brincando, manotiando, jodiendo. ¿Y la mamá? Ella en la luna, como si nada, poniendo cara de Mona Lisa la delincuente, la desgraciada, convencida de que la maternidad es sagrada, en vez de aterrizar a meter en cintura a sus dos engendros. ¿No se les hace demasiada desconsideración para con el resto de los pasajeros, una verdadera falta de caridad cristiana? ¿Por qué berrea el bebé, señora? ¿Por estar vivo? Yo también lo estoy y me tengo que aguantar. Pero hasta cierto punto, porque si bien es cierto que en esta vida abusan del inocente, también es cierto que siempre habrá una gota que llenó la taza. Y con la taza llena hasta el tope, rebosada hasta el rebose, he aquí que en Wílmar encarna el Rey Herodes. Y que saca el Santo Rey el tote y truena tres veces. ¡Tas! ¡Tas! ¡Tas! Una para la mamá, y dos para sus dos redrojos. Una pepita para la mamá en su corazón de madre, y dos para sus angelitos en sus corazoncitos tiernos. Si hace dos mil años se le escapó a Egipto el impostor éstos no, ya el Santo Rey estaba curado de engaños. "¡Y no se muevan, hijueputas, ni vayan a mirar porque los mato!" La frase era la misma, exactísima, que había oído tiempo atrás en un asalto, de suerte que nadie tuvo que decirla esta vez en el bus, se fue diciendo sola por el aire. Como el chofer se tardó unos segundos más de la cuenta en abrirnos la puerta, cuando la acabó de abrir, también, piró: difuntico. ¡Y quedaban dos chumbimbas en el tote para el que no le gustó la cosa! El radio, sin dueño, siguió cantando por él, en su memoria, los vallenatos, que aquí se están volviendo ritmo de muertos.

Esta sociedad permisiva y alcahueta les ha hecho creer a los niños que son los reyes de este mundo y que nacieron con todos los derechos. Inmenso error. No hay más rey que el rey ya dicho y nadie nace con derechos. El pleno derecho a existir sólo lo pueden tener los viejos. Los niños tienen que probar primero que lo merecen: sobreviviendo.

Cuentan que poco antes de mi regreso a Medellín pasó por esta ciudad destornillada un loco que iba inyectando en los buses cianuro a cuanta perra humana embarazada encontraba y a sus retoños. ¿Un loco? ¿Llamáis "loco" a un santo? ¡Desventurados! Dejádmelo conocer para darle más de lo dicho y un diploma al mérito que lo acredite como miembro activo de la Orden del Santo Rey. Ah, y una buena provisión de jeringas desechables, no se le vayan a infectar sus pacientes.

¿Y la policía? ¿No hay policía en el país de los hechos? Claro que la hay: son "la poli", "los tombos", "la tomba", "la ley", "los polochos", "los verdes hijueputas". Son los invisibles, los que cuando los necesitas no se ven, más transparentes que un vaso. Pero el día en que se corporicen, que les rebote la luz en sus cuerpos verdes, ay parcero, a correr que te van a atracar, a cascar, a mandar para el otro toldo. Un japonesito que vino a industrializar a Colombia murió así, sin poderlo creer.

Otro muerto en un bus: un mendigo alzado. Uno de esos basuqueros solivantados por Amnistía Internacional, la Iglesia católica y el

146

comunismo más los Derechos Humanos, que se la pasan el día entero fumando basuco y pidiendo, exigiendo, con un garrote en la mano: "Que déme tanto, jefe, que hoy no he desayunado. Tengo hambre". "Que te la quite tu madre que te parió", les contesto yo. O el cura papa que es tan buen defensor de la pobrería y la proliferación de la roña humana. ¡Mendiguitos a mí, caridad cristiana! Odiando al rico pero eso sí, empeñados en seguir de pobres y pariendo más... ¡Por qué no especuláis en la bolsa, faltos de imaginación, desventurados! O montáis una corporación financiera y os vais a Suiza a depositar y a la Riviera a gastar. ¡O qué! ¿Creéis que el mundo se acabó en Medellín y que todo es sancocho? Bobitos, el mundo sigue y sigue, se va redondiando, dando la vuelta hacia las antípodas hasta que llegas, por la parte de abajo de la naranja, en jet propio o primera clase a la Côte d'Azur, donde hay salmón, caviar, pâté de foie, y putas de a quinientos dólares que no habéis olido en vuestras míseras vidas. Bueno, sin más preámbulos se subió uno de estos asquerosos al bus con su garrote y se pronunció tamaño discurso de cuatro cuadras para informarnos que: Que como él era tan buen cristiano y no tenía trabajo, que prefería pedir a andar robando o matando. Y arrancó de puesto en puesto blandiendo su garrote perentorio, recogiendo su cuota. Para que acabara como dijo, como buen cristiano, cuando llegó a nosotros Wílmar desenfundó su rayo de las tinieblas y le aplicó de limosna su pepita de eternidad en el corazón, no se le fuera éste a dañar el día menos pensado y le diera por robarnos y matarnos… Y curado de basucos y miserias, manu militari, nemine discrepante, minima de malis, entró el pobre, el pobre pobre en el reino del silencio donde reina la más elocuente, la que no habla, ni en español ni en latín ni en nada, la Parca. Basuqueros, buseros, mendigos, policías, ladrones, médicos y abogados, evangélicos y católicos, niños y niñas, hombres y mujeres, públicas y privadas, de todo probó el Ángel, todos fueron cayendo fulminados por la su mano bendita, por la su espada de fuego. Con decirles que hasta curas, que son especie en extinción. Se quería seguir con el presidente… "Muchachito atolondrado, niño tonto, ¿no ves que este zángano está más protegido que ni que fuera la reina de las abejas? Déjalo que salga". Pobres de este mundo, por Dios, por la Virgen, por caridad cristiana, abrid los ojos, razonad: Si se cruzan una pareja de enanos ¿qué pasa? Que tienen el cincuenta por ciento de probabilidades, fifty fifty, de que sus hijos les salgan como ellos, midiendo uno veinte. ¡Uno de cada dos hijos les nacerá con el gen de la acondroplasia, enano! Pues una cosa sí os digo, desventurados: que el gen de la pobreza es peor, más penetrante: nueve mil novecientos noventa y nueve de diez mil se lo transmiten, indefectiblemente, a su prole. ¿Estáis de acuerdo en heredarles semejante mal a vuestros propios hijos? Por razones genéticas el pobre no tiene derecho a reproducirse. ¡Ricos del mundo, uníos! Más. O la avalancha de la pobrería os va a tapar.

D'iái, del bus, nos seguimos pal barrio de Boston a que conociera Wílmar la casa donde nací. La casa estaba igual y el barrio igual, tal como los había dejado hacía tantísimos años, como si una mano milagrosa los hubiera preservado, bajo campana de cristal, de los estragos de Cronos. Sólo que lo que no cambia está muerto… "Mira niño, en esta casa, en este cuarto de esta ventana que da a la calle, una noche despejada, estrellada, promisoria, mentirosa, nací yo". Y ahí mismo me quiero morir para redondiar el epitafio, que en mayúsculas latinas ha de decir así, en aposición a mi nombre y a este lado de la puerta: "Vir clarisimus, grammaticus conspicuus, philologus illustrisimus, quoque pius, placatus, politus, plagosus, fraternus, placidus, unum et idem e pluribus unum, summum jus, hic natus atque mortuus est. Anno Domini tal…" Y ahí ponen el año de instalación de la placa, no los de mi nacimiento y muerte porque soy partidario de no meter a la eternidad en cintura entre fechas, como en camisa de fuerza. No. Déjenla que fluya sola, que ella sola se irá pasando sin darse cuenta. Calle del Perú, barrio de Boston, ciudad de Medellín, departamento de Antioquia, República de Colombia, planeta Tierra, Sistema Solar, Vía Láctea y todas las galaxias, en la casa donde nací contra mi voluntad pero donde me pienso morir por mano propia.

Después llevé a Wílmar a conocer la iglesia salesiana del Sufragio donde me bautizaron, y salvo el bautisterio todo estaba igual, sin cambios. El bautisterio, no sé por qué, lo habían eliminado, sellado con un muro de cemento ciego. Mejor. Cuando uno se arrimaba ahí soplaba un chiflón de eternidad, un como vientecito frío, siniestro. Luego le fui explicando a Wílmar, que era un ignorante en religión, los pasajes del Viejo y del Nuevo Testamento que estaban escenificados en el techo. Y bajando la mirada: "¿Ves ese santo que se sonríe ahí, con sonrisita de falsía atroz? Ése es Juan Bosco, corruptor de

150

menores. Yo me le conozco su trayectoria". Y le conté cómo instalaron la estatua actual en reemplazo de la vieja, que se descabezó cuando volvíamos de una procesión en carroza. La historia sólo yo la sé y nadie más en este mundo. Regresábamos a la iglesia del Sufragio, nuestro punto de partida, manejando el cabrón chofer a toda verraca nuestra carroza cuando ¡pum!, que se enreda en un cable de la luz la estatua, se suelta de su base, y pasando por sobre mi cabeza rozándome, a punto de matarme, va a dar en vuelo libre contra el pavimento de la calle a romperse la suya. Quedó el santo hecho un lamento, un Nazareno, desastillado, descabezado, como para sacarlo del santoral (porque santo que no es capaz de protegerse a sí mismo ¡qué nos va a proteger a nosotros!). Esa mañana habíamos desfilado por el centro de Medellín en la procesión del Corpus Christi. Lentamente, pausadamente, a vuelta solemne de rueda, había avanzado nuestra carroza por entre la multitud admirada, incrédula, que se negaba a creer lo que veían sus ojos, que se pudiera dar tanta majestad concentrada en este mundo. En nuestro cuadro pío, inmóvil aunque semoviente, que se deslizaba etéreo por entre las nubes, como navegando sobre un mar de cabezas humanas, yo hacía de misionero salesiano. ¿Me imaginan ustedes a mí, de ocho años, mintiendo así? Cuánto tiempo no ha pasado y aún no olvido esa mañana en que el delincuente de Juan Bosco me quiso matar. Reconozco, eso sí, que el santo que se descabezó, con todo y lo ñato que era, se veía menos mal que el que entronizaron en su lugar, en su altar, con perfiladita nariz aguileña, griega, y sonrisita marica, falsa, pérfida. Y mientras salía con Wílmar de la iglesia, por asociación de narices se me vino a la memoria ese detective criminal que andaba por Junín persiguiendo maricas y que le decían El Ñato. ¡Cuánto hace que se murió, que lo mataron, también! En el cruce de Maracaibo con la que es hoy Avenida Oriental, disparándole desde una moto…

"Mira Wílmar, fíjate ahora que lleguemos a la estatua, que tiene en el pedestal, entre los leones, el mármol rajado". Y efectivamente, el mármol del pedestal de la estatua de Córdoba del parque de Boston seguía rajado donde indiqué, desde hacía años y para toda la eternidad. Y es que mármol quebrado no se junta, como no se puede reinstalar en su cáscara un huevo frito. "Ese mármol, de una pedrada, yo lo quebré". Y no había tampoco vidrio de casa que resistiera una andanada nuestra de piedras y de maldad.

La niñez es como la pobreza, dañina, mala. Entonces, cuando estábamos en estos razonamientos profundos, que se nos aparece ¿saben quién? ¡El Difunto! "Difuntico, ¿tú por aquí? ¡Qué milagro! ¡Y fuera de tus dominios, en mi barrio de Boston! Yo te hacía ya muerto". Que no, que andaba de vacaciones en La Costa. Que el que sí se murió, esta mañana, fue El Ñato. "¿Cuál Ñato?" "Pues el tira de Junín, que detestaba a los maricas". Que en el cruce de Maracaibo con la Avenida Oriental, desde una moto unos sicarios lo quebraron. "¡No puede ser! —exclamé asombrado—. Al Ñato sí lo mataron, y ahí, en ese mismo punto del espacio, pero hace treinta años, cuando ni siquiera habían abierto la Avenida Oriental, que era una calle estrecha. Más aún: él fue de los con que inauguraron esta modalidad de disparar desde una moto. Fue el pionero". Que no, que ése sería otro, que el que él decía lo acababan de matar donde dijo, esta mañana. Que fuera al entierro a ver si no era cierto. Y me dio la dirección de la casa donde lo iban a velar. Le dije que pensaba ir por la tarde, pero que aparte de eso ¿qué más? ¿No irían a venir enseguida también, por nosotros, los de la moto? Que no, que por hoy no me preocupara. Me despedí de El Difunto reconfortado por sus palabras aunque a la vez inquieto por la perspectiva insidiosa de que al Nato, y en general al ser humano (pues a juzgar por su maldad sin duda era eso), lo pudieran matar dos veces. ¿Podía eso ser? Por la preocupación se me olvidó preguntarle al Difunto por sus vacaciones en La Costa. ¿Vacaciones de qué?

Irreconocible, espléndido como a veces me gusta aparecer, salí esa tarde con Wílmar de mi apartamento como el rey Felipe, todo de negro hasta los pies vestido. Wílmar no daba crédito a sus ojos. Nunca estuvo más orgulloso de este su servidor con que andaba. ¿Los mendigos? Ni se atrevían a pedir. Se abrían en abanico para darnos paso. ¡Qué tipazo! Con decirles que el taxista cuando nos subimos al taxi apagó instintivamente el radio. ¿Que adónde deseaba ir el señor doctor? Le di la dirección que me dio El Difunto: a la falda tal de Manrique Oriental. "Falda" llaman en esta ciudad insensata a una subida, a una calle en pendiente. ¡Díganme si están o no están de atar! Falda, hasta donde yo entiendo, es la de las mujeres, corta o larga, larga o corta, ¿pero una subida? En fin, que ahí vamos por Manrique que es un barrio cuesta arriba como esta vida, una pared parada, buscando entre sus faldas esa falda. En Manrique (y lo digo por mis

154

lectores japoneses y servo-cróatas) es donde se acaba Medellín y donde empiezan las comunas o viceversa. Es como quien dice la puerta del infierno aunque no se sepa si es de entrada o de salida, si el infierno es el que está p'allá o el que está p'acá, subiendo o bajando. Subiendo o bajando, de todos modos la Muerte, mi comadre, anda por esas faldas entregada a su trabajo sin ponerle mala cara a nadie. Es como yo, su ahijado, que carezco de reparos idiomáticos. Todo me gusta.

Llegamos a la casa del Ñato, y puesto que la puerta estaba abierta entramos, sin llamar. El ataúd lo tenían instalado en el corredor para que se pudieran explayar más a gusto los dolientes por el patio. Instalada entre cirios la caja negra, y un Cristo doliente enfrente. Un rumor sordo de rezos nos recibió, con olor a pabilos chamuscados. Eran los cirios quemándose, preludio efímero de la eternidad. Recibían las condolencias las dos hermanas del muerto, unas señoritas ancianas muy dignas, muy respetables, cosa que jamás hubiera sospechado yo en tratándose de quien se murió. Bueno, "se" murió aquí no me gusta, lo quito: lo murieron. Ante el asombro unánime, la expectativa general, me acerqué a darles el pésame. "¿Quién sería ese señor de

155

negro con esa pinta, con ese porte, con esa dignidad?" se preguntaban todos. Yo. Yo era. Y el que dice "yo" habló: "Somos nada, señoritas, briznas en el huracán, pavesas, un espartillo en las manos del Creador —(un "espartillo" es una especie de yerba seca)—. Que El que Todo lo Puede lo haya acogido en su seno". Me agradecieron con dignidad sobria, sin aspavientos, sin alharacas. Entonces les pedí, en nombre de la amistad que me había ligado en vida al difunto, y del cariño que por él sentí (mentiras, mentiras, mentiras), que me lo dejaran ver por última vez. Con breve gesto de cabeza asintieron y me acerqué al ataúd. Lo abrí. Y en efecto, era El Ñato, el mismo hijueputa. Las bolsas bajo los ojos, la nariz ñata, el bigotico a lo Hitler... Igualito. Era porque era. Pero si habían pasado treinta años, ¿cómo podía seguir igual? Ahí les dejo, para que lo piensen, el problemita.

Al levantar mi cabeza del muerto y apartarme ligeramente del ataúd, dos loras que había en una percha lo vieron. Y que lo ven y se sueltan: "¡Hijueputa! —le gritaban—. ¡Malparido! ¡Marica!", y se la remachaban con sus lenguas gruesas. Y un rosario de insultos, una andanada pero de vulgaridades tales que no las puedo repetir aquí por pudor de idioma. Una de las dos señoritas viejas se acercó entonces a la caja, y discretamente le bajó la tapa. Y santo remedio, dejaron de verlo las loras y el chaparrón de insultos escampó.

Salí de esa casa con Wílmar y la mente confusa. Una de dos: O el que tuve ante mis ojos no era mi Ñato, o la Muerte de ociosa se había puesto a repasar a sus muertos. Pero si no era el Ñato de mi juventud, ¿por qué era idéntico? ¿Y por qué lo mataron igual, y en el mismo sitio y a la misma hora? ¿No sería que la realidad en Medellín se enloqueció y se estaba repitiendo? Ahora bien, si el Ñato que tuve enfrente era mi Ñato, ¿cómo le podían decir "marica" las loras a semejante foboloca? ¿No sería pura inquina de ellas, una calumnia postmortem? No, los animales no mienten ni odian. No conocen el odio ni la mentira, que son inventos exclusivamente humanos, como el radio o la televisión. Y en efecto, nunca se le conoció mujer al difunto. Ni hijos, ni por lo tanto nietos. ¡Pobre Ñato! Haber nacido marica y vivido y muerto sin poder serlo… A pocos les ha ido tan mal en este paseo.

Y ahora viene lo insólito: bajaron por la falda una carroza de funeraria y dos motocicletas dando chumbimba a toda verraca, ametrallando la fachada de la casa del Ñato. ¿Para qué le disparaban si no era una fachada de cartón, si era una fachada de cemento? Las balas no podían pasar rumbo a los deudos del interior… No, es que no era para que pasaran, era por su valor simbólico. Una especie de gesto de afirmación. Y que casi nos cuesta la vida de paso a Wílmar y a mí porque por un pelo no nos llevan, nos arrastran, en su bajada endemoniada el carro fúnebre y sus dos motos. Lo más preocupante de esto es que: Que aquí te disparan desde donde menos lo piensas. ¡Hasta desde un carro de funeraria!

¡Ay Manrique, barriecito viejo, barriecito amado! Se puede decir que ni te conocí. Desde abajo, desde mi niñez te veía, tus casitas como de juguete y tu iglesia gótica. Una iglesia alta, gris, espigada, de un gótico alucinante, estirándose sus dos torres puntudas como queriendo alcanzar el cielo. Las nubes negras, cargadas, pasaban, y al pasar se pinchaban en sus pararrayos y se soltaba la lluvia. ¡Qué aguaceros! La lluvia en Medellín se puede decir que prácticamente nace en Manrique. En ese barrio donde hoy empiezan las comunas pero donde en mi niñez terminaba la ciudad pues más allá no había nada —sólo cerros y cerros y mangas y mangas donde a los niños que se desperdigaban se los chupaba El Chupasangre— allá en Manrique tuvo mi abuelo una casa que yo conocí, pero de la que no recuerdo nada. O sí, una sola cosa que se me había borrado de la memoria: su piso de baldosas rojas por las que me ponían a caminar derecho, derechito, siguiendo la línea, la raya que separaba dos hileras de ellas para que después, cuando creciera, continuara igual por el resto de mi vida, recto, derecho, siempre derecho como un hombre de bien y que nunca se torciera mi camino. ¡Ay abuelo, abuela!…

Esa historia del Nato que he contado fue la última cosa bella que viví con Wílmar. Después el destino se nos vino encima como esa carroza fúnebre y sus dos motos, atropellándonos envenenado.

La noche fue siniestra. Lloviendo el cielo alienado la noche entera sin parar. El río Medellín se desbordó y con él sus ciento ochenta quebradas. Las unas, las subterráneas, que habíamos metido en cintura en atanores bajo las calles entubándolas a costa de tanto sudor y peculado, se abrían iracundas sus camisas de fuerza, rompían el pavimento y frenéticas, maniáticas, lunáticas, se salían como locas descamisadas a arrastrar carros y a hacer estragos. Las otras, sus hermanas libres —arroyos risueños en tiempos de cordura, mansas palomas— saltaban ahora vueltas trombas rugientes, endemoniadas, de las montañas, a volcarse sobre nosotros, a inundarnos, a ahogarnos, a desvariarme y hacerme subir la fiebre. Y desventrado el cielo, desbordado el río, desquiciadas las quebradas, se empezaron a alborotar las alcantarillas, a rebosarse, a salir a borbotones, y a subir, a subir, a subir hacia mis balcones el inmenso mar de mierda. Conste. Lo advertí. Que íbamos a acabar en eso.

En eso o en lo que fuera, el día amaneció normal, asesino. Ni rastro de la noche borrascosa. Poniendo cara de inocente la luz del día, hipócrita, mentirosa. Fuimos a comprar el refrigerador para la mamá de Wílmar, y me dio por pasar de regreso por el Versalles dizque a comprar pasteles. Esos pastelitos "de gloria" que hacía mi abuela, y que no se comen ni en la misma Viena. Se hacen así: se pone la pasta hojaldrada a inflar la noche anterior al sereno bajo cielo estrellado, y al día siguiente simplemente se mete al horno con relleno de dulce de guayaba. No mucho porque, como decía mi abuela, "el dulce empalaga". Cruzamos el parque, tomamos por Junín y llegamos al Versalles. A la entrada de éste nos tropezamos con La Plaga. "¡Ay Plaguita, qué alegría verte! —exclamé—. Yo ya te hacía muerto…" Que no, que todavía no, que seguía en la racha de suerte. "¿Y tu hijito?" Que ya estaba por nacer, que era cosa de días pero que se había tomado nueve meses. "¿Tanto así? ¡Qué despilfarro! Yo en nueve meses me escribo una ópera…" Wílmar entró a comprar los pasteles y yo me quedé afuera con La Plaga conversando. Entonces me hizo el reproche, que por qué andaba con el que mató a Alexis. "Por qué dices eso, niño tonto —le contesté—. ¿No ves que yo ando con Wílmar y a Alexis lo mató La Laguna Azul?" "Wílmar es La Laguna Azul", respondió. Por unos segundos se me detuvo el corazón. Cuando volvió a andar ya sabía que tenía que matarlo. Claro que era, claro que sí, claro que lo conocía, eso lo sentí desde el primer momento en que nos tropezamos por Palacé, allí abajo, cerquita de Maracaibo. ¿Que por qué lo llamaban así, con ese apodo tan absurdo? le pregunté por preguntar, por decir algo, por seguir hablando sin pensar, y me contestó que porque se parecía al muchacho de esa película. "Ah… —repliqué—. Nunca la vi. Hace años no voy a cine". Entonces salió el otro con los pasteles y me despedí de La Plaga. Tomamos por

Junín rumbo a La Playa, esa avenida donde una tarde como ésta me había matado a mi niño, y de paso a mí. Me ofreció un pastel de la bolsa pero no se lo quise recibir. Sin sospechar él nada iba comiendo pasteles y pasteles que iba sacando de la bolsa. "¿Tú ya conocías a ése?" le pregunté refiriéndome a La Plaga, a quien habíamos dejado atrás. "Ajá", contestó con la boca llena. "¿Porque también es de tu barrio?" "Ajá", volvió a contestar, asintiendo con la cabeza, y siguió comiendo pasteles. Le dije que tenía que ir a La Candelaria a pedirle al Señor Caído, pero no le dije a pedirle qué. Tenía que ir a esa iglesia a rogarle a Dios que todo lo sabe, que todo lo entiende, que todo lo puede, que me ayudara a matar a este hijueputa.

Le dije que me esperara afuera y entré a la iglesia sin él. Las veladoras del Señor Caído chisporroteaban fervorosas elevando al cielo su plegaria, mi súplica: que me iluminara cómo. Cuando salí de la iglesia ya lo sabía. En el atrio, entre los puestos de lotería y los mendigos él seguía esperándome. Vino hacia mí. Le dije que nos iríamos a dormir esa noche a cualquier motel de las afueras. Me preguntó la razón y le contesté que por supersticiones, que porque sentía que si me quedaba esa noche en mi casa me iban

162

a matar. Como esta impresión la puede tener cualquiera en cualquier momento en cualquier parte de Medellín lo entendió. Le había dado una razón incontrovertible, una que no acepta razones. Cruzamos el parque y al pasar junto a la estatua se alzó un revuelo de palomas que me avivó el recuerdo. Y recordé la tarde en que volví a esta iglesia a rogar por mí y a llorar por él, por mi niño, Alexis, el único. Abanicada su indiferencia por las palomas, ajeno a todo, más allá de las miserias humanas, seguía sobre su pedestal Pedro Justo Berrío, el viejo gobernador que gobernó a Antioquia por el tiempo inconcebible de cuatro años, un récord Guiness. Aquí lo usual es que duren meses; se tumban los unos a los otros en su rapiña, en su voracidad burocrática. Frente al prócer se alzaba en su desmesura idiota el tren elevado, el dizque metro, inacabado, detenido en sus alturas y convertido abajo en guarida de mendigos y ladrones. No lo han podido concluir, tienen años con él detenido: endeudaron a Antioquia para hacerlo y se robaron la plata. Hicieron bien: si no se la hubieran robado ellos se la habrían robado otros. Y al que no le guste la impunidad que no la respire, que siga su camino sin mirar, tapándose las narices. Unos roban y a otros los roban, unos matan y a otros los matan, así es esto. Todo estaba dentro de la más normal normalidad, la vida seguía su curso en Medellín. Algún día acabarán lo inconcluso y cruzará el tren elevado sobre mi ciudad deslizándose por sus aceitados rieles como volando, transportando gente y más gente y más gente. Yo ya no estaré para preguntarles: ¿Adónde van con tanta prisa, ratas humanas? ¿Qué se creen que se volvieron? ¿Pájaros?

Entramos al motel sin registrarnos, como se estila aquí. Aquí no es como en Europa donde se violan a todas horas los derechos humanos y a hotel adonde uno vaya le piden descaradamente identificación presumiendo lo que no se debe, que el ser humano es un criminal. Aquí no, aquí la confianza pública no está tan envenenada. Además aquí los moteles son de putas, y ellas y los que van con ellas no tienen identidad. Así, sin identidad como el hombre invisible cruzamos por la recepción, entramos al cuarto, nos desvestimos, nos acostamos y él se durmió y yo me quedé despierto meditando sobre los atropellos europeos a los derechos humanos y el eterno silencio del papa… El revólver, su revólver, lo había puesto, como siempre, sobre su ropa. Eso él. En cuanto a mí, yo simplemente estiraba, como me aconsejó el santo caído, el brazo, lo tomaba, le ponía sobre su cabeza la almohada y disparaba, y a ver si alcanzaba a oír el tiro su puta madre que lo parió. Después me iría yendo tan tranquilo, con estos mismos pies con los que entré… Y yo inmóvil y él durmiendo y así empezaron a correr las horas y el revólver no venía solo hacia mí volando por el aire ni mi brazo se me alargaba a tomarlo. Entonces descubrí lo que no sabía, que estaba infinitamente cansado, que me importaba un carajo el honor, que me daba lo mismo la impunidad que el castigo, y que la venganza era demasiada carga para mis años.

Cuando empezó a entrar el sol por la ventana entreabrió los ojos y entonces le pregunté: "¿Por qué mataste a Alexis?" "Porque mató a mi hermano", me contestó, restregándose los ojos, despertando. "Ah…" comenté como un estúpido. Nos levantamos, nos bañamos, nos vestimos y salimos. Al yo pagar en la recepción nos ofrecieron un café. Un "tinto", como dicen en este país absurdo.

Mientras esperábamos que pasara un taxi por la autopista le dije que yo iba con Alexis la tarde en que él lo mató. Que sí, que él ya sabía, que desde esa misma tarde me había quedado conociendo. "¿Entonces desde la primera noche que pasaste conmigo en mi apartamento me habrías podido matar?" Se rió y me dijo que si a alguien él no podía matar en este mundo era a mí. Entonces pensé que él era como yo, de los que dejábamos pasar, que éramos iguales, perdonavidas. Le pregunté por el que manejaba la moto desde la que él le había disparado a Alexis y me contestó que a ése lo habían matado al día siguiente. Le pregunté que quién, que por qué. Me contestó que no se supo, que eso se había quedado en veremos…

De los muertos que cargaba Alexis en su conciencia (si es que tenía) cuando nos conocimos, yo no soy culpable. De los de este niño, los suyos propios, tampoco. Allá ellos con sus muertos que de los que aquí tenemos compartidos ustedes son testigos. Le dije a Wílmar que en mi opinión ya no tenía objeto seguir en Medellín, que esta ciudad no daba para más, que nos fuéramos. ¿Que para dónde? Para donde fuera. El mundo no se acababa aquí, era bien grande. En cuanto a la humanidad, en todas partes sería la misma, la misma mierda, pero distinta. Aceptó. Simplemente tenía que ir antes a su barrio a despedirse de su mamá y a constatar que de veras le hubieran enviado la nevera, y a mi apartamento a sacar su ropa. Le pedí que se olvidara de la ropa y la nevera, que nos fuéramos de inmediato y que se despidiera de su mamá por carta que el correo era tan milagroso que hasta el mismísimo barrio de La Francia llega. Que no era en La Francia, que era en Santa Cruz y que a ninguna de las dos llegaba cartero: de una cuadra a otra los "bajan", los "quiebran". Eso lo entendí muy bien, en los barrios de las comunas la única que tiene paso libre es la Muerte. Nos despedimos. Yo me fui a mi apartamento a esperarlo y él tomó hacia las comunas. La despedida fue para siempre, vivos no nos volvimos a ver. Al amanecer sonó el teléfono: del anfiteatro, que fuera a identificar a alguien que llevaba consigo mi número.

"Anfiteatro" llaman aquí a la morgue, y no hay taxista en Medellín ni cristiano que no sepa dónde está porque aquí los vivos sabemos muy bien adónde tenemos que ir a buscar los muertos. Está saliendo de la ciudad, donde empieza la Autopista Norte, frente a una terminal de buses.

Un gentío se agolpaba afuera contra la valla de alambre de gallinero que cercaba el lote esperando entrar. Yo pasé ante los guardias de la caseta de entrada sin mirar, volviéndome a mi esencia, a lo que soy, el hombre invisible. Seguí a una antesala. Por sobre el llanto de los vivos y el silencio de los muertos, un tecleo obstinado de máquinas de escribir: era Colombia la oficiosa en su frenesí burocrático, su papeleo, su expedienteo, levantando actas de necropsias, de entradas y salidas, solícita, aplicada, diligente, con su alma irredenta de cagatintas. Mis ojos de hombre invisible se posaron sobre las "Observaciones" de una de esas actas de levantamiento de cadáver, que habían dejado sobre un escritorio: "Al parecer fue por robarle los tenis —decía—, pero de los hechos y de los autores nada se conoce". Y pasaba a hablar de heridas de la vena cava y paro cardiorespiratorio tras el shock hipovolémico causado por la herida de arma cortopunzante. El lenguaje me encantó. La precisión de los términos, la convicción del estilo… Los mejores escritores de Colombia son los jueces y los secretarios de juzgado, y no hay mejor novela que un sumario.

Al que iban dejando entrar de la calle le mostraban un álbum de fotografías en color acabadas de tomar y revelar de los muertos calienticos: primeros planos como de Hollywood, close-ups. Si alguna se parecía al desaparecido vivo, entonces podían pasar por la siguiente puerta, a la siguiente sala, a reconocer al apare-

168

cido muerto. El hombre invisible pasó. Era una sala alta, espaciosa, la de necropsias, con unas treinta mesas de disección ocupadas todas por los del último turno. Todas, todas, todas y todos hombres y casi todos eran jóvenes. Es decir, fueron. Ahora eran cadáveres, materia inerte. Desnudos, rajados en canal como reses, les habían extraído las vísceras para analizarlas y no les habían dejado nada de sustancia qué comer a los gusanos. El hombre invisible se enteró de que todos esos corazones, hígados, riñones, pulmones, tripas irían a una fosa común. Lo que aquí dejaban, para reconocimiento y consuelo de los deudos y estímulo a nuestra industria funeraria, era el casco del que fue, cosidos el pecho y el vientre en cremallera, con unas puntadas burdas, chambonas. Algunos tenían a sus pies el acta correspondiente de levantamiento del cadáver, pero no todos: Colombia nunca ha sido muy regular en sus cosas; es más bien irregular, imprevisible, impredecible, inconsecuente, desordenada, antimetódica, alocada, loca... El hombre invisible les fue pasando revista a los muertos. Tres cosas en especial le llamaron la atención de esos cuerpos desnudos sin corazón que pudiera volver a sentir el odio: la cabeza (y la de algunos con los pelos revueltos, erizados)

F= "el hombre invisible"

169

vaciada de sesos y rencores; el sexo inútil, estúpido, impúdico, incapaz de volver a engendrar, hacer el mal; y los pies que ya no llevarían a nadie a ninguna parte. Entonces reparó que sobre los pies de uno de esos cadáveres había otro, pequeñito, orientado en sentido vertical como los brazos de una cruz: el de un bebé recién nacido y recién rajado. Por un instante el hombre invisible pensó que el cadáver de la persona adulta era el de una mujer, la mamá, a la que le habían hecho la cesárea puesto que también tenía el vientre rajado. Pero no, era un hombre, otro más, y le habían puesto encima el cuerpecito del niño porque simplemente no tenían mesa vacía donde acomodarlo. El hombre invisible recordó esas combinaciones de objetos mágicas, insólitas con que soñaban los surrealistas, como por ejemplo un paraguas sobre una mesa de disección. ¡Surrealistas estúpidos! Pasaron por este mundo castos y puros sin entender nada de nada, ni de la vida ni del surrealismo. El pobre surrealismo se estrella en añicos contra la realidad de Colombia.

Entonces lo vi, sobre una de esas mesas, uno más entre esos cuerpos inertes, fracasos irremediables. Ahí estaba él, Wílmar, mi niño, el único. Me acerqué y tenía los ojos abiertos. No se los pude cerrar por más que quise: volvían a abrírsele como mirando sin mirar, en la eternidad. Me asomé un instante a esos ojos verdes y vi reflejada en ellos, allá en su fondo vacío, la inmensa, la inconmensurable, la sobrecogedora maldad de Dios.

A sus pies estaba su acta de levantamiento del cadáver. La leí de prisa. Nada especial. Que iba en un bus atestado y le habían disparado por la ventanilla desde una moto. Que cuando el agente de la fiscalía llegó al bus detenido a levantar el cadáver, salvo al chofer ya no encontró a nadie: se habían ido todos a sus casas a oír el partido de fútbol, y a comer, a fornicar, a parir más hijos. En cuanto al chofer, ni vio ni oyó nada, él estaba en su trabajo, manejando y cobrando. Se anotaba en las "Observaciones" que el presunto cadáver llevaba en el bolsillo del pantalón el número de un presunto teléfono: el mío, al que me llamaron. Para que no se fueran a enredar siguiendo pistas falsas pues si alguien no lo pudo matar ni mandar matar era yo, que lo quería, saqué mi bolígrafo y taché el número veinte veces: a ver si la ciencia forense colombiana era tan competente que alcanzaba a leer por sobre veinte tachones.

Si en un principio, de entrada, el hombre invisible pensó, por su color translúcido, que los cadáveres de la sala de necropsias estaban refrigerados, después descubrió que no. No. Era la transparencia de la muerte que nos deja a todos como santos coloniales de madera policromada, pero con colorcitos discretos, lívidos, de opalino a alabastrino. Los que sí están refrigerados son los N.N., o no identificados, que van a una cava o frigorífico desnudos, colgados de unos ganchos como reses por tres meses, al cabo de los cuales, si nadie los reclama, el Estado los entierra por su cuenta. El Estado, esto es, Colombia, la caritativa. Cuando el hombre invisible salió, ya era un experto en todo esto. Lo último que vio fue un cadáver boca abajo en una mesa chorreando sangre de la cabeza sobre el piso, y en el mismo piso, en un rincón, una ropa tirada: unos pantalones, una camisa y unos zapatos. Un moscardón pasó zumbando, alborotando el olor fresquecito de la Muerte.

Salí por entre los muertos vivos, que seguían afuera esperando. Al salir se me vino a la memoria una frase del evangelio que con lo viejo que soy hasta entonces no había entendido: "Que los muertos entierren a sus muertos". Y por entre los muertos vivos, caminando sin ir a ninguna parte, pensando sin pensar tomé a lo largo de la autopista. Los muertos vivos pasaban a mi lado hablando solos, desvariando. Un puente peatonal elevado cruzaba la autopista. Subí. Abajo corrían los carros enfurecidos, atropellando, manejados por cafres que creían que estaban vivos aunque yo sabía que no. Arriba volaban los gallinazos, los reyes de Medallo, planeando sobre la ciudad por el cielo límpido en grandes círculos que se iban cerrando, cerrando, bajando, bajando. Es la forma que tienen ellos de aterrizar, con delicadezas, con circunloquios sobre lo que les corresponde pero que el hombre necio, enterrador, les quiere quitar ¡para dárselo a los gusanos! Yo pienso que es mejor acabar como un ave espléndida surcando el cielo abierto que como un gusano asfixiado. Bueno, digo yo... Bajé el puente y entré a un galpón inmenso que no conocía. Era la famosa terminal de buses intermunicipales atestada por los muertos vivos, mis paisanos, yendo y viniendo apurados, atareados, preocupados, como si tuvieran junta pendiente con el presidente o el ministro y tanto qué hacer. Subían a los buses, bajaban de los buses convencidos de que sabían adónde iban o de dónde venían, cargados de niños y paquetes. Yo no, no sé, nunca he sabido ni cargo nada. Pobres seres inocentes, sacados sin motivo de la nada y lanzados en el vértigo del tiempo. Por unos necios, enloquecidos instantes nada más… Bueno parcero, aquí nos separamos, hasta aquí me acompaña usted. Muchas gracias por su compañía y tome usted, por su lado, su camino que yo me sigo en cualquiera de estos buses para donde vaya, para donde sea.

Y que te vaya bien,
que te pise un carro
o que te estripe un tren.

"Come on," Ryan coaxed. *"Stay, just a little while."*

She looked right at him. He smiled. He had the kind of smile that seemed unwilling, as if he didn't do it often—which made it special, made *her* feel special.

Ronni had heard it said that Ryan Malone could get money out of a stone. He'd spearheaded the plan to raise millions so that Honeygrove Memorial could add on a much-needed wing. Everyone marveled at him, wondered how he'd done it. But looking into his eyes right now, Dr. Ronni Powers understood the mystery completely.

The man possessed a commanding presence, a natural reserve—and a reluctant knock-'em-dead smile. An unbeatable combination, whether it came to convincing wealthy donors to put their money in his hands—or coaxing a woman to stay up all night talking to him....

Dear Reader,

Happy Anniversary! We're kicking off a yearlong celebration in honor of Silhouette Books' 20th Anniversary, with unforgettable love stories by your favorite authors, including Nora Roberts, Diana Palmer, Sherryl Woods, Joan Elliott Pickart and many more!

Sherryl Woods delivers the first baby of the new year in *The Cowboy and the New Year's Baby*, which launches AND BABY MAKES THREE: THE DELACOURTS OF TEXAS. And return to Whitehorn, Montana, as Laurie Paige tells the story of an undercover agent who comes home to protect his family and finds his heart in *A Family Homecoming*, part of MONTANA MAVERICKS: RETURN TO WHITEHORN.

Next is Christine Rimmer's tale of a lady doc's determination to resist the charming new hospital administrator. Happily, he proves irresistible in *A Doctor's Vow*, part of PRESCRIPTION: MARRIAGE. And don't miss Marie Ferrarella's sensational family story set in Alaska, *Stand-In Mom*.

Also this month, Leigh Greenwood tells the tale of two past lovers who must be *Married by High Noon* in order to save a child. Finally, opposites attract in *Awakened By His Kiss*, a tender love story by newcomer Judith Lyons.

Join the celebration; treat yourself to all six Special Edition romance novels each month!

Best,

Karen Taylor Richman
Senior Editor

Please address questions and book requests to:
Silhouette Reader Service
U.S.: 3010 Walden Ave., P.O. Box 1325, Buffalo, NY 14269
Canadian: P.O. Box 609, Fort Erie, Ont. L2A 5X3

CHRISTINE RIMMER
A DOCTOR'S VOW

Published by Silhouette Books

America's Publisher of Contemporary Romance

For the ones who take care of the children...

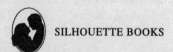 SILHOUETTE BOOKS

ISBN 0-373-24293-X

A DOCTOR'S VOW

This edition published by arrangement with Harlequin Books S.A.

® and TM are trademarks of Harlequin Books S.A., used under license.
Trademarks indicated with ® are registered in the United States Patent
and Trademark Office, the Canadian Trade Marks Office and in other
countries.

Visit us at www.romance.net

Printed in U.S.A.

Books by Christine Rimmer

CHRISTINE RIMMER

came to her profession the long way around. Before settling down to write about the magic of romance, she'd been an actress, a salesclerk, a janitor, a model, a phone sales representative, a teacher, a waitress, a playwright and an office manager. Now that she's finally found work that suits her perfectly, she insists she never had a problem keeping a job—she was merely gaining "life experience" for her future as a novelist. Those who know her best withhold comment when she makes such claims; they are grateful that she's at last found steady work. Christine is grateful, too—not only for the joy she finds in writing, but for what waits when the day's work is through: a man she loves who loves her right back, and the privilege of watching their children grow and change day to day. She lives with her family in Oklahoma.

Dear Reader,

My first PRESCRIPTION: MARRIAGE book, *Dr. Devastating,* was so much fun to write. I loved working with Christine Flynn and Susan Mallery, creating the doctors and nurses of Honeygrove Memorial. Naturally I was thrilled when our editors at Silhouette asked us to do it again.

And that wasn't all. Our editors also informed us that the twenty-year anniversary of Silhouette was coming up.

Chris, Susan and I started brainstorming. We thought, what if Honeygrove Memorial Hospital was planning its own twenty-year celebration? What if a big new wing was being added? And what if, this time around, instead of three doctor heroes, we chose three heroines with M.D. after their names?

We also decided to make our heroes three powerful, determined men, each with his own part to play in the creation of Memorial's new wing—and each destined to find love where he least expects it. And then we agreed that our heroes would have more in common than they realized, that this group of stories would be about a family—a family once torn apart by tragedy, reunited at last.

We hope that in these three new PRESCRIPTION: MARRIAGE stories, we've given you a little bit of everything you look for when you choose Silhouette Special Edition: love, laughter, passion, fulfillment, heroes you can fall in love with—and heroines who face life and relationships with humor, heart and honesty.

All the best,

Christine Rimmer

Chapter One

A bright flash of hard light cut through Ronni's dreams. Then the sound of a drum, a huge drum. Someone pounding on it. Hard.

With a small, disgruntled moan, Ronni turned over in bed, thinking disjointedly, *Lightning. Thunder. A storm coming…*

Another harsh flash. More ominous drumming. Ronni opened her eyes—and saw the figure standing beside her bed.

A burglar, she thought. There's a burglar in my bedroom.

A very *short* burglar.

All at once, as if a huge hand had ripped a hole in the belly of the sky, the rain began. A downpour. It beat on the roof. A sudden angry gust of wind sent it spraying at the French doors to the small patio beyond the bedroom, making a sound like gravel thrown against the panes.

More lightning. A blinding burst of it, flooding in through the gauze curtains, casting the bedroom—and the undersized intruder—into sharp relief.

She thought, not only small, but young—too young to be involved in a life of crime. Eight, maybe. Or nine. In striped pajamas and a dark-colored robe, standing by her bed at—she shot a glance at the clock—one-thirty in the morning.

Recognition dawned.

Not a burglar at all.

Ryan Malone's son, the older one. She'd met him the afternoon before, when she'd stopped by the main house to pick up the keys. "This is Andrew," the boy's grandmother had said. "And this is Lisbeth. And here is Griffin...."

In the harsh wash of light, the boy's blue eyes widened; he had seen that *her* eyes were no longer shut.

Thunder cracked, roared out and faded off beneath the heavy thrumming of the rain. The boy stepped back as the room plunged into shadow once more. He whirled for the French doors.

"Wait!" Ronni called, the sound a sleep-rough croak.

The boy froze.

"Please." She spoke more gently. "It's okay. Stay."

The boy didn't turn toward her, but he didn't try to run again, either. He remained poised—waiting, no doubt, for what she might do next.

Very slowly, so as not to send him fleeing, Ronni reached over and turned on the bedside lamp. The boy flinched when she did that, but he stayed where he was.

"Andrew." Ronni schooled her tone, made it soft, nonthreatening. She pulled herself to a sitting position. "That's your name, isn't it?"

The boy squared his shoulders, sucked in a breath—and resolutely remained facing away. "My name is Drew," he corrected her, speaking to the French doors. "My dad and my grandma still call me Andrew. I keep telling them I'm Drew now, but they keep forgetting."

"Drew, then," Ronni said. "I like that. Drew."

With a deep sigh, the boy turned toward her at last. They studied each other as the rain drummed away and lightning flared again, a boom of thunder following seconds after.

Ronni asked, "What are you doing here in the middle of the night, Drew?"

The boy chewed on his upper lip for a moment, then replied gravely, "I couldn't sleep. I had to check and be sure about you."

Ronni frowned. "Be sure?"

"Yeah." He was defiant now, the dark head held high. "Be sure. That you're really okay. That you won't...hurt anything. Here in the little house—or at my house, either." He glanced again toward the French doors—and escape.

"Did something make you think I might not be okay?"

"No. I don't know. I'm the oldest, that's all. I should be watching out. But I guess it was a bad idea."

He was way too far away, in the shadows. "Drew, I can hardly see you." His shoulders tightened, his body tensed. She thought again that he would bolt. But no. He was caught and he knew it. "Won't you come here?"

He took three reluctant steps in her direction. "What?"

She pushed back the covers and swung her feet to the floor. "I'm a doctor, did you know that?"

He answered with a careful nod. "I've seen you. At Dr. Heber's office. He's my doctor."

"Yes." She dared to stand, to reach for her robe at the end of the bed. "And did you also know that when you're a doctor, you take a solemn vow?"

His eyes narrowed. "A solemn vow?"

Quickly, she stuck her arms in the sleeves of the robe, flipped her thick braid out from under the collar and tied the belt. "Do you know what that means—a solemn vow?"

His black brows drew together. "*Solemn.* That's like...very serious, and *vow* means like a promise you can never, ever break."

"Exactly. A serious, unbreakable promise to 'First, do no harm.' That means, more important than trying to help someone get well, is not to harm them. Not to *hurt* them."

Was he buying? She couldn't be sure. And right then, even her five feet two inches felt a little too tall. She sat again and gave a small pat to the edge of the bed.

He looked at the space she'd patted, mauled his upper lip some more—and then gave in. He came and sat beside her—but not too close, nearer the end of the bed than to her.

"Do you see what I mean, Drew?"

"Yeah, but you don't need to help me get well, because I'm not sick."

"I can see you're not. And what I'm saying is, that as a doctor, I've taken an oath not to hurt people no matter what."

"An *oath?*"

"An oath is the same thing as a vow."

He peered at her closely, gauging the truth of her words. At last he conceded, "Well. Okay. Since you made a solemn vow like that, I guess you have to keep it."

"I do. It's a promise I will never break."

He went on staring at her. He looked so... dignified. So young to be so old.

She longed to reach out and put her arm around him, to comfort with a touch. But she sensed a deep reserve in him. And a desire to be considered mature. A hug would be too much—too forward, and too patronizing.

All right, she thought, if hugs are out, what next?

In the silence, the rain sounded even louder and harder than before. Lightning flashed twice, and thunder rumbled in the distance. It would be a wet walk back across the big yard to the main house.

"Drew, how did you get in here?"

He squirmed a little, as if the edge of the bed had suddenly become an uncomfortable place to sit. Then he admitted, "My mom always kept a key under the flowerpot outside there." He pointed toward the French doors. "I put it back where I found it." Another sigh, a gusty one. "But you're gonna say I shouldn't have used it, huh?"

"That's right. You shouldn't have."

He sniffed, and pulled his shoulders square once

more. "Well, I'm sorry. I won't do it again." He stood. "And I'll just go back to my own house now."

Nice try, kid, she thought. She rose to stand beside him. "Fine. Let's go." As she said that, she thought of the boy's father, her temporary landlord, Ryan Malone. Chief administrator of Honeygrove Memorial Hospital, Ryan Malone was an imposing man, a man who wore designer suits and came across as both cordial and aloof at the same time.

Ronni had only really talked to him once—at a fund-raising dinner about two weeks before. Marty Heber, Drew's doctor and one of the two other pediatricians in her practice, had made the introductions. Somehow the talk had gotten around to her new condo, which wouldn't be ready before her apartment lease was up.

"I have a guest house. You're welcome to use it," Ryan Malone had said. He'd pulled out a gold-embossed business card. "Call my secretary at Memorial. She'll handle the details with you."

She hadn't spoken to Ryan Malone since. She'd called the number on the card. His secretary had described the little house to her and told her no rent would be required. Ryan Malone's mother-in-law had shown her around a week ago and turned over the key just yesterday.

And now here she was, about to wake a virtual stranger in the middle of the night to return his wandering son to him. The idea did not thrill her. But what else could she do?

Evidently, Drew's thoughts mirrored hers. "My dad won't like this. I think it's better if I just go back alone."

"Drew. You know I can't let you do that."

"Yes, you can. Nobody has to know I was here. And I promise I'll never do it again."

Ronni gave the boy a long, patient look. Drew stared back, his eyes pleading. Ronni kept her expression firm.

Finally, the boy muttered, "Oh, all right."

She granted him a smile, then instructed, "Give me a minute. I'll see if I can dig up some coats and an umbrella."

He slumped to the edge of the bed again as Ronni hurried out to the small front closet, where she got the trench coat and the boots she'd put there just the evening before. She'd thought she'd left her umbrella there, too, but now it was nowhere in sight.

The coat and the boots would have to do. She rushed back to the bedroom with them, half-afraid that Drew might have taken advantage of her absence to make an escape.

But no. He was still there, perched on the side of her bed, looking grim. She went to the small stack of boxes in the corner, found the one with Outerwear scrawled on it and got him her old hooded anorak. "Here. Put this on."

He rose and trudged to her side. She handed him the anorak. He tugged it over his head as she yanked on her boots and donned her trench coat. "I don't know what to do about your feet," she said, shaking her head at his slippers.

"It's okay. Let's just go." He was peering up at her. He had to tip his head way back to see, since the hood of the anorak covered all but the tip of his nose. She had to hide her smile at how cute he looked.

He demanded, "I look ridiculous, don't I?"

You look adorable, she thought, knowing that if she said that aloud, it would thoroughly insult him. "You look fine." She marched over and got her flashlight from the bed stand drawer. "Let's go."

Outside, the wind had died. The lightning and thunder seemed to have stopped. But the rain was a cold curtain of water, coming down so hard and thick it poured off the branches of the pines and the hawthorns in relentless small streams. From the back porch of the main house, lights showed on either side of the patio, bright enough to light their way.

Tucking her unneeded flashlight beneath her arm, Ronni flipped up her coat collar and hunched her shoulders. "Let's run for it."

They bolted across the patio, through the small back gate and down the long driveway that ran between the guest cottage and the gracious two-story brick colonial where Ryan Malone and his family lived. At the back of the main house, they went through another gate, across a now-soaked stretch of lawn, to the back door. Ronni reached for the door handle.

"Wait," Drew said. "It's locked." He lifted the hem of the anorak, dug in the pocket of his robe and produced a key.

The door opened onto a large service porch. Drew shoved the anorak's hood back off his head as he closed and locked the door behind them. Ronni flipped her collar down and brushed at her wet hair. Through the darkness, she could see tall pantry doors on one wall and the big, square shapes of a washer and dryer. A small light shone on a panel of buttons right next to the door: the alarm system.

Drew saw where she was looking. "It's okay," he whispered. "I turned it off when I went out."

She whispered back, "You can work that thing yourself?"

He gave a small snort. "Ronni. I'm nine years old." He seemed to think that explained everything. And maybe it did. For "the oldest" in the family, a bright, too-responsible boy who had lost his mother—when? About two years ago, Ronni thought Marty Heber had said.

Sympathy moved through Ronni, bittersweet and tender. She did understand this boy. She had spent most of her childhood feeling like a miniature adult, herself.

"Okay." Drew's whisper had turned bleak. "What are we gonna do now?"

Good question, Ronni thought as they stood there dripping water on the service porch floor. Whatever they did would be awkward at best. She probably should have led Drew around to the front door. Ringing the doorbell and giving the dignified Mr. Malone a chance to throw on a robe and come down to answer would be marginally less awkward than having to seek him out in his bed.

But they were already inside and it was pouring out there. Her hair was drenched and poor Drew's house shoes were soaked through. Neither of them needed to get any wetter.

"Well?" Drew demanded, his whisper edged with impatience now. Clearly he thought that if she wanted to run things, she ought to know what she planned to do next.

An idea came to her. "Show me to the front door."

"What for?"

She sent him a put-upon glance as she turned on her flashlight. "Drew. Please. I'm doing the best I can, all right?"

He looked at her sideways for a moment. "Why are we whispering?"

And why did kids always ask so many questions? "I don't know. We can stop."

He thought about that. "No. We can whisper, it's okay. And I guess if we turn on the lights, it will only scare everyone."

"That's pretty much what I was thinking."

"Actually, Ronni, you could just go on back to the little house now, if you wanted, and I could—"

She gave him a look similar to the one she'd given him when he'd suggested coming back here alone.

He stared at her stubbornly for a moment, then complained, "But if we have to wake them up, anyway, why can't we just..." He must have read her expression correctly, because he let the sentence fade away unfinished. He decided to try bargaining. "At least give me the flashlight, since I have to go first."

Oh, right, she thought. Great idea. Give a flashlight to a nine-year-old. He'd be shining it everywhere but in front of them.

Still, he did have to take the lead. She handed it over.

Drew's slippers made soft squishing sounds as he led her through a huge kitchen and a dining room with a big cherry table and a gleaming parquet floor, into an expansive living room with Oriental rugs on the floors and artfully draped curtains framing the windows. The whole way, Drew never once sent the flashlight's beam anywhere it didn't need to be. Again, Ronni found herself feeling tenderly toward him—so young to be so grown-up.

Finally, they reached the spacious front foyer, where a curving staircase led up to the second floor. The front porch light glowed softly through the beveled glass windows on either side of the big door.

"Okay, we're here." Drew turned the flashlight on her, shining it right in her face, proving himself to be a bona fide nine-year-old, after all. "What do we do now?"

"Give me that." She took the thing from him and turned it off.

"Well? What do we do now?"

"Just wait."

"For what?"

"Until I can see again. You blinded me."

"Oh. Sorry."

"Right." By then, her eyes had adjusted somewhat. She tiptoed to the door, where she disengaged the dead bolt and pulled the door open.

The bell, tucked into the door frame, had a little light inside it. She pushed it. A melodic, startlingly loud series of chimes rang out. Both Ronni and Drew winced at the sound. When the chimes faded, Ronni rang once more for good measure, then shut and locked the door and went back to stand beside Drew.

"He's not gonna like this," Drew warned, still whispering. "He works really hard and he needs his sleep."

"You should have thought of that a little earlier."

Drew was silent for a moment. Then he muttered, "Well, you weren't supposed to wake up."

She muttered right back, "That's no excuse for sneaking into a person's house in the middle of the night—and I think you know it, too."

"I said I was sorry." Now he actually did sound contrite. "And I meant what I said, Ronni. I'll never do it again."

"I'm glad to hear that. And I'm sure your father will be, too."

Right then, a light burst on at the top of the stairs. Ronni and Drew gasped in unison and looked up.

Ryan Malone stood on the landing above, his hand on the light switch, wearing a robe very similar to his son's. His thick dark hair was mussed and his eyes drooped a little, still heavy with sleep. But even startled from his bed in the middle of the night, he looked terribly commanding. A man who took charge, a man to be reckoned with, even in his pajamas.

He started down the stairs.

Chapter Two

At the foot of the stairs, Ryan Malone paused.

He had no idea yet what was going on here, but he could see it had something to do with Andrew—who, it appeared, had been out wandering around in a rainstorm after midnight.

The little redheaded pediatrician, who was using his guest house for the next month or so, smiled at Ryan gamely. "Drew decided to come over and check me out."

The woman clutched a flashlight in her left hand. Her trench coat was rain-dark on the shoulders. Flowered pajama bottoms showed beneath the coat, tucked into a pair of calf-high rain boots. Beads of water gleamed in her hair—that hard-to-tame Raggedy Ann kind of hair. She had it tied into a single braid down her back, but little bits of it had burst free, to curl in a damp halo of corkscrews around a face that belonged on a pixie—or maybe an elf.

She was too cute. Too cute by half. It hardly seemed possible that a woman who looked like that could have made it through the grueling grind of medical school, internship and residency.

But then again, there were her eyes. Wise eyes, with humor in them and faint blue smudges marring the tender skin beneath.

Ryan turned his gaze to his son. Andrew wore some kind of light pull-on jacket, obviously borrowed from the woman. The jacket was wet and Andrew's head was down. He stared at his water-logged slippers and chewed his upper lip.

"Ryan, what is it?" Lily, his mother-in-law, had appeared at the top of the stairs. Ryan felt a degree of relief. Lily would deal with this. "Oh, my!" Lily's hand flew to her throat. "Andrew, you are drenched."

Ryan stepped aside as Lily rushed down the stairs, headed straight for his son. "Oh, just look at you. What *have* you been up to?"

Ryan said, "Evidently, he paid Dr. Powers a visit."

"A visit? To Dr. Powers? In the middle of the night in this weather? That's not like Andrew, it's not like him at all." Lily glanced from Ryan to the redhead and back again, her mouth pursed in disbelief. Then she turned to her grandson and accused in an injured tone, "Andrew. I just cannot believe that you would do such a thing."

Andrew said nothing. He went on staring down at his soaked bedroom slippers and continued to gnaw away at his poor lip.

Even Ryan, who knew less about children than he probably should, given that he had three of them, could see that his son wasn't about to explain himself now. He suggested, "Lily, it really is late. How about putting him back to bed now? Let him sleep on this tonight. And we'll discuss it tomorrow."

"Well, of course." She held out her hand, and wiggled her fingers impatiently. "Come with me, young man." Andrew's jaw had that mulish set it sometimes got. Still, he pushed back the sleeve of the too-big jacket and put his hand into his grandmother's. Lily sent the doctor an embarrassed smile. "I am so sorry about this."

Ronni smiled back. "There's no harm done."

Clucking and sighing, Lily led Andrew back upstairs.

Once the two had disappeared on the upper floor, Ryan turned to the little doctor. She looked at him as if she wasn't sure what to do next.

He felt the same. He should probably thank her and tell her good-night. But then again, maybe he ought to see if she could provide a few details about what his son had just done. He cleared his throat. "I know it's late. But do you think you could give me a few minutes before you go back to the guest house?"

"Sure."

"Do you...want to take off your coat?"

She blinked and put her hand protectively against her chest. "Oh, no. It's fine. I'll need it again in a few minutes, anyway."

"Right." He probably shouldn't have asked. He could see the collar of a robe beneath the coat, but still, taking it off might have felt too much like undressing.

Undressing.

What had made him think of that, for pity's sake?

Damn, this was awkward—the two of them standing here by the front door in their pajamas, at two in the morning.

Maybe if they got more comfortable...

"Come on," he said. "Let's go into my study. We can sit down in there."

She looked at him for a moment, her head tipped to the side. He was absolutely certain she was going to say no. But then she said quietly, "That would be fine."

He gestured toward a door a few feet from the bottom of the stairs. "Right through there." He led the way at first, but then stopped to open the door for her and flick on the light. "Have a seat." She went on ahead. He smelled the cool dampness of rain as she passed. Rain and something else, a faint perfume, as inviting as it was subtle and fresh.

She took one of the two leather wing chairs opposite the desk.

He went around the desk and dropped into the big, deeply tufted swivel chair behind it.

Once he'd sat down he said, "So..." And then he wasn't quite sure how to go on.

She pulled herself straighter and cast a glance around—at the leather-bound books that lined the bookcases, at the arrangement of family photos that stood in contrasting frames on the credenza a few feet away. At the broad expanse of desk between them, which was empty except for a leather blotter and a marble pen stand.

He knew what she was thinking. "I don't use this room too much," he said. "I have my office at Memorial."

She made a small sound of understanding. "It's a good room for work. Attractive, masculine...and comfortable. Or it would be comfortable, with a little more clutter."

"It's hard to clutter up a room you're never in."

"Yes, I suppose you're right." She shifted a little in the chair. And then she waited, giving him a chance, he knew, to take the lead. As a general rule, he was a man who had no problem taking the lead.

But for some reason, right now, he didn't seem to know quite where to start. He cleared his throat. "I guess I'm hoping that you know something I don't—about what my son just did."

She looked down at her flashlight—and then leaned forward a little to set it on the edge of the desk. "There honestly isn't much to tell. He came over to check me out—in the middle of the night. It was a case of iffy judgment and bad timing, that's all."

"Wait a minute. The way I see it, he broke in to the guest house."

She shook her head sharply. "No, he didn't. Not exactly, anyway. To him, the guest house is part of his home. He didn't really think of it as someone else's house. He even knew where the key was—where his mother had left it, under a flowerpot outside."

"Fine. He didn't *break* in. He had a key. But I think the real question is, why did he let himself in at all?"

"He said he wanted to make sure about me. He

wanted to be certain I was no threat to him or his family.''

''Where would he get the idea that you were a threat?''

She sat back again then and smoothed her coat a little more neatly over her knees. ''My guess? He didn't think I was a threat, not really. But he still had to be sure.''

''But you said that *he* said—''

''Mr. Malone, your son is a very mature, very responsible little boy. I really do think he was only doing what he said he was doing—making certain that I was okay, that I wouldn't do harm to him or his family. He's realized now that, at least while I'm staying there, the guest house isn't part of *his* house. He sees that letting himself into my bedroom in the middle of the night is not acceptable. And he's promised me he'll never do such a thing again.''

''He promised you.''

''Yes. He did.''

''You sound as though you believe him.''

''I do believe him. And since we're on the subject, there's another thing…'' He wasn't sure he wanted to know what, but she told him, anyway. ''It would mean a lot to him if you would call him Drew.''

''He said that?''

''Not in so many words. He asked me to call him Drew—and he said he keeps telling you and his grandmother that his name is Drew now.''

Ryan caught her implication. It didn't particularly please him. ''But we don't listen, right?''

She shrugged. ''Often, children of Drew's age feel a need to improve on their names. Maybe it's the urge to take more control of their lives as they mature. Or maybe just part of the natural process of self-definition. Whatever. All of a sudden, Arlenes become Leenas. Jasons insist that you have to call them Jake." She had a dimple on the right side of her mouth. He watched it deepen as she grinned. "I modified my own name at about Drew's age, to tell you the truth. I remember constantly telling people, 'Not Veronica. Ronni. Ronni with an *i*.' The change has stuck, too."

She looked so pleased with herself. He couldn't resist prodding her a little. "It made that much difference to you, to be called Ronni instead of your real name?"

She came right back. "Ronni *is* my real name."

He shrugged. "I'm only saying, what's wrong with Veronica?"

"Nothing. I just wanted to be called Ronni."

"With an *i*."

"Right."

"But why?"

She let out a slightly irritated little grunt. "I thought I just told you. I needed...to redefine myself. On my own terms."

"When you were Drew's age, you thought of that? That you needed to *redefine* yourself?"

"Not consciously, no. But in retrospect, I know that's what I was doing."

"And that's what Drew's doing?"

"I think so, yes."

Ryan let a moment pass before remarking, "You got a lot out of my son tonight, about how he feels and why he did what he did—which you really seem certain he won't do again."

"Is that an accusation?" She laughed then, a laugh with a purpose he easily recognized: to soften the challenge in her question. She definitely knew how to handle herself, this red-haired elf with the knowing eyes.

"No." He looked at her levelly. "It was not an accusation. It was merely an observation. And a compliment."

She thought that over, then said softly, "A compliment. Well, all right. Thank you, then."

"You're welcome." He wanted to smile, but he didn't. To smile right then would have felt like an admission of something—an admission he wasn't quite ready to make. "You're good with children. But then, I suppose it goes with the territory."

She frowned—and then caught his meaning. "You mean, being a pediatrician?"

"Yes."

"You know what? You're right. I'm an expert on kids." She flashed that dimple at him again. "So listen to the expert. I really think Drew just feels responsible. He wants to look out for the people he loves. And I don't think that's a bad thing at all."

"He's nine years old." Ryan spoke more gruffly than he meant to. "It's not his job to be responsible."

Ryan himself had felt responsible from the age of four. He didn't want that kind of crushing emotional burden laid on his children. Perhaps he wasn't as involved with them as he should have been. But he provided well for them. There was no reason they shouldn't feel safe and well cared for.

"Drew might only be nine," she said gently. "But his age doesn't change the way he feels. And as I keep telling you, I don't think what happened tonight is anything to get too concerned about—unless it's a part of a pattern.''

''No. I'm sure it's not. My mother-in-law said it—tonight was completely unlike him.''

''Well, good then. As long as it doesn't happen again, my advice is…'' She paused. ''Wait a minute. Do you even want my advice?''

''That's why I asked you in here.'' Or at least, a voice in the back of his mind whispered, it was the reason I gave myself for asking you in here….

She leaned toward him once more. ''All right, then. My *expert* advice is to talk it over with him—and then let it go.''

He couldn't hold back any longer. He let himself smile. ''All right. I'll do that.'' She smiled in return. He looked at her wide mouth, at that dimple. She had a true redhead's skin—pale, creamy pink, with light freckles dusting her brow and the bridge of her nose. She really did look so young, especially right now with her face bare of makeup, still damp from the rain.

He was staring again. And he shouldn't be.

Just as he shouldn't be thinking how cute she was. Shouldn't be thinking that maybe he'd had more than goodwill on his mind when he'd offered her the guest house for a month.

At the time, right after Marty Heber had introduced them, when she'd mentioned her housing problems, he'd told himself that it never hurt to do favors for other professionals in the medical community. A lot of his job was about raising funds—and funds were always easier to come by when a man had the sense to hold out a helping hand at every opportunity.

Besides, he had reasoned, she would present no inconvenience to himself or his family. The guest house had its own separate access and its own small yard. Other than the occasional polite wave when they met in passing, he'd foreseen no other contact between them.

Yet here they were, on her first night in the little house, sitting across from each other in their pajamas, discussing the uncharacteristic actions of his older son.

And here he was, staring too much. Thinking that he could sit here for a long, long time, just looking at her, just watching her smile.

Dr. Powers must have decided he'd gaped at her long enough. She started to reach for her flashlight.

And he realized he wasn't going to let her go. Not yet. He said, "You're finding everything in order, then? Over at the little house."

She left the flashlight where it was. "Yes. It's lovely. Thank you for offering it to me."

"No problem. No problem at all."

"Good. Well then, I—"

"Tell me more."

"Excuse me?"

"About Ronni. About how she's different from Veronica."

She laughed, a slightly nervous sound. "Oh, come on. It's very late and I should—"

"I'm interested. I really am. And besides, it's raining hard out there. Too hard. You can't leave yet."

"I can't?"

"No. You have to wait till it eases up."

She was watching him doubtfully. "What if it doesn't ease up?"

"It will. Eventually. And I honestly do want to know all about why you changed your name."

"You're serious?"

"I am." He leaned forward a little. "Come on. The difference between Ronni and Veronica."

She hesitated—and then she confessed, "Veronica is…a little shy."

"Shy?" He made the word an encouragement.

And she volunteered a little more. "Veronica lacks confidence. She…worries too much."

"You were like that? As a young child?"

She tipped her chin at a defiant angle. "Yes. But I got over it."

"By changing your name?"

"No, the name was just the outward manifestation of the change."

"Sounds very deep."

"You asked."

They laughed together then. And she challenged, "What about you? Didn't you ever want to change your name, or change something about yourself?"

"Now you've got me thinking about it, I believe at one point I really wished my name was Bud." He pretended to glower at her. "Don't laugh. When you're in fifth grade, Bud can sound like the name of a really manly kind of dude."

"So Ryan wasn't manly enough?"

"I've learned to live with it."

"Good. I like it a lot better than Bud."

"Then I think I'll go ahead and keep it…as long as you like it."

She blinked—and her expression turned wary. Her hand started edging toward the flashlight again.

Before she could touch it, he commanded, "Forget it. Stay here. It's still raining hard."

"But I—"

"Uh-uh. Stay here." He glanced around at all the gold-tooled leather volumes that lined the walls. "This is a comfortable room. You said so yourself. We might even get a little reading done."

"Great idea. Two strangers. Reading in your study in their pajamas. In the middle of the night."

"We're not strangers. We're neighbors, remember?"

"Oh, that's right. Neighbors."

"And I've just shared with you my deepest personal secret."

"You have?"

"Yes. That once I wished my name was Bud— and now you should reveal something about yourself."

"I already did, remember? Ronni and Veronica? Why I changed my name?"

"I remember. And what I meant was, you should reveal something *more.*"

"Like what?"

"How about telling me why you went into pediatrics?"

She didn't have to stop and think about that. "The usual reason. I like kids."

"As opposed to adults?"

"Not as opposed to. It's a preference. Children are so…naturally optimistic. I like their sense of wonder, and their simplicity. And they are incredibly resilient."

"Which means fewer of them die on you."

It was a hard way of putting it, but she didn't argue with his assessment. "That's right—and now it's your turn. What made you choose hospital administration, of all things?"

"I like being in control."

She made a face at that. "And that's all?"

"I like working with people. I enjoy organizing projects, seeing things through from conception to completion."

"You mean you like running things."

"That's right. Is there something wrong with that?"

"Not a thing." She grinned.

A moment passed where the only sound was the rain outside.

He saw her glance at that flashlight, so he asked her another question about her work.

She sat back, getting more comfortable. And for a while, they talked about their jobs, the challenges and the rewards.

Eventually, she got up. He didn't try to stop her, since she didn't reach for the flashlight first. She went over to the credenza to look at the family photos there. One by one, she picked up the pictures, studied them, then set them down.

When she came to a studio shot of Patricia, she asked, "Your wife?"

He nodded. "It's been a little over two years since she died. Acute myelogenous leukemia."

In her eyes, he saw a doctor's understanding of the words: cancer of the white blood cells, starting in the bone marrow, multiplying swiftly until they disrupted the production of normal blood cells. And then moving out, into the bloodstream, invading organs and tissues, especially the spleen and the liver.

"We thought she had a bad case of the flu. Not four months later, she was dead. It was…hard on all of us. And on Andrew—I mean, Drew—particularly, I think. He was seven, old enough to understand what was going on a little better than Lisbeth and Griffin could, old enough to have some idea that he was actually losing his mother, to know that when she died, she really wasn't coming back."

Ronni made a low, musing sound in her throat. There was a world of understanding in that sound. And sadness. Very carefully, she set the picture of Patricia in its place with the others. She returned to her chair, but then didn't sit down in it.

"I should—"

He put up a hand. "Hear that? Still raining…"

"It may never stop."

"It'll stop. Eventually."

They shared a long look, at the end of which she dropped into the chair again. "So what now? Should I choose a book to read?"

He considered, then replied, "No. You should tell me what movies you like."

And she did. She liked comedies.

He preferred action-adventure, and said so.

They moved on to favorite foods and dream vacation spots. To the schools they'd each attended, to the professors they each remembered.

She talked about med school, and how she didn't believe she'd ever slept more than two hours at a stretch through the whole of her residency.

Finally, they got onto the subject of the things that really bugged them.

"Price stickers that won't come off," she said.

He opted for "Voice mail. I really hate voice mail. It's just another excuse for people not to answer their phones."

"But I bet you *have* voice mail."

He had no defense against that. "Guilty as charged."

The rain was still drumming away when she glanced at the clock on the bookcase near the window. "Omigod. It's 4:00 a.m."

It couldn't be 4:00 a.m. But it was.

And still, he wanted her to stay. "Listen. Hear that rain? You can't leave yet. You need to give yourself a little more time, see if it slows down some before you slog back across the yard."

"I've already been here for two hours."

"And maybe you'll just have to stay for two more."

"Right. And then I might as well just stay for breakfast...."

"Why not?"

"Because..."

"Because why?"

Ronni stared at him. There were surely a hundred reasons why she should leave now, why she should have left a long time ago. She just couldn't think of one.

She cut her eyes away from him. Had two hours really passed since she'd entered this room? It didn't seem possible. He had started her talking and then...time had just melted away.

"Come on," he coaxed some more. "Stay. Just a little while." She looked right at him again. He smiled. He had the kind of smile that seemed unwilling, as if he didn't do it often—which made it special, made *her* feel special.

Ronni had heard it said that Ryan Malone could get money out of a stone. He'd spearheaded the plan to raise millions so that Honeygrove Memorial could add on a much-needed new wing. The new wing was under construction, scheduled to open in September, just eight months away.

Everyone marveled at him, wondered how he'd done it. But looking into his eyes right then, Dr. Ronni Powers understood the mystery completely. The man possessed a commanding presence, a natural reserve—and a reluctant knock-'em-dead smile. An unbeatable combination, whether it came to convincing wealthy donors to put their money in his hands—or coaxing a woman to stay up all night talking about everything from the tragic death of his beautiful wife to why she preferred the name Ronni over Veronica.

Say you have to go, and say it now, her wiser self insisted. But when she opened her mouth, what came out was "Well, maybe I could—"

"Oh! Ryan. I never imagined the doctor would still be here."

The mother-in-law to the rescue, Ronni thought. The woman was standing in the doorway to the entry hall, clutching her robe at the neck and squinting as if she'd just been awakened from a sound sleep—which she probably had.

"I woke up and thought I heard voices, so I came down to check. I…I do hope I'm not interrupting anything."

Ronni scooped up her flashlight and started toward the door and the woman standing there. "I was just leaving."

"Well, I'd imagine. It is *so* late."

"Wait." Ryan Malone stood from his swivel chair. "I'll walk you back across the yard."

The mother-in-law piped right up. "Ryan. It's *pouring* out there."

"She's right," Ronni agreed quickly. "No reason for both of us to get soaked."

"I'll walk you back," he said again, his tone allowing no room for argument. "Let me grab an umbrella." He came out from behind the desk and walked between the two women, commanding over his shoulder as he went out the door, "Lily, you go on back to bed."

Five minutes later, Ryan and Ronni stood before the French doors that led to the guest house bedroom. She cast a rueful glance down at his feet. "Now your slippers are ruined, too, just like your son's."

"They'll dry out." The rain poured off the overhang above them and landed hard on his umbrella, flooding off the back side, splashing the slippers in question, soaking his pajamas to mid-calf.

She looked up at the umbrella, at the rain coming off it in sheets. "Don't you just love Oregon? If it isn't raining, it's getting ready to rain—but why am I complaining? I did my residency in Seattle, did I tell you? It was even worse there."

"And here," he reminded her, "we actually get sun in the summer. And then there's the salmon fishing. And the gorgeous, rugged Pacific shoreline less than two hours' drive away."

"And the tulips in the spring, miles and miles of them spread across the valley floor..." She laughed, a breathless little laugh. And then the laugh trailed off. "I..." She didn't know what to say next, he could see that in her soft green eyes. At last, she continued shyly, "Thank you for ..."

He helped her out. "Keeping you up all night?"

"Yes. And not only that. For walking me back here. For being so...gallant."

"Gallant," he said, rather idiotically. "That's me."

"Well, Mr. Malone, I—"

"Don't you think we've reached the point where you can call me Ryan?"

She hesitated, then surrendered. "All right. Ryan. And you'll call me Ronni."

He already had called her Ronni. Repeatedly. In his mind, anyway. But if she wanted to think he'd been waiting for permission, that was just fine with him. "It's a deal."

Her hair looked so bright and alive. He wanted to touch it, to rub it between his fingers and feel the wetness of the rain in it. He wanted to bend down and bury his face in it, to let that faint, seductive perfume of hers invade all his senses. Then he wanted to kiss her.

Slowly and thoroughly.

She said, "Well. Good night—Ryan."

He had to step back so she could open the door. She slipped in with a wave of her flashlight.

"Goodnight, Ronni," he whispered as she pulled the door closed. It took him a minute to remember to leave. He stood there, the rain thudding on his umbrella, his shoes and pajama legs soaked clean through, looking in at her as she gave another quick wave and began shutting the curtains, first the filmy ones and then the outer drapes, too.

Finally, when it became utterly preposterous for him to stand there one second longer staring at a glass door and drawn curtains, he made himself turn and stride swiftly away toward the gate to the drive.

Chapter Three

Back in the main house, Ryan reset the alarm that his son had left disengaged. Then he climbed the stairs to his own bedroom, changed into dry pajamas and tried to sleep. But he couldn't. He felt too edgy. Too…energized, in spite of the fact that he'd only slept for a couple of hours before Ronni and his son had disturbed him.

At a little before five, he threw back the covers and got out of bed. He found another pair of slippers and a second robe and then didn't know what to do with himself.

He decided to check on his children.

Both of the younger ones were still sound asleep. Lisbeth was wrapped up tight in her blankets, only her button nose peeking out. Griffin had kicked the covers down and then curled himself into a ball against the nighttime chill.

Looking down at him, Ryan thought of Tanner.

Tanner, his younger brother. Tanner used to kick the covers down on winter nights sometimes. Before Tanner was five, they were separated for the first time. But during that initial year and a half after they lost their parents, they'd slept in narrow beds, side by side, in the state home. And when Tanner would kick his covers down, it was easy for Ryan to slide from his own bed and cover him back up again.

Carefully, so as not to wake him, Ryan pulled the covers close around his four-year-old son. Griffin let out a small sigh, his little body relaxing as the blankets banished the cold.

Ryan peeked in on Andrew—correction: Drew—last. He turned the doorknob slowly and pushed the door open with great care. Once he'd slid inside the room, he closed the door without letting the latch hook, to avoid the small click that might have disturbed a light sleeper.

He was halfway across the floor when Drew sat up in bed. "Dad?"

All he could think to whisper was a rebuke. "You should be asleep."

"Dad, I'm sorry. About what I did."

Ryan sat on the side of the bed and looked at his son through the predawn darkness. He was thinking that he should spend more time with him, and that he really ought to say something meaningful and profound right now. But all he could think of was "It's okay—as long as you don't do it again."

"I won't."

"Well, all right."

"Ronni wasn't mad. She's nice."

Ryan felt a thoroughly witless smile try to pull at the corners of his mouth. "You like her, huh?"

"Yeah."

"I like her, too." *A lot.*

"Dad?"

"What?"

"You can go back to bed now. Everyone's safe."

Ryan still felt as if he should say something. Perhaps about Patricia. About what his son had lost, what they had all lost. The one who tied everything together, the unifying thread.

"Drew, I…" What? *I'm sorry your mom is dead. Sorry I'm not a better father.*

Sorry the right words won't come…

So many damn things to be sorry about.

He stood. "Lie down, now. Go on back to sleep."

Obediently, Drew stretched out again and pulled his covers up under his chin. Ryan started for the door.

"Dad?"

"What?"

"You talked to Ronni about me, didn't you? She told you to call me Drew." Ryan hesitated before answering, long enough that Drew said, "It's okay with me, Dad. If you talked to her."

"Yes. I talked to her. Now, go to sleep. Pizza Pete's tomorrow."

"With Uncle Tanner?"

"That's right."

Ryan's mother-in-law tapped at the French doors to the guest house the next day at noon.

Ronni looked up from the open box of jeans and heavy sweaters she'd just set on the bed. The curtains were drawn back, letting in the thin gray light of a cloudy—but so far rainless—day. The mother-in-law held up two foil-covered plates, one in each hand. She also had Ronni's anorak slung over her shoulder. Ronni went and opened the door.

"I didn't see you leave this morning, so I thought that just maybe, since it's Sunday, you might be taking the day to unpack."

Stepping back, Ronni gestured her in and closed the door behind her.

"It looks like you're making headway," the woman said.

Ronni cast a glance at the box on the bed. "There's really not that much to deal with. I put most of my things in storage for the month."

"Ah. Until your own home is ready..."

"Yes."

"I'll bet you're really looking forward to that."

"Yes. Yes, I am." They smiled at each other, rather forced smiles, Ronni thought. She reached for the anorak. "Here. Let me take that."

"Oh. Certainly." Ronni slid the weatherproof shell off of the other woman's shoulder, then turned and tossed it on a chair. That accomplished, she turned back to her guest. "Mrs...."

"It's Underhill. But please. Call me Lily."

"And I'm just Ronni."

"Good enough. Ronni." The woman hefted the plates again. "I was putting my own lunch together and it occurred to me that maybe you might enjoy a little break yourself."

"That's thoughtful of you."

"Oh, it's nothing."

They smiled at each other some more. Ronni felt

a little like an interviewee at that moment. An interviewee for a job that really didn't exist—which would make Lily the employer. An employer determined to conduct a pleasant interview, no matter that she had no intention of hiring anyone.

Well. Nothing to do but get the interview over with. "Let's go on into the kitchen."

"Good idea."

In the kitchen, at the cute round pine table with its pedestal base, Lily took the foil off the plates, revealing a pair of sandwiches cut in half diagonally. Matching mounds of pasta salad sat neatly between the halves.

"This looks good," Ronni said.

"It's roast beef. With just a touch of horseradish sauce. I hope you're not a vegetarian."

"No. Roast beef is great."

"And horseradish?"

"I love horseradish."

"Well, then, this should work out fine."

They used paper towels for napkins. Ronni apologized. "I'm afraid I haven't had a chance to get to the store yet."

"Oh, I know you must be busy. A doctor's schedule is just killing, isn't it?"

"It could be worse. I do have my Sundays, now I'm in private practice. And today, I'm not even on call. How about coffee? I have that."

"Just a glass of ice water."

"Water, I've got."

"And forks, for the pasta salad?"

"No problem. All the kitchen things were here when I got here."

Lily sighed. "This little house. Always ready for

visitors.'' She went to a drawer and took out the flatware they needed.

They sat down and started to eat. The sandwich *was* good, the beef thin-sliced and tender. Ronni told Lily so.

Lily waved a hand. ''Oh, it's just a sandwich. But I must confess, I do love to cook. Patricia…that was my daughter, Ryan's wife?'' Ronni did not miss the slight emphasis on the word *wife*. ''Patricia loved to cook, too.'' Lily chuckled. ''And she was much more self-disciplined than I am when it came to sampling what she cooked. I'm a size twelve now, myself. Have been for years and years. But my daughter…aside from her pregnancies, never in her life did she go above a size eight.'' Lily's eyes changed, lost their brightness. ''And then, at the end, she was *so* thin.'' Lily blinked and spoke flatly. ''She died two years ago. Cancer, in case you hadn't heard. It's been…such a challenge, without her. For the children. For Ryan. For all of us.''

The usual condolences rose to Ronni's lips. She held them back. It seemed the wrong moment for a kind cliché.

''You never met my daughter, did you?'' It was almost an accusation.

''No. I did my residency up in Washington. And only moved here two and a half years ago. This is my first practice, with Marty, and with Randall Sheppard.''

Lily swept a hand out, indicating the whole of the cheerful, pretty room. ''Patricia did all of this. Country French, she called it. She wanted the guest house to be cozy and casual. Blue-checked curtains for the kitchen. Blue willow plates on the plate rails." Lily looked up at the rows of blue-and-white china plates that lined the narrow shelves above the cabinets. "And she did the main house, too. All of it. She chose everything, all by herself. She had a real sense for what makes a home an inviting place."

"Yes," Ronni said, for lack of something better. "The main house is quite beautiful."

"But *comfortable,* too," Lily said sharply. "A place where a family actually *lives.*" Lily's eyes looked suspiciously moist.

Though the older woman's mission here was painfully clear, Ronni couldn't help but feel compassion for her. "You must miss her terribly."

Lily drew in a long breath and smoothed the paper towel in her lap. "I...raised her alone, for the most part. Her father died when she was only two."

"It sounds as if you did an excellent job. Of raising her, I mean."

"I did my best. We were so close. I wanted so much for her. And she...lived all my dreams for her. For a while, at least, for as long as...she was with us. She was twenty-three when she married Ryan. Oh, you should have seen them on their wedding day. Patricia so fair, slender and tall. And Ryan beside her, dark and handsome, and proud. I knew from the first the kind of husband he would be. True and responsible. A good provider. Everything a woman could want." She smiled then and leaned toward Ronni. "Good enough even for my precious daughter, if you know what I mean."

Ronni's smile didn't feel forced at all this time. "I do."

Lily pulled back. She seemed to draw into herself.

"Listen to me. Rambling on. You're—" a flash of bewilderment clouded her eyes "—a very easy person to talk to...."

For a few minutes, they were silent, each concentrating carefully on her meal.

Then Lily spoke again. "Ryan told me that you feel we shouldn't be too concerned...about Andrew."

"That's true. I think your grandson is a great guy. And I really don't believe he'll be dropping in on me in the middle of the night again. But just in case, I did put that key away—the one he used to let himself in?"

"Good." Lily sipped her ice water. "Andrew is a fine boy. A lot like his father, did you notice? So responsible—" she let out a small, self-conscious laugh "—most of the time, anyway." She picked up her fork, then set it down without using it. "The truth is, Ryan's the one I worry about. He works such *long* hours. But then you know how that is, don't you? I imagine your schedule is pretty grueling, too...."

Oh, Lily, Ronni thought. I get the message. And I know that you're right. Ryan and I are both way too busy to let anything get started between us.

Lily continued, "He hardly has time for the children at all." Her smile was indulgent. "But he does try. He's spending the afternoon with them today, as a matter of fact. It's a family event. Ryan and the children—and Ryan's brother, Tanner. They always go to Pizza Pete's one Sunday a month."

Ronni had heard of Pizza Pete's. More than one of her small patients had raved about it. Besides the pizza its name promised, Pizza Pete's provided carnival games, a video arcade and a number of other tempting amusements.

"Sounds like fun," Ronni said. Then she heard herself offering, "Are you sure you wouldn't like a cup of coffee, after all?"

"Oh, I shouldn't. I know you want to get back to your unpacking...." Lily looked just a bit lost. And a little lonely, too.

Knowing she'd probably regret it, Ronni insisted, "Come on. Just one."

"Well, all right. It is *so* nice to have another woman to talk to, for a change."

Lily stayed for another half an hour, during which time she talked a lot more about Patricia, about what a darling child she'd been, and what a beautiful adolescent. About how she'd worked in an insurance office to help out while Ryan was getting his start.

"But then, of course, as soon as Ryan was on his feet financially, Patricia stayed home. She was just old-fashioned that way. She believed that being a wife and mother was a full-time job in itself, that her children needed her, every day, all day. That making a gracious home and providing tasty, nutritious meals for her family were very important, meaningful ways to spend her time.

"And she was such a tremendous benefit to Ryan in his work. They entertained a lot, especially in that last year or two before she became so ill, when he had become chief administrator at Memorial and he had a certain image to maintain. There were a number of important people he needed to get to know socially, in order to help raise the money for the new wing...you've heard about the new wing?"

Ronni made a noise in the affirmative.

Lily chattered on. "And did you know that Ryan's brother, Tanner, is the general contractor for the entire project? We're very proud of Tanner. He's done so well for himself with his construction company. And the wing is moving right along. Maybe you haven't had a chance to see it. I imagine your patients go to Children's Hospital?"

Ronni nodded. "But I do drive by Memorial now and then. And every once in a while, I even drop in."

"Drop in?"

"To do postnatal checkups of new patients. It looks very impressive—the new wing."

"Yes. The work on the interior is just getting under way now. One hundred million dollars, it's taking. From the Pembroke Fund. That was Ryan's doing, of course, the funding. He was a Pembroke scholar in college, and that connection was helpful. And he did play a lot of racquetball with Axel Pembroke, the president of the Pembroke Foundation— still does play racquetball with him, as a matter of fact. Have you ever met Axel Pembroke? What a strange little man." Lily shrugged. "But the one who controls the purse strings, the one who had to be dealt with. And Ryan did deal with him, and so effectively, too.

"And Patricia did her part, you can be certain. Such lovely dinner parties she gave, preparing everything herself, from the perfect food to the arrangement of the flowers. She just wouldn't hire a caterer. But that was understandable. No one could put a party together the way Patricia could. And then, when everything was ready, she'd sweep her beautiful blond hair up into a simple twist, put on a little black dress and look as if she'd never lifted a finger to put the whole thing together. What a hostess she was. I actually believe Mr. Pembroke had something of a crush on her...."

When Lily finally ducked out the back door with her two empty plates and a jaunty last wave, Ronni was only too glad to see her go.

I can see it all now, she thought, as she pulled jeans and sweaters from the box on her bed. Every time I wave at Ryan in the driveway, Lily will come flying over armed with a pair of foil-covered lunches and an endless stream of stories about the irreplaceable Patricia, loving wife, doting mother and hostess extraordinaire.

Not that Ronni had any intention of trying to supplant such a paragon. No. Ronni had very distinct plans for her life.

Those plans did include a man, of course.

But not for a while yet. Not for a year or two, at least.

Right now, all her attention had to be strictly focused on establishing herself in her practice—and on her condo, her own home at last, to which she would be moving by the end of the month.

Lily could have saved that roast beef sandwich. Ronni wasn't after Ryan Malone. Yes, he was attractive. Incredibly so. And it had been disconcertingly easy to stay up talking with him all night.

But it wasn't going to go anywhere. The timing just wasn't right.

"You're looking way too serious today, big brother," Tanner said. They were sitting at one of the picnic-style tables at Pizza Pete's. Across the crowded room, Griffin and Lisbeth jumped around in a netted pit full of plastic balls as Andrew stood a few feet away, watching them.

Ryan grunted. "Just thinking. About Andrew—I mean, Drew. I've been instructed that it's Drew from now on."

"Instructed. By who?" With his left hand, Tanner picked up his jumbo-size plastic cup of Dr. Pepper.

Ryan watched his brother knock back a big gulp and then set the cup down. Tanner had the body of a linebacker, while Ryan was leaner and taller by a couple of inches. But they were both southpaws. And they both had the same blue eyes. Malone-blue, people who knew both brothers were always saying. Drew had the Malone eyes, too—and he was left-handed, as well.

"Something about my hand?" Tanner asked.

"What? No."

"They call you the miracle man," Tanner razzed. "You can charm dollar bills out of the trees. Real big on social skills, that's what they say about you. But look at you now. Staring. Oblivious."

"I said I'm just thinking."

"Right. Come on. Who's giving instructions to call Andrew Drew?"

Ryan drank, then set down his glass. "Drew himself. Several times, apparently. But I didn't listen."

"I can see we're headed on a long trip here."

"Trip?"

"Yeah. A guilt trip."

"Very funny."

"So what's going on?"

Ryan glanced over at his children. The two younger ones were still rolling around in the ball pit and Drew remained on guard. It looked likely that Ryan and Tanner would have a few more minutes undisturbed.

"Did I tell you that there's a woman staying in the guest house?"

Tanner leaned on the table and raised both eyebrows. "You've got my full attention. Go on."

Ryan told him what had happened last night—a slightly edited version. He didn't mention the part about how he and Ronni had sat in his study for two full hours talking about nothing in particular, or how he'd walked her back to the little house and then stood there in the driving rain staring at her closed door after she'd gone inside. "So I guess I'm a little worried about Drew," he concluded. "That he's…taking too much on himself, that he thinks he has to—"

Tanner didn't let him finish. "Wait a minute."

"What?"

"Give yourself a break here. The way it looks to me, his only problem is he's just like his dad. He wants to take care of his family. There are a lot worse things in this world than that."

"Well, I know, but—"

"What I want to know more about is the kindhearted, good-looking pediatrician with the red hair."

Ryan tried not to wince. "Did I say she was a redhead?"

"Yep."

Ryan shifted on the picnic bench. Pizza Pete ought to think about getting some cushions for the damn things. "There's nothing more to tell. I liked her. She was very…understanding about the whole episode.''

Tanner wasn't fooled. "Right. Understanding.''

"Don't look at me like that.''

"You're interested.''

"All right. Maybe I am. But where can it go? I work a sixty-hour week, and I'm always thinking I should spend more time with the kids.''

"It doesn't have to *go* anywhere. You ask her out, that's all. If you have a good time, you ask her out again.''

"Right, but—''

"I've got it. The Heart Ball.'' The Heart Ball was a major annual fund-raiser put on by the Friends of Memorial. "It's two weeks away. Have you got a date?''

"No, but—''

"You *are* going, aren't you?''

"Of course.'' He was on the agenda, as a matter of fact, to give a little look-how-far-we've-come speech about the new wing.

"So ask her,'' Tanner said. "Do it today. I want a commitment, and I want one before our family-size pepperoni pizza arrives.''

Ryan decided he'd better make a joke of this. "Commitment? That's an interesting word, coming from you.''

Tanner's eyes went dark as the middle of the night. And Ryan felt like a jerk. Tanner had always played the field. And Ryan had always ribbed him about it, just as Tanner always gave *him* a hard time for being a one-woman man.

But commitment jokes were in bad taste these days. Tanner had a big problem concerning the issue of commitment. He was dealing with it as best he could, but the whole situation had him tied in knots.

"Tanner, I—"

Tanner shook his head. "Don't apologize. Sometimes, the truth hurts. That doesn't mean you can't tell it." He drummed up his best give-'em-hell grin. "Besides, I know your tricks. And they're not gonna work this time. We're talking about *you* right now. You and a cute little redheaded M.D. And that date you really do need for the Heart Ball."

"I'll think about it."

"Don't think, act."

"Tanner. I'll think about it."

"Well then, think fast. Here comes our pizza. And don't look now, but three hungry kids are headed this way."

Ryan did think about it. For the rest of the afternoon and into the evening. He thought about how he had no business getting involved with anyone right now. He thought about how, if he *did* get involved with someone, she ought to be like Patricia, a woman ready, willing and eager to do big-time duty on the home front.

And he thought how he'd met a number of women in the past year or so who would have been happy to try to fill Patricia's shoes, lovely, graceful women who had good educations and undemanding careers. Women who would have done their best to mother his children and take care of him, too.

He'd had zero interest in the subtle overtures of those women.

He also thought about what Tanner had said.

*It doesn't have to go anywhere. You ask her out.
If you have a good time, you ask her out again....*

That night, once the kids were finally settled into
bed and Lily had retired to her room, Ryan let himself out the back door, sprinted down the driveway
and around to the front porch of the little house.

Chapter Four

"Oh!" Ronni said, when she opened the door. "Ryan. Hello."

"Hello."

Ronni stared. He looked so...pulled together. So unbelievably handsome and self-possessed. He was wearing chinos and a soft, dark-colored sweater.

Her own attire consisted of a stretched-out sweatshirt, black leggings with a little hole in the knee and a heavy pair of gray thermal socks. Her hair was a mess, sticking out all over the place the way it always did when she went too many hours without combing it. She hadn't bothered with makeup, either, since she'd only spent the day puttering around, putting things away.

Just like last night. She'd been a walking fashion emergency then, too, with her hair coming out of its braid, her boots dripping water all over his Oriental rugs. He'd end up thinking she always looked like something the cat wouldn't bother to drag in the house.

Not that it mattered.

No, it didn't matter at all.

He was her temporary landlord, and nothing more. Not a man she hoped would notice her as a woman, not a man for whom she would want to look her best at least two-thirds of the time.

And what was he doing here, anyway?

She gulped and resisted the powerful urge to start patting at her hair and straightening her sweatshirt. "Um. Come on in."

She fell back and he entered the tiny entrance hall, which was really much too small for two people. He smelled of some nice aftershave—a lot fresher than she did, of that she was certain.

She gestured toward the kitchen a few feet away. "Have a seat."

"Thanks." He went where she pointed, pulled out a chair and sat at the quaint country French table, which his gracious and beautiful wife had chosen with such loving care. A notebook computer and a stack of medical journals and scribbled pages of notes cluttered the surface.

"You were working?"

"Just brushing up a little." Ronni leaned against the blue-tiled counter by the sink, feeling too edgy to sit down herself. "Friday, one of my three-year-olds came in with an itchy, scaly-looking rash on her face and the backs of her knees. Infantile eczema. I prescribed an antihistamine and ordered a few tests for common allergies, but it never hurts to examine other options—can I get you something?

Coffee? Or something else?'' She'd fit in a trip to the supermarket a few hours before and picked up the basics. She even had napkins now. She'd be ready when Lily came knocking—probably first thing tomorrow morning, armed with fresh-baked croissants or fragrant cinnamon rolls, and more tales of her perfect, lost daughter, more reminders that her son-in-law was a busy, busy man.

Ryan shrugged. ''I'd take a beer, if you have it.''

''Beer?'' Too bad she hadn't thought to buy any.

''Wrong choice, huh? Never mind. I'm fine.''

''Sure?''

''Positive.''

So much for refreshments. Back to the original question. What was he doing here?

A smile so faint it was little more than a shadow lifted the corner of his mouth. ''You're wondering why I'm here, aren't you?''

''Well, as a matter of fact…''

''I'd like to take you to the Heart Ball.''

She was not prepared for that. Not prepared at all. ''The Heart Ball,'' she repeated, like a fool. Like someone who'd never heard of such a thing.

''Yes. It's the twelfth. Of February.''

She knew that, of course. The Heart Ball was a very big deal in Honeygrove. It took place every year, around Valentine's Day. Memorial's auxiliary put it on and most of the doctors in town made an effort to attend.

He was looking at her so intently. ''You have a date,'' he said, his tone flat.

''I…'' Lie, her mind ordered. Tell him you do. But she didn't have a date. And she just couldn't lie about it. ''No. No, I don't have a date.''

''Then?'' He waited, his face composed, his eyes anything but.

The problem was, she wanted to say yes.

''If you say no, you'll destroy me.'' He spoke lightly, but still, somehow, the statement rang true.

And she found herself thinking, Why not? It's only one evening....

''Come on.'' There was that shadow of a smile again, haunting the edges of his mouth.

It actually might be fun, she rationalized. And it was an event she really should attend. Both Marty and Randall had been after her not to back out this year.

''Say yes.''

''All right, yes.''

''There. Was that so difficult?''

The question sounded rhetorical, but she answered, anyway. ''No. It wasn't. Not at all.'' In fact, it had been much easier than it should have been—given that she was a woman with a plan for her life. A plan that did not include a man at this point.

But one date. For the Heart Ball. What harm could that do?

He stood. ''Well. I guess I should let you get back to that rash.''

She should have said, Yes, I really do have to work now.

But she didn't. She asked him, ''So how was Pizza Pete's?''

And then he asked her how she knew about that.

And then she had to tell him of Lily's visit—the bare facts of it, anyway. That Lily had returned her anorak and brought along a nice lunch. That they'd had a pleasant conversation and Lily had mentioned that he and the children were off with his brother at Pizza Pete's.

That was just the beginning.

It was so strange. Once they started talking, they somehow never seemed to stop. He told her more about his job. He really did seem to love his work as much as she loved hers.

She'd just never met a man who was easier to talk to. Time seemed to melt away, as it had the night before. When she followed him to the entrance hall and said goodbye, it was almost 11:00 p.m.

Lily made no appearance at Ronni's door the next day. Not that Ronni would have been likely to know if she had. She was up at six and out the door by seven. She didn't get home until eight-thirty that night.

On Thursday, she bought a new dress to wear to the Heart Ball. She had no time for shopping sprees, really. But still, somehow she managed to fit in a trip to the mall between her office hours, the three patients she needed to check on at Children's Hospital and the stop at her condo, where she argued with the electrician and tried not to have a fit when she saw they'd delivered the wrong bathtub—a pink one, for heaven's sake. She had ordered cobalt blue.

At eight o'clock that night, when she finally got back to the guest house, she hung her new dress in the closet and reminded herself again that it was only one date.

Her beeper went off about five minutes later. She called the office exchange and got the number: a distraught father calling to report that his six-year-old daughter, who'd been suffering from the flu, had been vomiting with scary regularity for the past several hours. Ronni made arrangements to meet them at Children's Hospital.

It was well after midnight when she once again pulled into the long driveway beside the imposing brick house. A big black Lincoln swung in right behind her. Ryan. His headlights shone hard and white through her rear window, almost blinding her as she glanced in the rearview mirror.

Ronni blinked, focused front and kept going, steering her little Toyota around the curve to the front of the guest house and nosing it into the small carport there. She grabbed her purse and emerged from the car, shivering a little as she stepped out into the cold night air.

Ryan's headlights had vanished. He had pulled into the garage, near the main house, on the opposite side of the drive.

Ronni shoved her car door shut. It closed with a *ka-thunk* that sounded way too loud in the late-night stillness. She went around the end of the car and came out from under the shadow of the carport.

Once she reached the driveway, she paused, knowing she was easily visible in the light from the pole lamp about thirty feet away at the rear edge of the property. She was waiting. She shouldn't have been, but she was. Hoping he might decide to stroll back here and—what? Keep her talking all night again?

Take her in his arms and kiss her until she couldn't think straight?

Oh, stop this, she ordered silently. You don't need to talk all night. You don't need to be kissed. You need to go inside, Ronni Powers. Go inside right now.

But she didn't move. She just stood there.

And she heard footsteps. Coming in her direction. Ryan appeared around the curve of the driveway, so tall and commanding, in a finely cut suit, with a wool town coat slung casually across his wide shoulders. He saw her and kept coming, stopping at last just a few feet from where she stood.

"Working late?"

She clutched her purse a little tighter, wished she were taller, wished her lipstick hadn't worn off hours ago. "It's part of the job—and I could ask you the same question."

"You'd get the same answer. A meeting ran over. And I had a few things to catch up on."

She smiled at him cautiously, wanting to ask him inside—wondering what was the matter with her. She'd said yes to one date. But no more. It was supposed to be a casual thing.

Casual.

Hah!

"Well," she said. "At least we're not in our pajamas this time."

"Shall we call it progress?"

"Sure. Why not?"

He studied her for a moment.

Her heartbeat accelerated. "What are you staring at?"

"You. I'm hoping you're going to ask me in."

She said nothing. She was thinking how unwise that would be, how late it was, how if she asked him in, they'd only start talking and she'd start forgetting how this wasn't going to go anywhere.

One of his strong shoulders lifted in a half shrug beneath that fine wool coat. "I know. It's late. But opportunities are limited. Maybe we should snatch them when they come along." He reached out. His hand whispered along her cheek, and then dropped away. She felt seared right down to the center of herself.

"All right," she said, thinking that her voice sounded slightly dazed—and that she could still feel his touch, burning there, on her cheek. "Come on."

He followed her inside.

He didn't stay long. Only an hour. Before he left, he asked her to lunch the next day.

Should she have protested? Probably. But she didn't. She thought, Lunch. Tomorrow. What a lovely idea.

He offered, "I could come to your office."

"No."

He actually looked stricken. She couldn't bear that, and hastened to add, "I'll...meet you at Memorial. *Your* office. About twelve-thirty?" It all felt a little more casual that way, with her going to him. And she *was* keeping it casual. She added, "You could give me a quick tour of that new wing of yours."

"It's a big wing," he warned. "A whole floor just for pediatrics. There'll be a day-care center and a new playground, too. More medical-surgery beds. And a roof garden. It could be a long tour. Maybe too long for a lunch hour. But we could play it by ear." That last sentence seemed to be about a lot more than a building in progress.

"All right. I'd like that." Too much. Way too much...

They gazed at each other. For too long. Then at last he said, "I guess I really do have to go."

She wanted to cry out, *No! Please, I want you to stay. Stay all night…*

But of course, she said no such thing. She turned and led him to the door.

At 12:25 the next day, Ronni entered the outer office beyond the door with Ryan's name on it. She introduced herself to his secretary, a pleasant, motherly looking woman in a mauve blouse with a big bow at the neck.

"Have a seat. He'll be right out," the secretary said.

Ryan appeared at exactly twelve-thirty. He wore a different suit from the one he'd worn the night before, and he carried his town coat over his arm. His eyes warmed at the sight of her. She set aside the *Hospital Quarterly* she'd been pretending to read and stood.

He shrugged into the coat and spoke to his secretary. "What have I got next?"

She studied her desk calendar. "Policies meeting, Room A off the boardroom, at one-thirty."

Ryan turned to Ronni again. "Sorry. Looks like we'll have to skip either the tour or the lunch."

"I think I'd prefer a little food."

"Good enough." He strode across the plush gray carpet, took her hand and wrapped it over his arm. The proprietary action felt way too natural. And his arm was so warm and strong, even beneath all the layers of winter clothing. Her head barely reached his shoulder. He smiled down at her. "Ready?"

It seemed like a loaded question, somehow. But she answered brightly, "As I'll ever be."

They took the elevator to the basement level, where she suggested Granetti's, the Italian place where a lot of Memorial's staff hung out. The food was good there, and it was just a short walk across the parking garage to the back entrance.

He frowned. "We're not going to get a lot of privacy at Granetti's."

Which was just fine with her. They didn't need privacy, did they?

No, give her the bustle of a busy place like Granetti's. It would help to keep her from forgetting that she and Ryan Malone were friendly neighbors sharing a casual date—and nothing more.

"We've only got an hour," she reminded him. "By the time we get in the car and drive somewhere…" She let the thought finish itself.

He agreed that Granetti's would have to do.

They managed to get a table in a corner. She ordered the chicken cacciatore and he chose the veal parmesan.

They talked about everyday things. About mutual acquaintances, and about how she was getting along in her practice with Marty and Randall.

"Marty's a sweetheart," she told him. "And Randall is…"

He grinned. "One hell of a good doctor, or so I've heard."

"Beloved by his patients," she said, somewhat automatically. "And their parents, too." Of the two doctors, she preferred Marty. But she and Randall got on well enough.

Ryan asked how her condo was coming along.

She told him that she and her electrician were not the best of friends. "He seems to have forgotten I'll need outlets in the kitchen. And the ones in the spare room, which I'm planning to use as an office, are all in the wrong places."

"Sounds like you should look around for someone else to do the job."

"I would, if I had anything to say about it. But this man has the contract on the whole complex— don't worry, though. I promise I'll be out of your hair by the first of next month."

"Did I say I wanted you out of my hair?"

She looked down at the second piece of garlic-cheese bread she shouldn't have been eating, then back up at him. "No. No, you did not."

"Stay as long as you need to. Please."

Please. He'd said it almost tenderly.

She stammered like a fool over her answer. "I...I will."

"Ronni," another voice said then. "How are you?"

With some difficulty, Ronni dragged her gaze away from Ryan. Dr. Kelly Hall, an OB-GYN who worked over at the Honeygrove Women's Medical Center, was standing by their table.

Ronni made the introductions. "What's up?" she asked the other doctor, who was dressed in green scrubs with a lab coat thrown on top.

"The usual. Six pounds, four ounces. Born—" Kelly glanced at her watch "—exactly fifty-five minutes ago."

"Boy or girl?"

"Girl. And they haven't chosen a pediatrician yet."

"Recommend me?"

"Absolutely. Got a card?"

Ronni dug in her purse and handed one over.

"Great. You're off the hook for the postnatal exam. I'll get it handled by staff. But you should be hearing from the proud mother some time in the next week."

"That's fine."

Kelly stuck the card in the pocket of her lab coat. "And now, since I haven't eaten in approximately eighteen hours, I'd better grab some lunch."

"Try the chicken."

Kelly said she would and left them, striding purposefully away on her long, athletic legs.

When Ronni looked back at Ryan, he was watching her. "Kelly's a pal," she said rather unnecessarily.

Across the room, someone waved. Ryan lifted a hand in acknowledgement, then muttered, "As I said, no privacy. Not at Granetti's."

Ronni made a low sound of agreement as she picked up her fork to finish her chicken.

He walked her to her car about fifteen minutes later. She unlocked her door and turned back to him, started to make the right noises. "Thank you. I enjoyed—"

He put up a hand.

She fell silent.

He stepped closer. Too close. Those blue eyes held her.

The warmth and size of him took up the world. And the car was at her back.

She couldn't have moved away if she'd wanted to.

Which—oh, my goodness!—she did not.

He touched her cheek. Her skin, where his hand brushed it, felt on fire again, just like last night. His hand slid back, to cradle her head. She felt his fingers, cool and firm, at her nape beneath her hair.

And his mouth came down.

It settled on hers. So lightly.

And then more firmly.

And then…

Oh, she thought. Lovely. Too lovely for words…

Ronni sighed. And felt him smile.

And then he was pulling back.

She started to speak again. He put a finger against her lips. "I wanted to do that the first night. And the second, when I asked you to the Heart Ball. And last night, too."

"You did?" Breathless. She sounded breathless….

He nodded.

She heard voices and the echo of footsteps on concrete: two men walking to their own cars. No one she knew. But Ryan waved at them.

He turned back to her.

She knew just what he was thinking. "No privacy…"

"Right." He reached around her, took the handle of her door and pulled. "Come on. Get in."

She slid behind the wheel and he moved in a bit closer, leaning into the car a little, resting his arm on the open door. "Fasten your seat belt."

Obediently, she reached up, pulled the thing across herself and hooked it at her right side.

"Drive carefully," he warned.

And she promised, "I will."

Chapter Five

It was only a kiss, she kept telling herself all through the rest of that day. Only a kiss, she said to herself as she lay down to sleep.

And in the morning, on Saturday, as she made coffee and ate her breakfast and got ready to go to the office for a few hours.

Only a kiss...

No big deal. One sweet, tender moment.

Between friendly acquaintances.

Only a kiss. Nothing to obsess over...

She stopped in at her condo around three. The workers had the day off, of course. But she walked through the rooms, pushing thoughts of Ryan aside, trying to put all her attention on her new home. Trying to picture what it would look like, when the cobalt-blue tub had arrived and was finally installed in the bathroom, when the kitchen had a sink and cabinets and tile.

She returned to her temporary quarters at four-thirty. The front door of the main house opened just as she swung into the driveway. Drew came flying out. He ran up beside her car and she rolled the window down.

"We're decorating," he announced. "Come see."

His enthusiasm was contagious. She found herself grinning. "Decorating for what?"

"Valentine's Day. We do it every year. We do all the holidays. Christmas, Easter, St. Patrick's, Fourth of July. Halloween. That's my favorite, Halloween. Valentine's is my *least* favorite. All that love stuff, you know. But I do Odie and Garfield and stuff. Funny stuff." He started to open her door. "Come on. I'll show you."

She thought of Lily, wondered if Lily knew about the Heart Ball, about yesterday's lunch date. About a kiss in a hospital parking lot between friendly acquaintances...

Probably not. Ryan didn't seem the sort of man to tell his mother-in-law more than she needed to know.

Drew hauled the door open. "Come on, hurry up."

Ronni laughed. "Do you mind if I park my car first, instead of leaving it in the driveway for your dad to run into?"

"My dad wouldn't do that. He's a good driver."

Kids, Ronni thought. Literal to the bone. "What I meant is, it would be in his way if he came home."

Or maybe he was home right now. She asked Drew, "Or is your dad already home?"

"No, he's not here. I think he went to play racquetball at his club."

Shamelessly, she pumped the child for more information. "Will he be home soon?"

"Ronni, you just never know about when my dad is coming home. Are you going to come in or not?"

She simply couldn't resist the appeal in those eyes, which were really way too much like his father's eyes. "Sure. Just let me put my car away."

Axel Pembroke pounded across the court, trying his damnedest to return Ryan's serve. He didn't make it. The ball hit the front wall, ricocheted off, flew at the left side wall and then the right, finally bouncing to a stop parallel to the back wall.

"A perfect Z serve," panted Axel. "Game and match. You've killed me. Again." He staggered over to where he'd dropped his towel, scooped it up, wrapped it around his neck and began blotting up sweat. "Why do I play with you?" He made a show of rolling his eyes, which appeared huge and slightly protruding behind his thick sports goggles. "You never have sense enough to let me win, even though I am the man directly responsible for seeing that you get those huge Pembroke Fund checks you need to finish that new wing of yours."

Ryan laughed. "Come on, Axel. It's not 'my' wing. And besides, you wouldn't respect me if I let you win."

"How would you know? You've never tried it— but then again, I'm not really complaining." Axel took off his sport goggles, mopped sweat from around his eyes and slid them back on. "The truth is, I always knew that if I ever did beat you, it would be a real win."

Ryan picked up his own towel and slung it over his shoulder. "Knew? Past tense? Is this your way of telling me we've just played our last game?"

Axel hesitated. Then he chuckled again. "I'm afraid you're never really getting off the hook where I'm concerned."

Ryan wasn't about to let that remark pass. "Wait a minute. Did I say I wanted to get off the hook?"

"No," Axel conceded. "You didn't. You're a paragon of patience, when it comes to me." They left the court together, Ryan leading, Axel close behind—and still talking. "In fact, you're a paragon, period. A superior man in every way. My analyst says I envy you. You're everything my dear departed father thought *I* should have been."

Ryan said nothing. He understood that Axel's father was a sore spot with him. The Pembrokes were an old and powerful Honeygrove family. When Axel Pembroke III had died, he'd willed the bulk of his estate to the foundation that bore his family's name. His only son, Axel IV, had been left a modest trust fund—and the job of administering for good works the money that he surely must have believed should have been his. It had been something of a local scandal that Axel had been left with so little.

Their racquetball bags waited against the wall beside the door to the court. Ryan knelt beside his to tuck his racket away.

Axel stood over him. Ryan glanced up at the other man. Axel's expression was eerily thoughtful.

"Yes," Axel said. "That's the word—*paragon.*

You started with nothing—and, as they say, just look at you now. Whereas I, well, I started with *everything*. I had all the advantages—at least as far as the brains and the money go. And what did I make of them? Not a whole lot."

Ryan zipped up the bag. "Axel. Why don't you just tell me what's on your mind?"

Axel bent to get his own bag. "The thing is, a man has to grab his chance when it comes along."

What in hell did that mean? "Axel. Are you trying to tell me something here?"

The other man seemed to shake himself. Then he chuckled for the third time. "No. Not a thing. Just thinking out loud."

All the way home, Ryan wondered what was going on with Axel.

He was still wondering when he let himself in the back door. Then he heard voices coming from the kitchen. He paused on the service porch, listening.

"See, it's Garfield," his older son was saying. "I'm going to put one of those bubble things over his head. He's going to be thinking, Who needs love? I want dinner."

An adult laugh followed. Ryan recognized that laugh. It was Ronni's. Ryan drank in the sound. Then she spoke. "Sounds exactly like something Garfield would think."

"My, we have made a lot of decorations." That was Lily's voice. "Where will we put them all?"

"Gramma, look." That was Lisbeth. "A big green heart. Just for you."

"Oh, honey. It's beautiful. But I think the hearts are supposed to be red."

"I like green, Gramma."

"I like purple!" Griff. Ryan smiled. Everything his youngest said lately had an exclamation point after it.

"We need to start putting them up," Drew said.

"Soon," Lily replied. "But first—"

"I know. We have to clean up our mess."

"That's right." Lily's tone changed, deepened a little. Adult to adult. "Patricia started this, of course. A family tradition. Decorating for every holiday."

"It's a great idea." Ronni sounded polite now, careful to say the right thing.

And Ryan realized he was eavesdropping. He hadn't even closed the back door behind himself. He pushed it shut—harder than required.

He heard Lily say, "That must be Ryan...."

He strode into the kitchen, where everyone sat around the table. Construction paper, colored pens and scissors, bits of paper doily, tubes of paste and glitter-glue cluttered the broad surface. Ronni had her back to him. She turned her head, those green eyes so bright he felt blinded when they met his.

Griff jumped down from his chair. "Daddy, look!" He held out a big sheet of purple construction paper, inexpertly cut, but clearly a heart. "Purple! I like that!"

Ryan dropped his racquetball bag in the corner and knelt by his younger son. "Yes. This *is* purple. A fine purple heart."

"Look at mine, Daddy." Lisbeth held up her creation.

"Looks good," he said, nodding.

"We have to clean up first," Lisbeth said. "Then we get to do the decorating part. You can help us."

Drew spoke then. "Dad's probably too busy."

"No," Ryan said firmly, though he'd been planning to grab his briefcase and head for his office at Memorial where a tall stack of purchase orders had been awaiting his signature for days now. "I'm here. And I'll help."

"Oh, Ryan," Lily protested. "That isn't necessary. We can handle this. Truly."

"Yes, it is," he said. "It's very necessary."

Ronni stood. "Well, I think these decorations are just incredible. And I also think I'd better—"

No way he was going to let her escape. Not yet. "Stay." It came out sounding like an order. But what the hell? It *was* an order.

"Yeah," said Drew. "Come on, stay."

"Yes," Lisbeth chimed in. "Daddy can get the ladder, to reach the high places, and you can hold the tape."

"Stay!" shouted Griff.

"Oh, now, children," Lily chided. "If Ronni has to go, we shouldn't—"

"She doesn't." Ryan met those eyes, held them. "Do you?"

"I..." She smoothed the loose-fitting skirt she was wearing and tried to look away.

He said it one more time. "Stay."

And she gave in. "All right. I'd love to."

Within the hour, the front windows were covered with hearts of all colors and sizes, not to mention Garfields and Odies, and Drew's interpretations of the Rugrats cartoon characters. By the time Ryan put the stepladder away, it was six o'clock. Lily said she'd have dinner ready in a half an hour.

And Ronni started making goodbye noises again.

"You have to eat," Ryan told her. "It might as well be with us."

"But I—"

"Stay!" Griff jumped up and down. "You eat with us!"

Ronni gave in again.

But at seven-thirty, after the food was cleared away and the kids had settled down in the family room to watch *The Lion King* for the umpteenth time, Ronni insisted that she really did have to go.

"Fine," Ryan said. "I'll walk you over."

She opened her mouth—to protest, he knew damn well.

He didn't give her the chance. "I'd like to walk you over. Do you have some problem with that?"

"Well, no, but—"

"Good, then. Say good-night to the kids and let's go."

It was cold outside, the stars overhead obscured by the ever-present blanket of clouds. Ronni wrapped her arms around herself and took off across the lawn to the driveway at a pretty fast clip. Ryan almost grinned. She might try to hurry off, but he had the longer stride by far. It presented no problem for him to keep up.

And he intended to keep up. In fact, he'd just decided that it was time for them to talk about a few things—things other than pet peeves and how much they each loved the work that they did.

When they got to the front door of the little house, she turned to him, shivering a little, her mouth turning up in a see-you-later smile.

"Don't say it."

She blinked. "Excuse me."

"Don't say 'Good night.' I'm coming in."

She stiffened. He feared she might actually tell him no.

But in the end she only took the key from her pocket and opened the door. She led him to the living room, where she slid behind the coffee table and sat on the couch.

He took the small easy chair opposite her, leaning forward, bracing his elbows on his knees. He got right to the point. "You're avoiding being alone with me."

She shifted a little, sat forward herself, and then looked down at the table between them.

"Look at me."

She dragged in a breath—and then raised her eyes to his at last. "Ryan, I..."

"You've been thinking that somehow we're going to keep this casual, haven't you? That you're not going to let it become anything...too important."

In a small voice, she confessed, "Yes. I suppose so."

"Why?"

She sighed, sat back against the cushions.

"Come on, Ronni. Talk to me."

"I just...don't think we're a good match. We've both got demanding jobs. I'm not ready for anything serious right now. And you've got three children. It's a lot to consider."

There he was. Looking down at the coffee table himself. He forced his gaze upward. "You know what? For some crazy reason, I don't give a damn."

She sighed again, said his name again, softly, in a low, lost-sounding tone. "Ryan..."

He found he couldn't sit still for one second longer. He stood, stuck his hands in his pockets. "Damn it, Ronni."

She looked up at him. "I wish I could make you understand."

He did understand. She'd just told him she didn't want a man right now, and when she *did* want a man, it wasn't going to be him. But understanding didn't change the way he felt. He wanted to reach out, across the barrier of the coffee table she'd put between them. He wanted to pull her close, feel her small, sweet body against his, to put his mouth on hers, lose himself in sensation.

But he kept his hands in his pockets. "Tell me more," he said. "I'm listening."

She shook her head. "It's just…old stuff. How I grew up, what that made me want for myself."

"Tell me."

"Oh, Ryan…"

"Stop saying 'Oh, Ryan' and tell me."

She rubbed her upper arms, as if warding off a chill. "Would you…sit back down, then? I hate it when tall people insist on looming above me."

He dropped to the chair again, sat forward, waiting.

She made a small, reluctant noise in her throat— and then at last, she began. "My mother died when I was about Lisbeth's age. My father was…he just had no idea how to take care of a little girl. So he parked me with relatives. A long series of relatives. Looking back, it seems as if I spent my whole childhood trying to fit in to other people's lives. I never…had my own room." She laughed, a slightly embarrassed sound. "Boy. That makes sense. I want to keep things casual because I never had my own room.''

To him, it made perfect sense. But he didn't say that. He didn't want to interrupt, to give her any excuse to stop telling him whatever she was willing to reveal.

She went on. "I... Everything was going along just as I planned it. I made it through med school, my internship and residency. I went into partnership here, with Marty and Randall. Six months ago, I paid off the last of my loans. I bought my condo.''

"Your own room at last.''

Her wide mouth tightened. "Are you making fun of me?''

"No. I am not. Go on.''

She stared at him for a moment, and then continued. "Everything is right on track. The way I see it, in a few years, I'll be ready to meet someone special. Someone nice and fun and easygoing. Someone less career-focused than I am." She laughed again; he knew that particular laugh was at herself. "Someone who likes to cook. Someone who might even consider the idea of being a househusband.''

"A househusband. I'm getting the picture. A nice, single guy with no children, no...previous encumbrances. And definitely no high-powered job taking up a huge chunk of his time.''

"That's it.''

"I'm afraid that's not me.''

"Exactly. And then, yesterday, you kissed me. I really wish you hadn't done that.''

"Why?''

"Because now, even though I keep telling myself

that it was just a kiss, it's not working. I keep thinking about you. Wishing that…''

"Wishing what?''

"Oh, Ryan…''

"Wishing what?''

"I am trying to tell you that *I* need what *you* need.
Someone to cook my dinner and do my laundry.
Someone to be there for me after a hard day at work.
Someone to look after the kids.''

He reminded her gently, "You don't have any
kids.''

"But you do. Three of them. Three really great,
adorable, demanding kids.'' Defiance flashed in her
eyes. "And someone is going to have to take care
of them, to do all the day-to-day things with them.
Right now, you're very fortunate. You've got Lily.
But will Lily want to keep taking caring of your
children once you've found someone else to take her
daughter's place?''

He had no answer to that question. Or if he did
have an answer, he didn't want to get into it right
then. "You're thinking way too far ahead.''

"No. No, I'm not. It's not a good idea, to let
myself start something that will only get me hurt in
the end.''

"Is this Ronni talking—or scared, shy Veronica?''

"In this case, they're both the same person.''

"I wouldn't hurt you.''

"No, you wouldn't. Or at least, you wouldn't
mean to. But I…just don't want to get into something that isn't going to go anywhere.''

He decided he'd had about enough of that coffee

table crouching between them. He knew how to give orders, so he gave one. "Come here."

She sat a little straighter, and she swallowed. "I...that's probably not a good idea."

"I don't give a damn. Come here."

"Oh, Ryan..."

"There you go again with the 'Oh, Ryans.' Come on. Come here."

She stood. He didn't move. He didn't even let himself breathe as she came around the end of the table and took the few steps that put her right in front of him.

Slowly, he reached out both hands and took her by the waist. She made a small, helpless sound. Her body tightened, then went still. He felt the warmth of her beneath the soft wool skirt, felt the firm outward curve where her slim hips began.

He asked in a whisper, looking up into her pixie's face, "Is there anyone else?"

She closed her eyes briefly, then let out a small, tortured sound. "No."

"Was there ever?"

"There was someone in college. I thought it was serious, at the time. But then I decided to go on to med school. He wanted to settle down, start on a family. It didn't last...."

Ryan slid his hands upward, loving the feel of her. She drew a startled breath, her small rib cage expanding sharply, then contracting as she exhaled. Slowly, tenderly, he moved his hands back down to her waist again.

He said, "I haven't been with anyone, not since my wife became ill. I guess I...don't do 'casual' very well."

She lifted a small, pale hand and laid it against his cheek. A swift arrow of pure heat shot through him, bringing full arousal, so stunning he had to suppress a hard gasp.

He tightened his hold on her, commanded, "Bend down to me."

"Oh, Lord," she murmured on a long, sweet breath.

He pulled her closer, opening his thighs so that she could stand between them. Her legs brushed the inside of his, sending desire rolling through him in waves.

"Ronni. Kiss me."

Still she hesitated. So he reached up, slid a hand around her neck beneath the thick, heavy warmth of her hair and brought her mouth down to his.

Chapter Six

A taste was not enough. It only drove him to want more. He ran his tongue along the tempting seam where her lips met. She moaned. And then she let him in.

She had some scrunchy rubber-band thing holding back her hair. He caught it, pulled it down, dropped it to the floor. And then he buried his fingers in the thick curly mass, straining his mouth upward to hers, tasting the moist, sweet secrets beyond her parted lips.

He knew he should stay down there, in the chair, below her. That he should let her keep some measure of control.

But he couldn't. His body ached too much. He had to have her against him, had to feel the whole length of her, pressed close, straining to get closer still....

He rose, pulling her up with him, wrapping his hands around the firm curve of her bottom. She cried out, a yearning, needful sound, slightly bewildered, as if she wanted to call a halt.

But she couldn't. No more than he could.

He pushed up her loose skirt, felt the thick, stretchy fabric of the dark tights she wore. He guided her legs around him, went on kissing her hungrily, as he pushed himself against her, so she could feel how much he wanted her, the friction of their straining bodies increasing the heat and need.

She wasn't that heavy, so small and compact. Easy for him to hold. The kiss went on and on as he started walking. He could have gone to the bedroom. Right then, she would have let him.

But he didn't.

He carried her to the kitchen, to the long counter by the sink. He eased her onto it. And then he took her face in his hands.

She opened her eyes, looked at him.

He pressed his forehead against hers, let his hands trail down, over her slim shoulders and her arms. He caught her hands, twined their fingers together against the tiles and silently counted to twenty-five.

When his breathing had slowed somewhat and he felt he had his arousal under reasonable control, he let go of her hands so that he could pull her closer, so that he could bury his face in her hair.

She wrapped her arms around him, held him close. He whispered, "What can I tell you? Except I do know. I know exactly what you've earned, what you need from your life. It's the same with me. I lost both my parents when I was four. There was no one else who might have taken us, my brother and me. We ended up in a state home. And then in and out of foster care..."

She pulled back, looked at him. Her eyes told him more than words ever could have.

Gently, he touched her skirt, smoothed it more modestly over her thighs. "I know what it is. To want to make a life that's safe, where you...have your own room. Where nothing really bad can happen. I've tried to make just that kind of life, for myself, and for my family."

She said the next part for him. "But then...you lost your wife...."

He ran his hand down her hair, caressed her pale, soft cheek. "So much for safety. So much for what we can really control."

They gazed at each other for a long time.

And then he said, "Maybe I'm not the man you were looking for. But here we are." His hands rested on her thighs. He fisted them, wrinkling the skirt he'd smoothed so meticulously only moments before. "I want you so damn much...."

She put her own hands over his, gave a gentle squeeze. "I want you, too...."

"But?"

"I need a little time. To deal with this."

He took her chin, tipped it up, kissed the tip of her nose. "Time."

"Yes. Please."

Her lips were so close. He could have taken them again. But he didn't. He said, "All right. It's exactly a week until the Heart Ball. Maybe you don't believe I can do it, but I'm going to leave you alone until then—unless you decide to come looking for me.'' She tried to speak. He put a finger against her sweet mouth. ''No. Don't say 'Oh, Ryan.' ''

He felt her sigh against his fingers. ''All right.''

He touched her hair, because he couldn't stop himself. ''Aren't you going to ask me what happens then?''

''I would, if I thought you really knew. But you don't, do you?''

He shrugged. ''Maybe this…attraction between us will just fade away, all by itself.''

''Do you think so?''

''No.'' He put his hands at her waist, helped her down to the floor. ''Walk me to the door.''

He kissed her one last time before he left her, then whispered, ''Eight o'clock, next Saturday?''

''Eight. That's fine.''

And he went out the door.

When Ryan got back to the main house, he found Lily in the kitchen wiping down the counters with a big sponge. He could hear *The Lion King,* still going strong in the other room.

Lily glanced over, nodded, went on rubbing with her sponge.

He noticed his racquetball bag, in the corner, where he'd dropped it earlier. He bent and grabbed the handle. ''Lily?''

''Um?''

''The chicken tonight was terrific.''

She kept scrubbing.

He tried again. ''Maybe I don't tell you enough how much I appreciate all that you do.''

''I'm glad to be of help. Did Dr. Powers get back to the little house safe and sound, then?''

He caught the hint of sarcasm. The guest house was less than a hundred yards away. Ronni could have made it back there just fine on her own.

"Well, did she?" Lily prodded.

He kept his voice level. "Yes. Safe and sound."

"Good." Grudgingly, Lily added, "She's...very nice."

"I think so."

"Well, that's pretty obvious." She scrubbed at one spot, as if something had gotten stuck there, her lips pursed tightly together, her face drawn and tense. At that moment, she looked older than her fifty-eight years.

Ryan thought of Axel Pembroke, that afternoon, not saying whatever was on his mind. Now he was getting the same treatment from his mother-in-law. "Lily?"

"Um?"

"Is there something you'd like to say to me?"

At least she stopped that damn scrubbing. She straightened and turned to him. "Is there something I *should* say?"

"What kind of answer is that?"

She set down the sponge. "I'm sorry. Your private life is your business, of course."

And what should he say to that?

You're right. So stay out of it...?

Or something gentler.

I loved your daughter. But she's gone. We can't bring her back. And now I've met Ronni. I want her. In my life.

In my bed...

No, he just couldn't do it, not right then. He gave

her the facts. "I'm taking Ronni to the Heart Ball next Saturday."

She folded her arms over her middle. "Well. Thank you for telling me. I hope you two will have a lovely time."

Before he could think of what to say in response to that, there was a loud wail from the family room. Griffin came running in. "Gramma, Gramma! Lizzy won't share!"

Lisbeth pounded in right after him, clutching a half-full bowl of popcorn in her chubby arms. "He's eating all the popcorn. And then he went and tried to spit in it. So I took the bowl away from him."

"Where's your brother?" demanded Lily. "I thought he was keeping an eye on you two."

Drew spoke up from the doorway to the family room. "I just went to the bathroom for a minute. Sheesh."

Griff jumped up and down. "Share, Lizzy! Share!"

"Griffin," Lily commanded. "You stop that now."

"I want popcorn! She's gotta share!"

"Give me that bowl," Lily said to Lisbeth.

Lisbeth stuck out her lower lip—but she did hand it over. Lily set it on the counter next to the sink.

Griffin kept shouting, "Share! She's gotta share!"

Lily said, "Griffin, time out for you."

Griff puffed up his little chest. "No! I won't! I want popcorn! She's gotta share!"

Ryan wondered how Lily bore all this, day to day. How Patricia had stood it. He loved his children dearly, but two minutes of them in crisis had him longing to grab his briefcase and head straight for the door.

"Share! Share! Share!" Griffin jumped up and down some more.

Lisbeth put her fingers in her ears and stuck out her tongue.

Ryan couldn't take any more. He said, "Griffin," low and hard.

His younger son stopped jumping, shut his mouth and turned to his father, eyes round as full moons.

"Go sit at the table. Now."

It worked, thank God. Griff trudged to the table, pulled out a chair and climbed onto it.

Ryan looked at his mother-in-law, seeking a hint as to what to do next. "Five minutes," she said.

Griff slumped his shoulders and stared at his Keds.

Lily said, "Lisbeth, go on up and take your bath."

"But *The Lion King...*"

"You've seen all you're going to see of it tonight."

Lisbeth's eyes filled with tears. "Griff ruined *everything.*"

"Go on, now."

Lisbeth sniffed and turned for the hall to the stairs.

"Can I get up now?" Griff pleaded, the minute his sister was gone.

"Not until I say so," his grandmother replied. She looked at Drew. "Do you want to watch the rest of that movie?"

Drew grunted. "No, thanks. I've seen it about a hundred times."

"Then go on in and turn it off."

Drew ducked back into the family room again, leaving Ryan and Lily alone with a very sulky Griff.

Lily shot Ryan a long-suffering look. "Go on. I can handle this."

He felt just a little bit guilty at how eager he was to be gone. "Are you sure?"

She only sighed. So he took her at her word and made his escape, running upstairs first to exchange his racquetball bag for his briefcase.

It was a little after nine when he reached his office at Memorial. He let himself in and switched on the lights and sat down at his desk to tackle the stack of purchase orders.

As a rule, Ryan liked to put in hours at night. He did it a couple of times a week, as a matter of fact. There were no interruptions, and he usually got a lot done in a short space of time.

But that particular night, his concentration kept wandering. He kept recalling the tender, astonished way Ronni had murmured "Oh, Lord" when he'd told her to kiss him, kept remembering the taste of her mouth and the glorious feel of her body against his.

Then he'd think of Lily, with her face so drawn, scrubbing the counter that was already clean. And of Griff shouting "Share! Share! Share!"

More than once, he threw down his pen, got up and paced the room, feeling like a man trapped in a cell. Finally, he gave up and went home.

Monday at Ronni's office, it was business as usual. Ronni thumped tummies. She listened to heartbeats and the sound of breathing, to air whistling in and out through slightly congested lungs. She took medical histories, gave routine shots and answered an endless list of common questions: Why is my toddler such a picky eater? Is my six-month-old gaining enough weight? Will it spoil my newborn if I pick her up when she cries?

After office hours, she went to Children's Hospital, to check on her patients there. When she left the hospital, she did a little grocery shopping. She got home at seven and made herself dinner.

And then, at last, she allowed herself to think about Ryan.

About the way he had kissed her, the things he had said, the tenderness in his touch, in his eyes...

She shouldn't get involved with him. She knew it.

The timing was wrong for her—and he needed a wife, not another breadwinner.

And yet...

Never in her life had she felt the way she did when he touched her. She loved to talk with him, to just *be* with him. Could something that felt so good really be wrong?

True, he would never be the househusband of her dreams.

But then, she was certainly no Patricia, either.

He'd given her a week to think about it.

A week. Unless she sought him out beforehand.

Her mind thought that a week was a very good idea.

Her heart, on the other hand, wasn't so sure. She wanted to go to him.

But she knew that she wouldn't.

It was only five more days, after all, until the Heart Ball.

Ryan got the call from Tanner on Tuesday.

"We've got money problems on the new wing." Tanner's tone was flat, expressionless.

"Explain."

Tanner took a deep breath and let it out hard. "I had my accountant hand-carry the papers for the construction draw to the bank on the first," Tanner said. "And then I waited, the way I always do, for the bank to call back and say the funds were available. The bank didn't call. Two days later, on the third, *I* called *them*. They told me the account set up with them by the Pembroke people had an insufficient balance to cover the draw."

Ryan could not believe what he was hearing. "Insufficient," he repeated with great care.

"Yeah," Tanner said. "Extremely insufficient. As in they could give me ten thousand and change, max. They'd already been in touch with the people at the foundation. And gotten a runaround. So *I* called the foundation on Friday, the fourth."

"Why didn't you call me?"

"Ryan. I *am* calling you."

"I mean Friday. You should have called me then."

Tanner let out another hard gust of air. "Look. You might be my older brother. But we're both all grown up now. I don't call you every time there's a glitch. If I did, we'd be on the phone twenty-four hours a day—and do you want to hear this or not?"

"Sorry. Go on."

"All right. I called the Pembroke people. They

said they'd get back to me. They did. Today. They told me what I'd already figured out—they've got a problem.''

''But what the hell *is* the problem?''

''I got a bunch of mumbo jumbo. About cash flow and certain miscalculations. The upshot is, we're having a meeting. Tomorrow. At the foundation offices at 10:00 a.m.''

''Who, specifically, did you talk to at the foundation?''

''The project officer for the wing.''

''Bill Langley.''

''Right.''

''Did you try to reach Axel?''

''I did. No go. I thought maybe—''

''I'll call him myself, see what I can find out.''

''It doesn't look good.''

''No, it doesn't.'' Ryan knew his brother had to be in the hole pretty deep at this point. According to his usual procedure, Tanner would have paid his employees and subcontractors up front, expecting to be reimbursed by the money from the fund. ''I'll be there for that meeting tomorrow.''

''Fine. Right now, see what you can find out. And call me back if you learn anything.''

''Will do.'' Ryan disconnected the call and dialed Axel's office.

''Pembroke Foundation. Mr. Pembroke's office.''

''This is Ryan Malone. Let me speak with Axel Pembroke.''

''I'm so sorry, Mr. Malone. Mr. Pembroke is not available at this time.''

''When will he *be* available?''

"If you'd like to leave a number, someone will get back to you."

"Someone? Axel isn't returning his own calls anymore?"

"I'm sorry, Mr. Malone."

He wanted to shout at her, to demand a few answers, right now or sooner. But he held his tongue. Whatever the hell disaster was going on there, it wasn't the secretary's fault. She was only repeating what she'd been told to say.

He hung up and tried Axel's home phone. A machine answered. He left a message, tried Axel's cell phone. No luck.

He called Bill Langley himself—and got the same evasive answers that Tanner had heard.

He asked Langley point-blank, "Where's Axel? I can't seem to reach him."

And Langley started tap-dancing, repeating the same things Axel's secretary had said. "Temporarily unavailable…tied up right now…"

Ryan demanded, "How long is 'temporarily'?"

"I'm sorry. I just can't say."

"I'll be there tomorrow, at the meeting you've called with Tanner Construction to talk about this."

"That's a good idea, Mr. Malone."

Ryan had a meeting with a couple of department heads at nine-thirty, which was five minutes away. As he stalked past his secretary's desk, he told her to page him immediately if Axel Pembroke called.

She didn't page him. When he returned to his office at eleven, he tried Axel's home number and his cell phone a second time. No answer at either number.

So he called his brother back. "I got nowhere,"

he said without preamble when Tanner picked up the phone.

"I was afraid you'd say that." Tanner swore. "Got any ideas about what's really going on?"

Ryan remembered that racquetball match with Axel last Saturday, replayed in his mind the strange things Axel had said.

"Ryan? You still with me?"

"I'm here."

"I asked you a question."

"Let's wait until that meeting tomorrow. See what they tell us."

"That's no answer."

"It's the best one I can give you right now."

Ryan and Tanner arrived at the Pembroke Building at nine-fifty the next morning. Bill Langley met them in the front office and then led them into a small conference room where two other men, attorneys for the foundation, were waiting. Coffee was served. Ryan passed on that. He had enough adrenaline racing through his system to get him through the rest of the day as it was—and no doubt far into what would probably be a long, sleepless night.

Langley started right in with a smoke screen. "I'm afraid we have a difficult situation here. As I'm sure you're aware, projecting the income for a fund the size of ours is not an exact science. Decisions were made based on our best knowledge. And it appears that a few of those decisions were... unwise. There have been miscalculations. Huge miscalculations."

Ryan glanced at the two lawyers. He knew exactly what their presence meant. Whatever had gone wrong, the foundation would be playing it close to the vest. This was damage control, big time. And Tanner and Ryan would get no real answers right then.

Langley took off his glasses and massaged the bridge of his nose. "Of course, we intend to do our best to honor our commitment to the Honeygrove Memorial Twenty-Year Wing. We've checked into a number of options. Unfortunately, according to the terms of the Pembroke Trust itself, we are not allowed to liquidate the principal. Also, the Trust cannot actually borrow money against itself. As a hedge against depletion in just such a situation as this one, the Trust was set up so that all projects would be funded strictly out of the income from investments."

"You're saying there's no money, and there isn't going to be any money anytime soon," Tanner said with slow precision.

"I am saying that we are going to have to declare a moratorium on all funding, at least for the next few weeks, until we can fully calculate the extent of the shortage and discover how best to recover our cash position."

Tanner muttered an oath.

Ryan picked up the ball. "The fund has so far provided us with sixty million dollars. We were to have received another forty over the next six months. How much do you project we will see of that?"

Langley slid a glance at the two legal eagles, and then cleared his throat. "I simply cannot project anything at this particular point. The foundation does have a few assets outside of the fund. And we do intend to liquidate those assets, as quickly as we can."

"How quickly will that be?"

"It's just impossible to tell right now. I'm sorry. But at this point, I really can't promise you anything. The truth is, there are other projects in just as dire a need as yours. It's a terrible mess, I know. And it's only going to get worse before it gets better...."

Ryan and Tanner left twenty minutes later, after having been assured by Langley that the foundation would get Tanner a few hundred thousand, somehow, within the next two weeks. "It's our hope that that will help you a little."

"Little," Tanner said. "That's the operative word."

"I'll get together with my board right away," Ryan said. "We'll be in touch with you to set up more meetings."

"Of course."

When they got outside, where the sky, for once, was incongruously clear, Tanner turned to Ryan. "Get that thought out of your head."

"What thought?"

"That it's all your fault. It's not."

His brother's generous denial didn't help. "I'm the one who focused on the Pembroke Foundation, and you know it. I was so damn proud of myself, to get everything we needed from one source."

"The Pembroke Fund was always solid as a rock. It's *still* solid as a rock. That's the problem. They lose their cash flow, and that's all she wrote. They can't honor their commitments. And they still didn't

give us a damn hint about what's really going on.
Their income projections just couldn't logically
have been this far off. I can't see any possibility but
theft, can you? That someone's been dipping a hand
in the till?''

Ryan had to admit, "That's what it looks like."

"Did you ever reach Axel?"

"No."

"Are you thinking what I'm thinking? Axel
would be the one, wouldn't he, with enough access
and authority over the money coming in? He'd probably need an accomplice, though. Someone high up
in the foundation's accounting department.'' Tanner's conjectures made sense. Way too much sense.
More and more, it looked as if Axel Pembroke had
seen his chance and grabbed it but good.

Tanner went on, "The foundation and its lawyers
can't sit on this forever. Too many people are going
to be affected. Word will get out. And the press will
be on it. Soon.''

Ryan nodded. "I give it another twenty-four
hours at most.''

"It's going to be ugly," Tanner said.

"*Ugly*'s too mild a word.''

Tanner muttered, "If Axel's the one, I will personally eliminate that little weasel from the gene
pool.''

"If it's Axel, you and I both know he's already
left the country.''

"Ryan..."

"Say it."

"I'm in damn deep here. Until you can come up
with some alternative plan for funding—''

"How far are you extended?"

"Too far. I've got insurance. But it's not going to cover all of it."

"What about if you call an immediate halt to construction?"

"It depends."

"On?"

"How long it takes to get going again. Even if I cut my losses, I'm in too damn deep. I need money, and I need it soon—or I'm looking a Chapter 11 in the face."

Debt reorganization, Ryan thought. A polite word for bankruptcy. His own brother bankrupt, because of *his* baby, his twenty-year wing...

"Look," Tanner said tightly. "Maybe I can keep things moving for another few days."

"What would you do if I wasn't your brother?"

Tanner didn't answer.

Ryan spoke for him. "You've got no choice. Shut the damn project down."

Chapter Seven

After she did her rounds at Children's Hospital Thursday afternoon, Ronni stopped by her condo and admired her cobalt-blue bathtub and its matching sink. Then, since she was having all her mail delivered to a P.O. box until she made her permanent move to her new home, she ran by the post office.

She got back to the guest house at a little after eight and went through the stack of bills and junk mail as she heated up a can of soup. Then she sat down to eat with the evening's edition of the *Honeygrove Gazette* to keep her company.

She'd barely smoothed the paper out when the headline jumped out at her.

Pembroke Fund in Trouble. President of Fund Vanishes...

Ronni set down her spoon.

Millions of dollars are missing from Pembroke Fund coffers. And Axel Pembroke IV, president of the foundation that bears his family's name, is nowhere to be found. Also missing is Ms. Rhonda Jagger, CPA, and Pembroke Foundation accounting manager...

Ronni scanned the next few paragraphs quickly. Apparently, Axel Pembroke and Rhonda Jagger had been diverting income from the foundation's investments for a number of months. Neither had been seen since Sunday, February 6.

Ronni read on.

Hardest hit by the news is Honeygrove Memorial Hospital. The new wing at Memorial, scheduled for completion in September of this year, in time for the twenty-year anniversary of the hospital's present building, was to be paid for by a hundred million dollar arrangement with the fund....

The new wing. Ryan's pet project. To most of the medical community in Honeygrove, the twenty-year wing and Ryan Malone were synonymous.

What had Lily said that Sunday when she dropped in with roast beef sandwiches and endless tales of the incomparable Patricia?

"One hundred million dollars, it's taking. From the Pembroke Fund. That was Ryan's doing, of course, the funding...."

And Marty, when he first introduced them, at that fund-raiser almost a month ago now: "This is Ryan

Malone, the man personally responsible for all the construction you see going on at Memorial lately.''

The man personally responsible...

He must be devastated by this.

Ronni left the newspaper on the table next to her untouched bowl of soup. She grabbed a jacket from the hall closet and went out the French doors in the bedroom.

She had to knock several times at the back door of the main house before Lily answered.

''Is Ryan here?''

Lily shook her head. She didn't look friendly. But then, maybe she was just worried about Ryan.

Ronni said, ''I saw the news...about the theft of the money from the Pembroke Fund.''

Lily pressed her lips tightly together and nodded. ''I'm afraid there's not much I can tell you. I've hardly talked to Ryan since this all happened. He called me around dinnertime yesterday, from the hospital, and told me a little about what was going on. He said that he'd be late coming home. He *was* late. Very late. This morning, he left before eight. He said he'd be in and out of meetings all day....''

''Oh, Lily, I'm so sorry....''

''I'm just...trying to keep things going. Trying to get the children bathed and ready for bed.''

''Is there anything I can do?''

''We're fine. And I really do have to get back to the children. Griffin's in the tub now. There'll be water everywhere.''

''Yes, of course. Would you tell Ryan that I stopped by?''

''I do have to get back upstairs....''

''Please tell him, Lily.''

"Yes, yes. I will. Now, I have to—"

"I know. Call me if there's anything—"

"Thank you. I will." Lily shut the door.

Ronni stood on the back step, staring at the closed door, feeling dismissed. Lily's obvious reluctance to pass on Ronni's simple message grated.

It also made the situation all too clear. Lily would present a real problem if Ronni and Ryan took their relationship any further than it had already gone.

But right now, Lily wasn't the primary issue.

Ryan was.

Ronni knew he had to be blaming himself for the catastrophe of the vanished funds. She wanted to reach out to him, to hold him, to tell him things he wouldn't believe but needed to hear, anyway.

It's not your fault. You'll find a way to get through this. You'll find the money. Somewhere...

Ronni ran back to the guest house and called Memorial. The switchboard put her through to Ryan's desk, but all she got there was his voice mail.

She stumbled over her message, not knowing quite what to say. "This is Ronni. It's 8:45 p.m. Thursday. I'm at the guest house, if you need to talk...."

After that, she couldn't think what else to do to try to reach him. So she reheated her soup and ate it. Then she retired to the bathroom. She took a long, hot bath, hoping to relax, to make herself stop worrying....

Ryan let himself into the silent house at a little after midnight. At that point, he was functioning completely by rote. He locked the door and punched the correct buttons on the alarm. He set his briefcase down, shrugged out of his overcoat and hung it in the closet by the stairs.

Lily had left his newspapers, the *Gazette* and the *Oregonian,* on the foyer table where she always set them. Ryan didn't pick them up. There had been copies waiting on the side credenzas at two of the emergency meetings he'd called that day. He didn't need to read it all again.

He bent, grabbed his briefcase and started up the stairs. Halfway to the landing, the light came on. It was Lily.

"Ryan. Is everything…all right?"

"It's fine," he lied automatically. "The kids?"

"Sound asleep."

"Good."

"You look exhausted."

"I am."

"Ryan…" She was frowning, the faint lines on her face etched deeper than usual. He wondered what the hell else might have gone wrong.

Some crisis with the kids, most likely. "What?"

Her gaze slid away, then she drew her shoulders back a little. "Oh, nothing. It's not important."

He just didn't have the energy to press her, though he probably should have. "Go on to bed. Get some sleep."

"Yes. I will. Good night."

"Good night."

Lily turned and went off down the upper hall to her own room. He heard her door close, then realized he was just standing there, halfway up the stairs, holding on to the banister as if he'd fall on his face if he let go. He started climbing again.

In the master suite, he didn't bother to turn on a

light. The drapes were pulled back. He could see well enough by the outside lights. He left his briefcase by the door, tore off his tie and tossed his jacket on the bed. Then he dropped into a big overstuffed chair in the sitting area near the wide front windows. He rested his head back and stared at the ceiling.

He had never in his life been so tired.

He should take off the rest of his clothes and go to bed.

But he knew he wouldn't sleep. He'd only lie there, staring at the ceiling, random and infuriating phrases playing through his head.

Pembroke Fund In Trouble...

"...liquidate assets, as quickly as we can..."

"...can't promise you anything..."

"...fully calculate the extent of the problem..."

"The thing is, a man has to grab his chance when it comes along...."

With a groan, Ryan dragged himself upright. He stared around him at the big, attractive room he had once shared with Patricia. It looked way too empty tonight. Way too quiet, too gloomy, too cold.

He couldn't stay there, in the gloomy silence, listening to mocking phrases echo through his head. He strode to the door, quietly let himself out and went back down the stairs.

The light was on in her bedroom. He could see it—shining a welcome through the trees.

He probably should have gone around the front and rung the bell. But that light seemed to beckon him. He couldn't turn away from it. He went through the back gate and straight to the patio.

The filmy under curtains were drawn. He couldn't

see anything but vague shapes inside. For a moment, he just stood there, staring at the source of the light—the lamp by her bedside, he could make that much out—a pool of greater brightness within the general glow.

He lifted his fist.

And he knocked.

Then he waited.

She didn't take long. He saw movement, near the lamp. And then a figure approaching the doors. A hand lifted the curtain.

And there she was, on the other side of the glass, wearing the same pajamas she'd been wearing that first night, flannel ones with little flowers on them. As usual, her hair was pulled back, but still coming loose in little corkscrews all around her freckled face.

She drew back the curtains, turned the lock and pulled open the door.

He started to explain himself. "I know I promised I'd stay away until Saturday, but…" He didn't finish. He realized he didn't have to. He could see in her eyes that she understood.

And she did. She more than understood. For Ronni, something momentous had occurred, right at the moment when she'd pulled back the curtain to find him waiting on the other side.

She'd seen his face and it had hit her.

She loved him.

She, Ronni Powers, loved Ryan Malone.

This was happening too fast and he was not the kind of man she'd planned to love.

But maybe love didn't work on a timetable. Maybe love wasn't something a woman could plan.

And she was Ronni, after all. *Ronni* who was willing to take chances. Who bravely stepped forward
to meet every challenge.

Ronni. Not scared, cautious Veronica...

And maybe it was crazy and yes, it was too fast.
Maybe it wasn't going to be easy.

But still, she knew—*this was love.*

And somehow all her doubts and hesitations, all
her well-laid plans for her life, meant nothing anymore. Not in the face of his need for her. Not in the
face of her love.

"Oh, Ryan..."

"There you go again." Ryan smiled. It felt
strange. He didn't think he'd smiled one time in the
past three days.

She reached out, took hold of his arm and pulled
him inside with her. Then she shut the door, drew
the curtains.

"You must be freezing," she chided. "You don't
even have a jacket on."

"I'm all right."

"I was so worried you wouldn't get my messages."

"Messages?" His brain felt slow, thick. "You
left messages for me? When?"

"Tonight. One on your voice mail at the hospital.
One with Lily...."

"I didn't check the voice mail. And Lily didn't
mention it. I...what did your messages say?"

"Just that I was here. If you needed me."

Her words sent warmth spreading through him.
He hadn't consciously realized how much he needed
warmth. Until now, when he was here, with her.

"I read the news in the *Gazette.* About the

money," she said softly. "I...couldn't stop thinking of you. Worrying about you. Hoping you were all right."

It occurred to him that he'd feel even warmer if he had his arms around her. So he held them out.

She came to him, soft and small and firm, smelling of soap and shampoo, wrapped in flowered flannel. He lifted her off the floor so that he could bury his face in her wild red hair.

For the first time in days, it seemed to him, he felt alive. The blood coursed through his veins, hot and swift. He lowered his mouth to hers.

She wrapped her slim arms so tightly around him. He felt...a change in her. There was no reluctance in her now. She returned his kiss without hesitation.

It was just what he needed. That frank eagerness, that honest hunger matching his own.

He shifted her higher, taking her hips in his hands, raising her up enough that he could kiss her smooth white neck, and then lower. He nuzzled the collar of her pajama top. She knew what he wanted and helped him, holding tight to his shoulder with one hand as she undid two buttons with the other.

Her breast, small and firm, traced with fine blue veins, was bare to him. He took it, pressing his lips into the soft curve, drawing the tight nipple into his mouth.

She moaned and held his head, helping him, holding him where he wanted to be as he swirled his tongue around and around. She moved against him, the muscles of her hips tightening and then relaxing in his cradling hands.

He wanted her mouth again. He kissed his way back up her pale throat, over her jaw to her softly parted lips. As he drank from her mouth, he lowered her a little, until he held her at the waist.

She clutched him tightly with her arms, her legs dangling against his thighs, as he carried her to the bed. The covers were already down. She must have been lying there, unable to sleep, waiting....

He dared to think it: waiting for him.

She slid to the floor, there beside the bed. And she took him by the shoulders, guided him down to sit on the edge.

He looked up at her. Her lips were swollen, her pale skin flushed. One pretty breast peeked out at him from between the sides of her unbuttoned top.

He didn't want to say it. But the man he was had to say it. "I...didn't bring anything."

She knew what he meant. And she said, "It's all right."

But it wasn't. In spite of how his body ached for her, he couldn't let them be that irresponsible. "Ronni..."

"It's all right. Honestly. I can take care of it."

"You can?"

She nodded. "You remember Kelly Hall, that OB-GYN I introduced you to the other day at Granetti's?"

"I remember. What about her?"

"Well, some doctors pass out suckers to well-behaved patients. Kelly passes out—"

He grunted. "You're kidding."

"No, I'm serious. She does. To everyone. I think she's seen the results of one too many unplanned pregnancies in her line of work."

"You're saying she passed them out to *you?*"

"She did."

So that problem was solved. Still, there remained the deeper question. Did she really want this? Her eager kisses, her yearning body, her sighs and her moans had all told him yes.

But he wanted her to say it—needed her to say it.

"Ronni, are you sure?"

She whispered, so sweetly, "Yes, Ryan. I am."

Chapter Eight

He didn't know what to say next.

But it didn't matter.

She knelt at his feet. She took his shoes away, and then his socks. He just sat there, looking down at her bright head, thinking that somehow he'd found heaven, in the middle of an endless, gloomy night.

She rose, took his hand, made him stand. And then she undressed him, took everything away and set it neatly on a straight chair a few feet from the bed.

When he was naked, she kissed him, pressing herself all along his bare body. Her pajamas felt warm and fuzzy, and she felt so soft, so fantastically willing.

He ached at the feel of her, at the heat of her....

"Get in bed now," she whispered, and gently

pushed him down again. He could do nothing but obey. She pulled the blankets around him and then, still standing by the side of the bed, she bent over him, her face only inches from his.

He reached up, behind her head, found the band that held her braid. He tugged it free and tossed it aside. He pulled her down, so their lips could meet. And as he tasted her mouth again, he worked his fingers into the coiled strands, until it was all free and wild down her back, falling over her shoulders, making a red veil around them as the kiss went on and on.

He wanted her body against him. He cupped the back of her head and tried to bring her down, onto the bed with him. But she resisted, reluctantly breaking the kiss. "Wait. Only for a minute. I'll be right back, I promise...."

He knew a hard flash of stark fear, no less real for its absurdity, that she would vanish—into the bathroom or down the hall—and that she wouldn't come back.

He'd be left alone.

He didn't know why the hell that should scare him. He'd been left alone before. You'd think he'd be used to it by now.

And he *had* become used to it. Until just recently.

Until Ronni...

Even with Patricia, whom he *had* loved, it hadn't been like this. He'd never looked into Patricia's eyes and felt that jolt of recognition, that sense that here was someone exactly like him.

Except female.

Gloriously, utterly female...

He wanted to command *No, stay here,* but then

he knew it wouldn't come out as a command; it would come out as the cry of a child, lost in the dark....

She kissed his cheek—and then his mouth one more time. And then she left him. He turned his head away from the sight of her going. He looked at the far wall, closed his eyes.

She didn't take long. Two or three minutes. He heard the soft brushing of her bare feet on the hardwood floor.

He rolled his head to look at her. She had a small box in her hand. She flipped back the top, took out a foil packet and set it on the nightstand. Then she opened the nightstand drawer and dropped the box inside.

He couldn't wait for her any longer. He shoved the covers aside and reached for her, snaring her arm, pulling her down to the bed with him. He kissed her again, and while he kissed her, he unbuttoned her last buttons, pushed the pajama top off her shoulders and down her arms. He threw it on the floor.

And then he cupped one sweet breast, lowered his mouth, and tasted her there as he had when he was holding her high in his arms on the other side of the room.

He slid his hand down her flat belly and under the elastic waist of her pajama bottoms. He felt her stomach jerk, when he reached the warm nest of curls there. She sucked in a gasp, pulling air from his own lungs as she did it, since their mouths were still joined.

He touched her, delving in, feeling the silky wetness, the hot, needful readiness that matched his own. She helped him, pushing the hindering flannel off and down, kicking it away.

He rose up, reached for the foil packet on the nightstand, got the thing free of its covering and slid it on.

And then, at last, he sank down upon her, into her. She welcomed him with a cry.

After that he was lost. She surrounded him, all warm, soft skin and cradling arms. She pushed herself up toward him. He took what she so freely offered, losing himself, forgetting everything but the hungry rhythm of their moving bodies, the red cloud of her hair, and the feel of her hands, stroking him, clutching him, urging him on.

At the last, she stiffened, cried out his name. He felt her climax pulsing around him. That sent him over the edge into the long free fall of total release.

A few minutes later, he eased himself to the side. Then they lay there, facing each other, idly sharing caresses, content, for a while.

But the time did come when he got up and went to the bathroom to throw the condom away. When he came back, she had put on her pajama top.

All at once, he felt just a little too naked. So he got his Jockey shorts from the pile on the chair and pulled them on.

She watched him, crouched on her knees in the center of the rumpled bed. He reached for his shirt.

She said, "You're going?"

He let his hand drop to his side. "I…no, I don't want to go. But I wasn't sure if you—"

She stopped him in midsentence by the simple act

of holding out her hand. He went to her, sat on the side of the bed and pulled her into his lap.

She cuddled right up against him, looping her arms around his neck, her bare legs to the side, her cute pink feet brushing his calf. He rocked her a little, rocked them both, to be truthful.

She spoke first. "You've hardly said a word about what you've been going through the last couple of days." She chuckled. "But then again, we have been busy...."

He nuzzled her hair. "Way too busy for talking...."

Her tone grew more serious. "But maybe we should talk, don't you think? Or rather, *you* should talk. And I'll just listen. Sometimes it helps, to have someone to listen."

"It's pretty damn grim."

"That's okay."

He didn't know where to begin—wasn't sure he even wanted to begin. So he just held her, close against his heart, his cheek resting on her curly head.

A sad little memory drifted into his mind.

Ordinarily he would have let it drift right back out. But instead, he heard himself say, "When I was little, I used to have a recurring dream...."

And she made a small, encouraging sound, enough that he continued, "I remember having that dream a lot in the year or two after I lost my parents. Maybe that's impossible, for me to remember that long ago. I was so young. But I do remember."

She snuggled even closer to him, whispered, "Please tell me about it."

So he did.

"It would start with my father. With...the sheer

size of him. He was a huge man. Or it so seemed
to me. Built like my brother Tanner is now, powerful. Thick through the arms and chest. I'd dream
that he would hoist me onto his giant-sized shoulders, and I would feel…just as strong as he was,
and safe.''

She put her hand on his forearm, brushed it lightly
back and forth in a soothing caress. ''It sounds like
a good dream.''

''It *was* a good dream. At first. I'd see my father,
he'd lift me up onto his shoulders. And then I'd hear
my mother. Singing to me, the way she always sang
to us. An Irish song. 'Molly Malone.' It was my
favorite of all of her songs. I thought it had been
written just for us.''

''Just for you.'' Her face was resting against his
shoulder. He couldn't see her expression. Still, he
knew she was smiling. ''For the Malones…''

''Yes. And then, in the middle of the song my
mother's voice would fade. My father would vanish.
And I'd hear a baby crying. I'd look over and I'd
see him. The baby. Crying in a crib, lying there all
alone, waving his fat little arms, with no one to hear
him.'' He rubbed his chin against the top of her
head. ''I don't know why I dreamed of a baby. Tanner was three when our parents died. And I was four.
We weren't babies then. Not anymore.''

She suggested softly, ''Maybe you felt like a
baby. Defenseless…''

He kissed her temple, ran his hand over her hair.
''Maybe so. I know I felt…connected to that baby.
As if I should have been there, to pick him up, to
hold him, to whisper the things you whisper to a

baby, those little soothing noises, so that he'd feel safe. And protected. And loved...

"But I wasn't there. And for that, I hated myself. I know there was no logic to it. But I'm not talking about logic here."

She made another small, tender sound, then moved her head against him. He felt her lips brush the side of his neck. She cuddled closer once more.

He said, "About then, with that baby I couldn't touch wailing through my dream that had somehow turned into a nightmare, I'd wake up sweating and moaning. Tanner would be standing over me, with his thumb in his mouth, holding the little dirty scrap of a blanket he slept with until they took him away to his first foster home.

"Tanner would pull that soggy thumb from his mouth and he'd put his hand on me, on my shoulder. Or over my heart. And he'd say, 'Bad dream. It's okay. Go back to sleep...'

"Not even four years old, younger than Griff, and he'd say that to me. The same as, if I woke up and he'd kicked the covers down, I'd sneak over and cover him back up so he wouldn't be cold. We...took care of each other."

She raised her hand, stroked the side of his face. "I'm glad you had that. Each other..."

He thought of himself and Tanner, just the day before, standing on the street in front of the Pembroke Building beneath an incongruous clear blue sky.

I'm looking a Chapter 11 in the face, his brother had said.

"Did you know that Tanner's the general contractor on the new wing?"

He heard a small, regretful "Yes…"

"He could go belly-up from what's happened. A general contractor pays his people up front."

"I understand."

"Do you? And do you know how many jobs this project created, how many it would have created in the future?" He didn't wait for her answer. "All of those jobs. Lost. A lot of people out of work right now, and a lot more who won't get jobs in the future because the jobs won't be there. A lot of sick people who won't get the kind of treatment they deserve. Services we won't be able to provide because we simply do not have the facilities."

She stirred. "Ryan, don't—"

He couldn't stop. "And then there's me. I'm a little…tarnished. Yeah. Tarnished. That would be the word. Not the golden boy, the fund-raising genius I was a few days ago. But I've still got my job. It's unlikely I'll lose it. No one would ever say this mess was my fault."

She lifted her head, gave him a stern look. "Because it isn't."

He wanted to shout at her, which was truly pitiful. She hadn't done anything but make tender love to him—and then offer to listen while he went against all his ingrained ideas of himself and poured out his woes.

"Shh." He smoothed her hair again, until she went still in his arms. Then he confessed, "I should have known."

"You should have known what?"

"What Axel was up to."

"How? How *could* you have known?"

So he told her. She sat very still, hardly breathing,

it seemed to him, as he repeated the details of his final racquetball match with Axel Pembroke.

At last, he said, "That little bastard just couldn't resist the temptation to rub my nose in what he'd done. I should have been alerted."

She kissed him again, this time on the edge of his jaw. And then she slid off his lap before he could grab hold of her and make her stay. She planted herself in front of him, propped her hands on her hips and demanded, "This...suspicious behavior of Mr. Pembroke's. It occurred when?"

"Saturday."

"And he disappeared when?"

"Sunday, from what the papers say."

"Well." She threw up both hands. "Isn't hindsight a marvelous thing?"

He scowled at her. "You're defending me. I don't need defending."

"Yes, you do. You need someone to look at the facts here. Someone who isn't you, with your exasperating tendency to feel responsible for things you can't possibly control—not that I don't completely understand that tendency. As a doctor, I spend a lot of my professional life feeling exactly what you're feeling now. Because there are so many things we just don't know yet about the human body and what can go wrong with it, things we can't help feeling we *should* know, when our patients look at us for all the answers we simply do not have."

"This isn't the same thing."

"It is. Oh, it is. You hooked up with those Pembroke people in good faith. And from what I understand, that foundation is an old and respected organization. It's never reneged on its commitments before, has it?''

"Of course not."

"Well, there you have it. You did a fabulous thing, to get that huge amount of money out of them. And that last encounter you had with that Pembroke fellow, well, no one—I repeat, *no one*—could have known by the things he said to you then what he had up his sleeve. And even if you *had* known, what could you have done about it in the time between your conversation with him and his disappearance? Obviously it was already too late to stop him from stealing the money.''

She flashed a triumphant little grin. "But maybe you could have gone to the police. You could have told them, 'I played racquetball with Axel Pembroke a few hours ago, and he said some things that have been preying on my mind. Things like how I should understand if he grabs his chance. And how I'll never be off the hook where he's concerned.' Big deal. I'm sure they would have run right out and arrested him from that." Her red-gold eyebrows drew together. "That does bring a point to mind. You probably should tell the police about it. He might just have said something that meant nothing to you, but could give them a lead.''

He let out a long breath. "I already have. I called them yesterday.''

"And?''

"They took my statement over the phone and said, 'Thank you very much.'''

"Okay then. You've done what you reasonably could have done when it comes to Axel Pembroke.''

"Except to track him down and kill him with my bare hands."

She pretended to consider that idea, then let out a delicate grunt. "Not your style. And besides, you haven't got time for revenge."

"It wouldn't be revenge, I'd think of it as justice."

"Call it what you want, it's a luxury you can't afford. You've got too much to do here in Honeygrove, trying to find a way to get the funding you need to finish that new wing."

He swore under his breath. Right then, that task seemed just about impossible. "I think I'd rather just take off after Axel."

"But you can't. And you won't."

They both knew she was right.

She came back to him then and pushed him down on the bed. She crawled in beside him and pulled the covers up over them both. She kissed his ear and then whispered into it, "And right now, you shouldn't do anything—except get a few hours' sleep."

"Right now, I should go back to my own bed."

She sighed. "Probably so." She pushed the covers back. "Go on. I won't stop you."

But he didn't want to leave. Not yet. He grabbed the covers and hauled them up around his neck. "Maybe just for a couple of hours."

"I could set the alarm."

"Do it. Set it for four."

She rolled over and reached for the clock, then she settled under the blankets with him, turning her back to him, so he could wrap himself around her.

He actually dozed a little, a feat he would have deemed impossible a couple of hours before.

But eventually, the feel of her so close was too tempting by half. He caressed her shoulder, smoothed her hair out of his way and kissed the side of her neck. She turned to him, sighing, wrapping her sweet arms around him, pushing her mouth up to his.

Her beeper went off before the alarm. It was three-thirty. She slid from the bed and fumbled around until she found her pajama top—which he'd tossed halfway across the room the second time they made love. He watched her through the shadows, still barely awake, as she pulled it on. Then she disappeared into the other room.

He sat up, turned on the lamp and waited for her to return. She didn't take long.

"Sorry," she said wryly, stopping at the dresser just inside the door. "Three-year-old girl with a high fever. The parents are frantic. I'm meeting them at Children's Hospital right away." She pulled out a pair of underpants and a bra, opened another drawer, found some socks.

He watched her, enjoying the sight immensely as she tossed her pajama top on the end of the bed and put on the underwear. Then he pushed back the covers and reached for his own clothes.

She let him out the back door, kissing him one last time before he left, promising, "Tomorrow night, if you need me, I'll be here."

"I'll need you."

"Then I'll be here."

He couldn't resist teasing, "Barring any emergencies with your patients."

She wrinkled up her freckled nose. "That's the way it goes when you get involved with a doctor."

"As long as the doctor is you, I'm willing to put up with it."

"Good. Now, I—"

"I know. You have to go. And so do I."

When he got back to his own room, he actually fell asleep again. He woke at seven, cleaned up, got dressed, grabbed his briefcase and went downstairs.

Lily was standing at the stove, scrambling eggs. "There you are. I'll have these ready in a jiff."

Ryan set his briefcase on a chair. "Never mind. Just coffee. I'll get something later, at the hospital."

"You're sure? You have to eat."

"I *will* eat. Later. I promise."

She got a mug, poured him coffee. He took the cup from her. "Thanks."

She went back to the stove. He stood at the counter, sipping. "The kids?"

"Getting dressed. Or they'd better be." She slid him a glance. "Oh. I forgot to mention last night that Dr. Powers dropped by."

Had she really forgotten? He doubted it. More likely she'd decided that Ronni's message could wait.

Lily continued, "She said she'd read about the Pembroke Fund in the newspaper. She was... concerned."

He went ahead and told the truth. "I know. I've already talked to her."

Lily stopped stirring the eggs and shot him another look, this one accompanied by a tight frown. "You talked to her since *midnight?*"

He set his mug on the counter. "Yes, Lily. I did."

"Well," she said, then repeated "Well" again.

His gut felt as if some unseen hand had grabbed it and tied it into a long chain of hard knots. He had another hellish day of what-do-we-do-now meetings ahead of him. And his mother-in-law, his mainstay on the home front, was looking at him as if he'd committed adultery.

And maybe, to her mind, he had.

He made himself say it. "Ronni has become very important to me, Lily."

She glared at him. "Do you really think you have time for such nonsense right now?"

Her question came at him like a slap in the face. He spoke quietly. "That was uncalled-for."

Her face crumpled. He felt like a heel.

Lily turned away, switched off the flame beneath the eggs and muttered miserably, "I…you're right. It's none of my business."

No, he thought, that's not so. Lily was a very important part of Ryan's and his children's lives.

But if he and Ronni went on together—and right now, he couldn't imagine giving her up—and if Lily refused to accept Ronni…

Well then, big changes would have to be made. Tough changes.

Lily had collected herself. She turned a tight, brave smile on him. "Let's just let this subject go, for now. You have enough to worry about as it is. And we have no way of knowing what the future will bring."

She was letting him off the hook, temporarily,

anyway. He shouldn't have felt such utter relief. But he did.

Right then, Griff came bouncing in, waving an action figure, with his shirt on inside-out. "Gramma! Daddy! I'm all dressed! And I'm *hungry!*"

Lily glanced at him, then gave a weary sigh when she saw his shirt. "Go on. Sit down. Your breakfast is ready."

Ryan picked up his briefcase again. "Gotta go." He went to his son, kissed the top of his blond head. "Be good for Grandma."

"Daddy! I'm always good! Have a nice day working!"

A nice day. Right. "I will." He turned to Lily. "I'm afraid I'll probably miss dinner again."

"All right."

He headed for the back door.

The day wasn't quite as bad as the two before it had been. The first frenzy of hair-tearing was over. They were starting to focus on what to do next. Community efforts had raised more than ten million toward furnishings and equipment, earmarked for spending after the wing itself was complete. They were now looking into rechanneling that money, trying to free it up for immediate use. And since Memorial was a not-for-profit institution, they could probably dig up some emergency government funding. But whatever they did, it wouldn't bear fruit tomorrow or the day after. And construction couldn't get going again until Tanner had some money in hand.

Ryan met with the doctors' wives and society matrons from the hospital's auxiliary, Friends of Memorial, at one. They were very concerned about the problem with the new wing—and about the speech their chief administrator was expected to give at the Heart Ball the next night. What could he possibly say about the situation right now that wouldn't put a damper on the evening they'd worked so long and hard to plan? Perhaps he should just skip his little talk....

Personally, Ryan would have liked nothing better. He did not relish the idea of getting up before Honeygrove's best and brightest and admitting that the loud sucking sound they heard was Memorial's new wing going down the drain. But they couldn't pretend it wasn't happening, either. He said he'd prefer to remain on the program.

Murleen Anniston, wife of a prominent cardiologist and this year's chairwoman of the Heart Ball Committee, threw up her plump hands and cried, "But we've worked so hard! We've chosen an Oriental theme this time, and everything is just beautiful. You have no idea what it's like, every year, trying to make this a special, one-of-a-kind event. We're looking forward to a lovely evening, an evening people will remember in a positive way, in spite of this recent catastrophe. We just don't want to invite any more discomfort than everyone's already feeling over this."

"I understand, Mrs. Anniston. And I promise you I will not deliver any gloom and doom." That's a hell of a promise, Malone, he thought bleakly. One he was going to be hard-put to keep.

"How can you *help* but deliver gloom and doom?" Mrs. Anniston demanded.

He had the urge to say *Trust me* but quelled it. He already felt too much like some two-bit snake-oil salesman lately, someone who'd promised miracles and then hadn't delivered. No need to sound like one, too.

He said carefully, "I think it's important that we face this situation head-on, that we don't try to pretend there's nothing wrong when everyone knows that's not true."

Murleen Anniston's ample bosom rose and fell visibly with her agitated breathing. "But it was all supposed to be so *beautiful*. A truly gala event, an evening to remember!"

Maggie MacAllister, the wife of Memorial's chief of staff, spoke up then. "Murleen. I think Mr. Malone is right." Ryan cast the trim brunette a look of sheer gratitude, to which she responded with a gracious smile. "We can't bury our heads over this," she said. "Our chief administrator must remain on the program, just as we originally planned. He is a highly skilled speaker, as we all know. I'm sure he'll say just the right thing to put everyone's mind at ease."

Ryan waited for Mrs. Anniston to cry, *Like what?*

But she didn't, thank God. She laid her hand over her heaving bosom. "Well. I am very nervous about this. But if you really think there's no other choice…"

"That is exactly what I think," Maggie said.

The other ladies started talking then. Their comments amounted to a chattery chorus of agreement with Maggie MacAllister's point of view.

Ryan's "Look How Far We've Come" speech remained on the program for the Heart Ball.

* * *

He had three more meetings after the one with the auxiliary. By then, it was seven at night. His secretary had gone home and the office was quiet. He settled in at his desk to write a new speech.

By ten, he had started and dumped a countless number of drafts.

He simply couldn't figure out an angle. Each approach either dripped the gloom and doom he'd sworn he would avoid—or sounded as if he was singing "My Heart Will Go On" when everyone knew the damn ship was sinking.

At ten-thirty, he gave up. He shut down his computer, turned off the lights and went home, where the Garfields and Rugrats and crooked purple hearts danced in the front windows.

Lily and the kids had already gone to bed. The house seemed too big, too silent, too dark.

He got out of his business clothes and into chinos and a sweater. The damn speech he hadn't written nagged at him. He stood before the windows that looked out on the front lawn and tried to think of what the hell to do about it.

Nothing came to mind. So he went out, across the backyard, to the light that glowed through the French doors at the back of the little house.

Chapter Nine

He tapped on the glass and she answered immediately. She opened the door, pulled him in, shut it and drew the curtains as she had the night before. She was still in her clothes—a pair of green leggings, fat socks and a big red sweater. He thought she looked like one of Santa's elves.

A very sexy elf, to his mind.

He reached for her. She came into his arms, lifting her mouth to his. He kissed her all the way to the bed and down onto it. In no time at all, with two sets of eager hands working at it, they were both without clothes.

He looked into those wide, wise eyes as he entered her, taking her hands and holding them over her head. Her hair fanned out in a coiling halo on the white pillow, and her mouth beckoned him.

He took it, and pressed into her. She moaned. He

drank the sound. She pressed upward, taking him deeper. And he pressed back, deeper still.

They rolled, together, and she was above him, riding him, stroking his chest with those wonderful, small hands, making little hungry noises in her white throat as she tossed back her head and moved slowly, rhythmically, driving him wild.

He closed his eyes, let her have him, let her do what she would, only daring to clasp her hips, to follow her as her rhythm grew frantic, racing to a hard finish, where the world fell away beneath them and they spun into free-fall as one.

Finally, she relaxed on top of him. He put his arms around her and buried his fingers in the wild tangle of her hair. She felt so good, from the warm, slight weight of her to the silky hair trailing over his arms, to the soft breasts pressing into his chest. Even the rhythm of her breathing pleased him, slowing now, in sync with his.

Her skin was like satin under his hands, and down where they remained joined, he could feel...

Everything.

Because they'd forgotten to use a condom.

The realization must have hit her at the same time it did him. She stiffened, then turned her head and lifted up enough that she could look at him.

"Oh, God..." she said.

They both gulped.

And then she groaned. "We forgot—"

"I know."

They stared at each other. Finally, she slid to the side and pulled the sheet up around herself.

He felt like an idiot—a first-class fool to have been so careless. "I'm sorry. I should have—"

She sat up. "Don't."

"But I—"

She laid a finger against his lips, shook her head. "We were both at fault."

He captured her hand and kissed the fingertips. "How…bad a time is it?"

"You mean how likely am I to conceive?"

He nodded.

She hesitated, then gently pulled her hand free of his. "It's the right time."

He closed his eyes, muttered an oath.

Her hand brushed his shoulder. "Listen. The odds are still against it. Let's not borrow trouble, okay?"

He knew that was sound advice. "Okay."

"And I'll see about getting a script for the pill. That way we won't have to worry that this might happen again."

"Good idea."

She was leaning over him, clutching the sheet, her hair spilling over her shoulders. He wanted her closer, so he reached up and pulled her down again. She didn't resist, exactly, but she didn't let herself relax, either.

Settling her head on his chest, he stroked her hair and caressed her smooth back. Finally, she let out a long breath and her body went pliant in his arms.

He kissed her temple—and resolutely introduced a new subject. "How did things work out with that three-year-old last night?"

She laughed, a good-humored sound. He took that as a positive sign; she really didn't intend to dwell on the dangerous mistake they'd just made.

He teased, "What is so funny?"

"Turned out the father had misread the thermometer. Her temperature was one hundred *point* eight, not one hundred *and* eight.''

He grunted. ''A trip to the hospital in the middle of the night for nothing.''

''It's part of the job. And when you've seen as many really sick children as I have, you become rather grateful for the false alarms.''

He pulled the covers closer around them, wished he could stay with her, that he didn't have that unwritten speech hanging over his head. His preoccupation must have communicated itself to her, because she lifted her head and frowned at him. ''You're still thinking about that condom we didn't use.''

''It's not that.''

''Okay, then.'' She pulled away.

''Wait a minute…''

''No.'' She dragged herself up against the headboard and folded her hands on top of the sheet. ''Talk to me. I'm listening.''

So he told her about his meeting with the ladies from the auxiliary. ''And now I've got to write a new speech,'' he said once he'd explained it all. ''I worked on it for over three hours this evening. And got nowhere. I don't know where to start.''

She studied him for a moment, then asked briskly, ''You want my advice?''

''You have some?''

''Yes.''

He sat up beside her and adjusted his side of the sheet. ''All right. Hit me with it.''

''The way I see it, you start with making them believe.''

''Believe in what?''

"In the project itself. A new wing for Memorial. Space for Pediatrics. And a day-care center. More medical and surgery beds. More *parking,* for heaven's sake."

"We've already got the extra parking."

"That too, then. You have to remind them how much of the project is already completed. That you're not starting from zero. You're...halfway there—and don't shake your head at me. Listen. I'm serious. You need to make it all real for them. Bring visual aids, maybe. A giant-sized model of the completed wing would be perfect. But if you can't manage that, how about some scale drawings, in color preferably? Can you get those?"

Grudgingly, he admitted, "I suppose."

"And some charts and graphs."

He groaned. "What? You want me to run them on an overhead?"

"It's a thought. But if that's too tacky for you, just get the lights low and get a spotlight on you and...inspire them."

"Inspire them. I don't feel very inspiring right now."

"Ryan Malone. Are you whining?"

"I do not whine."

"I'm so glad to hear that."

"And this wasn't supposed to be any big deal. It's just a simple little speech."

"You said you wanted my advice, and you're getting it. A simple little speech won't do it right now. You need...a good show. You want *drama.* You want to make them remember..."

"What?"

"The dream. The dream of what could have been.

What was supposed to be. What is actually halfway there. And what can *still* be, if only everyone, the whole community, will all pull together to get the project back on track.''

''You want me to do all this by tomorrow night?''

''I do. And I know you can.''

She kicked him out shortly after that. Sent him back to the other house to sit in his mostly unused study there, writing himself an outline for his presentation on a yellow legal pad.

In the end, he had to reject a lot of Ronni's suggestions as just too complicated. He couldn't collect a lot of materials and rehearse with them within the allotted time.

At seven in the morning, he called Murleen Anniston to tell her that he would need two screens, one on either side of the podium, as well as two slide projectors. Then he called Tanner, who said he could dig up the slides Ryan needed and also agreed to pinch-hit as projectionist.

''You'll need help setting up,'' Tanner added.

''I was hoping you'd say that. Meet me at the ballroom? One this afternoon?''

''I'll be there.''

Ryan made more calls. To a reporter he knew at the *Gazette* and a talk-show host for a local television show.

Right after lunch, he drove to the Honeygrove Golf and Country Club. There, in the club's ballroom, with the setup crew milling around them, he and Tanner enlisted the aid of a few harried auxiliary ladies to help them relocate some of the tables and put the projectors where they needed them.

Murleen Anniston had the screens ready, masked with red velvet curtains to be drawn by hand when the time was right. Tanner even managed to talk the busy workers into shutting the drapes across the high windows for a half an hour, so they could try a couple of run-throughs of dimming lights and raising curtains, followed by bringing up the single spot and the two projected slides slowly and smoothly.

By three, they had it all set up. Ryan went home, where he shut himself in his study, put a straight chair up on his desk to represent a podium and gave his new speech three times to the door across the room.

Drew was sitting at the foot of the stairs when Ryan came out of the study at five. "Dad? Who were you talking to in there?"

Ryan looked down at his son and thought what he always thought: that he needed to spend more time with him. The truth was, in the past few days, he'd barely seen the boy—or Griff or Lisbeth, either, for that matter.

"I was practicing the speech I have to give tonight."

"What kind of speech?" Before Ryan could frame an answer, more questions followed. "Is something wrong with your job or something? Grandma keeps saying you've got a lot on your mind. She always says that about you, but lately, it seems like she's saying it lots more than usual. And you've been gone so much. I mean, even more than you are most times. And Dad, in school, we have current events, you know? My whole class read in the paper about Mr. Pembroke and how he ran away with the money that Uncle Tanner was supposed to use to make the hospital bigger. I guess what I'm asking Dad is, what is going on?''

Ryan resisted the urge to glance at his watch. He knew what time it was. He also knew that he needed to explain a few things to his son. He probably should have done it before now. But late was better than not at all. ''Scoot over.''

Drew made a place for him on the step.

Ryan dropped down beside him and set about laying out a simplified version of the problems that had confronted him for the past several days.

At the end, Drew said, ''Dad, I want you to know. I will help you any way that I can.''

Ryan's first response was, There's really nothing you can do. But he knew that would sound patronizing. He said, ''Thank you, son.''

''And this ball you're going to, are you taking a girl?''

''Yes, I am.''

''Who?''

''I've asked Ronni and she said she'd go with me.''

''Ronni? Really?'' The look of pleasure on his son's face did Ryan's heart good. ''That's great. Ronni's cool.''

''Yes, I think so, too.''

''If you want to marry her, it's all right with me.''

''Well. I'll…bear that in mind.''

''I mean, you probably have to marry someone again someday, don't you?''

''I don't *have* to, no.''

''But, I mean, I think you should.''

''You do?''

''You seem…a little lonely to me, Dad. Like you

could use a good wife. And I think you should pick the right one. Someone who likes me and Lizzy and Griff. And Grandma, too. Ronni likes all of us, even if she is a little nervous around Grandma. Ronni would be a good choice. I really think she would."

"I'll bear that in mind."

"You already said that, Dad."

"Oh. Well. So I did."

That night, when Ronni and Ryan approached the towering red lacquer gate that marked the entrance to the ballroom, they were greeted by Murleen Anniston in a snug-fitting, very Chinese-looking creation of gold-embroidered red silk. The dress was not terribly flattering to a woman of Mrs. Anniston's generous proportions, but no one could say that the Heart Ball Committee chairwoman hadn't gone all out to capture the spirit of the evening. Even her coiffure fit the mood. It towered a foot above the top of her head, jet-black for the occasion, adorned with a crossed pair of gold chopsticks, Mylar streamers—and a rather astonishing number of small blue birds.

The chairwoman's husband, Dr. Clark Anniston, wearing a tux with a gold cummerbund, stood at her side.

"Welcome, welcome." Mrs. Anniston smiled and bowed in what she must have considered true Oriental fashion, as the guests approached the entrance after checking their wraps.

Ronni and Ryan smiled their hellos at the Annistons. Then they went through the gate and over the small arched, very Oriental-looking bridge just beyond it.

Inside the ballroom, the tables were set with red linen and gleaming black china. The chairs were gold brocade. The centerpieces, placed on black lacquer platforms, had been created of spread fans and Chinese vases filled with artfully twisted sticks and birds of paradise.

The twelve-piece orchestra in the corner was playing something atonal that made Ronni think of water rippling over smooth stones. Or perhaps she thought of water because there were six good-sized portable rock fountains burbling away in strategic spots along the walls, interspersed with papier mâché statues of scowling temple dogs, which had been skillfully spray-painted to look as if they were carved of jade.

Ronni and Ryan mingled for a while, moving between the tables, greeting people they saw every day in scrubs and lab coats, all of whom had dressed to the nines for the Heart Ball. Ryan introduced her to three of Memorial's most well-known couples: Katie and Mike Brennan, Dana and Trevor MacAllister, and Lee and Derek Taylor. Katie, Dana and Lee were all nurses—and lifelong friends. Mike, Trevor and Derek were M.D.s. Both Lee and Katie were pregnant—well into their third trimesters, Ronni judged. Ryan asked after Dana and Trevor's little girl. The proud parents beamed at him. They said the child ran their lives—and they wouldn't have it any other way.

All three handsome doctors looked so happy, so in love—and so pleased at the idea of having children in their lives. Ronni wondered how Ryan would feel if—

But then she quickly reminded herself not to borrow trouble. The slip-up they had made would probably come to nothing in the end.

A few minutes later, Ronni spotted Kelly Hall, standing over by a big brass gong next to the raised dais with the podium in the center—where Ryan, no doubt, would be giving his speech later. Kelly saw her, too, and signaled her over.

"This makes two times I've caught you with Ryan Malone," Kelly teased. "Is something going on I should know about?"

"Oh, I hope so."

"You should see your face."

"Dead giveaway, huh?"

"Nobody looks that happy—unless they're in love."

"It's all...very new."

"New or not," Kelly said wryly, leaning closer and pitching her voice low. "I hope you'll make use of those samples I gave you...when the time is right."

"I will." Ronni felt a slight twinge of conscience about the night before. But what was done was done. She added, speaking only for Kelly's ears, "The truth is, I *have* made use of them. And, now you mention it, I need an appointment."

"The pill?"

"Uh-huh."

"Call the office Monday. We'll get you in this week."

"Great."

"And I wish you both the best of everything."

Ronni murmured a ridiculously breathy "Thank you."

Kelly leaned closer still. "I heard about the problem with the new wing."

Ronni let her expression speak for her.

Kelly made a sympathetic sound. "Pretty bad, huh?"

"Awful. But he's working through it. He's a very determined man."

"I heard he's on the program tonight." Kelly raised a golden eyebrow. "'Look How Far We've Come'?"

Ronni squared her shoulders and put on a peppy smile. "Yep. Time to mobilize the troops."

Kelly laughed. "You do believe in him. That's a good thing."

Ronni could see him, about a hundred feet away, talking to another man who looked a lot like him, only thicker through the chest and shoulders, with midnight-black hair. "Oh, look. I think that's his brother, Tanner. Can you believe, I've never actually met him?"

"Well, you'll meet him tonight." Kelly's tone had changed. It sounded vaguely disapproving. "I'll bet he's feeling the pinch."

Ronni turned back to her friend. "Considering the situation he's in, having to shut the whole thing down after putting up a lot of money he may never get back, I'd say he seems to be holding up pretty well."

"My guess is he's just highly skilled at hiding whatever's going on inside." There it was again, that judgmental edge. Very unlike Kelly.

"You know Tanner, then?"

"I know *of* him, that's all."

"You sound as though what you know isn't good."

Kelly's usually direct gaze slid away, then back. "I'm sorry. That wasn't my intention. As I said, I don't know the man." Ronni saw a change of subject coming. That was fine with her. If Kelly did have something negative to say about Tanner, she didn't really want to hear it. He was Ryan's brother, and Ronni felt a certain automatic loyalty toward him.

Kelly asked, "So, how's progress on the condo?"

"The condo is coming along just fine. Of course, the paper-hanger hates me because I've gone geometric rather than floral. Floral patterns are *so* much easier to match on a wall."

"Oh, I'll just bet."

"And then there's the grout color I chose for the kitchen counter tiles." She pretended high drama. "I'm just agonized over that. Should I go darker? And should I or should I not have it sealed?"

"Big questions. When's your move-in date?"

"The first of March." Or it had been, until two nights ago. Now, with what was happening between her and Ryan, Ronni wasn't so sure. At this point, she couldn't even imagine moving out of the guest house—unless it was to move in with him.

And would she be doing that? Moving in with Ryan? *Marrying* Ryan?

Right now, she couldn't see her life going in any other direction.

But there was so much to consider. His demanding job. Her demanding job. The children. Lily.

Oh, God. Lily.

So many challenges. Too many to deal with all at once.

And really, she didn't need to deal with them all at once. It might feel to her as if she'd loved Ryan Malone forever. But she had to remember. It had only been two days. Two days since he'd come to her in the middle of the night, needing her, forcing her to admit to herself that she was in love.

Kelly was talking to her. She ordered her wandering mind to pay attention. "What was that?"

Kelly grinned. "You're about a light-year away."

"Just thinking."

Kelly chuckled. "Well, someone you like a lot is trying to get your attention."

Again Ronni glanced over to where Ryan stood with Tanner. She met Ryan's eyes—and experienced the loveliest sensation of mingled expectation and delight, just to look at him, to have him look back at her. Oh, she'd simply had no idea what she'd been missing all these years.

"Gotta go," she said to Kelly, then paused and suggested, "Want to join us?"

"No, I've got a date around here somewhere. I'd better go find him. They'll be serving up the chow mein before you know it. Through careful observation, I have deduced that the black lacquer platforms on the tables are actually lazy Susans. Looks like Chinese potluck to me. Do you think we'll get fortune cookies?"

"Only time will tell."

Ronni left Kelly and began working her way through the crowd to Ryan's side. He put his arm around her when she reached him. Lovely. It felt so lovely. A little slice of heaven, just to stand beside him, as his hand moved down to rest lightly at the small of her back.

"This is Ronni," he said, as if she were the most important person in the world.

Tanner Malone smiled at her, an easy smile, one Ronni imagined made him very popular with the ladies. "I've heard about you," Tanner said.

"All good things?"

"Absolutely."

She met Tanner's date, a woman who worked for the architectural firm that had been responsible for the design of the half-finished wing. Then Ryan led them all to their table, which wasn't far from the dais and the big brass gong where Ronni had been standing with Kelly a few minutes before.

"What'll you bet Murleen Anniston will beat on that thing?" Tanner muttered. "I've got a headache already just thinking about it."

"Have some tea," his date suggested. There was a big, steaming pot of the stuff waiting on the table.

There were also several uncorked bottles of wine. "I'll try some of this instead." Tanner poured himself a glass, then offered the bottle around.

Two other couples shared their table, members of Memorial's board of directors and their wives. Ryan introduced Ronni to them. She smiled and made small talk, thinking that both of the men seemed distracted, their wives slightly nervous.

But why wouldn't they be nervous? They'd probably already had to field a lot of questions tonight concerning the new wing. And they had to know that Ryan intended to get up in front of them all and address the subject directly.

Well, Ryan was going to set all their minds at

ease. Ronni felt absolutely certain of that. She couldn't have said exactly *why* she felt so positive. It was probably just blind devotion, something she wouldn't have understood in the least a few days ago. But now blind devotion made absolute sense to her.

She loved Ryan. She *believed* in him. He would work a miracle, and that was that.

A few minutes later, Murleen Anniston hit the big gong. The orchestra stopped playing.

"What did I tell you?" Tanner grumbled.

His date said, "Have some more wine."

He waved the bottle away. "No, thanks. Maybe later."

"Welcome, welcome." Mrs. Anniston beamed, repeating the same words she must have said hundreds of times already, back at the red gate in front of the ballroom doors. "It brings us a thousand delights to have you all here tonight for Honeygrove Memorial's Nineteenth Annual Heart Ball. We'll have a short program later—a few exciting talks about our hospital, about our plans for the future. And after that, dancing. Oh, and I do hope you'll all make time to drop in and bid on the silent auction in the Oak Room next door. But for now, please, enjoy the feast!" She hit the gong another time, good and hard.

The orchestra began playing again. Streams of waiters wearing black silk pajamas and little black slippers appeared at all the entrances, holding huge trays high. Each waiter stopped at a table, unfolded his tray base, balanced his tray on it and began shuffling the steaming bowls of Chinese delicacies to the black lacquer lazy Susans.

"White rice, spring roll, egg roll, Szechwan scallops, paper-wrap chicken, shrimp with lobster sauce, hot pepper pork..." The waiters named off each dish as they set them on the tables.

Ryan leaned close to her. "Hope you like Chinese." The warmth of his breath against her ear sent a sweet shiver down her spine.

"I love it." She picked up her black lacquer chopsticks and peeled them apart.

They spent an hour on the meal, as the orchestra played softly and the rock fountains burbled in the background. Ryan seemed relaxed. He talked easily with the board members and their wives, until soon enough, they, too, got into the spirit of the evening, spinning the lazy Susan, sampling the various dishes, saying yes to second glasses of wine.

One of the wives even got a bit tipsy. She seemed to consider herself something of an expert on the use of chopsticks. She announced that in China, the way one held the sticks defined social caste. The closer to the base, the lower on the social scale.

"Chinese aristocrats hold their chopsticks very near the top," she declared as she tried to pick up an egg roll and failed. The thing rolled off her plate and into her lap. She sighed. "Oh, dear..."

Her husband suggested rather sourly that maybe she ought to just use a fork. She shot him a wounded glance, picked up the wandering egg roll with her fingers and set it on her plate.

Right away, Ryan asked her about some project that she was apparently chairing for the auxiliary. She brightened instantly and launched into a description of how exciting and challenging she found it to do a job and do it well. "Worth the effort in personal satisfaction alone, that's the way I think of my volunteer work,'' the woman said.

The other wife unequivocally agreed and good cheer was once again established—thanks to Ryan.

At one point, he captured Ronni's hand, under the table where no one could see. He gave it a squeeze. She squeezed back. If only he did half as well with his upcoming speech as he did with his dinner companions, the evening would be an unqualified success.

Eventually, the black-clad waiters reentered. They took away the dinner plates and served an orange-ice confection sprinkled with red-dyed coconut. A fortune cookie garnished each dessert.

Everyone began cracking open the cookies, eager to read what the future might bring.

You will meet an important person who will help you advance professionally.

Your talents will be recognized and suitably rewarded.

Love is like a flower. It requires the water of attention to make it grow.

Ryan broke his cookie open last.

''What does yours say?'' asked one of the wives.

Before he could answer, Murleen Anniston got up and banged the gong again. The lively chatter in the big room faded to an expectant hush.

The chairwoman mounted the dais and moved behind the podium. The chandeliers dimmed and a spot came up. Light winking off the Mylar streamers on her headdress, she began to tell them all of the good they had done by the large checks they'd written for the privilege of attending this event.

People who needed expensive treatments and

couldn't afford them would have their care paid for. State-of-the-art equipment would be purchased. Home nursing would be provided for many elderly people who didn't require hospitalization but needed medical assistance nonetheless.

Mrs. Anniston introduced two more speakers. One described the new physical therapy equipment, which receipts from the Heart Ball would provide. The other went into a rather lengthy explanation of the various volunteer programs that the Friends of Memorial's efforts helped to fund.

When the chairwoman took the podium for the second time, Ryan snared Ronni's hand again under the table. "This is it. Wish me luck."

"I do. Though you don't need it. You're going to do us all proud."

Tanner pushed back his chair. "That's my cue," he whispered. "I'm the technical crew." He left them.

Up behind the podium, Murleen Anniston drew in a deep breath. "And now, we come to a very important part of our program. None of us can help but be aware of the upsetting events that have transpired in the past week concerning our hospital's new wing."

As she spoke, four women in evening dress mounted the steps to the dais. Two went left and two went right. Slowly and carefully, they pulled back two sets of red velvet curtains and anchored them to the side. Beneath were twin white screens.

Murleen Anniston continued, "As I mentioned earlier, it has been nineteen years since our first annual Heart Ball. The year of the first ball, our hospital had just moved to its present site. Before that, as many of you may remember, Honeygrove Memorial was called Honeygrove General and housed in that ancient brick monstrosity over on Willamette Way, which has since become a museum. It is our hope that by next year, our twentieth Heart Ball, we will be aiming our auxiliary efforts at Honeygrove's children, who will find the care and comfort they need in our expanded ability to serve the ill and infirm. I speak of Pediatrics, ladies and gentlemen, which is to be a major part of our new twenty-year wing.

"Recent events put our efforts in jeopardy. And our chief administrator, Ryan Malone, is here tonight to speak to us all about what's been done—and what we need to do—to get this important project back on track. Let's give him a warm welcome. Ladies and gentlemen, our own Ryan Malone..."

Polite applause filled the room. The lights, including the spot on Murleen Anniston, dimmed to black as Ryan slipped out of the chair at Ronni's side.

Slowly, twin images took form on the white screens. On one side, a photograph of Memorial as it stood right then, including the half-finished new wing. A raw-looking projection off the east side of the original structure, the new wing was a naked two stories of unpainted, preformed concrete slabs and glass.

The other screen revealed an artist's rendering of Memorial as it was supposed to look seven months hence, when the finished new wing would blend right in with what was already there. The rendering showed a new front entrance, complete with a canopied projection that drew the eye and brought everything together. The entire structure had been re-painted. Now the whole thing was a salmon-accented dove gray. A beautiful roof garden topped the new wing, greenery spilling over the walls, soft-ening all that concrete, making the whole massive structure look alive and inviting.

The polite applause hit its modest peak and began to fade as the spotlight came up on the podium once more. Ryan waited there. He looked out over the ballroom, saying nothing at first, as the applause died to silence. Two bright flashes went off—mean-ing photographers in the audience. Perhaps from the *Gazette,* Ronni thought.

Ryan began quietly, his low, rich voice amplified to perfection, filling every corner of the hushed, shadowed room.

"Thirty-four years ago, on a winter night much like this one, a man and a woman were hurrying home to their children after an emergency visit to a sick relative in the Bay Area. Their car hit a patch of black ice, spun out of control and into a concrete piling. Both the man and the woman died within minutes of the crash. They never got home to the three..." he faltered, coughed. Ronni's heart froze in her chest.

But then he smiled, that wonderful, unwilling smile of his. "Excuse me. Make that two. Two young sons. That couple never got home to the two young sons who were waiting for them.

"Until their parents were killed, those boys had everything. A loving home. Two people dedicated to the job of seeing them to adulthood. But then, their world changed.

"No family members stepped forward to claim

those two boys. No one adopted them. They were raised by the state, and in foster care—with all the odds stacked against them, a lot of people might say.

"Yet, today, one of them runs his own construction company. And the other is the chief administrator of *your* hospital: Honeygrove Memorial."

Ryan paused, let that sink in.

Then he continued, "Those two boys—myself and my brother—are living proof that no one—*no one*—can predict what will be. Those boys floundered, they failed sometimes. They often felt very much alone.

"But they weren't alone. Helping hands were extended, the state did provide for them. And both of them received Pembroke scholarships, money to go on to college, provided by the very organization that is so much in trouble now."

He paused again, looked out over the ballroom, his eyes seeming to connect with every person there.

He went on, "What I want you to understand tonight, if you believe nothing else, is that, though the odds do seem stacked against us right now, we *can* still build our new twenty-year wing. You see behind me—" he gestured with a sweep of his right arm "—how far we've come. We are halfway there, ladies and gentlemen. Construction is halted now. We need to get going again. We need to mobilize the press and the various branches of the media in our favor." He smiled again. "Are you out there, ladies and gentlemen of the press? I hope so. Right now, you're reporting a scandal. We want more out of you. We need you focused on the future, on the forty million dollars we plan to raise.

"We have ten million, from our community fund,

which was originally intended for later use. We think within the next few weeks we'll be able to rechannel that money. We'll get construction moving again. But we'll need more. Much more. We'll need a massive fund-raising drive—and I do hope I can count on all you ladies from the auxiliary to work with me on that.''

There was a smattering of applause. Ryan said, ''Good. And I will be exploring a number of other avenues. There *are* state and federal monies to be had. We just have to contact the right agencies and fill out the right forms. The people from the Pembroke Foundation are working night and day to try to get us at least some of the money they originally promised us. And other charitable institutions are being approached.''

He gestured with his left hand. ''This is what we can have, by September, in time for the twentieth anniversary of Honeygrove Memorial as we know it now.

''Our community needs to see this project completed. This is the new millennium. Projected population growth in our city is astounding in the next decade. Children's Hospital is overburdened. When we're providing pediatric care ourselves, we can take on some of that load. We need more medical and surgery beds, and our new wing will have them. More services, and *better* services, for the people of Honeygrove. With your help, and the help of the whole community, we can get there. We can do it.

''The worst may have happened. We've been orphaned. We've lost what we thought we could count on, and it's been a crushing blow. But we are not beaten. The future is not set. And here, tonight, I know, are many of the people who will see us through this rough time. My door is open, at Memorial. Come and see me, or pick up the phone and give me a call. I want to hear your ideas. And yes, I want you and everyone you know to get out your checkbooks. Again.'' A ripple of laughter went through the room. ''I see you know just what I mean. I will do what I have to do, to bring us through this tough period and on to success. But I cannot do it alone.'' He looked down at the podium, seemed to gather himself, then lifted his dark head to face them all once more.

''Ladies and gentlemen, look how far we've come. And look where we're going. It won't be easy, but we will get there. I'm not a man who believes in what fortune cookies tell me. But tonight, mine said, 'Being faithful to a trust brings its own reward.' I'm going to choose to believe that. I'm going to make a promise to you. And you're going to help me keep it, just as this community helped my brother and me to grow up, to forge productive lives, after our parents were lost to us.

''We will succeed.

''And in September of this year, the Friends of Memorial will throw a party as terrific as this one. A party where we will celebrate the completion of Honeygrove Memorial's twenty-year wing.

''We can do this. And I promise you. We will.''

Ryan said no more. There was a huge and echoing silence.

And then the slow, building roar of deafening applause.

Chapter Ten

The *Gazette* ran a recap of Ryan's speech in its Sunday edition the next day, complete with nice, big color photos and a notice in bold print explaining where to send donations. On Monday, Ryan went on the local six o'clock news to explain to the community at large about the major fund-raising drive they were mounting. He also did two guest spots on radio during the week. Beyond that, he accepted invitations to speak to the Elks, the Masons, the Knights of Columbus, the University Boosters, Catholic Daughters and the ladies of the Eastern Star.

And his door *was* always open. If he wasn't in a meeting or giving a speech, he was answering phone calls or welcoming visitors who knew of this or that avenue for funding they wanted him to be sure to explore.

Ronni never saw him until late at night. But she had her own work to keep her good and busy. Yes, once or twice, she found herself thinking wistfully that she would like just a little more time with the man she loved.

They had so many things to talk about—where they were going together, the children, the problem with Lily, how to mesh their mutually complicated lives. But by the time he would come to her, at the late-night end of an inevitably exhausting day, he would want to make love. And so would she. And then, after that, well, she couldn't really blame him for falling asleep in her arms. Most of the time, she fell asleep right along with him, only to be wakened by the alarm at four, to watch him gather his scattered clothes and pull them on. Then he'd bend over her. She would kiss him a drowsy goodbye and he would slip away, back to his own house. His own bed.

They hadn't even shared words of love yet. They were just getting through each day now, holding on to each other whenever they could. Everything had happened so fast between them. And right now he carried an enormous burden, trying to pull off a miracle and save his hospital's new wing.

Also, she sensed that he felt the same reserve she did. When the words *were* said, Ronni wanted them to be...leisurely. Special. She wanted a candlelit dinner and roses on the table, soft music playing in the background. And then, as they talked and kissed and laughed together, on an evening when, for once, hours stretched out before them, she would tell him, "I love you."

And he would say he loved her, too.

On Thursday of that week, Ronni went to Kelly Hall's office. She took a routine pregnancy test, a required procedure for any patient seeking birth control. The test came out negative. Of course, Ronni knew that if she were pregnant, it wouldn't be likely to show up in a test yet. Like a home test, the office urine test worked by detecting the hormone HCG, which became present in the urine of a pregnant woman about two weeks after conception. Only six days had passed since the night she and Ryan had made that dangerous mistake.

Kelly went over her medical history with her and then began the physical exam.

"Sensitive?" Kelly asked when Ronni grimaced as Kelly gently prodded her left breast in the familiar circular pattern.

"A little."

"Period due...when?"

They'd just gone over Ronni's history. And the date of the start of her last period had been included.

"Not for another week or so yet," Kelly said, answering her own question. "Hm..."

Ronni jumped to explain the sensitivity away. "Maybe it's coming a little early this month."

"I thought your periods were normally quite regular."

"They are. But we both know there are any number of reasons for sensitive breasts."

"Foremost among them, imminent menstruation...and pregnancy. Lower that arm, and raise the other one. That's good."

Ronni looked down at her friend's slender, capable fingers as they moved gently around the slope of her right breast.

That one was tender, too. Kelly glanced at her face when she winced.

"All right," Ronni confessed. "We had unprotected sex. One time. Last week."

"Put your arm down." Kelly helped Ronni to rearrange her paper gown so that it covered her breasts again. "Put your feet up now." Kelly performed the pelvic exam, which both women knew would be unlikely to reveal signs of pregnancy right then.

"Everything looks fine," Kelly said when she was done. "We'll have the results of the Pap smear in a day or two."

Ronni knew the drill, of course. She wouldn't hear anything about the Pap smear results unless abnormalities showed up.

Kelly peeled off her latex gloves and dropped them into the trash. Then she walked around the examining couch to stand by Ronni's shoulder. She put her hand on Ronni's arm. Ronni recognized the touch: a doctor's touch, meant to soothe, to reassure. It felt just a little strange, to be on the receiving end of such a touch this time.

Ronni let out a hard breath and said what she was thinking. "Pretty stupid, huh? *Incredibly* stupid. And me an M.D. Someone who should know better."

Kelly's eyes were so kind. They didn't judge at all. They really did seem to understand. "It happens." Her voice was low, warm. A little sad. "And even an M.D. is human, you know. Like everyone else, sometimes we're just not as careful as we ought to be—and let's not jump to conclusions." She spoke more briskly. "The only symptom we have right now is breast sensitivity. It could very well be a false alarm. I can run a serum test if you want me to, right now. We get virtually one hundred percent accuracy a week after conception on those—barring lab error, of course.''

"No," Ronni said. "It's all right." She didn't need to know this minute. She wasn't even sure she *wanted* to know right now.

"Okay," Kelly agreed. "Wait another two weeks. We'll run the serum test then—or you can take a home test, if your period doesn't start when it's due. A positive result on a home test after a missed period is just about as accurate as the serum test.''

Pregnant, Ronni thought. *I could be pregnant....*

Now, that would add a whole new dimension to an already extremely challenging situation.

Not that she didn't want to bear a child. Someday. But right now?

She *had* three children to deal with already. Ryan's children.

And then there was Lily. And two time-consuming careers.

So much to work through.

Too much to work through, to be honest.

And then to add pregnancy. A new baby...

It made her palms sweat and her head spin. "Oh, God, Kel. It would be...a truly tough time to have a baby. I can't believe this. I don't *want* to believe this.''

"Hey. Slow down. You won't know for a week or two, at least. And nothing has to be dealt with today. It's quite likely that you're not pregnant, after all. And if you are, there will be options.''

"You're right." Ronni sat up. "I'm not going to start worrying about this now. There is no point."

"Smart thinking." Kelly patted Ronni's shoulder. "Go ahead and get dressed. And I'll go write you up a script for Ovral. You can start taking them on the fifth day after the onset of your next menstrual period."

My next menstrual period...

Please God, let it show up right on schedule: a week from tomorrow, Friday, the twenty-fifth...

She decided not to tell Ryan. Not yet. Not until she found out for certain either way.

He had enough on his mind. There was no reason to worry him with this, too—especially if it turned out to be a false alarm.

That night, when he came to her, she behaved no differently than the other nights. She opened her arms to him. They made love—safely, using a condom.

And when he fell into an exhausted sleep, she held him close, felt his heart beating against her own, and told herself that everything was going to work out just fine.

The next day, Friday, Ronni got home early for once. She pulled into the driveway at a little after five. By five-thirty, she'd thrown on a big sweater and some jeans. She was staring into the freezer, trying to decide which Marie Callendar delicacy to call dinner when the doorbell chimed.

It was Drew, standing on the front step with his hands stuffed in the pockets of a red-and-black bomber jacket, his cute nose red from the cold.

"Ronni, I really need to talk to you, and since you never come over to see us, I decided I better come and see you."

Kids, she thought with the usual admiring amusement. They always faced directly what adults tried to sidle around. She did need to make more of an effort to get together with the children, to get to know them better, to start getting them accustomed to the idea of having her in their day-to-day lives. But she knew that Lily would resist her efforts. And she'd been putting off forcing the issue, hiding behind her own busy schedule, telling herself she'd stop in at the main house one of these days very soon.

Drew shivered and hunched up his shoulders. "Ronni. It's *cold* out here." His breath plumed on the air.

She stepped back. "You'd better come in then, hadn't you?" She led him to the kitchen, where he took off his jacket and hung it neatly over the back of a chair.

Then he sat down and looked around. "I guess you have to start cooking soon, huh?"

"As a matter of fact, I was just looking in the freezer, trying to decide what to have."

"Grandma's making a roast. With mashed potatoes and carrots. You like roast?"

"Roast is great. Did you tell your grandma that you were coming over here?"

A frown. "Oh. No. I forgot. I'd better call her, huh?"

She gestured at the phone on the wall by the sink. He went to it and dialed. "It's ringing," he said after a moment, then, "Grandma? It's me." He listened. "Well," he said, "that's what I called for, so you would know where I am. I'm over at Ronni's. I'll be back in a little while.... No, it's okay. Ronni doesn't mind." He put the mouthpiece under his chin and asked seriously, "Am I bothering you?"

"No, not at all."

"Did you hear that, Grandma? She said, no, not at all.... Yeah, okay. I won't stay very long. And you know what? Ronni hasn't had dinner yet, and she really likes roast." Ronni tried not to cringe as he asked, "Can I invite her?" He listened some more, then instructed, "Hold on." He spoke to Ronni. "She says you're too busy to come over and you have lots of things to do."

Poor Lily, Ronni thought with a moderate degree of irony. Forced into a corner by a clever nine-year-old. Ronni felt a little sorry for her.

But not that sorry.

"Here, let me talk to her." Ronni held out her hand. Drew passed her the phone. "Hi, Lily."

Lily's reply was cautiously polite. "Hello. How are you?"

"I'm just fine. And you?"

"Fine."

"Good. And thank you so much for inviting me. I would love to come. We'll be over in a few minutes. How's that?"

"Oh, well, I—"

"Did you need to talk to Drew again?"

"I don't...no. No, that won't be necessary."

"Is there anything you'd like me to bring?"

"No. No, there's nothing."

"See you in a few minutes, then."

"Yes, all right..."

Ronni hung the phone back on the wall. Drew had already plunked himself down in the chair again and was sitting with his legs spread, his hands gripping the edge of the chair between his knees. He grinned. "She'll get used to you. Eventually."

"Well. That's really good to know."

The grin faded. "She still misses my mom."

Ronni spoke softly—and honestly. "I'll bet you do, too."

"Yeah." He shrugged, looked down at his hands. "But my mom is gone, you know?"

"It's…one of the hardest things, I think, to lose your mom. I lost mine when I was seven."

He looked up again, his eyes wary and hopeful at the same time. "Your mom died, like mine?"

"Uh-huh."

"What about your dad?"

"He died a few years ago."

"But after you were all grown-up, right?"

"Yes."

"My dad lost both of them—his mom *and* his dad—when he was real little."

"I know. He told me."

"We've got a lot of lost moms around here, Ronni."

She'd never really thought of it that way, but Drew was right. "We certainly do."

"You did okay, without your mom, didn't you?"

"Yes. But I missed her a lot."

"And my dad did okay."

"Yes, he did. He did wonderfully."

Drew put his weight forward onto his hands, then rocked back. "So do you want to know what I had to talk to you about?"

"Yes, I do. Very much."

"It's about helping my dad. To raise the money he needs for the hospital." His hair had fallen over his forehead. She couldn't resist. She moved forward, reached out, brushed it back from his face. He let her do that, but then demanded, "Are you listening to me, Ronni?"

She slid into the chair opposite him, thinking, *If Ryan and I had a child, could he possibly be as wonderful as this one?*

"Ronni, you look funny. Are you gonna *cry?*"

"Of course not."

"Then are you listening?"

"I am."

"I've already talked to the principal at my school. She says they don't allow fund-raising there, except to bring in money for school things, you know?"

Ronni nodded.

"So I've been trying to think of something I could do, you know, to help? Something that can't be at school. I thought about selling lemonade and those bake-sale things and car washes. The high school kids do car washes a lot. But people don't want lemonade in the winter. And I'm not in high school. And how would I get all the stuff to make cookies? I mean, it's a problem that I'm only nine."

Ronni really wanted to grab him and hug him. But she didn't. She knew this was serious business. "Yes, I see what you mean."

"And I want to *help* my dad, not bother him. I don't even want him to know what I'm doing until it's all done. I want to go out and get the money. Lots of money. Maybe a hundred dollars or something. And then I want to just give it to him. I want it to be a surprise. You know?''

''I do. Yes, I understand perfectly.''

''But Ronni, I have to admit. I'm gonna need an adult to help me with this. And Grandma has to watch Griff and Lizzy. I know you're real busy, taking care of sick kids and all, but you have some time Saturdays, don't you? And Sundays?''

She admitted, ''Yes, I do.''

''Well good, 'cause I was thinking. I bet we could get a table and set it up outside the Superserve Mart. They let people do that. For Girl Scout cookies and Jerry's Kids and stuff like that. We could sit out there. And we could talk to people, just a couple hours, you know, on Saturdays and Sundays? You could wear one of those white coats.''

''A lab coat?''

''Yeah. So they would know you're a doctor. You could even wear that thing around your neck.''

''My stethoscope…''

''Yeah. A stethoscope. And you wouldn't have to do that much, I promise. Just *be* there. I would stand by the big glass doors and catch the people while they were going in and out. And I would tell them about the new wing and how we really need money and they could just give a dollar or even fifty cents if they wanted to. We could have a big glass jar for that, you know? Or if they want to write a check, they can do that, too. I copied the stuff from the paper, about what to write on the check when you make a donation.'' He stopped, dragged in a breath and looked at her with burning eyes. ''Ronni, don't tell me it's a dumb idea. Don't tell me I'm a kid and not to worry about it. Just tell me you'll help me and you won't tell my dad.''

She stared at him. He had never looked so much like a miniature version of his father as he did at that moment.

''Ronni, will you do it?''

''Have you told your grandmother about this?''

He bounced impatiently in the chair. ''No, not yet. I was waiting. To talk to you first.''

''I see.''

''I just want to know. Will you help me or not?''

''I would have talk to your grandmother first, to get her okay.''

''I know. I said that. We could talk to her tonight.''

''It's going to be cold,'' she warned, ''sitting out in front of the Superserve Mart in February, and it'll probably rain.''

''So? We'll wear jackets.''

''And it's not always easy, asking people for money. Sometimes they're rude. And most of the time they say no.''

''But sometimes they say yes. And that's what I'll think about. Making them say yes. I'll tell them it's only fifty cents or a dollar. Or even a quarter. If they can just give a quarter, that will be great. And if they say no, I'll tell them thank you, anyway.''

She couldn't keep herself from smiling. ''It sounds like you've given this a great deal of thought.''

''I have. Say yes, Ronni. Please.''

''Let's talk to your grandma and see what she says.''

"That means yes, if Grandma says it's okay, right?"

Ronni hid her smile. "No, you don't. We talk to your grandmother, see what she says, *then* I'll make my decision."

"Oh, all right—and we can't tell her in front of Griff or Lizzy."

"We can't?"

"No, because then they might say something to my dad, and that would ruin everything. We'll have to wait till after dinner. We'll let them watch *Aladdin,* or something. And then you, me and Grandma will talk."

Lily was cool but polite through dinner. She asked Ronni twice how her condo was coming along. The message seemed pretty clear to Ronni: *When will it be finished so you can move there and away from my son-in-law?*

Ronni resolutely took Lily's questions at face value. She joked about her troubles with the paper-hanger and her current quandary over window treatments.

"I think I'll end up going with wood blinds throughout. They're simple and attractive, and they even have some insulation value, I understand."

Lily allowed stiffly, "With the right valance, a wood blind can be very nice."

"I think I'll skip valances. They have that little carved strip at the top. That's enough for me."

With precise movements, Lily cut herself another bite of roast. "Well, as long as you choose what you like. After all, you do live alone. So you've no one to please but yourself."

Ronni sipped from her water glass, thinking, *Lily, we do need to talk.*

But what would she say?

I won't be living alone for long, Lily. Ryan and I...

What?

We haven't actually discussed our plans yet, but we are *in love and...*

No. That wouldn't work. She couldn't say much at all to Lily until she and Ryan had figured a few things out. He was the one she needed to talk to.

And in spite of all the pressure he was under, they really ought to find the time to do that soon.

Within a week or two, they might *have* to find the time. If she took that second test and it came out positive.

"Are you awright, Ronni?" Lisbeth was staring at her.

"I'm fine, honey."

"You look funny. Kind of sick."

"Well, I'm not. Honestly."

Lily warned sharply, "Eat your carrots, Lisbeth."

Lisbeth made a face, but then dutifully speared a slice of carrot on the end of her fork.

After the meal, all three children helped to clear the table. As Ronni watched little Griff scrape his plate and set it carefully on the drain board, she couldn't help but admire the job Lily was doing. Ryan's children had lost their mother and didn't spend enough time with their father. Still, all three of them seemed happy, full of enthusiasm and reasonably well-behaved—because of their grandmother, who provided consistency and stability, not to mention love and support. A full-time, attentive caregiver meant a lot to a young child.

How happy would those children be if their grandmother moved out? If they had a too-busy father and a doctor for a stepmother and they ended up in day care until seven or eight at night?

How happy would a newborn baby be, in the same situation?

They weren't easy questions to consider.

But they might *have* to be considered, if—

No. Ronni said to herself. Stop this. Take a page from the twelve-step programs: one day at a time.

She picked up Griffin's plate, rinsed it and put it in the dishwasher.

"You don't have to do that," Lily said.

"I don't mind, really."

Drew said, "Time for a movie."

"Yeah!" Griffin exclaimed. "*Lion King,* yeah!"

"No, I want *Aladdin,*" said Lisbeth.

"Lion King!"

"Aladdin."

Lily cut in. "Children. Stop bickering. Or it will be bath time right now."

"I have an idea," said Drew in a voice clearly intended to entice. "How about *Land Before Time, Part Two?*"

Griffin wrinkled up his nose—then grinned. "Yeah!"

Lisbeth gave in, too. "Oh, all right."

Drew led the younger ones into the other room, leaving Lily and Ronni alone. Ronni began rinsing another plate.

Lily looked on. As Ronni bent to prop the plate in the dishwasher's lower rack, she slid Ryan's mother-in-law an oblique glance—a glance she immediately regretted. The older woman's expression was far from friendly.

"I really couldn't tell you what time Ryan will be home tonight." As she spoke, Lily edged in at the sink, elbowing Ronni aside.

With a sigh, Ronni reached for a towel, dried her hands and tried to decide how to reply to that remark, given that any second now, Drew would be popping back in to pitch his grandmother his fundraising scheme.

"Lily." Ronni spoke low, taking care that her words wouldn't carry to the other room. "It so happens I didn't come here tonight to see Ryan." Lily made a little harrumphing sound as she grabbed a handful of flatware. Ronni made herself go on. "Although I do care for him. Deeply."

Lily turned on Ronni, the flatware still clutched in her hand, fork prongs and knife points out. "I trust you'll inform me, if any…important decisions are made?"

"Well, of course. We—"

"Then, fine. Until that happens, I really don't think what goes on between you and my son-in-law is any of my concern." She turned back to the sink.

"But, Lily—"

"Shh. Drew."

Ronni glanced toward the door to the family room. Sure enough. There he was, wearing a big, nervous smile. "You're whispering. Did you tell her already?"

Lily dropped the flatware into the basket, pushed in the rack and firmly shut the dishwasher door. "Tell me what?" She was scowling.

Drew's eyes widened. He looked askance at his grandmother, then turned to Ronni again. "She's mad?"

Lily made another of those harrumphing sounds. "I am not mad, young man. And haven't I taught you that it's rude to speak of others as though they weren't in the room?"

Drew stubbed the floor with his shoe. "Sorry. Sheesh."

Ronni rushed into the breach. "Lily. Drew has something important to talk to you about."

Lily was drying her hands. "What?" She hung the towel back on the rack.

Ronni smiled encouragingly at Drew. "Go on. Tell her what you told me."

Lily looked more closely at her grandson. Her pinched expression softened. "Something important, is it?"

Drew chewed his lower lip and nodded.

Lily sighed. "Come on. Let's sit down." The three of them pulled out chairs and settled in at the big breakfast table. "Now," Lily said, "tell me what's on your mind, Andrew."

Drew launched into the same spiel he'd given Ronni at the guest house. Lily let him say it all without interrupting. When he was finished, she looked at Ronni. "Have you told Drew you would help him, then?"

"I told him we would talk to you, get your opinion—and then I'd decide."

"So, you'll help him if I give the okay?"

"Yes, I'd be proud to."

"But how will you realistically find the time for it?"

"As Drew pointed out, I do have some time on the weekends. And that's when he wants to do it. I can manage."

"You're sure?"

Ronni couldn't help but admire Lily right then. In spite of the older woman's exasperating determination to keep Ronni at a distance, she could still see the value of her grandson's proposal. She wanted him to have the satisfaction of doing this thing.

"I'm positive," Ronni said. "And I'll be willing to contact Superserve Mart to get their permission to set up a table. And I'll call around. I'm sure we can find some posters and official-looking donation jars to put on the table."

"This is...very good of you," Lily said.

"Grandma." Drew was squirming in his chair. "Come on. Please say yes."

And Lily said, "All right. It's a lovely idea and I'm proud of you for wanting to do it."

It was after eleven when Ryan came to Ronni that night. The little house was dark.

He let himself in with a spare key. They were past the point where she expected him to knock.

He locked the door behind himself and she called to him in a sleepy whisper from the bed. "Ryan?"

He stalked across the carpet, taking off his clothes as he went. When he reached the bedside, he finished undressing, tossed everything toward the corner chair and slid in beside her.

He gathered her close. She was so warm and soft and she smelled of soap and that special light fragrance she always wore. She shivered at the contact with his cooler skin. "Brr..."

''Warm me up.''

She cuddled closer. He felt her breasts, the taut peaks brushing his chest. She slipped a leg between his. The endless chain of meetings he'd held that day, the speech that night at the Lions Club, all of it seemed blessedly far away right then.

That past week, he'd driven himself like a man possessed. He kept his attitude positive, his mind open and his eyes on the prize. He had made a promise to see the damn wing to completion by September. He would keep that promise or kill himself trying.

Every waking moment was spent focused on the job he had to do.

Except when he was here with Ronni.

With Ronni, for a few brief hours, he didn't have to do anything but feel, but touch and be touched. He didn't have to listen.

And he didn't have to hear himself talk.

She was his haven. Whenever he started thinking that he couldn't sit still for one more money-raising suggestion or get up in front of one more group and announce enthusiastically, ''Look how far we've come....'' Whenever it all seemed impossible, he would think of her. Of her cradling arms and tender kisses, of her wise and understanding eyes.

He tipped her chin up and kissed her. She sighed.

He ran his hand down over the silky curve of her back, cupped her bottom and pulled her up tight. He was hard, aching for her.

She moaned. He deepened the kiss, trailing his hand over the curve of her hip, seeking the sweet secrets between her slim thighs.

She murmured his name again as he touched her,

pushing her hips up toward him, offering him all that he longed for, all he that needed: an explosion of pure sensation. Total release. And then peace.

A little later, she tried to talk to him. Something about Lily. She'd had dinner over at the main house. Roast beef, she said.

"That's nice," he muttered. Sleep was pulling him down.

"Ryan, about Lily..."

"Um?"

"She's not...happy, about you and me. She resents me, and I think it's really something you and I should... Ryan? Are you listening?"

He smoothed her hair.

"You're going to sleep, aren't you?"

"So tired..."

"Ryan?"

He forced his eyes open, squinted at her through the darkness. "Um? What? About Lily...?"

She was still for a moment. Then she kissed his shoulder. "Never mind. Go to sleep."

His eyelids drooped again. He knew that he should keep them open, that they did have to talk about Lily. They had to talk about so many things.

Talk. That was all he did all day....

Talk, talk, talk, talk.

"I know," he heard himself whisper. "We have to talk...."

And she whispered back, "It's all right. We will. Later. You go on to sleep."

Sleep. A beautiful word.

He smiled and gave up the effort to keep his eyes open.

Chapter Eleven

The next day, Ronni contacted Superserve Mart and got permission to set up a table near their front doors. From her office, she called Maggie Mac-Allister, whom Marty Heber had said might be able to help her find the materials she and Drew needed. Maggie met her at Children's Hospital at one and gave her three big Save Our New Wing jars, a couple of "official fund-raiser" lapel pins and two stand-up posters.

At three that afternoon, she and Drew were all set up in front of the store, shivering in their heavy jackets. By five, when they closed up shop, Drew had become adorably adroit at marching up to perfect strangers and asking them for "Just a dollar, or fifty cents, or a quarter. We can really use whatever you can give...."

They raised forty-eight dollars and twenty-seven

cents. Drew was ecstatic. They drove home at five and he chattered the whole way.

"If we do that every time," he said, "every Saturday and Sunday, that's..." Ronni took her gaze off the road long enough to cast him a glance. He was frowning, fiercely calculating. "Forty-eight and forty-eight. Ninety-six. Ninety-six dollars and fifty-four cents a week. Wow. Almost a hundred dollars a *week*, Ronni! In a month, we could have five hundred. And in two months, we might get a *thousand!* Jeez, if we could get a thousand! Wouldn't Dad be proud of us?"

She was feeling that urge to hug him again. "Oh, yes, he *will* be. Very proud."

"This is somethin', Ronni. This rules. And I really think it helped to have a real doctor there, even though it was kinda hard to see your lab coat under your big jacket. But I think they could see the stethoscope."

"Oh, yes. I'm sure the stethoscope worked wonders. But the most important element was you."

"It was?"

"Yep. You were...indefatigable."

"I was?"

"Uh-huh."

"Uh...what's indefa...you know."

"Indefatigable. That means untiring. You knew what you had to do and you did it. Without slowing down or acting tired. For two whole hours."

"Indefatigable." Drew savored the word. "Never getting tired. That's how you just have to be sometimes. Like my dad."

Like my dad...

A small, tight band of wistfulness seemed to wrap

around Ronni's heart. She remembered the night before, how desperate and hungry Ryan's kisses had been—and how total his exhaustion later. He was driving himself so hard now—too hard, really. Every day, he worked until he had nothing left to give.

It wouldn't always be this way. She knew that. But still, she was starting to worry about him a little, even to worry about the two of them, about how in the world they would move on from here. Now that he was so driven to keep his promise about the new wing, it seemed they never talked anymore. He came to her so late. They made love. And they stole a few hours of sleep. She hungered for nights like those first ones again, when they had talked and laughed for hours on end.

At the same time, she understood that it would be unfair to push him too much to open up to her now. She really had to be patient, to let him get through this.

There would be time, in the future, to say the things that needed saying. She had to remember that.

And what if you're pregnant? a harsh mental voice demanded. *You're going to have to do a little pushing, then.*

"Ronni?"

She ordered the nagging worry to leave her alone. "Hmm?"

"You better keep all our stuff—and the money— at the little house, where Dad won't see it."

"All right." The card table they'd used was hers, anyway. And the rest, she could stick in the back of the bedroom closet. Ryan would be unlikely to look in there.

Drew let out a long whoosh of a breath. "Tomorrow, I hope we make as much as today—or even more."

"Me, too."

"I wish we could set up the table on Monday."

"That's a no-go, and you know it. I have to work. And correct me if I'm wrong, but I believe you have school."

"Well, I was just wishing, you know?"

"Wishing. Yes, I do know."

"Ronni?"

"Yes?"

"You rule."

She glanced over, smiled at him, felt a flush of pleasure at such high praise. "Thank you."

"I hope you and my dad get married, Ronni."

Her throat felt tight. She swallowed—and swung her gaze back to the road before she got them in an accident.

"Did you hear me, Ronni?"

"Yes, I did."

"*Are* you and my dad getting married?"

"I…hope so."

"Did he ask you yet?"

"Drew, this is something that…"

"What?"

"Something that your father and I have to talk about ourselves, before we can talk about it with you."

"Well, *when* will you talk about it?"

I wish I knew. "Drew…"

"Oh, all right. I get the message. I'm being annoying."

She smiled at that. "Not annoying so much.

You're just...asking questions I can't answer right now.''

He was silent, then he said, ''Ronni?''

''What?''

''I still think you rule.''

The next day, it rained. Ronni sat at the card table, huddled in her trench coat under the overhang in front of the supermarket as Drew approached one shopper after another. People seemed more impatient than they had the day before, in more of a hurry. No one seemed to want to linger out in the rain long enough to pull some change from a pocket and toss it in the jar for a good cause. But Drew didn't give up. When they counted the take at five, they had thirty-seven dollars and nine cents.

''Not as good as yesterday,'' Drew said, looking a little glum.

''Hey, it's thirty-seven dollars and nine cents more than you would have had if we hadn't come out here at all.''

Drew brightened a little and agreed that was so.

By the time they got home, the rain had stopped. Ronni made a point to drop in at the main house for a few minutes. They found Lily in the kitchen at the counter, several bundles of cut flowers spread out on newspaper in front of her and a row of crystal vases waiting to be filled nearby.

''Hi, Grandma, we're home!'' Drew headed straight for the stairs to his room.

''How did you do today?'' Lily asked his retreating back.

''Not as good as yesterday. Thirty-seven dollars

and nine cents.'' He called that from the central hall. Ronni could hear him start up the stairs.

Lily shrugged, picked up a carnation and began stripping away the lower leaves. ''That sounds pretty good to me.''

''Yes,'' Ronni said. ''I thought so, too—listen, are the other two kids upstairs?''

Lily considered her row of vases, chose one, pulled it in front of her and set the lone carnation in it. She reached for a sprig of greenery. ''Yes, they are.''

''I think I'll just run up and say hi.''

Lily shot her a look, then shrugged again. ''Suit yourself. Once you get past the landing into the upper hall, Lisbeth's door is the first one on the left. Griffin's is right next to it.''

Upstairs, in Lisbeth's pretty mint-green-and-white room, Ronni was introduced to Bead Blast Barbie. A few minutes later, she proceeded down the hall to Griffin's room, where he showed her his latest creation made of Duplo blocks.

''It's a castle!'' he told her. He pointed at a ramp made of green oblong blocks. ''That's how you get in! And when you get in, you might never get out!''

''Sounds scary.'' Ronni pretended to shiver.

Griff let out a monster laugh. ''Ha-ha-ha! It is!''

Back downstairs, Lily was still arranging flowers. She'd filled two of the vases with bright blooms and feathery fern branches.

''They look beautiful, Lily.''

''The truth is, there's absolutely no substitute for fresh-cut flowers in the house. Yes, they are expensive. And doing the arranging takes time. But they provide that special, extra accent that tells the world a woman cares. Patricia always said so.''

''Patricia was right.''

''Well, of course she was.''

On Tuesday evening of the week that followed, Ronni stopped at the main house for another visit with the children before she settled in at the guest house.

Lily treated her with distant courtesy, as if she were some stranger who'd dropped in unannounced, someone who got the benefit of her hostess's good manners, and nothing else. Ronni gritted her teeth and bore it. At least the kids seemed glad to see her.

Wednesday, after she'd made her rounds at Children's Hospital, Ronni checked in at her condo, where she found everything as it should be.

The wallpaper had been hung in the kitchen, the baths and the master bedroom. The other rooms had been textured and painted. The carpets were in, the floors laid, the appliances in place. The wood blinds had been installed that day.

It was all ready for her to move her things in.

She sat on the pale Berber carpet in the bright living room and felt just a little bit sad.

If things went as she hoped, she'd never live here—in her own single-woman version of a dream home. She should probably start making arrangements to sell it.

But then, with nothing really decided between her and Ryan, contacting a Realtor felt just a tiny bit premature.

No, she wouldn't do anything right now. She got

up off the floor, turned off the lights and let herself out the front door.

That night, when Ryan came to her, they made love as they always did. And then afterward, for once, they did talk just a little.

Ronni explained how she'd been making an effort to spend time with the children—and that Lily was less than enthusiastic about her presence in the main house.

"She's not welcoming me with open arms, Ryan. You have to know that. She never misses an opportunity to ask me when my condo will be ready—so that I can move out and away from you."

Anger made his eyes ice-blue. "She said that?"

"Not in so many words, but—"

He pulled her close. "I know, it's awkward. And hard on you. I'll talk to her."

She pushed away enough that she could look at him. "Oh, Ryan. Until we figure out where we're going together, there really isn't much to say to her. She's polite to me. And she never tries to stop me from seeing the kids. It's not an intolerable situation. And it won't be...up to the point that she and I try to live under the same roof together. Then I think it would become just about unbearable, unless she made a drastic attitude adjustment."

Ryan cupped her face, kissed the tip of her nose— and thought about what she'd just said.

Until we figure out where we're going together...

An important subject, one he knew begged for discussion.

And he intended to discuss it.

Very soon.

But now, he needed to get Tanner back in the

black, to get construction started up again on the new wing. As soon as he got a little breathing room, as soon as he could take his concentration off the whole scary house of cards that was his fund-raising scheme, then they could talk about the future. Then they would tackle the formidable problem of what to do about Lily.

Then he could relax a little, let down his guard a little, give Ronni the time and real attention she deserved.

He pulled her close again.

Ronni snuggled her head into the curve of his shoulder—and almost said it: *Ryan, my condo* is *ready....*

But she held the words back. What would they mean to him, but some sort of threat? Emotional pressure, applied strategically: *My house is ready now; I can* leave *here now...*

She knew he didn't want her to leave.

What she feared deep in her heart was that he wanted her to stay. Right here. In the little house. His guest.

And his lover.

And nothing more.

It was an immature, insecure little fear, and she knew it. A fear born of the child she had once been, the one who had never really belonged. The one who existed on the edges of other people's lives, the one who, once her mother died, had never been the center of anyone's world.

Ryan said, "This Sunday is Pizza Pete's day."

She idly threaded her fingers through the crisp mat of hair on his chest. "Right. The monthly family event."

"And we won't miss this month, even though I'm up to my ears in meetings, grant applications and fund-raising speeches. I want you to come, too."

"You do?" She felt guilty, for her own childish fears. Of course, Ryan wanted her in the center of his life. And he was showing it every way that he could.

He stroked her shoulder, his hand trailing down beneath the covers. "You'll love Pizza Pete's. Lots of loud video games and kids screaming. And you can get right up and refill your own soda when it runs out."

"Sounds delightful."

"So. You'll come." He kissed the top of her head, a sweet and chaste gesture that didn't even hint at the things his hand was doing under the covers.

Ronni moaned.

"Is that a yes?"

"Umm..."

"I can't hear you."

"All right. Yes. I will definitely—" she moaned again "—come...."

Drew must have been watching for her in the front window, because he ran out the door and down the steps as Ronni pulled into the driveway the next evening. She rolled her window down.

"Ronni, we have to talk...."

Lily appeared in the open front doorway. "Andrew! What are you up to? You've left the door open—and get back in here this minute, you don't even have a sweater on!"

"I'm coming!" He tossed the words over his

shoulder, then turned back to whisper urgently at Ronni. "Get parked and come to my house. I'll get rid of Griff and Lizzy. Then you, me and Grandma can talk."

"About what?"

"About Sunday."

Lily commanded, "Andrew! Now."

He glanced over his shoulder again. "Coming..." Then turned back to Ronni. "Please..."

"Okay, I'll be right over."

The minute Lily let Ronni in the back door, Drew rushed over and shut the door to the central hall.

Lily planted her hands on her hips. "What is going on?"

"I don't want Griff and Lizzy to hear." Drew spoke in a theatrical whisper. "And we have to hurry. Lizzy's reading a book to Griff. You know how long that's gonna last."

Lily pulled out a chair for Ronni, gestured her into it, then demanded of her grandson, "*What* don't you want Lisbeth and Griffin to hear?"

"About Sunday..."

"*What* about Sunday?"

"Grandma, if you'll quit asking questions and let me just talk, I'll explain everything."

Lily marched over to a chair opposite the one she'd given Ronni and sat down herself. "All right, young man. Explain."

Drew shifted from one foot to the other.

"Do you have to go to the bathroom?" Lily demanded.

"No! I just want to *talk*. And I want you to listen."

"We're listening."

"Okay. Dad told me this morning that he invited Ronni to come with us to Pizza Pete's this Sunday and—"

Lily's head whipped around. She pinned Ronni with a glare. "Ryan invited *you*...to Pizza Pete's? But that's strictly a *family* activity."

Drew tried to cut in. "Grandma, come on. We don't have that much—"

Lily whirled on her grandson again. "*I* certainly didn't hear your father tell you he'd invited Ronni for Sunday afternoon."

"You were upstairs, fixing Lizzy's braid, or turning Griff's shirt right side out, or something. It doesn't matter. What matters is, she's supposed to go, and so am I. And we *can't* go, not this time. Because we need to be at the Superserve Mart raising money for the new wing."

"But are you *sure* your father said he invited Ronni?" Lily sounded like a stuck record.

And Ronni was experiencing a number of conflicting emotions—exasperation and frustration first among them. Still, she spoke gently, "Ryan asked me to go last night. I said I'd enjoy it. I hope you'll be coming with us, too."

Lily made a small, disapproving sound. "I never go to Pizza Pete's. It's for Ryan and his brother and the children—and of course, Patricia, when she was alive."

"Well, this time, I'll be going, too."

Drew stamped his foot. "Will you guys quit talking about what we already *know* and help me try to figure out what we're going to *do?*"

Ronni looked at him and spoke as gently as she

had to his grandmother. "I think we're just going to have to skip the fund-raising Sunday—or maybe we can go a little later, after we're finished at Pizza Pete's."

"We *can't* skip it. We only get two days a week. We can't miss any of them. And I bet we won't be able to go later. On days when we go to Pizza Pete's, Dad almost always comes home for dinner, so we're not gonna be able to go, that's all, not without him finding out what we're doing."

"Then maybe you'd better just *tell* him what you're doing."

"No, I don't want to do that. I want it all done when I give him the money. I want to show him that I can really help."

"I can understand that. Truly, I can. But you only have two options that I can see. You can skip it for one day—or tell your father what you're doing."

"Ronni's right." Lily spoke up at last, albeit somewhat grudgingly. "You'll have to do one or the other."

"No, I won't. That's why I wanted to talk to you guys."

"Drew," Ronni said, "there's no other choice."

"Yes, there is. We could tell Dad I'm sick."

Both Ronni and Lily demanded in unison, *"What?"*

"No, wait." Drew bounced up and down on the balls of his feet. "Let me explain. I could act sick, see? And then I could stay home. And then as soon as you're all gone, Grandma and me, we could still do the fund-raising. It wouldn't be as good as having you there, Ronni, in your lab coat and everything. But you said it was mostly up to me, anyway. I'm the one that goes up to the people and asks for the money. And I could still do that. And then we could get back to the house before you guys come home. And I could go back to bed, and keep being sick for the rest of the day. And then, by Monday, I could be well and everything would be back to normal again." He glanced from Ronni to his grandmother and back to Ronni again. Then he raised both hands, palms up. "That's it. And I know it would work."

Ronni shook her head. Lily was doing the same.

"Andrew," Lily said. "That would be a lie."

"But it would be for a good reason! It would be to help with Dad's new wing. And anyway, I'm already lying for a good reason, because I'm not telling him what I'm doing."

Lily was not convinced. "That's different."

"It's *not* different."

Ronni didn't envy Lily right then. It was inevitably a losing proposition, to argue ethics with a nine-year-old.

Lily said, "Do not push your luck, young man. Keep talking. You'll convince me that we have to tell your father what you're up to right now, after all."

"No, we don't have to tell him. There's nothing wrong with surprising him. It's *good* to surprise him—even if it is a lie. It's a good lie, just like me pretending to be sick would be a good lie."

"No," Lily said. "Absolutely not. I am not going to allow you to fake being sick—not even for a good cause. It's just…not acceptable."

"But I *have* to!"

"No, you do not. Ronni and I have told you what you can do." Ronni actually felt a twinge of gratification. For once, Lily considered the two of them on the same side. Lily finished, "You can skip it for a day—or you can tell your father what you're up to."

"But that's not *fair!*" Drew grabbed a chair by the back, yanked it out from under the table and dropped down into it, hard.

"Gramma, Gramma, Griff spit on the book!" It was Lisbeth, calling from the other side of the door to the hall.

"She stopped reading!" Griff shouted. "Drew said she has to read to me!"

With a long sigh, Lily rose to let them in.

Ronni left about ten minutes later, by which time Griffin and Lisbeth had been sent to take their baths, with strict orders not to fight anymore—or else. Drew was still sulking. When Ronni said goodbye to him, he turned his head away.

Ronni returned to the little house feeling bleak.

But then, three hours later, when Ryan came through the French doors, he was grinning.

"Bioventure Pharmaceuticals has donated five million," he announced. "The ten million from the Community Fund went to the bank today. Tanner should have the money he needs by tomorrow—and on Monday, construction starts up again."

Chapter Twelve

Ronni let out a whoop and ran to him. He hoisted her high. She wrapped her legs around his waist and he spun them both around in circles until her head swam.

They fell to the bed together, laughing and kissing and holding on tight. Then he was taking her sweater, tugging it over her head, tossing it away, unclasping her bra. And she was slithering his belt off, sliding his zipper down.

He reached for the condom just in time. They were still half-dressed when he rose above her. She pulled him down, wrapping her legs around him, drawing him into her fully with a joyous sigh.

Joined, they lay still, matching breath for breath. He braced his elbows on either side of her head, looked down at her, whispered on a ragged breath, "Tomorrow night. Not a single damn speech to give. We're going out, you and me. Like—'' he groaned ''—normal people do....''

She pushed her hips toward him, pulled him tighter with her arms. "Sounds...lovely...."

He kissed her. For a while, there were only soft moans, hungry sighs—and at last, one low, rough groan of release, followed by an answering feminine cry.

The next night, Friday, was Ronni's night on call, but she managed to talk Marty into trading with her. She and Ryan went to the best steakhouse in town, where they ordered filet mignon.

It was a lovely romantic evening, exactly the kind of evening Ronni had been waiting for: hours together, just the two of them, to talk and laugh, to make love—and to plan for their future.

And they did talk. They laughed. Later, in the little house, they made beautiful love.

She woke when he left her. He kissed her so tenderly before he slipped out the door. She lay there for a moment in the dark alone after he was gone.

And then she sat up, switched on the light.

They'd had such a perfect evening.

But there had been no talk of the future. And no talk of love, either.

And whose fault is that? she asked herself.

At any time during the evening, she could have spoken up for her own needs; she could have made a few demands.

She could have said, "I understand you're under pressure. That the main thing on your mind is all the money you still have to raise. But I don't want to go on like this forever. I want us to be *really* together. I want us to be man and wife...."

She could have confessed, "Oh Ryan, today is the day my period was due. It didn't come."

But she had said nothing.

She was *afraid* to say anything. Afraid he might...what?

Reject her?

No, he would never do that. Ryan Malone was a man who always kept his promises, who lived up to his responsibilities.

If she *was* pregnant, he would marry her.

He would see no other choice.

And that was what bothered her.

If she was pregnant, and they married, she would never know with complete certainty if he really wanted marriage with her—or if he only felt obligated to make a commitment to the woman who carried his child.

So she was waiting. Holding off on telling him that she loved him, that she longed to spend a lifetime at his side.

She was holding off until she knew for sure about the baby.

Holding off on the chance that it was a false alarm, that she could tell him of her love without simultaneously dumping another giant-sized responsibility in his lap.

The whole situation tied her stomach in knots.

Literally.

Why she almost felt as if she might—

Ronni sat straight up in the bed. She gulped, moaned, "Oh, no..."

And then she tossed the covers out of the way and dashed for the bathroom.

She made it just in time to lose her filet mignon dinner in the toilet bowl. When the retching finally stopped, she dragged herself to her feet, brushed her teeth and rinsed her face.

"Tomorrow," she said to her pale, rather hollow-eyed reflection in the mirror over the sink, "you'll buy a home test and you'll take it." It still might come out negative at this point, even if she was pregnant. But a positive result would tell her what she needed to know.

Ronni turned off the bathroom light and went back to bed, where she resolutely closed her eyes and called up a habit of her internship and residency—the habit of dropping off pretty much on reflex, of grabbing every minute of sleep she could get.

She did go right to sleep. Unfortunately, it was a hospital kind of sleep. Not deep at all, with the expectation of sudden waking threading through her anxious dreams.

Ronni bought the test on her way to the office the next morning.

She picked Drew up at two. They were set up in front of Superserve Mart by two-thirty and they stayed until five, giving Drew an extra half hour to approach every customer who went through the big glass doors.

One elderly man wrote out a check for fifty dollars. When they added that to the rest, they were well over a hundred just for that day.

As they were driving home, Ronni said, "See? It

all worked out. You've hit your weekly goal today. You can afford to go to Pizza Pete's tomorrow.''

He shot her a pouty look. ''I'm still behind because of last week.''

She was beginning to become really irritated with him. ''Oh, come on. You've made forty-eight, thirty-seven and one hundred and twelve—plus change. You add those three together and you get what?''

His brow beetled up, then he grunted. ''It's too big a problem to do just in my head.''

She did it for him. ''You've made one hundred ninety-seven, plus the change. You seem to have set a goal of fifty dollars a day, right?''

He grunted again. Apparently the bad-tempered sound was supposed to serve as an affirmative.

''Fifty dollars a day, and if you'd had tomorrow, you would have had four days total.''

''I feel like I'm in math time at school.''

She went on, undeterred by the nine-year-old attempt at sarcasm. ''The point is, you wanted to have raised two hundred dollars by tomorrow. And you've already raised one hundred ninety-seven as of today. That's less than three dollars short of your goal.''

''But I could be *ahead*.''

''Well, keep sulking. I'm sure that will help a lot.''

He hunched his shoulders, stuck out his chin. ''You don't understand.''

''Sure, I do,'' she shot right back. ''You're not getting your way—and you don't like that.''

''This is *important*. I can go to Pizza Pete's any day.''

"No, you can't. You only go once a month, and you go with your family and that's a special thing. When I was a child, I would have given just about *anything* to have had a family to take me to a place like Pizza Pete's."

"I really hate when grown-ups start talking about when they were kids. That was a long time ago and it doesn't have anything to do with me."

"Fine. You know your options. If you really want to raise money instead of spending the day with your family, just tell your father what you're doing, and you and I will go to Superserve Mart."

"I told you a hundred times. It has to be a surprise."

"No, it doesn't. You *want* it to be a surprise, that's all."

"You just don't understand."

"I think you said that before. I also think you'd better let this go, because you are not going to get your way and that is that."

He let out a long, wounded sigh and was fumingly silent for several minutes. But then, at last, he straightened in his seat. "Okay. You're right. We got one hundred and twelve dollars and thirty-three cents today and that's really good. It's excellent, even."

"It certainly is."

"And next week, we'll probably get a hundred more."

"Right."

"So I guess I'll stop being mad at you."

"Good."

He slid her a look. "Did you have a nice time going out to dinner with my dad last night?"

"He mentioned that, did he?"

"I heard him tell Grandma."

She could just picture Lily's reaction: an expression of distaste and a muttered "All right, then. I won't prepare anything for you."

"Well?" Drew prompted.

"I had a wonderful time." And she had, even if they'd never quite gotten around to discussing love and marriage. Even if she'd thrown up after he left and had to buy a pregnancy test this morning...

"Good." Drew sounded very satisfied, and that made her smile. She glanced over, met his eyes. He said, "We're having meat loaf tonight. You like meat loaf?"

"Oh, no you don't."

"Ronni. I can get her to ask you, I can."

"You have excellent manners, Drew. And I know you've been taught to get an okay from your grandmother before you invite people to your house."

"But you're not just *people*."

"I think that was a compliment. Thank you."

"I mean it. I can get her to ask—"

"I think I've already made myself clear on this point. Not tonight. And in future, I want you to talk to your grandmother *before* you bring up dinner to me. Understood?"

"Oh, all right."

She turned onto their street and pulled into the driveway.

"You're gonna come in for a few minutes, aren't you? You *always* come in and say hi to Griff and Lizzy."

Ronni parked the car and they went into the main house together. She met another of Lisbeth's Barbie dolls and played a few minutes of Yoshi's Island on Griff's Nintendo 64. It was business as usual with Lily, a polite hello and a frosty smile. The house smelled enticingly of meat loaf, but Lily did not invite her to stay.

The next morning, first thing, Ronni took the pregnancy test.

It was positive, exactly what she'd expected.

Still, as she stared at the twin red lines in the viewing holes, she felt as if someone had kicked her forcefully in the solar plexus.

A baby.

She was going to have a baby.

She and *Ryan* were going to have a baby.

She moved through the morning by rote, thinking about things she'd never really thought of in terms of herself before—how she'd like a cup of coffee, but caffeine wasn't good for the baby. How she'd need to stock up on neonatal vitamins, take better care of herself, start eating more nutritious meals...

"There will be options," Kelly had said—Kelly, who would now be her obstetrician as well as her gynecologist.

But to Ronni, the choice was already made. She was thirty-two years old and reasonably well-established in her career. It wouldn't be easy, but she could juggle things around enough to handle having a baby.

She could handle it, and she *would* handle it.

And anyway, she wouldn't be doing it alone.

Ryan would help.

Ryan...

She would have to tell him, lay a whole new burden on him.

Her mind turned away from the idea, immediately began handing her excuses to put off saying anything to him.

After all, it was so very early. For heaven's sake, she was only—she counted backward—seventeen days pregnant. She had time to deal with this herself for a while. To...become accustomed to the idea that she was going to be a mother.

Yes, eventually, Ryan would start to wonder if there had been any repercussions from that one doozy of a mistake they'd made. He'd ask her about it. But that wouldn't be for a while yet. Probably a week or two at least.

She didn't have to be in any great rush, she must remember that. For a week or two, anyway, her secret could remain hers alone.

The phone rang at eleven-thirty. "Ready?" It was Ryan.

They'd agreed she'd come to the main house and they'd all drive to Pizza Pete's from there.

"I'll be right over." She tried to sound happy and normal—and she thought she succeeded pretty well. Which thoroughly surprised her. She didn't *feel* happy and normal. She felt bewildered, dazed, thoroughly confused....

She put on her trench coat, grabbed her purse and went out across the lawn to the other house. Ryan let her in—or rather, *pulled* her in.

He reached out, took her hand and hauled her over the threshold right into his arms. Once he had her there, he pushed the door shut behind her with a quick shove of his fist.

"I missed you."

"Since last night?" Oh, he felt good. Her breasts, which ached a little all the time now, felt eased somehow, the ache soothed by the pressure of being held against his chest. Really, now she thought about it, the pregnancy-induced sensitivity wasn't all that unpleasant, anyway.

"Yes," he said. "I missed you since last night."

She tried to see beyond his shoulder, to look for the others. But it wasn't easy, since he was so much taller than she.

He teased, "Don't go looking for anyone else. We're alone. They're all upstairs, putting on their coats. Kiss me."

"Oh, Ryan…"

"Don't start that. Just kiss me."

So she lifted her mouth and he bent down enough to cover it with his. He tasted of coffee and his body felt so hard and good through all the layers of their clothing. She closed her eyes. Sighing in delight, she sparred with his tongue as it slipped beyond her parted lips.

"Umm…" he said, as if the kiss were an edible thing, a tasty morsel they were sharing.

Deftly, without breaking the kiss, he turned her a little. Then he eased his left hand between the wrapped sides of her coat. He cupped her breast, massaged it. It felt good, the soothing of a pleasant ache. Good. And arousing. Heat pooled in the center of her and radiated out in a long, delightful shiver of pleasure.

She stood on tiptoe, pressing herself closer into him, reveling in the sweet, lustful intimacy of the moment, lovely, naughty images playing through her mind: if he pulled her coat open. And pushed her up against the door. And lifted her. If she boldly wrapped her legs around him...

"Well. *Excuse* me."

It was Lily. Her voice had come from behind Ryan—in the doorway to the kitchen.

Ronni froze. She opened her eyes. Ryan pulled away. Slowly. He didn't hurry, didn't seem the least embarrassed. He slid his hand out of her trench coat and gently ran his palm over the wide collar, a caress that reassured, as it staked its claim.

Ronni thought, Oh, yes. If I had to go and get myself accidentally pregnant, I am so glad it was with this man.

He turned, reaching for Ronni as he did, pulling her firmly into the shelter of his arm. "Something we can do for you, Lily?"

Lily blinked. Her mouth worked for a minute, then she announced tightly, "The children are coming."

Ryan shrugged. "Great. It's time to go."

"I...this is totally unacceptable...."

Ryan frowned. "What are you talking about?"

"You know what I'm talking about." Lily spoke in a charged whisper. "The two of you carrying on like this. It's...not good for the children."

"Oh, come on. We *thought* we were alone."

"That doesn't matter. You shouldn't be behaving this way when they might see."

"Lily." Ryan spoke more softly. "It was only a kiss."

Lily put her hand against her throat. "Well, I just...I think you should keep such displays to yourselves. And I...I really think it's about time you two decided if you plan to marry or not. If you do, I'll be leaving, of course. It's only fair that you let me know, so that I can make arrangements to go elsewhere.''

Before Ryan could respond to that bombshell, they heard the pounding of small feet on the stairs.

''We'll talk about this later,'' Ryan said.

Lily nodded, a tight little jerk of her head.

Ten seconds later, the three children spilled into the kitchen, each bundled up in a nice, warm jacket. Lily kissed them goodbye and warned them to behave. They promised they would.

''Let's get a move on,'' Ryan said.

Lily stood at the door, waving goodbye as they left. Ronni glanced back at her, wanting to be angry with her—and then only thinking how lonely she looked.

Halfway to Pizza Pete's, Ronni's beeper went off. She took out her cell phone, called the exchange and got the number of a frantic mother whose little girl had just fallen down a flight of stairs.

''Dr. Ronni, I called 911. The paramedics will be here any minute. She's unconscious. I'm so scared....''

''Is she breathing normally?''

''Yes. I think so...yes.''

''Don't leave her. Watch her closely.'' Quickly, she told the mother what to do should the child's breathing become labored or if she made gurgling sounds.

The mother said, ''Yes. All right. I will. Yes.''

''And stay calm. That's very important. You're doing everything you can do, and help is on the way.''

"All right. Yes. I know. I'm calm."

Ronni said, "I'll meet you at Children's Hospital." She disconnected the call. Ryan glanced across the console at her. "Sorry."

"Part of the job, right?"

"'Fraid so."

"Why don't you drop us off and take the car? If you can't get back before we leave the restaurant, I'll get Tanner to give us a ride home."

"Okay."

He reached over, snared her hand and gave it a squeeze. She tried not to think of Lily or the baby, not to dwell on how she, Ronni, was managing to make Ryan's already-difficult life more complicated still. They couldn't even enjoy a family outing without her beeper going off.

But no. She shouldn't think that way, and she knew it. They would work through it. They would. They just had to take things one step at a time.

Chapter Thirteen

At Children's Hospital, Ronni learned that her patient had regained consciousness during the ambulance ride to the hospital.

Ronni performed a thorough exam. She was always very wary when it came to injuries and sudden falls. She'd seen more than one case where a "bad fall" had actually been something much more sinister.

But Ronni saw no indications of child abuse this time. The girl's bumps and bruises were consistent with a fall down a flight of stairs. And she had no prior history of mysterious injuries.

Ronni ordered a CAT scan, then arranged to have the patient admitted overnight, mostly for purposes of observation.

"It's all my fault," the mother kept insisting. "Oh, I hate those stairs. And I should have been paying better attention. I ran down to check on my chocolate chip cookies. And she must have tried to follow me....''

Ronni said the things she always said in such situations. ''These things happen. And it really does look like she's going to be fine.''

''When can she come home?''

''If there are no complications—and I really don't believe there will be—she'll be going home tomorrow.''

''Oh, Doctor. Thank you. Thank you so much....''

Ronni got back to Pizza Pete's at a little after one. Inside, as Ryan had promised, computer games zinged and whizzed, classic rock music played good and loud, and children roamed freely from one entertainment to the next.

She saw Ryan and his brother, sitting alone at one of the redwood picnic tables near a corner of the room, the remains of a huge pizza and several half-finished sodas nearby. Their dark heads were close together. Whatever they were talking about, it looked serious. Ryan's back was to her, but judging by Tanner's intense and unhappy expression, Ronni didn't think they'd appreciate being interrupted right then.

So she hesitated, still standing by the door, not wanting to break in on them, remembering something she hadn't thought of in years: a certain conversation between her Uncle Stan and her Aunt Mildred. Ronni had lived with them for several months, after her mother died. She'd tried to be good, to be everything they wanted her to be.

But then, one morning, she'd come downstairs early and Uncle Stan and Aunt Mildred were talking softly at the kitchen table. Ronni had huddled close to the wall, listening, though she knew that she shouldn't.

"You'll just have to tell him," Mildred was saying. "We've kept her for six months. It's long enough. He'll have to take her himself, or find somewhere else to put her."

"Mildred, come on. You know how he is. Always with the big schemes that never pan out. He can hardly take care of himself. He's never going to settle down and be a decent father to the poor kid."

"Well, I can't help it. It's just not fair to Laurie." Laurie was Ronni's cousin, their daughter. Laurie was older, almost twelve, and didn't like having a little kid in her room. "You're going to have to talk to him, Stan. He hasn't sent any money in three months. And we have our own children to take care of...."

"But—"

"Don't give me any 'buts,' Stan. It's enough. You call him and talk to him."

Ronni had turned then and crept back up the stairs. A few days later, her father had come to get her. He'd driven her straight to her Aunt Ida's in Salt Lake City. She'd stayed there for almost a year.

Tanner looked up. He spotted Ronni and smiled, his brooding look fading as if it had never been.

Still half in thrall to the sad, old memory, Ronni pasted on a smile of her own and found herself thinking of what Kelly had said about Tanner the night of the Heart Ball: *My guess is he's just highly skilled at hiding whatever's going on inside.*

Ryan turned, saw her, waved her over. Still wearing her resolute smile, she moved toward the two men.

They stayed for another hour. Ronni drank a Sprite and decided against trying the cold pizza. She watched Drew beat a very complex-looking video game and stood by admiringly as Griffin rode a bucking mechanical horse. And she tried not to wonder what Ryan and his brother had been talking about when she got there—tried not to let herself think it might have been something concerning Lily, or how difficult Ronni was making things by being in Ryan's life.

"Stay for dinner," Ryan said, when they got back to his house. And she thought of Drew, yesterday, his blue eyes shining as he declared that they were having meat loaf and he could get his grandmother to invite her.

She didn't really feel up to it. She'd had enough of Lily's barely masked hostility for one day. She wanted to go back to the guest house, to be alone for a while. To take a little break from feeling like an intruder, which had pretty much been her mental state since she'd walked into Pizza Pete's and seen Ryan and his brother talking so seriously about something they'd immediately *stopped* talking about as soon as they caught sight of her.

After all, she'd hardly had any opportunity to get her bearings after what she'd learned from the pregnancy test that morning. She needed time to herself.

Still, it didn't seem right to beg off. The whole point was for her and Ryan to be with the children whenever they could, wasn't it?

So she said yes. And tried to keep her attitude positive through the meal.

She finally managed to escape at around eight-thirty. Ryan whispered, "I'll be over in a little while" as she went out the back door.

For the first time, she actually wished he wouldn't.

Ryan must have sensed that. His dark brows drew together. "It's Lily, isn't it?"

It was. And it wasn't....

How could she explain? It all seemed so...totally overwhelming right then.

She said, "We'll talk, all right? Later."

"Give me an hour."

She went back to the guest house and threw up. Then, once her poor stomach was finished rebelling, she brushed her teeth and splashed water on her face.

After that, she paced the floor of the bedroom, lecturing herself.

She just had to tell him. That was all there was to it. She had to tell him she was pregnant, toss another major burden on his broad shoulders—and get the truth out there, where they could deal with it.

He came just when he'd said he would. He shut the door, drew the curtains and turned to her. He looked so...troubled.

The distance between them, not more than ten feet, seemed enormous. She couldn't stand it. She ran to him. He wrapped his arms around her, held her so close.

And he said it. "I love you, Ronni."

And she said, "I love you, too."

"I wanted it to be...better than this."

"I know."

"There's so much we have to talk about."

"I know. Oh, I know."

"I keep thinking things will...settle down, that we'll have some time. But it never seems to happen."

"No, it never does."

"I want us to...get married."

Joy, silvery and light, shimmered through her. "Me, too...."

"But after today, I don't think there's any way Lily's going to accept it. We're going to lose her."

The shimmery feeling faded a little. Ronni broke the embrace, sliding her hand down to clasp his. "Come on."

She led him to the kitchen, pulled out a chair for him. He dropped into it. She sat down opposite him, leaned forward, held out her hand. He took it, turning it over, brushing her fingers open, caressing her palm.

"I tried to talk to her," he said. "After we got the kids to bed, before I came over here."

"And?"

"She said what she said this morning. If I marry you, she's leaving."

Ronni said aloud what she knew he must be thinking, too. "It's going to be hard...on the kids. Lily is the one really stable element in their lives."

He made a low noise of agreement in his throat and muttered, "She's been a rock, since Patricia died."

"Ryan, I really hate the idea of just...kicking her out. Or having her walk out."

"So do I." He let go of her hand. "But what the hell else can we do?"

Ronni's stomach chose that moment to start acting up again. She took a slow breath, let it out carefully. The nausea receded a little. She pulled her hand back to her side of the table. "I wish I knew."

He shifted in his chair, speared his fingers through his hair. "We'll just have to find good day care. It's not impossible. People do it all the time. And at least I can afford to pay for the best."

"You know what our schedules are. It just doesn't seem fair to the children."

"We can't help that."

She put her hands in her lap, clasped them tightly together. "Maybe if we…gave it some time."

He looked at her across the table, his expression harder than before. "Damn it, Ronni. I want to marry you. You just said you wanted to marry me."

"I know. And I do, but…"

He waited for her to finish. When she didn't, he demanded impatiently, "But what?"

"But it's…not right."

"What the hell are you getting at?"

"I just…it's not right. People like us, who have to have *everything*. Demanding careers. And children. And…each other, too. I'm just saying that maybe we have to slow down a little here. Maybe we have to give some credit to a very important element in this equation. And that element is Lily."

He echoed her words. "Slow down." His voice had turned cold. "You want us to…slow down?"

She couldn't answer right then. She was too busy sucking in another long breath, ordering her stomach to relax.

He said carefully, "What, exactly, does that mean?"

"Oh, Ryan..."

He put up a hand. "Don't."

"What?"

"Don't start waffling on me. I can't take that right now."

"I'm not waffling."

"The hell you're not."

"There's more than just you and me in this." *So much more. More than you know, more than I seem to be able to tell you right now...* "I'm just trying to be fair."

"Fair." He growled the word. "Life is not fair."

"I know, but—"

"Look. You have some better plan?"

"I..."

"Do you have some better plan?"

She stared at him. He was so angry. All the pressure he'd been under in recent weeks was breaking out now.

He repeated for the third time, "Do you have a better plan?"

"I... Lily's a good woman, at heart."

"I never said she wasn't."

"And she and I could find...a common ground. I know we could. Eventually. She's just...having a hard time accepting me. Accepting what I represent. In a way, my coming into your lives is like...Patricia dying all over again. To Lily, it must seem as if I'm moving in on her daughter's territory, trying to replace her."

"Patricia *is* dead. It's a fact."

"And Lily needs more time to deal with that fact."

He stood then. "Say it. Whatever it is, just get it out of your mouth."

"Would you...would you just sit down? Please?"

He ignored her request. "You're backing out on me, aren't you?"

She started to say *Oh, Ryan* but bit it back just in time.

"Answer me. Are you going to marry me or not?"

"Yes."

He stared at her unbelievingly. "Yes...but what?"

"Yes, but I'm thinking that maybe we should give Lily what she wants. For a while..."

He spoke way too quietly. "I don't like this."

"You think I do?"

"Then don't do it."

"Listen to me. My condo is finished."

His eyes were as cold as his tone now. "So? Sell it."

"I will. In a while. But right now, I think it would be a good idea if I...moved in there. Just for a short time. This really has all happened so fast, between us. And we have to think of the whole picture. We have to give Lily, and ourselves, a little space to—"

"Wait a minute. Do you *want* to move in there? Do you want to get away from me?"

"No. That's not it. That's not it at all."

"Then forget it."

"Ryan..."

He braced his hands on the table and brought his face down to her level. "No. I don't need any space.

I'm tired of coming through that bedroom door after dark, of getting up in the middle of the night to go back to that big, empty room alone. I want you with me, where you belong. And I want you to marry me, right away."

Her heart felt so full, it hurt to hear him say that.

But the truth would not be denied. "And then Lily will leave us, abruptly. In anger and hurt. The children will suffer. Do you want that, too?"

"Of course not. I never said it was an ideal situation. But if you move out, then *we're* the ones who suffer."

"Yes. And we're also the ones who want to change everything."

He sank to the chair again, ran his left hand down his face. "God. This is one hell of a mess."

She leaned forward. "Ryan. Please believe me. I love you with all of my heart. And I know…that too many people have left you. But you are strong. And I'm strong. And sometimes, it's the strong ones who have to make a few sacrifices. This isn't forever. I swear to you. It will only be long enough for Lily to see what will happen if she gets what she thinks she wants."

He looked at her piercingly. "And what do you think she's going to see?"

"That I'm not the enemy. That her daughter really is gone. That…life has to go on."

"And your moving out is going to make her see that?"

"It's a good possibility. I really think it is. I think by giving her no choice, we are forcing her out. Discounting her, and all that she's done for you, for your children. I just don't think that's right."

He laid his hand on the table, looked down at it, then shot a telling glance up at her. "But if you're coming back, anyway, it's a false choice. Isn't it?"

She did not let her gaze waver. "No. It's…giving her time. And believe me, after she's thought about it for a while, she will know that's a gift, from people like us. A gift she's been giving you and the children for over two years now. Her time. *All* the time. To love and to nurture, to cook and to clean. To simply *be* there, when you couldn't. Don't you see how important that is? In some ways, what she's given is the most important thing in the world. The thing you didn't have as a child. The thing I didn't have. The thing I really don't want the children to lose if we can possibly help it."

He said warily, "She could choose to leave, anyway. She has money of her own. She used to sell real estate and she did pretty well at it. Then, when she decided to move in with us, she and I had a long talk. I pay her well. Not as much as she's worth, maybe. I realize I could never pay her that much. But enough that's she's able to save quite a bit. She could end up accepting you—and still wanting to leave."

Ronni's stomach roiled. She swallowed, breathed deeply, then spoke with all the conviction she could muster. "Yes. She could still leave. But if she accepted me first, we could make a smooth transition. Together. We could make it a good change. Instead of an ugly, painful one."

He didn't speak for a long time. Ronni spent the endless seconds breathing deeply, slowly, in and then out, mentally telling herself that she was *not* going to throw up.

Finally, when the silence had stretched out so long she wondered if he ever would speak, he said, "There's something else, isn't there?"

Her heart bounced into her throat—a physical impossibility, she knew that. Still, she could feel it there, beating hard and loud.

"I can see it in your eyes, Ronni. There's something else going on here. Something you're keeping from me. I want to know what it is."

She gulped. Her stomach churned. "I..."

"You *are* having doubts, aren't you? About us. About marrying a man with a twenty-four-hour-a-day job, three kids—and shaky prospects for child care."

Her heart was lodged there, in her throat, cutting off her ability to speak or to breathe. And her stomach... Oh, Lord...

"Tell me the truth, Ronni." His eyes burned into hers.

And she couldn't hold it, couldn't keep it down. She shot to her feet. "I...excuse me...."

He gaped at her. "Ronni?"

She turned and ran—down the short hall to the bathroom right next to the bedroom. She threw back the toilet seat and got over the bowl just in time.

There wasn't much left to come up. But what was there, she lost.

She dropped to her knees and let it happen.

In the middle of it, Ryan knelt beside her. He put his hand on her back. She moaned and heaved some more. Gently, he gathered her hair, held it out of the way for her.

When it was over, he wrapped his arms around her and rocked her. "Hey," he whispered. "Hey..."

She let herself lean against him, felt his warmth and his strength, listened to the lovely, even beating of his heart. Then she sighed, pushed him away a little.

He got up, wet a washcloth, bent down again and tenderly wiped her flushed, hot face. Her mouth tasted vile. She grimaced.

"Toothbrush, huh?"

She nodded. He stood. She pulled herself to her feet as he got her toothbrush from its holder, found the toothpaste and squeezed a line of it over the bristles. He handed it to her and stood back enough that she had the sink to herself.

She brushed. When she was done, he led her to the bedroom. She followed behind him obediently, too drained to do anything but go where he led her.

"Lie down."

She stretched out on the bed. He took her shoes off and then his own.

He lay down beside her, tenderly pulling her to him, so her head rested on his shoulder. "So that's it—what you weren't telling me?"

"Yes," she admitted in a tiny voice.

"Is everything…all right?"

"All right?"

"Should you be throwing up like that? It's only been, what…?"

"A little over two weeks. And yes, morning sickness is normal, from about the second week on. Plus, there are some arguments that stress exacerbates it."

"Stress." He seemed to consider the concept, then she felt his nod against the top of her head. "Plenty of that lately. You…took a test, then?"

"This morning. It was positive."

His arm banded a little tighter around her. "When were you going to tell me?"

"I've been arguing with myself, whether to wait a little...or to tell you right away."

"But your stomach decided for you."

"That's about the size of it." She lifted up, looked at him. "I...oh, I didn't want to do this to you."

He traced her jawline with a forefinger, so lightly. Still, the touch warmed her all the way to her toes. "The way I remember it, we did it to each other."

"I'm going to go through with it, to be a mother...."

"Did I say I didn't want that?"

"No. And I knew you wouldn't. I know how you are. But I...wanted to say my intention out loud. And clear."

"I get the message."

"I love you." She surged up a little, brushed her lips against his, then settled her head back on his chest.

He wrapped both arms around her. She felt the touch of his lips in her hair. Right then, she realized she felt better than she had in days. It was good to have the truth out, not to feel as if she lied to him every time she looked at him.

She felt certain at that moment that they would get through this. They would work it all out with Lily. Somehow. She was sure of it....

He chuckled. "I guess you'll have to marry me now."

She was actually relaxed enough to tease him a little. "*Have* to? This is the twenty-first century, in case you didn't notice. Women don't *have* to get married anymore.''

"You do. And we are. Right away.''

She lay very still. "Ryan. Didn't you understand anything I told you in the kitchen?''

"I did understand. I just don't agree with it. And this changes everything.''

"It changes nothing.''

"How can you say that? We love each other. You're having my baby. And we're getting married.''

"Eventually.''

She could feel the tension gathering in him again, even through their clothes, muscle and sinew going hard with resistance.

He said, "You're not moving out.'' It was an order.

"I am. Oh, please. Trust me. I want to give this a chance…give Lily a chance.''

"I'm against it.''

"I'm sorry. I love you. And I'm doing it.''

Chapter Fourteen

The next day, Ronni made arrangements to have her furniture taken out of storage and delivered to the condo. That same afternoon, she sent home the three-year-old who had fallen down the stairs.

She was also able to tell the parents of another patient, one who had been seriously ill, that after three and half weeks in the hospital, their daughter would be released the next day.

It was a good moment, the kind a doctor treasures. The parents looked at her with gratitude, relief— even joy. And Ronni felt the same emotions herself, as if she had guided them all through the minefield of a serious illness, and somehow, here they were on the other side, with the patient intact, almost ready to resume a normal life again.

She didn't realize it then, but that was the best thing that would happen all week.

After she finished at Children's Hospital, Ronni went to the condo and worked until past nine, putting away kitchen things and moving what pieces of furniture she could move without help. She was back at the guest house by nine-thirty, wanting to be there for Ryan when he arrived.

But by eleven, he hadn't shown up.

He was angry with her.

She felt terrible about that.

Still, she honestly believed the temporary move was the right thing to do. Their love was strong. A disagreement, and his ensuing anger, wouldn't kill it.

She went to bed and actually fell asleep sometime after eleven-thirty. She woke at twelve, when he slipped under the covers with her.

He pulled her close. She snuggled against him. "Ryan, please don't be angry with me."

Instead of answering, he kissed her. She kissed him back. For a while, she forgot everything—the problem with Lily, their disagreement over the solution she'd devised. She lost herself completely in the touch of his hands and the glorious feel of his body against hers.

The next day she called a handyman Marty had recommended. He met her at the condo at seven and helped her to move the heavier pieces of furniture where she wanted them. Then, for two more hours, she continued putting things away. She made it back to the guest house at ten.

Ryan came to her late again. They made slow, tender love.

Afterward, she told him she would make the move that Sunday.

All he said was "I guess you'll do what you think you have to do."

The nights that followed were much the same. She went to the condo, unpacked until nine or so. And Ryan came to her late at night.

They made love. But they hardly spoke. She tried more than once to reassure him that she truly wasn't deserting him, that the separation wouldn't last that long, that she really did think it was the right thing to do.

He would let her talk, but that was all. And then he'd change the subject.

Friday night, she suggested gently that they ought to discuss the best way to tell Lily and the children about her move.

He said, "There's nothing to discuss. You're leaving. You tell them."

"Ryan, I am doing this for *all* of us."

"Are you?"

Right then, she wanted to give in. To throw up her hands and cry "All right. Have it your way. We'll get married. Lily will walk out. And *you* can stay home with the children until you find someone trustworthy to take care of them!"

But she held her tongue. She knew she was doing the right thing. And if Ryan wouldn't help her, she would handle it on her own.

Saturday, Drew raised fifty-five dollars and eleven cents during their stint at the supermarket.

On the drive home, as he babbled away about how much they'd earned so far, Ronni considered the best way to tell him of her plans.

She almost began explaining right then.

But no. She really felt she ought to tell Lily first, then the children.

When they got to the house, they found Lily on the service porch, loading up the washing machine. Ronni waited until Drew had finished regaling his grandmother with the details of their afternoon's work. When he went upstairs, Ronni stayed behind, watching as Lily measured detergent and poured it over the clothes.

Lily shut the lid, turned the dials. There was the gushing sound of water pouring into the drum.

At last, Lily turned and forced a tight smile. "I believe Griffin and Lisbeth are upstairs."

"I...actually, I wanted a few words with you."

"Oh? About what?"

Where to begin? Ronni didn't have a clue. So she jumped right in with both feet. "My condo is ready. And I've moved my things out of storage. I'll be leaving. Moving in there. Tomorrow."

Lily put her hand on the washer lid, as if she needed the support. "Excuse me?"

"I just...wanted you to know. I'm moving out tomorrow."

"Moving out?" Lily looked truly stunned.

"Yes. Ryan and I..." Well now. There was the beginning of a lie. Ryan had nothing to do with it. Best to leave his name out of it if she could. "Well, I've decided that maybe what's needed here is a little...perspective. A little time for all of us to think about what we really want."

Lily put her other hand against her throat. "You have?"

Ronni's stomach chose that moment to start acting edgy. She sucked in a breath through her nose.

There. That was better. "Yes. I…just wanted you to know."

"Well. Well, thank you." Lily's glance shifted away. Could she be feeling just a little bit regretful at this turn of events? Or was Ronni only indulging herself in a bout of wishful thinking?

Lily drew her shoulders back and let go of the washer. "I think you're very wise and I hope… everything works out for you."

So much for regret. Ronni sighed. "I'm sure it will. I'll be gone by noon tomorrow. But I still intend to continue helping Drew with his fund-raising on Saturdays and Sundays."

"That's…very kind of you."

"I'll pick him up at two-thirty tomorrow and have him home by a little after five."

"All right. I…"

For a split second, Ronni actually thought Lily might say something straight from the heart. "Yes?" she prompted on a rising inflection of pure hope.

"Nothing. I suppose you'll want to tell the children now."

Ronni found both Lisbeth and Griffin in Griffin's room, playing Nintendo. She watched for a while, then said she had something she wanted to talk to them about.

It went very well. She sat on the floor with them and explained what a condo was, that she had one. That it had been being finished while she lived in the little house. That now it was done and she was going to go live there.

"But you'll come back and see us, won't you?" Lisbeth asked.

Griff jumped up and down. "Yes! Come back and see us! You come back soon!"

She promised she would.

She knocked on Drew's door next.

"It's open!"

She stuck her head in. He was sitting at the computer, his back to her. He turned, smiled.

"May I come in?"

"Sure." He pushed a button and a screen saver came down. Hundreds of little cartoon bugs leaped and danced across the screen.

Ronni dragged the spare chair over near him and sat down in it. And then she told him that she was moving the next day. He didn't say anything when she delivered the news, only tucked his hands between his knees and looked down at the chair mat under his feet.

She went on to explain that she still intended to continue the fund-raising project with him. "I'll pick you up the same as always tomorrow and we can—"

He looked up, Malone-blue eyes stricken. "Don't you like my dad anymore?"

She couldn't stop herself. She reached out. "Oh, honey—"

He flinched away before she made contact. "Just tell me. Don't you like my dad?"

Ronni carefully folded her hands in her lap. "Yes. Yes, I do like your dad. Very much."

"Don't you like *us*...me and Griff and Lizzy and Grandma?"

"Of course I do."

"Then why are you moving away?"

It occurred to her that she hadn't given this talk they were having enough thought. Not near enough...

"Why are you moving away, Ronni?"

For some reason, any answer she might have uttered would have felt like a lie.

She didn't want to lie.

"I...I think it's the best thing."

It was no answer. And Drew knew it. "But *why?*"

"Oh, Drew. It's not going to mean anything, not to you and me and our project. It's just that I have my house and it's ready and now I'm going to move there for a while."

"You're coming back, then?"

"I...yes. I am."

"When?"

"I don't know exactly. Soon."

His chair had a swivel base. He toed the floor, turning it—and himself—away from her.

Her stomach seemed to hollow out. There was no fear she might throw up now. Only an emptiness. And the beginnings of understanding.

Maybe Ryan was right about this. "Drew... please..."

He remained facing the far wall. "You promised," he said quietly. "You made a solemn vow, never to hurt anyone. But you're doing it, anyway. You're hurting us. You're leaving us. Just like my mother, you're leaving." He stubbed his toe against the floor mat, then whispered so low she had to lean forward to hear it. "I *hate* you."

The three words cut deep, clear down to her soul. "Oh, Drew, I—"

But he didn't let her finish. "I don't think I want to talk about this anymore, Ronni. I want you to go."

"Drew…"

But he only sat there, not moving, not looking her way.

After a minute, she stood. "I'll…be here. Tomorrow at two-thirty. To pick you up."

He said nothing. He still didn't turn.

So she went to the door, pausing there briefly, trying to think of one final, positive thing to say. Nothing came to her.

She left him, closing the door very quietly behind her.

In the kitchen, she found Lily peeling potatoes at the sink.

One glance at her face—and Lily knew. "Andrew didn't take it well."

"No, he didn't."

"He'll be all right." Lily manufactured another of her taut little smiles. "Don't you worry about him. Once he gets used to the idea, he'll be just fine. And good luck in your new home."

Ronni hated herself right then. And what she felt for Lily wasn't much better. She said bleakly, "I'll pick him up tomorrow as planned."

"That will be fine."

In the guest house, a last stack of boxes waited by the front door. She'd packed the rest up the day before and taken it over to the condo. Tomorrow, she'd put these last few things in her car, along with the suitcase and overnight bag that waited in the bedroom. And that would be that.

Except now, she didn't want to do it.

Now she was thinking that when Ryan came that night, she'd admit that she'd made a giant-sized error in judgment. She still believed that, eventually, this ploy might help to turn Lily around.

But at what cost? She and Ryan were hardly speaking.

And Drew. Lord, she should have given more thought to how Drew would take this.

As a betrayal. A desertion.

He had reached out to her—from that very first night, when she'd wakened to find him standing by her bed. He had reached out. And she had reached back. Together, they had been building something important. A bond. A trust.

And then, in the course of one conversation, she had shattered that trust.

"Bad move, Dr. Ronni," she muttered to herself. "Very bad move..."

Ryan arrived at a little after ten. Relief flooded through her, warm and sweet. Until she saw his tall, broad-shouldered form on the other side of the French doors, she hadn't admitted to herself that she feared he might *not* come.

She jumped from the bed, where she'd been curled up with a book she couldn't concentrate on at all. And she ran to him.

He caught her in his arms and kissed her. She kissed him back fervently, then put her hands on his shoulders and looked into his eyes. "I...I've been waiting for you to come, so afraid you *wouldn't* come...."

His eyes looked strange. A little sad. Way too knowing. "I'm here. This is your last night, right? Tomorrow, you're gone."

"Just to the condo."

"Right."

"Ryan. Please don't be like this. I…I *have* been thinking. I told Lily and the children today, about the move."

"Lily mentioned that. She was extremely… solicitous. I think she believes you've broken my heart—and also that I'll get over it."

She didn't want to hear anything about a broken heart. She asked urgently, "How's Drew?"

"Fine. A little withdrawn. Why?"

"He was very hurt when I told him."

"That doesn't surprise me. He thinks the world of you. He's even told me I should marry you."

"Yes, I…he's said as much to me."

"So why are you surprised that he's hurt at your leaving?"

"I'm not surprised. I'm just…maybe I didn't give how he'd feel enough thought."

Ryan spoke flatly. "It seems pretty obvious to me that, for him, no matter what you say, your leaving isn't going to seem temporary. His mother 'left' him, remember? And she didn't come back."

She dropped her hands from his shoulders and stepped back. "Look. All right. I was wrong. This was a bad idea. A really bad idea."

"You think so?"

She glared at him. "Yes. I think so. And I've changed my mind. I'm not going to do it."

He looked at her for what seemed like a century.

Then he said, "Because I'm angry. And because Drew is hurt."

"Yes. Yes, exactly. Isn't that reason enough?"

Another lifetime of a pause. Then he shook his head. "No. It's not."

She could not believe he had said that. She challenged tightly, "Well, then. What *is* enough?"

"That's a good question. And I'm betting you'll come up with the answer. For yourself. In your own time."

"Ryan. What are you saying?"

"That I don't think Lily's the only one who needs a little space here. I think you need it, too."

"No, I—"

"Would you mind letting me finish?"

She wanted to shout at him. But she didn't. She kept her mouth shut.

He said, "I've given this a lot of thought the past few days. And I've come to the conclusion that this move of yours is the best way to go, after all."

Chapter Fifteen

Ronni tried to argue with him, to make him see that she really had changed her mind.

But Ryan would not be swayed. He left within a half an hour of his arrival, still firm in his decision that he wanted her to leave.

She longed to ask him to please come to the condo tomorrow night.

But she didn't. She was too afraid of what his answer might be.

The next morning, not seeing any other option, she put her things in the car and locked up the little house. At the condo, it didn't take long at all to put everything away.

The place really did look good. All her choices, from the Dover white ceilings to the mauve floor tile, to the oatmeal-colored Berber, went well together. The rooms gave an impression of comfort and light.

She was pleased with it.

Too bad it felt so empty.

When she went to pick up Drew, she dropped off the keys to the guest house. Lily took them with a nod and an aloof "Thank you."

Ronni had been worried all day that Drew would refuse to go with her.

But he came down the stairs when Lily called him and marched out the front door to get in the car. He hardly said two words on the trip to the supermarket. When they got there, he ignored her completely and concentrated on catching every last shopper who went through the doors.

He raised seventy-two dollars and sixty-eight cents.

On the way home, Ronni tried to talk to him, about how well he was doing raising money for the wing, about how much she admired all the hard work he was putting in. He looked out his window and didn't reply.

Finally, she burst out with "Drew. It's all going to work out all right. Please believe me."

He only went on looking out his window, as if the sight of bare hawthorn trees and frame houses fascinated him.

When she pulled into his driveway, he got out and ran up the front walk without looking back.

She watched him open the door and disappear inside, and then, for several minutes, she sat there with the car idling, debating the idea of going in after him, of making another effort to bridge the gap of hurt and misunderstanding that yawned between them. She could see the other children, too. She could help Griff with his latest Duplo creation, and she and Lizzy could—

But no. It just seemed too false. Not to mention dishonest, to move out and then knock on the door that same day, wanting to play with the little ones as if nothing had changed—hoping to force Drew to forgive her and see things her way.

How could he see things her way?

By then, *she* couldn't even see things her way. What was to see, but the truth? She had moved out. And that made a much clearer statement than any of her protestations and promises of future reconciliation could ever do.

She drove back to the condo, where she put the fund-raising gear away and then actually found herself wishing for the irritating bleat of her beeper. For a worried parent calling, needing Dr. Ronni's sage advice. For anything to block out the memory of Drew turning away from her, whispering I *hate* you, and the sound of Ryan's voice, flat and final, announcing, *I've come to the conclusion that this move of yours is the best decision, after all.*

There was a knock on the door at a little after seven.

Ronni's heart went racing. "Ryan!" she cried aloud as she hurried to answer. She flung the door open. "Oh, I'm so glad you…"

It was Kelly Hall. The other doctor shrugged. "I know, you were expecting someone more interesting."

Ronni backpedaled. "No. No, that's not true. How *are* you?"

"Fine. I heard a rumor you were moving this weekend."

"A rumor?"

"Yes. From Marty Heber. I ran into him at Children's Hospital yesterday." She held out a brightly wrapped box. "I come bearing a housewarming gift."

"Come on in." Ronni accepted the box. "I'll give you the tour."

She led her friend through the rooms. Kelly made admiring noises. "I love this wallpaper. Geometric was definitely the way to go. And the wood blinds are just right."

Once the tour was through, they settled in the living room. Ronni opened Kelly's gift—a cobalt blue pottery jar.

"Oh, Kel. I love it."

"Thrown by a local potter. And now that I've seen your bathtub, I know it was the right choice—though I have to admit, I considered wrapping up a home pregnancy test kit instead. You know how I am."

Carefully, Ronni set the jar on the coffee table. "I already bought a test. Last week."

"And?"

"It was positive."

Kelly did not look surprised. "Have you...made any decisions?"

"Yes. I'm going to have this baby. And marry Ryan."

"Then may I ask you something?"

Ronni knew the question without having to hear it. Still, she muttered, "Go ahead."

"Weren't you staying at Ryan Malone's guest house?"

"Yes, I was."

"Then if you're marrying him, why even bother to move in here?"

"It's a very long story. And not a particularly pleasant one."

"I don't mind hearing it—if you want to tell it."

"Thanks. Not right now. But maybe later. If you're still available and willing to listen."

"I'm a doctor. I'm *always* available."

"Kel, you are a pal."

Kelly let out a long breath. "I'd suggest we get drunk, but alcohol is contraindicated in situations like yours."

"Darn."

"Call my office. Soon, okay? We need to give you a more complete physical, run the usual battery of tests and—"

"I know, I know. And I will."

Once Kelly left at a little after nine, Ronni waited, still hoping against hope that Ryan might appear.

He didn't. She went to bed at eleven-fifteen and spent a restless night, waking every time she heard a sound, hoping it might be Ryan at the door.

It never was.

Ronni spent the next three days focusing fiercely on her work, giving the best care she could to other people's children, really listening to the common mom-and-dad worries she heard every day. Soothing fears. Giving advice. Wishing she could work round the clock and never have to go back to the condo, where everything was just as she'd imagined it might be in all her years without a home. Beautiful and quiet, a haven after a hard day at work. A place all her own, her dream-come-true—except for the emptiness that echoed through the rooms.

Except for the memories that found her there.

Memories of Ryan…

Coming in the French doors of the guest house. Holding out his arms. Touching all of her so tenderly, sleeping for a few too-brief hours at her side.

And of Drew…

Announcing that first night, "My name is Drew. My dad and my grandma still call me Andrew. I keep telling them I'm Drew now, but they keep forgetting."

Then later, on their drives home from Superserve Mart, the way he'd chatter so happily about how much money they'd raised.

And later still, turning away from her, muttering, "I *hate* you.…"

And of Lizzy, with her Bead Blast Barbie. And Griff, making an exclamation out of everything he said.

She even missed Lily. Missed the smell of her meat loaf and the sight of her hands zipping up a small child's jacket. Missed her little speeches about Patricia, missed the sadness in her eyes—and the real goodness within her that she fought so hard to keep from showing to Ronni, the interloper in their lives.

Oh, she did know that she couldn't let this go on.

That she was going to have to go to Ryan, to reason with him, to argue with him, to shout at him—to get down on the floor and crawl to him if she had to, to make him see that she knew what a huge mistake she'd made. To make him understand that she'd had enough of the space he'd said she needed.

But then, somehow, she could never quite bring herself to pick up the phone. Somehow, just when she'd make up her mind to confront him, she'd start to wonder if, maybe, some part of him was angry at her for more than her desertion.

If maybe, he resented the coming baby just a little. If the last thing he'd wanted was another child.

She'd remember that afternoon at Pizza Pete's, when she'd seen Ryan and his brother, their dark heads together, talking so seriously, probably about her.

She'd think of all her childhood years, on the periphery of other people's lives, hoping so desperately for someone to love her. To think of her as unique and bright and wonderful, to *want* her to be with them.

And she'd ask herself, have I re-created my own childhood in this? Am I more Veronica than Ronni, after all?

Have I put myself in an impossible relationship, and then gotten myself pregnant, to drive the man I love away? Do I only know how to be the unwanted one, and will I end up teaching my child to be just like me?

Those grim thoughts took hold of her. And they wouldn't let go. Wouldn't let her act to clear up the confusion that made every night a restless one.

Thursday morning, it was raining. A hard, heavy rain. Ronni had the wipers on high all the way to the office. She and Marty Heber pulled into their neighboring spaces at the same time.

He waved to her as they both got out of their cars and ran for the shelter of the building. He reached the office door first, opened it and ushered her into the still-empty waiting room.

"I predict that this downpour will go on all day," he said as he shut the door behind them and smiled at Kara, their receptionist, who was already busy in the record-lined space behind the sliding glass window.

"I just *love* the Northwest." Ronni wrinkled up her nose.

Marty started undoing the buttons of his coat as they headed for the door that led to the exam rooms. "Looks like the Malone boy is going to be fine."

Ronni froze where she was. "Which Malone boy?"

He shot her a surprised glance—and then shrugged. "Sorry. I assumed you knew. The older one, Andrew. Appendectomy. Yesterday, in the late afternoon."

Ronni's mouth had gone dry as a cotton swab. "Perforated?"

"No. We caught it in time. Zero contamination of the abdominal cavity. The operation went well. Complications are unlikely. He'll be back home tomorrow or the next day."

"He's at Children's Hospital?"

Marty nodded.

She put her hand on his wet coat sleeve. "Marty, I..."

He tipped his head toward the outside door, the overhead lights gleaming off the lenses of his wire-rimmed glasses. "Go on. Randy and I can cover for you."

She probably should have said, "You're sure?" But she wasn't going to take the chance he'd say no. She turned and flew back out the door into the driving rain.

They'd put Drew in a single room in the east wing. Ronni poked her head in, not sure what she'd find. Perhaps Ryan, looking at her with distant eyes. Or Lily, ready with a cold and off-putting smile.

But Drew was alone.

And awake. He spotted her.

"Ronni." Those blue eyes filled. "Ronni, you *came...*"

She ran to him, forgetting all about how reserved he was, how he never seemed to like physical displays of affection. She bent down and pressed her cheek against his. He lifted his hand and touched her hair. His skin felt warm, but not fevered at all.

With some relief, she reached behind her, grabbed the chair there and dragged it forward so she could perch on the edge of it. Then she caught his hand, the one without the heplock taped to the back.

Tears were running from the sides of his eyes. She grabbed a tissue from the bed tray—two tissues, because she was crying, too. "Here." She pressed one of the tissues into the hand she was holding and used the other to wipe at her own eyes.

He didn't use his tissue. He just lay there, looking a little too pale, crying silently.

"Oh, honey..." She swiped at her eyes and tried not to sob aloud.

He said, "They cut me open and took out my appendix."

"I heard."

"It still kind of hurts. But I get medicine. So it doesn't hurt too much."

"You are going to be fine."

"I know. Dr. Heber told me." A small sob escaped him. "Ronni. Ronni, listen…I'm sorry, for what I said. I shouldn't have said that. I know that I shouldn't…"

She bent forward, to get as close to him as she could. "It's okay. You know it is. I…I love you. And I hurt you. And…I do understand."

"I…I did that to my mother. I did. Right before she died…" He was speaking so quietly. Not a whisper, exactly. But for her ears alone.

She leaned even closer. She could feel his breath against her face. "Oh, sweetheart. Did what?"

"I…I told her I hated her. I was so mad at her. Because I knew she was going away from me forever. And she asked me to take care of Dad and Lizzy and Griff. To look out for Grandma, too. And I told her that was stupid, I couldn't do that. I'm only a kid. And then I said it. 'I hate you.' Just like I did it to you. And she said, 'Well, I *love* you,' and I knew I should say I was sorry, that I loved her, too. But I was just so…I don't know. I just couldn't say it. I never said it. She died and I never said it.…" He balled up the tissue then and scrubbed it across his cheeks and under his nose.

Ronni captured his hand again, ignoring the soggy tissue still clutched in it. "Oh, honey. You listen. You listen to me. Your mother loved you. And she understood that you weren't really mad at her. You were just hurting bad, because you were losing her."

Hope and tears made his eyes shine so bright. "You think so? You think she *knew?*"

Ronni wrapped her other hand around their joined ones. "I *know* that she did."

Drew sniffed loudly. "Ronni. I know you didn't try to hurt us. I know you didn't break your solemn vow. And even if you're not going to live with us and be part of our family, can we be friends, anyway?"

"Oh, I would like that. I would like that so much."

"Good. You're keeping our money, aren't you? Keeping it safe?"

"I am."

"And I really am going to be well soon. Dr. Heber said so. We'll go out and get maybe a hundred dollars again, in one day."

"You bet we will."

"And we'll make my dad proud."

"Absolutely. So proud…"

Those shining blue eyes shifted away, focusing on a point behind her. She turned.

Lily and Ryan were standing in the doorway.

Lily's lower lip was quivering.

And Ryan was…just Ryan: the man Ronni would always love.

Lily caught her lip between her teeth, then released it. "Ronni. I wonder if I might have a moment with you alone."

Ryan started to say something.

But Ronni didn't let him. She gave Drew's hand a squeeze and answered, "Certainly."

* * *

They left Ryan with Drew and went down to the cafeteria.

Ronni got a glass of grape juice and Lily poured herself a cup of coffee. They took a table near one of the long, narrow windows next to a tall, shiny-leafed rubber plant. Outside, the rain kept pouring down.

Lily looked into her coffee cup. "I don't know why I took this. The last thing I need right now is more caffeine."

Ronni sipped her juice. "Coffee is…reassuring, I think. It's the warmth. And that little trail of steam that spirals up from the cup."

Lily drank, set the cup down. "Well," she said, "I don't know. I don't feel very reassured."

Ronni gave a small shrug. "How are…Griffin? And Lisbeth?"

"Fine. They're with the sitter now. She's fifteen, lives down the street. A very responsible girl." Lily pushed her cup away. "I just…"

"What?"

"I don't like myself very much right at this moment."

"Lily…"

"No. Just listen. Please."

"All right."

"On Monday, Andrew started complaining that his stomach hurt. I thought it was an act—like the one he wanted to put on for his father to get out of going to Pizza Pete's. Remember?"

They looked at each other. Ronni thought. My God. Lily and I. We have *memories* together….

She nodded. "I remember."

"I thought...he was just trying to get me to call you. You know how kids' minds work. I assumed he was thinking that if he got sick I would call you, since you're a doctor, even though Dr. Heber is his pediatrician."

"Yes, I see."

"Then, by yesterday morning, he was vomiting. He had a fever. And I realized what a terrible error in judgment I'd made."

Ronni could relate to that: to an error in judgment. She could relate to that too well....

Lily pulled her coffee back in front of her and drank some more. "Why am I drinking this? Don't tell me. For reassurance." She wrapped both hands around the cup and pressed her forehead against the rim. "I have to say it, I have to face it. If you *had* been there, he wouldn't have been forced to suffer for two days because his grandmother is a selfish, pigheaded old—"

Ronni reached across the table, took Lily's wrist and guided the cup back to the saucer. "Lily. Appendicitis is a tough call. Even the best doctors, ones with years of experience, sometimes fail to diagnose it correctly. Until it becomes acute, it's difficult to tell *what* it is."

Lily shook her head. "Still, I should have—"

"Listen. I talked to Marty. The operation was routine. Drew is going to be fine in a very short time."

Lily stared down at the half-empty cup again. "Is he?"

"Yes. He is."

"In every way?"

Ronni listened to the rain for a moment, giving Lily a chance to answer that herself.

And Lily didn't disappoint her. "Ryan is miserable," she said. "And even before he got sick, Andrew walked around the house like a ghost of himself. Both Griffin and Lisbeth have asked for you. More than once. Last night, when we got home from the hospital, Lisbeth demanded to know if 'Ronni was making Drew all well.'" Lily rested an elbow on the table, rubbed her forehead with her hand. "The truth is, you love Ryan. And Ryan loves you. And the children love you, too. They miss you."

Ronni pointed out the obvious, because she felt it needed to be said. "They all love *you,* Lily. They love you so much."

Lily dropped her hand away from her face. She looked directly at Ronni. "Yes. They do love me. And I love them. But it's time I stopped imagining I can bring my daughter back by keeping you out of our lives."

They sat there for a while, not speaking, watching the rain hit the window and slither in shiny streams down the glass. The rest of Lily's coffee grew cool in the cup and Ronni finished her juice.

Finally, Ronni said, "I'm coming to the house to see Ryan. Tonight. It will be late. So I can be sure he'll be there."

Lily closed her eyes and sighed. Somehow, the soft outward rush of air sounded like a benediction.

"Of course you are," she said.

Chapter Sixteen

Ronni pulled her car into the driveway of Ryan's house at ten-thirty that night. The rain had died to a misty drizzle by then. Ronni didn't bother with an umbrella as she ran across the front lawn and up the steps.

The door opened before she lifted her hand to ring the bell.

Ryan stood beyond the threshold. She looked into his beautiful eyes and she thought of that first night, of the way they had stood in the foyer, two almost-strangers, in their pajamas, wondering what to say next....

He spoke first.

"Lily said you would come."

"Yes. And here I am."

He stepped back. She went in and he closed the door. "Let me have your coat." She untied the sash and he slipped it off her shoulders, his fingers brushing the sides of her arms, sending awareness moving through her in a slow, warm wave.

He hung the coat in the entryway closet, then opened the door next to it, the one to his study, where he'd led her that first night.

She went in ahead of him, took the same chair she'd taken that other time.

He didn't sit, only stood near the edge of the big desk, facing her. Once both of them stopped moving the room seemed very quiet. Ronni listened to the faint clatter of rain dripping down the gutters outside, and tried to decide where she should start.

He started for her. "Drew told me. About the fund-raising you two have been doing."

"He did? When?"

"While you and Lily were down in the cafeteria. He said he wanted it to be a surprise, but it was also a lie and lies weren't a very good idea."

"He's...quite a kid."

"Yeah. One of the best. And he...told me what he'd told his mother before she died—and what he said to you when you told him you were moving out. That he hated you."

"I knew he didn't mean it. And I would bet my license to practice medicine that Patricia knew it, too."

"Still, he's decided to stop throwing words like *hate* around."

"A wise decision."

"Yes. I think so."

Another silence fell. Ronni thought, I love you. How I've *missed* you...

She said, "Drew came up with the plan to raise

money all by himself. And he does all the work, too. I just sit there, with a stethoscope slung around my neck. Looking official.''

"He couldn't have done it without you.''

"He would have figured out a way.''

"Maybe.'' There was a marble pen stand on the desk a few inches from where he stood. He touched it, as if to straighten it, bring it square with the leather desk pad. But then he pulled his hand away without moving it. "Drew tells me you're going to keep it up. Every Saturday and Sunday, once he's fully recovered, until you raise a thousand dollars.''

"That's right. That's our plan.'' She swallowed. All the important things she had to say seemed trapped there, in her throat. She coughed. "How's it going on your end? With the fund-raising.''

"Good. It looks like the Pembroke people can give us fifteen million by summertime. And another local foundation, the D. P. Wiley Children's Fund, has committed to putting up twelve million, because the wing will provide pediatric care. Government grants look good for a couple of million. And then there's the money we're getting straight from the community, things like what you and my son have been doing. We're still around ten million short. We need to replace the money we took from the Community Fund. But we're getting there.''

"That's wonderful.''

His eyes ran over her, seeing everything. "You look tired.''

"I'm fine.''

"You're sure?''

"There's nothing wrong with me that a good

night's sleep wouldn't cure." *A good night's sleep at your side...*

"How's the condo?"

"Perfect." She clutched the chair arm for courage. "And empty."

Something flashed in his eyes. Something bright. Something so lovely. That reluctant smile touched his mouth, then didn't quite take form. "This is the first time you've ever come to me." His voice was rough, low and husky with emotion. "Except for that first night, when you brought my son back. And that wasn't really for me, was it? It was for Drew."

"I...didn't even know you then."

"You know what I mean. It's always been me. Coming to you. *Pushing* you..."

"Ryan. It never felt that way to me."

"Maybe not. But it did to me."

"I've been wondering—" she swallowed again and made herself confess "—wondering if maybe you...resent the baby coming, just a little. You have three children already, and you're always so busy and—" She cut herself off. He was turning away from her, the movement so abrupt it felt as if something was tearing.

She watched, her hand over her mouth, as he went to the credenza and picked up a picture of Drew, Lisbeth and Griffin in front of a Christmas tree, piles of brightly wrapped gifts stacked around them. In the picture, Griffin was hardly more than a baby. Drew held him on his lap.

Ryan touched the picture, the pads of his fingers laid so lightly against the three beaming faces. "I...resented Griffin. Resented the fact that Patricia just had to have another baby. We already had our boy and our girl. It seemed like enough to me. But she wanted more. And she just kept after me. She could be relentless when she wanted something— relentless in the sweetest, most loving way. Finally, I gave in. She got what she wanted. And I felt...I don't know, as if she'd backed me into a corner, I guess. And a little bit guilty, because I knew I wasn't that good a father to the first two. And now another one was on the way..."

The two words came out before she could stop them. "Oh, Ryan..."

He turned to her, his expression rueful. "Wait. I'm not done yet."

She pressed her lips together, nodded.

His blue eyes held hers, a steady look and a sure one. "So I felt pushed into something I didn't really want. And inadequate, too, as a father. But then, when Griff was born, when I saw him...all of a sudden, it seemed impossible to imagine the world without him in it. I remember holding him the first time, thinking, This is what it's all about, Malone. This is what matters. This is what counts...."

He turned away just enough to set the picture down, then faced her fully once more. "Yes, I would have liked more time with you, before another baby came. But another baby *is* coming. And maybe I'm not the kind of father I *should* be. Not the kind I *want* to be. But I'm the father my children have. I love you. I love them. And I'll love our baby."

She wanted to jump from the chair and throw her arms around him. But she couldn't. Not yet.

She stayed where she was and made herself tell him the rest of the doubts she'd been keeping from him. "I...I saw you, that day in Pizza Pete's. You and your brother. You were talking about something. I don't know...it seemed like it wasn't good. I thought maybe it was about me."

"You didn't ask me about it."

"I was afraid to."

"You should have asked, anyway."

"I know."

He took one step toward her, and another. One more step and he was standing over her. He reached out, touched her hair so tenderly, then let his hand drop back to his side. "Tanner's having some trouble. And it's nothing to do with the new wing. He got a woman pregnant, and it wasn't like you and me. He doesn't want to marry her. She doesn't want to marry him. She doesn't even want the baby. But he talked her into having it. It's due pretty soon now. She's supposed to give it up for adoption. However, she's not the most dependable woman in the world. In spite of the agreement they've made, Tanner's never sure *what* she'll do. He says he's not ready for fatherhood. But then again, he's not ready to let that baby go, either."

"And...*that's* what you were talking about?"

"Yes."

Ronni stared up at him, amazed at how far astray her own fears had led her—and also reasonably certain that the mother of Tanner's child was getting the best possible prenatal care from Dr. Kelly Hall.

She thought of telling Ryan. But no. Not right now. Right now, they were talking of the two of them, of their own lives, their own child....

Ryan said, "The next time you decide I don't

want our baby, will you please come to me and ask me if it's true?''

"I...yes. Yes. I will.''

"You were right about Lily. She told me a few hours ago that she's been a stubborn fool. She said...she's changed her mind, about leaving. We're her family and she wants to stay. If that's all right with you....''

"Of course it's all right. It's exactly what I hoped for.''

"You'll have to tell her that.''

"Don't worry, I will.''

"Good." He dragged in a breath. "Lord, I've missed you.''

"Oh, and I have missed you....''

"I did believe it was important, that you go to that condo of yours for a while, that you have some time without me around, to make up your mind for certain. But damn it, you can't imagine how it's been. Every night. Without you.''

"Yes, I can. Just like it's been for me. Empty. Lonely. I can't sleep.''

"You need your sleep. You're sleeping for two now.''

"Oh, Ryan...and don't look at me like that. I am *not* waffling. I'm selling my condo. I want to move back to the guest house until we can get married—which I want to be soon. And then I want to move in here, with you and the kids, and Lily, too. How does that sound?''

He held out his hand. She laid hers in it.

Home, she thought. *This* is what home is. My hand in his hand. Loving. And loved.

Oh so gently, he turned her hand over—and placed a blue velvet jewel box in her palm.

She gasped and looked up at him. "Where did this come from?"

He gave her his marvelous unwilling smile. "I bought it today, after I saw you at the hospital. I guess I have to admit, if Lily hadn't told me you were coming here tonight, I would have come looking for you."

"You would?"

He nodded, then commanded, "Open it."

With fingers that only shook a little, she did. Inside, from its bed of midnight velvet, a large beautifully cut engagement diamond gleamed at her. A string of smaller diamonds sparkled along the matching wedding band.

"Do you like it?"

"I love it."

"Here." He took the case from her and removed the engagement ring. Then, with great care, he slid it onto her finger. "Marry me, Ronni," he whispered, his voice rough with emotion.

"Yes."

A gentle tug on her hand brought her out of the chair—and into his cherishing embrace. "I love you," he said on a low husk of breath.

She pulled away just enough to look right in his eyes. "I love you, too. And I will be your wife." Her gaze didn't waver. "Forever and always—or at the very least, for as long as we're both on this earth. That is my vow to you, Ryan Malone."

Epilogue

The check arrived four days later. It came via Federal Express, straight to the house, with no return address. It came in the afternoon, when Lily and the children were sitting around the kitchen table making decorations for St. Paddy's Day. It was made out to Ryan Malone.

A brief note, unsigned, came with it.

Congratulations on your upcoming marriage. Here's five million toward Memorial's Twenty-Year Wing.

"A cashier's check, for pity's sake," Ryan muttered in disbelief that night, when he and his bride-to-be were managing to steal a few precious moments alone. "There won't even be a damn tax write-off on it. Who would do such a crazy thing?"

Ronni hazarded a guess. "Someone who knows what you want more than anything else?"

He put a finger under her chin, tipped her face up to his. "I have what I want."

She grinned. "But five million sure helps. And now there's only five million to go."

"I'm telling you, Ronni, even though I've squeezed every cent out of every source I can think of, I still believe this is doable. Hell, my own son raised…what?"

"Three hundred twenty-five dollars and forty-eight cents. So far."

"We'll get the rest somewhere."

"I have no doubts at all about that."

His mouth hovered just inches from hers. "You have a lot of faith in us."

"I do. Would you please kiss me, Ryan?"

His lips met hers with tenderness and passion— and enough love to last a lifetime.

* * * * *

*To find out more about the renovations of the
hospital's new wing and Ryan's brother,
Tanner, the contractor on the project,
be sure to look for Susan Mallery's*
THEIR LITTLE PRINCESS
the next book in
PRESCRIPTION: MARRIAGE
*available from Silhouette Special Edition
in February.*

Back by popular demand!

CHRISTINE RIMMER
SUSAN MALLERY
CHRISTINE FLYNN

prescribe three more exciting doses of heart-stopping romance in their series, **PRESCRIPTION: MARRIAGE.**

Three wedding-shy female physicians discover that marriage may be just what the doctor ordered when they lose their hearts to three irresistible, iron-willed men.

Look for this wonderful series at your favorite retail outlet—

On sale December 1999:
A DOCTOR'S VOW (SE #1293)
by **Christine Rimmer**

On sale January 2000:
THEIR LITTLE PRINCESS (SE #1298)
by **Susan Mallery**

On sale February 2000:
DR. MOM AND THE MILLIONAIRE (SE #1304)
by **Christine Flynn**

Only from
Silhouette Special Edition

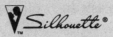

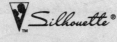

PAMELA TOTH
DIANA WHITNEY
ALLISON LEIGH
LAURIE PAIGE

*bring you four heartwarming stories
in the brand-new series*

So Many Babies

At the Buttonwood Baby Clinic,
babies and romance abound!

On sale January 2000: **THE BABY LEGACY**
by Pamela Toth

On sale February 2000: **WHO'S THAT BABY?**
by Diana Whitney

On sale March 2000: **MILLIONAIRE'S INSTANT BABY**
by Allison Leigh

On sale April 2000: **MAKE WAY FOR BABIES!**
by Laurie Paige

***Only from Silhouette* SPECIAL EDITION**
Available at your favorite retail outlet.

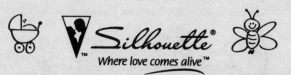

Silhouette®
Where love comes alive™

THE F RTUNES OF TEXAS

*Membership in this family has
its privileges…and its price.
But what a fortune can't buy,
a true-bred Texas love is sure to bring!*

On sale in January 2000…

Snowbound Cinderella

by

RUTH LANGAN

Ciara Wilde sought refuge in a secluded cabin after
hightailing herself away from her own wedding, but
dangerously attractive Jace Lockhart soon invaded her safe
haven. When they're forced together by a raging blizzard,
will their passions overheat their long-denied desires…?

THE FORTUNES OF TEXAS continues with
THE SHEIKH'S SECRET SON by
Kasey Michaels, on sale February 2000
from Silhouette Books.

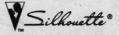

Available at your favorite retail outlet.

MONTANA MAVERICKS
Big Sky Brides

Legendary love comes to Whitehorn, Montana,
once more as beloved authors

Christine Rimmer, Jennifer Greene and Cheryl St.John

present three brand-new stories in this exciting anthology!

Meet the Brennan women:
SUZANNA, DIANA and ISABELLE

Strong-willed beauties who find unexpected
love in these irresistible marriage of
covnenience stories.

Don't miss
MONTANA MAVERICKS: BIG SKY BRIDES
On sale in February 2000,
only from Silhouette Books!

Available at your favorite retail outlet.

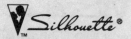